Red Snow

To Sharon
All Love
Julma

Red Snow

Wilma Hayes

In the Sticks Publishing

Ludlow, Shropshire

First published in 2014
© Wilma Hayes

ISBN 978-0-9576179-4-0

Author Photo by R D (Bob) Hayes

Red Snow is published by In the Sticks Publishing, Woodgate Cottage, Bleathwood, Ludlow, Shropshire, SY8 4LX

e-mail: Inthesticksbooks@aol.com

website: wilmahayes.co.uk

facebook: Wilma Hayes – Author

twitter: @BooksWilma

For my Mother and Dad
and all my family
who lived and worked in the snow

Wilma Hayes is a native of western Canada, but fled to England in 1985 to avoid snow and harsh winters. The memory of it has been very useful in writing this story albeit from a safe distance!

She is a Professional Home Economist and had a career the profession in Canada for several years. In England she worked in state and public school administration as Bursar until she finally escaped to the countryside. So far they don't seem to have missed her.

Her passion for writing is occasionally interrupted by the needs of three cats, a dozen chickens, a cottage garden and of course her husband.

Also by Wilma Hayes
Freeing My Sisters The Welsh Marches Series, Book 1
Things I Haven't Told You The Welsh Marches Series, Book 2

Tenbury and the Teme Valley, People and Places
I Wouldn't Have Missed It (written with William Hayes)

www.wilmahayes.co.uk

Acknowledgements

I am grateful to John Fender for advice on all things military and helping me with the spy issues, and to Bob Beasley for help with military tactical matters.

And to Ben Nock at the Military Wireless Museum, Kidderminster for showing me around the museum and helping me to understand (a little) about Morse code and war time radios. *www.qsl.net/g4bxd/introduction.htm*

For the Russian translations I owe eternal thanks to Natalia Wilson and Alena Harbon. Alexander Rudyk's comments on Russian society were invaluable too. Not being a Russian speaker I have relied heavily on their assistance and in spite of their expertise, I am sure that I have made some errors. I do hope that anyone with more language ability than mine will forgive me.

My wonderful readers JH, DA, JC, RY, AL and JF as usual have been a great help. Your advice was invaluable – as always.

And thanks to my amazing husband for all the IT help and endless encouragement!

Loss and Snow

The conjunction is alive. Snow has no movement, fire has all. At the edge where they meet, there is creation; light, smoke, steam, horror and life. No distinction among them. All is consumed – weapons, machines, armour and fabric, screams, silence, hate and love. Everything is gone. She is gone; they are gone. No one is left, but me.

PART ONE

1

April 1939

Love and loss: two faces of the same pain.

Sunday 9 April 1939: Hugely embarrassed today. Slipped going up the steps to the balcony at the chapel – new shoes, smooth soles – grabbed something to stop sliding all the way to the bottom. 'Something' was the ankle of a woman ahead of me. Embarrassing flurry and kerfuffle. Have large graze on my shin. Woman was kind and helped me up. She is very pretty.

A week later when Roy felt he could look her in the eye again, he made some kind of stumbling apology and thank you speech when they left the chapel. She was gracious. They introduced themselves and when she smiled broadly and said yes, he realised that someone, who must have been him, had asked if he might buy her tea later in the week. So there he was with very little money in his pocket, asking to take a very posh young woman to tea. Her name was Annie Carter.

At his lodgings he ransacked the pockets of all of his few clothes, drawers and cases, anywhere where coins might hide, borrowed a few more from John who had the room next to his and by doing some very quick mathematics looking at the tea shop menu ahead of time, he felt he might just avoid embarrassing himself again.

The tea shop was warm and full of steam; the tables arranged in a haphazard way across a small room with a black and red tiled floor. The chairs were an odd collection, but the table cloths and curtains were bright, clean and sun shone obliquely through a large bow window on the street. By accident or design, their

1

table was in the lovely window.

'Well,' she smiled as she put her little handbag on her lap. 'So far I know that your name is Royston Thomas and I can tell from your accent that you are Welsh, but other than that, I feel I would fail as a detective.'

'Good detectives ask questions I think, so you've made a good start. But please call me Roy.' She waited for more and so he was condemned to continue. 'I work at the Journal and write small bits of local interest; school fetes, what's happening in the council chamber. Things like that.'

She brightened visibly, 'Court sittings too?'

'No sadly. That goes to the police and court reporter. He's pretty long in the tooth – has done it for years. Rumour has it that he sleeps on the public bench and wakes up in time for the verdict then makes up the rest.'

That made her laugh – it was lovely and something inside him felt warm and happy.

The tea arrived and she took charge of the pot and cups. 'Why Worcester?' she asked pouring the first cup which she handed to him. By some miracle he didn't drop it. 'And why a newspaper?'

'I have an elder brother who will take over our farm and so that means, in time honoured tradition, that the younger brother gets sent out to make his way in the world. I just wrote to the editor and asked for a job and amazingly, here I am.'

'Farm?' He saw her eyebrow lower in a tiny flicker and he could see the vision of a five acre Welsh hill farm, long house hovel and dirty children outside looming in her mind.

'It is about 900 acres with ten tenants and a big cavernous house that my family lives in. It's near Aberaeron on the bottom of a lovely valley. Very pretty place.'

She seemed to relax, lowered her eyes and poured another cup of tea for herself. He may have imagined it all, but had to sympathise with her. What would her father say? His precious daughter was seeing the second son of a Welsh farmer.

She was gracious and asked him about himself. He was able to speak without too much embarrassment. Then he asked about her. He was a bit startled to find she was one of The Carters and worked at her father's bank – he being the manager. She was just a teller she told him and her father's only child. He began to feel a little overwhelmed. She was wearing a dark blue dress with a small collar, underneath which was a bow and under this began a long row of round buttons placed very close together. Her hat was the same colour and had a similar bow on the side. But when he looked at the quality of the fur wrap that she had draped over her arm he felt a long way out of his depth. He dearly hoped that the frayed collar on his shirt wasn't obvious.

Their conversation was light and comfortable in spite of Roy's nervousness and she waved gaily to several people who went past the window. Instead of feeling warm and kind he began to feel a little like a pet.

Mr Donaldson came in to turn the wireless on in the news office as he did every day at 1 o'clock. It was their signal to stop for dinner and to keep up to date with the worrying events in Europe. A short, round, balding man with large belly, he wore colourful braces on his trousers and always managed to look a little dishevelled - as if his role as editor was almost too much for him. In fact he was very good at it.

As always, the news reader began with the big national story of the day. Today, 27 April 1939, the government was introducing the Military Training Act. This meant that all men between the ages of 20 and 22 must register for six months military training. There were a list of reserved occupations that would be exempt; farming was one of them, but newspaper journalism was not. Roy's stomach turned to brick and he looked across the room. John, with whom he shared lodgings, was rising from his chair. His face was quite white. Eric who had been leaning back in his chair as if he didn't care, suddenly crashed his chair forward back onto the floor. He looked eager. Several others were obviously listening closely and the room fell silent. With every word from the newsreader, Roy felt increasingly weak.

Mr Donaldson turned the volume down on the wireless at the end of the announcement. 'Gentlemen,' he cleared his throat. 'These will be difficult times. I wish you all the very best luck in the world.' He went back to his office and Roy went out to keep his lunch appointment with Annie. He had no desire to hear the rest of the evil news today.

'Roy? You don't look well. Is anything wrong?' Annie was already at a table in the tea shop and he sat down with as much control as he could command.

'No.' Then remembering his manners, 'Thank you.' He tried to smile, but it felt as if he didn't manage it quite right. He took a menu from the waitress. 'I've just had a shock. That's all.' He stared hard at the menu.

Annie reached for his arm. 'What's happened? You don't look....'

'It's Hitler's fault!' He spoke more loudly than he meant and several people looked up. He leaned forward and spoke more quietly. 'The Military Training Act has just been passed in the House and all able bodied males between 20 and 22 have to register for six months military training.'

Annie visibly relaxed. 'Oh well, that's not so bad is it?' Roy must have looked shocked because she continued. 'I mean, it's only training and you might not even have to do anything with your training.'

He didn't quite know what to say next. The lovely Annie obviously hadn't paid much attention to world affairs lately. Where should he start?

He decided not to start at all. 'I think I'll have the soup. What would you like Annie?'

Registration a few weeks later was a demeaning affair of form-filling under the eye of a military man who appeared to size them all up for their ability to withstand his ministrations on a parade ground and who found them all wanting. The sight of that uniform was sobering and Roy felt quite ill when he got back to his lodgings. Mrs Elles, his landlady was surprised to find him home early in the afternoon and when he explained where he'd been, she made him sit down at the kitchen table and drink a very large cup of sweet tea.

'Don't be downhearted dear,' she murmured sympathetically. 'It may never happen.'

'But if it does Mrs Elles? What if it does?'

She was a tall, muscular woman who Roy felt would have made a successful, no-nonsense bus conductor. Today, she wore a house dress of faded flowers, with a little rim of lace showing beneath her hem, a large white pinny, with frills on the shoulders and a scarf tied as a turban over her head. He wondered what colour her hair was. He'd never seen it. She sat down at the other side of the table and poured a cup of tea for herself and then added a little milk. 'I'm old enough to remember the last war Roy, and I can tell you that we promised ourselves then that we would never do it again. But here we are and I suppose there is no other way to stop Hitler should he attack us, but to fight back.' She pushed the sugar bowl towards him. 'I don't know what else we can do.'

'Just throw all the best of the country's young men in front of the guns - again.' He spoke with more bitterness than he mean to and stirred the tea vigorously. 'I don't want it to sound like I'm afraid, Mrs Elles. I don't think I feel afraid. I just feel that - I don't know - that it's the wrong way to go about it.'

'What can we do?'

He had no answer for her, none at all.

Over the next weeks, he thought about it a great deal, trying to find an answer to his confused thoughts. Every day the post awaited him at Mrs Elles'. Every day, he dreaded the letter telling him where to report and when. Every day, he thrashed the options around in his mind. There weren't many to be honest, either obey or not and if not, then what? It was the 'what' that occupied his mind. There was no one to whom he could describe his anxieties – anxieties that were so woolly and so badly formed in his head that he would struggle to put them into words. Neither was there anyone who could help him clarify the risks and the challenges ahead. He just knew in his heart that the storm breaking was all wrong.

'Oh, Roy. Do come and sit down.' Annie patted the corner of the picnic blanket. 'You've become quite moody lately.' He sat down beside her, smiled as brightly and sincerely as he could at her and the two friends who had come to share their picnic. They had staked their little pitch of grass late in the game; the first overs were finished by the time they arrived. The friendly match on the little green was what England was all about he decided. His cricket career was limited to time at school, and it was not a game he played at all well. Frank, Annie's friend Joyce's current interest, was short, barely taller than Joyce, but a keen player and offered commentary on every ball thrown. When the players went off for tea, Roy took a chance that Frank might have some opinions on the conscription issue as he'd come to call it, and asked if he had registered. 'Oh yes! Everyone's keen to get going! Aren't you?'

'Well, no.' He tried to be ambivalent. 'I can't help but think that it's going to be a very nasty affair again.'

'Nonsense old man. We can have Jerry on the run in weeks.' He put more sandwiches on his plate and winked at the girls. 'Can't wait to get started.'

'Your enthusiasm is to be admired,' Roy ventured. Stupid, arrogant lizard, Roy thought. The world is yours to inherit and I fear for it if you do. 'I have to ask though: what if the force to be met in Germany is really as large and well trained as it is reported?' I fear more for the world if you don't.

Frank snorted in derision at the idea. 'Buck up old chap. We've beaten the Hun before and we can do it again.'

'But...,' he'd heard the numbers in the office many times and spoke with some confidence. '...the German Army has – right now – a million and a half men. We have about half that. I'd argue that we will have a hard time defeating that overnight. And Hitler's already taken over Austria. Who next? ' He glanced at Annie. Her face was still but her eyes were wide in alarm.

'All the more reason then to join up and get on with it. Don't you think?' Frank lay back on his elbow and grinned. Roy's vision of him as a lizard on a rock became sharper.

Roy looked at the empty cricket pitch. Is this what the war would be about – like it was last time? The English way of life – sportsmanship, fair play, civility and the gentle slowness of time. No, he knew it wouldn't be like that at all. This would be a war to the last man.

Saturday 15 July 1939: What a time to fall in love. Hitler occupied Austria in March; Jews are leaving in droves; he's making great noises about Sudatenland. It's becoming clear that Poland will be next on his list. Annie and I have just been to the pictures. Don't remember the film, only the Newsreel. Chamberlain has reaffirmed support for Poland. Am very afraid that this is a road going one way only. What does this do to love??

Mr Donaldson kept up the routine of turning on the wireless at 1 o'clock. But the young men in the office were coming to dread it rather than rejoice in an hour's break in the sunshine. Poor Chamberlain. One had to admit he was doing his best and he was probably a decent man. But opinion seemed to be on the point of public harassment.

Political loyalties were confused in Roy's home when he was growing up with his Mum voting one way and Dad the other. It meant that political discussions invariably ended with someone being aggrieved. His best option was to have no preference at all. So whatever colour Chamberlain wore it didn't matter to Roy. The poor man had crushing responsibilities and Roy didn't envy him. He would know better than any of the population that the country was in no fit state to take on Germany even if it was the right thing to do.

Today, Mr Donaldson turned the wireless on early. It had drifted off its usual BBC station and they heard a series of sharp blips, irregularly paced.

'What's that?' John threw some copy into a basket on Roy's desk.

'Just a call sign,' Roy answered. 'It's one station calling for another – a "here I am, where are you?" sort of message.' He listened for another few seconds. 'There are some German words, then it's just letters, probably code. A German station sending a weather report by the sound of it.'

John, Mr Donaldson and Jimmy the office boy, looked at him sharply. 'You understand it?'

'Yes, it's Morse.'

Mr Donaldson's eyebrows went up. 'How do you know Morse – and at that speed Thomas? And German?' He pulled up one of his braces that had slid off his shoulder. It snapped in the silence.

'I spent a few months at home when I was ill as a child and my father taught me as a way to keep me amused and quiet. We used it between us until I left home. He was with the Engineers - a wireless operator during the war. I learned a little German at school.'

Donaldson stared at him for a moment then retuned the radio and they joined the sainted BBC at the last pip of the time signal. The main news bulletin was about more of Hitler's overtures towards Poland. Roy put his head in his hands. Surely there could be no doubt now. How much longer could it go on like this?

Annie and Roy spent as much time together as they could and in due course he was invited to dinner. He looked at himself as he knotted the tie he wore to work as it was the best one he had. 'Here's my last chance to make a fool of myself and lose her forever. Pray to God that the old man doesn't ask me to say something in Welsh – 'because it sounds so lovely'. He looked closely at his reflection. The tie was badly wrinkled, but the knot was perfect. He pressed it down against his shirt. It would have to do.

He opened the door to the kitchen. 'I will be back later Mrs Elles. I have my key.' She was standing at an ironing board. He pulled his tie out of his jacket. 'Do you think you could iron this for me?

She looked at it. 'Take it off and I'll see what I can do.'

'I don't want to undo the knot. Can I just lay it – somehow?'

She licked her finger, picked up the hot iron with a pot holder and touched the surface. There was a satisfying sizzle and she beckoned him to the ironing board. 'Bend down, and give me the end.'

He put his chin on the end of the board and she ran the iron up the fabric, alarmingly close to his face. 'How's that?'

7

He straightened up and the tie fell into place, even covering the frayed button hole on his shirt. 'Thanks Mrs E. That's perfect. Don't wait up for me.'

'Have a nice time.'

Yes, he had to admit that he'd fallen in love with Annie. How could he not? She was sympathetic to his crashing deliberations and his frothing uncertainty. She tried hard to understand his dilemma and she saw how terrified he was. What she could not have realised was that it is not just dinner with her father and mother that terrified Roy, but how their lives, hers, his and theirs would evolve and just how helpless he felt in trying to do what he thought was right. He was not even sure what right was – not entirely sure at all.

Dinner with Mr and Mrs Carter was less terrifying than Roy thought it might be. He didn't have to make small talk with a father who was convinced that all young men wanted to do was seduce his daughter and that Roy was one of many he would have to put in his place. Mr Carter was tall and thin, greying floppy hair which he repeatedly tried to wipe off his forehead. As befitting a bank manager he was well dressed but tonight in an obvious attempt to look at home he wore a sweater buttoned over his shirt and tie. All four of them had a pre-dinner sherry in the parlour or living room or whatever they called it in these elevated layers of society in which he now found himself. Conversation was general but naturally drifted to the international political situation. Roy tried not to lay all his frayed cards on view at once, but having confided in Annie how confused he was about all of it, he could hardly come down on one side of the argument or the other.

At the dinner table, conversation did waver towards what Roy did for a living and his roots in Wales. Annie had obviously briefed them on the size of the farm and that gave him some relevance to lay in submission against his humble salary – of which Mr Carter would be only too aware. And to give them both credit, neither Mr nor Mrs Carter asked what his intentions towards Annie were. Roy had been dreading the question because he had not confided his feelings even to Annie yet and could hardly in good conscience, or best manners for that matter, announce it over the dining room table. However it was likely that the way they looked at each other gave all the information her parents required and they decided not to intervene – at least not at this stage.

'You must get a lot of very current information in your job Mr Thomas,' Mrs Carter deftly flicked open her napkin. She had black, well coiffured hair and a round rosy face. She was a smartly dressed with ear rings that seemed too large for her small face. She sat very upright as if the chair had no back to it and she smiled all evening.

'That's the business I'm in,' Roy started to say, then realised that this sounded a bit flippant, 'and it comes at us all the time, by telephone or teleprinter, radio...'

Annie interrupted then. 'Roy's office gets a great deal of information from its own reporters and from news services.'

Mrs Carter obviously wanted to know more, but Mr Carter spoke first. 'And what are they saying?'

Roy picked up his soup spoon. Why did it have to be soup? How many spots could his newly ironed tie accept before it began to be obvious? 'There seems to be deep concern about Hitler's intentions. They seem to be unambiguous, but I suppose no one in our government truly wants to believe them.'

'Is there any news about Russia?'

'Russia?' What an odd question.

'Nothing that you wouldn't already know, sir. Except that European governments seem to be of the opinion that a strong Germany will be a sort of bulwark against the Bolsheviks.'

'And will it?' Mrs Carter asked. Roy had misread the depth of her understanding in political matters. It clearly was an issue discussed around this very table.

As the main course was being cleared away and Mr Carter lit yet another cigarette, he asked if Roy had registered yet.

'Yes,' he was able to answer truthfully. 'But I haven't been called to go anywhere or do anything yet.'

'What would you like to do, if you were given the opportunity?'

The question stunned Roy for a second and he didn't know how to answer truthfully. The question for him was not what to do, but how not to go in the first place. He looked at Annie and she smiled with encouragement. Roy took this to mean that an honest answer would be best.

'To be honest, sir, I'd rather not have to make the decision.'

Mr Carter drew twice on the cigarette instead of once and the muscles in his face hardened. 'What do you mean?'

Roy looked at Annie. She was looking at her plate. No guidance from there then.

'I mean that I feel so much of this is wrong. I can't believe that we are lining up all the young men in this country to put them in front of the guns again. It was such a short time ago that we did just that and lost so much.'

'What do you suggest we do instead?'

'I wish I knew sir. If I did I would have communicated it to the Prime Minister by now and would have a very well paid job in Whitehall. But alas.' Mrs Carter laughed and her husband snorted through his cigarette smoke.

Roy felt that this was all going the wrong way for him, so collected what bravery he had left. 'I don't want you to think that I am a coward. I'm not afraid to be called up. But I do know that whatever skills I have or can be trained to have, will be of little use to anyone when I'm dead.'

The pudding arrived at that moment and Roy could have kissed the little woman who served it. He felt that she had just saved whatever relationship he might have had with Annie by appearing at that precise second. He was not to be let off the hook completely however because Mr Carter surprised him with his next question.

'Neville Donaldson tells me that you are quite good with Morse code. Is that right?'

'I don't know if I'm good or not Mr Carter. I was taught by my father and we – that is my father, my brother and I – used it as a sort of game for years.'

Roy obviously looked puzzled about the way this information had arrived at Mr Carter's plate, but Mrs Carter took pity. 'Arnold and Neville go to the same tennis club you see, Mr Thomas.' Ah, wheels within wheels then. 'So what?' Roy wanted to scream.

He was not put to any more interrogation then and the evening ended with the kind of silly conversation that he could not even remember when he came to leave.

Annie drove him home in her mother's roadster. He took off his hat and let the wind thrash through his hair. He desperately needed something to sift through all the loose ends, half thoughts, disorganised logic, rumours, facts and supposition in his head. He felt that it was only a matter of time before he said the wrong thing in the wrong place to the wrong person and condemned himself out of his own mouth before he'd even decided what his position on it all really was. Maybe it wasn't everything else that was wrong, maybe it was him. Maybe he just needed to buck up.

Roy looked at Annie, headscarf flying. It wasn't going to be that easy was it? She was sweet and pretty. She was fun, a little naïve and very pretty with a laugh that made him feel happy all over. She was perfect. And he loved her.

The idea of a commitment was terrifying enough no matter how much he wanted it. It was even more terrifying if he had to ask Annie to come with him into the decision he would have to make. But he was not yet ready to face that decision. He did not yet know for sure what it was going to be. Perhaps he was cannon fodder after all. He couldn't tell her yet how he felt. It just wasn't fair.

They stopped outside Roy's lodgings. Roy pointed to the front window. 'Wait five seconds.' They watched and then the curtain twitched at the side of the frame. 'Shall we give Mrs Elles something to discuss with her friends?'

'Yes please.' She leaned towards him, pulling the scarf from her hair. He put his arms around her and kissed her gently and with passion. He felt his soul fill with love for this woman and his body begin to stir. Then the stick shift dug into his ribs and laughing, they released each other.

'I had better not keep you out too late, or your father and Mrs Elles will be laying plans to keep us from seeing each other.'

She giggled into his shoulder. 'It was very brave of you to come to dinner. It can't have been easy – not the first time at least.'

'So, I presume from that comment, that I haven't disgraced myself too badly then.'

She smiled and pulled him toward her again. 'No.' They had the opportunity for one more kiss before the curtain began to move again.

2

September 1939

Tuesday, 29 Aug 1939: The news continues to push the political theme down a predictable but very slippery slope. On the 23rd Germany and Russia signed a non-aggression pact and on the 25th the British government agreed to assist Poland if it were ever attacked. It is just a matter of time now and not a great deal of time at that. It is very worrying and I feel quite ill.

Hitler's troops invaded Poland on Friday the first of September.

Annie did not seem to be terribly concerned two days later at Chapel. She smiled and squeezed Roy's hand as they went in. 'Everything will be all right.' He wanted to shout at her, at everyone around them that No! it would not be all right – ever again! The pastor announced that the Prime Minister would broadcast a message at 11 on the Home Service and so worship would be shortened to give them time to get home to listen. It was assumed that Roy would join the Carters and by 11 they were waiting in the parlour for what Roy knew would be the inevitable – the life changing announcement from which there was no return.

At 11:15 Mr Chamberlain began in serious tones with the weight of a heavy history and a terrible future on his shoulders: *'I am speaking to you from the Cabinet Room at 10 Downing Street.*

'This morning the British Ambassador in Berlin handed the German Government a final note stating that, unless we heard from them by 11 o'clock that they were prepared at once to withdraw their troops from Poland, a state of war would exist between us. I have to tell you now that no such undertaking has been received, and that consequently this country is at war with Germany.'

Roy felt Annie clutch his hand. 'It will be all right – it will all be over soon.' He squeezed her fingers hard, 'No! No it won't.' Annie and her mother looked at him with a mixture of surprise and disgust. His breath had disappeared somewhere and his voice had nothing to propel it out of his throat. 'I'm sorry.' He dropped Annie's hand and went to the door. 'Forgive me ...' Only Mr Carter's face showed him any empathy.

Early the next day in the news office, a message from the teleprinter made his heart stop.' The National Service (Armed Forces) Act 1939 has been enacted by Parliament on the day we declared war on Germany 3 September. It supersedes the Military Training Act 1939 passed in May this year, and enforces full conscription on all males between 18 and 41 resident in the UK. Men aged between 20 and 23 will be required to register to serve in one of the armed forces. They will be allowed to choose between the army, the navy and the air force.'

Mon 4 Sept 1939: Went to see Mr Donaldson this morning and by mid-day was on the train to Aberaeron.

In his mind was only one thing – safety - safety for his mind. He knew that he would find it at his home. There was also space there - space in which to search his conscience without complications; where he could look at the most important issues arising from the announcements, allocate them to his values and determine the ones that he could not reconcile. Here he knew he would find sympathy from his mother and he hoped to find understanding from his father. Whatever his decision was likely to be he hoped that they would not try to influence or prejudice what it would be. Even if, in their hearts they disagreed, he prayed for their support. He was wounded and disoriented. He needed help.

Monday

Dearest Annie,

I must apologise for my disgraceful action yesterday. I will write also to your parents to apologise to them. I badly misused their hospitality.

The Prime Minister's announcement was not a surprise. I think we knew it was inevitable given all that had happened in the last few months. But it shocked me in as much as I had not prepared myself for it at all well.

Mr Donaldson has kindly given me a few days away to consider and I

*am on my way to Aberaeron. I hope this will explain the very bad
handwriting and I will explain everything to you on my return. I will write to
tell you when that will be.*

Yours

Roy

Roy's mother fussed as mothers do on the unexpected return of their offspring.
His brother and father were concerned. It was obvious by Roy's face that
something was wrong. Coming home the day after war has been declared told
them as much as they needed to know.

They had a hastily assembled tea in the dining room. It was not a room saved
for special occasions and on a working farm it also served as meeting room,
office and laying out room when necessary. The dark wooden panelled walls
oozed time - an eternity of time. The old oak table had seen Roy's generation
and that of his father doing their prep and eating their Christmas lunch. The
wooden floor that his mother hated for having to polish it, glowed under her
efforts as it always did.

Roy knew that he would have to confront his family in words when he arrived
and the few hours on the train gave him a little time to rehearse his concerns. He
had yet formed no opinion on how deep they ran; what he should do about them
nor what the consequences might be.

'I don't know how you feel about it Haydn but I can't quite take it all in.'

His brother reached for another slice of buttered bread. 'I shall have to join up
I expect. I don't think there will be any option.'

'But being the eldest and on the farm ...'

'Dad is fit and well and there are tenants, I doubt that I could make much of a
case for exemption.'

'Will you try?'

Their father interrupted, 'That is something for Haydn to consider. All in good
time.'

'But,' Haydn cut the slice of bread in half. 'If I am not staying on the farm Da,
there may be an opportunity for Roy to take my place. It might be one way ....'
Roy knew that Haydn had intended to say 'out', but couldn't quite bring himself to
do so. 'That's what you want isn't it?' The abrupt accusation in his voice was no
less than Roy expected.

'Haydn!' Their mother dropped her knife onto the table cloth. 'We don't know what Roy wants.'

Roy laid his cutlery neatly on his plate. 'I don't know what I want either. I think that the whole country, the whole world is wrong. But there is nothing I can do about it. Nothing is right.' In spite of having had nothing to eat since morning, he could not face the food in front of him. 'I think I may refuse to go at all.'

My mother looked at him in alarm. 'What? Refuse to join up?'

Haydn, too, seemed surprised that he might go that far in support of his principles. 'Can you do that?'

Roy leaned back in his chair. 'I shall probably be jailed or painted white in every town I go to.'

My mother's skin had taken on the colour of ash and my brother stared. His father broke the sticky silence. 'I'll ask Glyn Andrews to come around in the morning.'

The ancient little lawyer had not changed in all the years Roy had known him. He had always been old and wizened, wore a coat too large for him and had pockets stuffed with papers, pencils, glasses and in the winter an assortment of scarves and gloves none of which matched. His eyes however were not in any way as confused as his demeanour suggested. They sparked with intelligence and he had a voice that could stop an unworthy line of argument before it even began. Roy had met him many times, when he was old enough to witness transactions on the farm; new tenancies, transfers and wills and before that, when he was allowed observe. Roy liked him.

They were shown into the library where a tea trolley waited. The dark panelling here glowed like the dining room. The shelves were stuffed with books and there were tables and delicate lamps. This was the room that his mother put her creative energy into. It was pretty and comfortable. Chairs and a settee in dark leather promised warm softness. A small grate, now clean with a pot plant sitting in front of it, provided the warmth in other seasons. Above it was an oversized mantel on which rested photographs of ancestors Roy could not remember from his living experience or from family legends. Roy's mother excused herself to see to the lunch. Glyn always stayed for lunch.

Mr Thomas shook hands, welcomed him, introduced him again to Roy and opened the drinks cabinet. 'Something for the tea, Glyn?' He squeaked the cork from a bottle. 'Thank you Peter, yes.' A goodly slug of golden syrupy whisky went into the tea cup and another into a small glass. His father rarely drank and this clearly signified the gravity of the situation. His mother on the other hand had never had so much as a drop in Roy's experience. Not even medicinally. His father raised an eyebrow in Roy's direction. He had never in his life offered Roy a drink. 'No thanks. It's a bit early for me.' The other two men smiled.

Glyn went straight to the issue. 'Now, my boy. What's the problem?'

Roy's words began to come out in the wrong order and he stopped and began again. 'I am not able to do the decent thing and join up. I can't. I can't agree that it is the way we should be going about it and ...' Here his logic began to unravel. 'I don't know what to do.'

'Are you afraid?'

How does one answer a question like that truthfully? To say yes, was to admit being a coward; to say no was to be seen to be lying. Roy opted for the middle ground. 'For this country? Yes, I'm very afraid.' He took a deep breath. 'For myself? Yes, but I believe that if you are going to get killed, you probably know very little about it, so that issue is not the important one.'

'What is important? Apart from the whole issue being wrong.' Glyn poured tea onto his whisky. 'I happen to agree with you, but politicians aren't about to change the course of history because you and I object to what they are doing.'

'I can't. I can't contribute to killing people. No matter who they are. The ordinary Germans who will line up against us don't deserve to die any more than the ordinary men from this country.' His father handed him a cup of tea – heavily spiked with sugar no doubt. 'The major-domos might be another matter.'

His father poured tea for himself and sat the cup beside his glass of alcohol. 'Does this mean that the boy will have to be a registered conscientious objector?'

Glyn pulled one of his coat tails out from under him and settled deeper into the chair, his tea and whisky balanced on his stomach. He addressed Roy rather than Peter. 'Is that what you are considering?'

Roy had to nod. It looked more and more like that's exactly what he was wanting.

'You can do one of two things as your first step. You can refuse to register for any kind of duty at all; or you can register as a CO. Have you registered for the Military Training?'

Roy nodded. 'That,' he went on, 'may complicate things. But we can deal with that if something comes of it.' He put the whisky laced tea back on the low table beside his chair and pulled a series of papers from his pockets until he found a blank paper and a pencil.

'If you are totally sure of this, and capable of registering as an objector, then it will be necessary for you to go to the registering office and let them know what your intentions are. In due course you will probably go to a tribunal.'

Roy saw his father sit up straighter.

'What happens to you then will depend a lot on what you say in mitigation.' He tapped the pencil on the paper on his knee. 'If, for example, you feel you are unable to use arms in any form, they could force you to go into active service anyway - or you could be sent to a non-combatant corps of some sort.'

'To do what?' Roy's father was frowning

'Much like last time I expect: dirty jobs, bomb disposal, stretcher bearers on battlefields, that sort of thing.' All Roy could do was nod. Glyn obviously hadn't expected an answer. 'But if you don't wish to wear a uniform at all, then you could be sent to work in essential civilian services, agriculture, forestry, hospitals, but, and this is important, you will have no choice in the matter.' Roy and his father were silent considering the possibilities. Glyn carried on. 'There is always the possibility that a tribunal could allow you exemption without conditions. I suspect that will be unlikely as you aren't a Quaker or Jehovah's Witness. And I don't think that being a devout Methodist will be taken into account.'

'Or?' Roy could tell by looking at him that there was more to come. 'The other alternative, of course is that you could be sent to prison for the duration and who knows how much longer.'

Roy's mouth was suddenly very dry and he took a large mouthful of tea. It was very sweet.

'There is a right to appeal. And,' Glyn returned to his tea, 'I don't think things will be as harsh in the tribunals or in the public eye as they were last time. I sense more sympathy in the judicial mobs than before.'

Roy turned to look out into the garden and heard Glyn's voice over his shoulder. 'The decision is yours, my boy. If you decide to register here as a CO and you wish me to go with you, I will be happy to do so. Alternatively, you could register in Worcester. Either way you can go back to work until you are called to the tribunal.'

Roy leaned on the frame around the big glass doors opened into the garden and tried to think. A few minutes later he felt his father take the tea cup from his hands. 'Go out for a while. Think. Come back when you are ready. I'll tell your mother not to wait lunch for you.'

Aware of his manners if nothing else, he thanked the little lawyer and went out into the farm.

The world outside was just the same as it had been for as long as his memory. His mother's roses were still in bloom in front of the house and the long track up to the main road was buttressed by hazels and rhododendrons; the sheep still grazed in the pastures and the farm hands were still tracing circular tracks around the corn field with the big horses and mechanical cutters. But it would never be the same again. Something huge and beyond the control of everyone on earth was about to break. Like a thunderstorm getting darker and darker on the horizon that would begin to crash down on everything in sight any second now.

But the sun shone and there was a light breeze – the storm about to break was of quite a different kind.

Roy noticed how colours seemed brighter this afternoon; how normal sounds were isolated in the stillness, never connecting with each other. His senses were keener and sharper than they had ever been. Is this what fear and deep concentration did in one's head? Is this what men 'going over the top' felt when the whistle blew?

He walked around the long range of farm buildings into the pasture, up the path to the top of the escarpment behind the buildings. There he sat in the sun at the top and made his breathing slow after the exertion of the climb. If he was to decide what direction his life was to take, he needed control. He knew he couldn't take another human life. He struggled with the slaughter of animals on the farm for heaven's sake and couldn't take part in it. Taking aim with a weapon against another living thing asked more of him than he was able to give. It was unlikely to matter how dangerous the situation, what the provocation was, he could not see himself pulling a trigger – ever. He thought about it very hard because he was wise enough to know that there was no other way to win this war other than to kill more of them than they killed of our lot, but he couldn't take part in that way.

So did he want to be part of winning this war or not? Could he wear a uniform? Could he join up and do some job that didn't require firing a gun? If he did, it would mean giving some support to the concept of armed conflict and he would be trained to fire the damn thing anyway. He lay down in the bracken. Little white puffs of clouds – little white puffs of muzzle smoke. Bomb disposal, stretcher carrying, being sent where he had no desire to go. No one in this war would have a choice of going where they wanted. Why should he be any different? He remembered his father telling him of the respect he had for the

Salvation Army stretcher bearers in the last conflict. Surely they had been objectors. Peter had told him that they had been on the battlefields collecting wounded and dead even before the shelling had finished. How much bravery did that take? How much courage? How much choice?

Feeling dampness from the foliage he was lying on, he got up and walked slowly over the upper fields to the small chapel where his family had gone forever to sing and pray. This was where Roy's faith had been born and where it had been nurtured and allowed to grow in him. He sat quietly in a pew at the back. The stone building was cool and mild to the eye. The hymnals were tucked into the back of the pew in front. What did God want him to be? Surely God didn't want the killing that everyone knew would come. Even someone as dim as Annie's friend Frank knew what was coming. So why was God insisting Roy be the one to say, 'No. It must not be this way'? But God wasn't insisting. There was still the issue of free will. Freedom to kill each other. So there must also be freedom to say no. What was freedom and what was conscience? He didn't know. But he prayed for the wisdom to know.

His thoughts were no clearer when he raised his head. Who did he confide in? Who did he not tell? Annie? Could he look her in the eye and tell her that he was a conscientious objector? How could he ask her and her family to tell their friends that she was seeing someone who refused to fight?

His father? Distinguished in the last war. His brother? Haydn would probably join up and distinguish himself as well. Roy would be asking them to lie for him or to take his disgrace onto themselves to redress the balance.

Perhaps compromising everything he felt and believed in and taking the King's shilling was the kinder thing to do for all their sakes.

His father was waiting for Roy in the sitting room when he got back. The colours that had been so sharp they hurt his eyes were becoming faded and dull. The farm workers were gone from the field, the horses put in their stalls for the night, the pigs in the yard had been fed and the chickens locked away.

'Come in.' From the tone of his voice, Roy knew there would be no choice in the matter. His mother was sitting by the lamp, a magazine loose on her lap. It was time for his reckoning.

His father started kindly. 'I hope you found Glyn was helpful.'

'Very.' Roy found that his voice worked and was surprised. 'I am very grateful.'

'So, now that you know what could be ahead of you, what have you decided?'

'Peter,' his mother interrupted, 'perhaps Roy hasn't had time to decide.' Mum was always good at giving Roy an honourable way out in front of his father.

'It is one of two choices Mum and they both affect you and Dad.' She folded the magazine and put it on the table under the lamp. Roy sat down on the leather settee. 'I can join up and do what everyone else will have to do. This will embarrass no one. You won't have to live with the shame of it.' He saw that she was about to speak. 'No Mum, please let me get this all out, before I lose the courage to do it at all.' She leaned back in her chair, but Roy could see that his father was leaning forward, needing to hear.

'Or, I can follow my conscience and go with Mr Andrews in the morning. That will be asking you to carry the shame of that for the whole of this war. It will also put more pressure on Haydn to join up and balance the equation for all of you.

'You also need to know that I have met a young woman and I am very fond of her.' Roy saw his mother's face flush; with pleasure or disgust he was not sure. 'Her family are well thought of in Worcester; her father is a bank manager; and so if I go with Mr Andrews in the morning, I will either end our relationship forever or I will be asking the same things of her and her family as I am asking of you. So, I think that on balance, it would be better for everyone if I just joined up and let the world unfold as it should.'

'No!' Roy had heard his father shout before, usually at his brother or the farm labourers, but this was not like that. It was a cry from his heart. 'No! You mustn't compromise your feelings on this Roy – just for other people. We, your mother and I, have brought you up to have a mind of your own and if the price for that is some embarrassment, then I think we will be able to bear it.'

Roy must have looked shocked. He certainly felt it. Dad carried on with no less emotion in his voice. 'If I am honest, I wish that I had been courageous enough to do the same thing last time.'

Wednesday

Dearest Annie,

I will be back tomorrow – late afternoon. Can I see you please? Shall I meet you at the bank after work? I have some things I must tell you.

Yours

Roy

20

He waited outside the bank and when Annie saw him she rushed up as if she were about to throw her arms around him. But she remembered who she was and where they were and put her arm in his instead. 'I was so worried when I got your letters, Roy. Whatever has happened?'

'Walk with me – to the river.' Roy felt relaxed for the first time in weeks. The weight of indecision had gone and he felt taller. He squeezed her hand and felt the warm light brown leather glove. She was wearing a wide tan coloured skirt with dark diagonal woven lines and a short dark jacket. He hadn't seen the hat before; it too was dark brown with a wide brim that covered her face. A long feather struck in Roy's direction.

She asked about his trip and what Aberaeron was like this time of year and when they reached the widest part of the path and were alone, he pulled her hand tighter across his elbow. 'Annie. There are things I must tell you.' They stopped and he turned to face her.

She looked pale and her eyes were wide. 'Roy, you are beginning to frighten me.'

Roy stroked her cheek. 'Don't be afraid. I do have some things to say that are not what you may want to hear, but first..,' he tilted her chin up so she looked into his face. 'I need to say that I love you. More than I have words to say. I want you all to myself forever. But more than that, I love you for who and what you are. You are my Annie.' He pulled her against his chest. She was warm and solid and all the qualities that he so desperately needed at that moment.

Her face flushed and she looked so relieved he thought she would crumple. 'Oh, Roy. I love you too.' She tilted up her face and kissed him then she leaned on his chest and put her head on his shoulder. 'You have just made me very happy. Can I tell mother?'

'You may want to hear what else I have to say first.' Condemned out of his own mouth, but the three seconds of joy he'd just experienced had to be worth it. They turned back to the path. 'I went to see my father, mother and brother because I needed to understand – in myself – how I would face the war that's coming. I'd very much like to join up, beat the Hun and come home, happy, to you.'

'Well then?'

'But I can't.' Her face flushed redder and if he needed to describe betrayal then this was it. He ploughed on. 'I can't take up arms – killing is not in my nature – I can't do it. Neither can I wear a uniform. I can't be part of a system that condones it, makes its citizens carry arms. I can't do that either.'

21

'But....' He saw such confusion in her face that he felt sick. Perhaps he had done the wrong thing after all. 'But, we have to fight. We have to beat Hitler. There is no other way.' Her words tumbled out.

'And you are right. I believe with all my heart that there is no alternative, and I will do whatever I can, within the limits of my conscience, to make it so.'

'I don't understand. If you can't carry a gun, or join up or - what else – what?'

They stopped by an open section of the path. There were swans on the river, serene and still. 'I don't know what will happen to me. I have registered as an objector. In due course I will have to face a tribunal.'

'Oh, Roy.' She began to cry and he put my arms around her. Neither of them cared any longer who might see them or what conclusions they might make.

She needed to know it all, so he carried on hoping that he wouldn't lose his nerve. 'I might go to prison, or if they think I have any skill they need, I could be sent to do some civilian work. But it won't be anywhere near either Aberaeron or Worcester. They won't make it comfortable for me.'

She cried and cried until Roy's handkerchief was wet through. 'That's so unfair!' Her indignation was a joy to hear and he smiled at her.

'Darling, I don't think that fairness has much part in all this.' He kissed her then. His heart was full of joy in spite of what tomorrow or the next day, or next week held for them. 'We now have some decisions to make. Come.'

There was a bench a short way along the path and it had just been vacated by an elderly couple who had been throwing bread to the ducks. No doubt trying to make sense of the new world in which they found themselves too.

They sat quietly for a moment. 'What sort of decisions Roy? I thought that loving you was quite enough.'

He put his arm around her and pulled her close. 'Annie, I would like to ask you to marry me.' Her head came up sharply and her eyes were wide and full, '... but I can't.'

'But, but, why not?' He saw her crush of disappointment. 'I'll wait for you. If it can't be now then ...'

He pulled her head against his shoulder. 'There are many reasons. We are still very young. I'm just 20 and you too. Who knows how the war will change us. Who knows how long it will go on. We may not be the same people when it's over.'

'We will. I can't change how I feel about you.'

22

'Sshh, my darling. There's more to consider. For one thing, when it gets out that I'm objecting to this war - and it will Annie, it will - then if we are engaged, you will be in the same place as I am.'

'I don't care. It doesn't matter.'

'But it will. How will your father take it? How will it affect him? And your mother, if you are seen to be engaged to a conchie?'

'A conchie? You are never that!'

'But I am Annie. That's exactly what I am.'

Monday 13 November 1939: Surely it will come this week. Not long ago I was sick with worry that a call up for training would be lying on the hall table. Every day I dreaded coming back to my lodgings in case the date for the tribunal was there. Now I rush home and am crushed when there is no letter. I want this to be settled; to know where I am to be; to settle Annie before I go.

The system should have taken care of him after his formal registration as an objector, but as usual it didn't. No system in the world prepared in peace time for a war that everyone knew was coming, would work perfectly when it did. Roy's registration in Wales should have resulted in him attending a tribunal and he sent draft after draft of his arguments to Glyn for him to comment on and they waited.

As soon as he had returned from Wales in September Roy had asked to speak to Mr Donaldson.

'Thomas. Feeling better?' Donaldson had bright yellow braces holding up his trousers today and he was perspiring in the autumn heat.

Roy closed the door to the office. The question had at least two meanings. 'No sir. In fact I think I am less well than I was last week.' Donaldson flapped a hand at the chair in front of his desk, sat down on the other side and pushed numerous papers aside with his elbows. 'I registered as a conscientious objector on Wednesday. Don't worry sir, I had legal advice on the matter and I know what I'm doing,' Roy took a deep shaky breath, '... and what is likely to happen to me.'

'Damn shame, Thomas. With your skills on the keypad, the Army would be damn lucky to have you.' He leaned back in the dangerously squeaky chair and put his hands behind his head. 'You may not even have to see active service.'

'It's not that that bothers me sir. It's the whole idea of war. I can't - I can't justify it - to myself I mean.'

Donaldson swung sideways in the evil chair and seemed to think for a few minutes. 'What do you want me to do Thomas?'

Roy was taken aback by the question. He expected to be thrown out or sent to become the office boy making the tea while promoting the office boy to Roy's desk, but no, he asked what he could do. Roy stumbled in answering. 'I don't know ... yes I do know. I would like very much to keep working as I am now, until the tribunal. If possible, I would like to keep this between us as far as possible; I don't want to upset the routine or the paper. Is that what you mean?'

'That's exactly what I mean, Thomas. Consider it done.'

And that was that. Roy came out of the office, a little stunned, but had done his best to smile at the others in the office who bothered to look at him with questions in their eyes. He and Annie agreed to keep his woolly status between themselves until the tribunal was over and he knew where he was to be sent. They didn't discuss what she would say to her parents or her friends. Roy did not want her to have made a promise to him that was too unkind to everyone else. They agreed to wait until the end of the war if necessary before they divulged any plans between them. But in the first place they waited for the Government to speak.

When the letter came, it wasn't at all what he expected. The small brown envelope was addressed by hand. The letter inside was from HM Laundry Services, Worcester.

15 November 1939

Dear Mr Thomas:

We understand that you are now living in Worcester. Will you please attend for an interview at 7 pm Thursday 23 November at the address above?

Yours faithfully,

A Millner (Miss)

Laundry? Roy had expected to at least have had the benefit of a tribunal before being sent to work winning the war. And he did not expect to be located at Worcester. He slowed his brain down. It was only an interview and he could still be sent anywhere. But he hadn't had the opportunity to have his say. Had he missed the letter? Had it gone to Wales? Why hadn't his father forwarded it? Nothing made any sense. Annie was as perplexed as he was.

When Roy saw the building where the interview was to take place, he was beginning to be suspicious about this 'laundry'. The address was a simple terrace house packed tightly among others on a silent street. He walked past it twice to be sure it was the right place and then knocked anticipating that he would have to make an apology for being at the wrong address. The door was opened immediately by a large woman with a scarf around her head, knotted at the front in a turban. She was wearing a printed pinafore over a printed dress, and large slippers. 'Mr Thomas?'

The hall led to stairs up to the next floor or past them to the back of the house. Doors to the two front rooms were closed. 'Next floor, room on the right – at the front of the house.' She turned and waddled down the corridor to the back of the house. Roy went upstairs feeling as if he could have been a burglar in other circumstances; a strange house, no real purpose for being there. It was as if he'd gone through the looking glass. A brusque 'Come' came through the door before he had time to knock. Inside was a desk and chair whose occupant was seated with his back to a low burning fire in a small grate. He rose and Roy saw a gaunt man of average height in a dark blue pin striped suit and college tie of a sort that Roy could not hope to know. He glanced at the clock on the mantle behind him. 'On time, I see.' He beckoned to another chair in front of the desk. 'Sit.' Roy felt as if he were in the Headmaster's study with no idea why he'd been summoned.

'You are Royston Thomas?'

'Yes, sir'. They both sat down.

'I know only three things about you Thomas.' His voice was thick enough to drive a nail through, but precise. 'You are very good with wireless, can speak German and you are a conscientious objector. Is that correct?'

Roy realised that his mouth was dry and he dearly wished there was a glass of water to hand. 'I know Morse code, sir, but I don't have much experience with transmission equipment - and yes, I am registered as a conscientious objector. My German is school boy level but I can get along.'

The man did not blink. 'Before we carry on with this interview, I'd like to give you a few short tests if I may.' He must have seen Roy's bewilderment. 'Don't worry. They are nothing to commit you to without your agreement - at this stage.' Roy was not able to answer before the man got up and gestured for him to follow him.

They went out of the office to a room across the landing. Inside were a radio receiver and a transmitter on a small table. The man gestured to the chair at the table and handed Roy some headphones. 'Please just write down, here, what you hear.' He tapped a pencil on a pad of paper on the table.

It was not a difficult test although the transmission speed increased and the letters ceased to make sense in English – or Welsh or German for that matter - after a few seconds. But Roy finished the test without missing any letters. Whether he got them all correct was another matter. Then he was given a paper with a short text on it and asked to transmit. He'd only transmitted with his spoon on a tea cup or soup bowl before, but after a few seconds he got used to it. When he finished, he removed the headphones. A man in dark suit came from behind a screen that Roy had not realised was there, took the paper on which Roy recorded the incoming message. He was well built of average height and had enormous bushy eyebrows. His host nodded toward the door 'My colleague will bring the results of the tests to us in a few minutes. Can we now go back to my office please?'

Seated again at the large desk, his host drew a printed form out from his desk drawer and with subtle ceremony laid it upside down in front of him. 'Now Thomas, we have great need of your skills and at the same time we understand your objections. We can terminate the interview at this stage and you will await the tribunal hearing in due course, or we can continue. What is your wish?'

There was a soft tap on the door and the other man came in, handing over a paper. The interviewer raised his eyebrows. 'You scored 100% on the incoming test and the transmission was 97% correct Thomas. For a man who had not used the device before, that is quite remarkable. But back to my question.'

Something told Roy this was about to be the adventure of his life. 'I'd like to go on sir.'

'In that case, I am Robert Smythe and before I tell you anything more ...' he turned the paper over, '... I need you to sign this. It is the Official Secrets Act.'

3

November 1939

Thurs 23 November 1939: Interview was quite unusual. As I left, Mr Smythe shook my hand and wished me good luck before shutting the door in my face. What happens now is unknown. I have again to wait.

'Not a lot happened, Annie.' This was a new experience for Roy, saying enough but not too much, even to the one he loved the most. That had been made abundantly clear. 'I had a little test on the wireless.' He was sure he could say that because it had been done before he'd signed on the dotted line, 'And then a chat. He knew I had objected of course, but that's about it.'

She was almost hopping up and down with interest and the thrill of the adventure. 'What was the chat about? What did you discuss? What will you be doing? Laundry? How did he know that you knew Morse code?'

That was easier to answer and Roy could tell the truth this time. 'I don't know what I will be doing. They will send for me, or send instructions when they want me. More than that, I don't know. As for how they knew about the Morse, I don't know that either. Many people in Wales know about it and all the people in the news office. Who can say.' Who indeed?

'But what about the tribunal?'

'I'm not sure, but I think that it may not happen, now that I've had this interview.' That was nearly true. It would definitely not happen; he had been assured of that.

'And so we wait again.' She squeezed his hand as they walked. 'And we have a little more time together.' For a few more weeks or days, the world would be a normal place. He could be with Annie and they could be a normal courting couple. Normal. What a wonderful sound. Would any of the world ever be normal again until the war was over?

But the tension in his mind did not make these weeks a happy time. Much as he loved her and being with her, it all seemed too abstract – so unreal, so lost in a sea of time.

'Roy! Over here!' There was a crush of people getting off – like him, going home for Christmas - and Roy was exhausted. Thankfully, Haydn grabbed his bag and clapped him on the back at the same time. Roy was never so glad to see him in all his life. 'Come on, let's get you home.' Words never sounded so good.

Mum fussed as Roy knew she would. 'You are not eating enough.' She could tell a lot from just a hug, but mothers are like that. 'Tell your landlady you need to eat better.' Roy couldn't tell her that they got what was given and although it wasn't bad food, it was what it was; fuel and nothing else and dictated by a ration book. Naturally, they wanted to know everything and naturally, Roy could only tell them that he'd had an interview. He really had no idea what it was all for and he didn't have to evade the question. He just didn't know.

They went to chapel on Christmas Day as they had done for as many years as Roy could remember – probably all his life. It was such a normal place – a place where everything was as it had always been without trying to be grander that it was. It was where life, love and the greatest good were the same thing. It was where Roy knew he could find God; where the deepest parts of his heart could be found even when he didn't entirely know what they were. It was a place of peace and at this time of year a place of joy. He knew that God would find him here and show him the way he should take. God would give him strength to be himself, believe in himself and confirm all his moral values to be right.

There was a special poignancy about the service, the music, the inside of the pretty little chapel. It was a time of birth – birth of a faith – a faith that had grown over centuries and had given families like his, strength, compassion and hope for whatever the future would be. In the strong old hymns, he felt like weeping as they stood together as a family in the small chapel on the wet hillside. It was as if the chapel itself knew the future. Outside, the colour of the countryside was brighter than he realised it could be; so green, so still and so Welsh. It made Roy want to sob with the possible loss of it all. For all the uplifting joy of Christmas, he realised there was a loss, a deep and infinite loss underneath all that he felt. He knew in the deepest part of his heart that he would never again find this kind of peace in his soul. The priceless youth that he had known in this eternal valley, on this ancient farm was over. Something broke in his heart and he knew it was the last link with his past. Even among all the people he held dear, he was alone. In another lifetime, he would have been looking forward to his life to come with excitement and anticipation. All he could feel now was dread but underneath all of that, he knew that what he was doing was right.

Haydn took Roy to the train in the evening. 'I haven't told Mum or Dad yet, Roy, but I've decided to join up.'

Roy felt as if he had been punched. 'Are you sure? Can Dad manage the farm by himself?'

'With help he can and there's plenty of that around.'

'Where will you go?'

'Probably the Infantry – wars always need cannon fodder.'

'Don't even joke about it Haydn.'

Haydn grinned at Roy. 'It will help to balance up local opinion for Mum and Dad I suppose.' Haydn helped Roy onto the platform with the boxes of food and socks and scarves that Mum had insisted he take. 'Come home again, Haydn.' Roy shook his brother's hand even though he was smarting by Haydn's last remark. He always had to throw the last punch.

'Come home Roy. Come home to Wales.'

The letter arrived on the 25 of January from the same Miss Millner – Roy doubted that she was the woman who had opened the door at the interview, but nothing about that place was what it seemed. The notification came from the same address, but it enclosed a rail ticket to Bridlington and instructions on when and where to report when he got there. A brief list of things to bring was included on a separate sheet, mainly personal items but no identification - that would be provided later, just the letter he held. It gave no indication as to when Roy might be home again.

He told Annie immediately, then went to see Mr Donaldson to tell him. Donaldson did not seem surprised and then Roy went to Wales. His father was not surprised either. From his family, he returned to Worcester and arrived at Annie's by mid-morning on Sunday.

'Roy! Come in.' Mr Carter greeted him on the front step. 'We are glad to see you.' He shook Roy's hand heartily. Annie greeted him with a hug and the briefest of kisses. But it was enough to make him feel totally awake and alive again. 'When did you arrive?'

'About 9 this morning. Mrs Elles, bless her, will let me stay an extra day with her before I leave.'

'You should have come to us. We could have put you up.' Roy saw her mother produce the briefest frown.

'I needed a place to stow all the stuff my mother has laden me with – oh here by the way.' He produced a cake in a box that his mother had insisted on sending for them. 'She gave me breakfast and let me brush up before I came round.'

Like Roy's family, they wanted to know all, and he was able to say with honesty, what he had said to his family. It was not a lot, but he turned the conversation to what was happening for them and what news if any there was from the paper or the bank. They found lots to talk about and no one seemed to be too embarrassed by the fact that he bore the unspoken badge of an outsider to the cause. He was now on a kind of active service. He felt that the Carters could still hold their heads up in their society. He had not let them down completely and they could describe his work and the secrecy of it in any way they liked.

Tuesday, 30 January 1940. Bridlington was merely a transfer point. From there I was taken in the dark another three hours. Have no idea where we are. Sixteen of us in the moors. Concrete buildings dug into the hillside for training and working; freezing huts for sleeping. Have done so many hours on a never ending series of wireless transmitters and receivers that I think my ears and my fingers are bleeding.

On arrival, Roy unpacked his little bag into the locker beside his designated iron bed. The wind outside flapped the corrugated tin siding on the hut that was designated as his sleeping quarters. There was a small iron stove in the middle of the large room, but the beds closest to it had been occupied long ago. Thankfully, his wasn't in the far corner of the room, but the heat the little stove put out was not making much difference to the ambient temperature. He put another jumper on under his jacket. Two or three of the bunks were occupied by sleeping figures; on another a sallow faced man slouched reading a newspaper. He nodded in Roy's direction and returned to the paper. Roy noticed that he was wearing gloves.

As he shut and locked the door on the cabinet beside his bed, the door to the hut opened and a fresh gust of cold air decimated the little heat there was inside.

'Ah, Thomas.' A tall man in the military uniform held out his hand. 'I'm Captain Arthurs. If you are stowed away, I'll show you where you are to be working, where the mess hall is and that sort of thing.' Roy could only nod. His chattering teeth would have chopped all his words into tiny fragments had he tried to speak.

Outside was a forest, not of trees, but of poles and pylons with aerials and wires making a cat's cradle of listening and transmitting possibilities. His new working room was at least warm. There was a wide table down the middle with tall office stools on both sides and wide benches and more stools around three of the walls. In front of each stool was a radio receiver and attached to it by heavy headphones was a young person, many of them women and most in military uniform of various kinds. Pads of paper and pencils were littered across the tables, along with tea mugs, ashtrays, scattered booklets. The walls were papered with diagrams and tables. Only one or two people looked up. All the others were concentrating, twitching a dial on the radio set with one hand and writing down what they heard with the other.

'Here, Thomas.' Captain Arthurs indicated an empty seat. 'Sit here for a few minutes and listen in. It will be an indication of what you will be doing.'

Roy sat down, picked up the headphones. As he brought them to his ear, he could hear the unmistakable ditditdahdit of Morse code. But it made little sense, in English or Welsh or German for that matter. He turned and frowned at Arthurs. Before he could comment, Arthurs explained. 'It's encoded. Makes no sense to any of us.' He leaned forward and lowered his voice. 'Bless them,' he nodded to the room behind him, 'they just keep taking it down and passing it on and that Thomas is exactly what you will be doing too.' He pushed a pad and pencil toward Roy. 'You have the required 90 letters per minute, so I'm sure you will be fine. You will be relieved for a break for dinner and at the end of the shift. Any questions? No? Well, good luck.' With that, he went to the door.

Roy turned to the desk with its threatening pad of squared paper and tin mug with two pencils in it, feeling as if he'd just been abandoned on an ice flow. As he struggled with the ear phones, a small WREN with brown hair came up to him, smiled and put out her hand. 'Hello. I'm Ellen.' The accent was clearly northern and Roy was never more than happy to meet someone who might, just might be able to sort him out.

'Hello,' he fumbled almost dropping the heavy headphones.

She retrieved the near miss and smiled. 'Don't worry about Captain Arthurs.

31

He's like that with everyone. We think he doesn't know what goes on here – so he doesn't try to explain.' But she did explain and in 20 minutes Roy had located the frequency he was assigned and was happily printing letters of nonsense onto the squares, dropping the finished sheets into a box for collection and watching the time on his wrist watch drag by while the cold wind from the sea, thrashed into the building. The sheets of paper were periodically gathered into bundles, tied up with string or packed in envelopes. Motorcycle couriers arrived regularly, day or night, took the packages and stowed them in canvas bags with long straps that they looped over their shoulders. With the snap of the motorcycle engine starting, the little slips disappeared. No one knew where they went or what happened to them. Roy continued to write down letter after letter after letter.

February 1940 The wind never stops blowing here. I swear it comes directly from the snow in Finland because it is terribly cold.

12 February 1940

Dearest Annie,

The wind continues without interruption and I have probably never been so cold in my life. We are sure that it comes directly from some very snowy place and is sent here by the Germans to sap every bit of heat out of us.

However, I am content and keep busy. I even have time when I'm not employed doing other silly things, to write a little for the paper. Mr Donaldson was kind enough to say I could continue to send articles from wherever I was. It helps me to pass the time and also in doing so, I can imagine the office as it was, full of activity, noisy with typewriters and warm.

Writing to you keeps me sane and warms my heart.

With all my love

Roy.

25 May1940 The air outside is warm and calm and we are all behaving wildly. There are games of rounders and tennis going on among the aerials. I am told that I can have three days leave but then to expect a new posting. I feel relieved – work that was more boring than this would be hard to find.

* * *

'I've left tea on the trolley for you and if that's all you need ...?'

'Thank you Mrs Rupert.' Robert Smythe got up from his desk. 'I'll look after things – have a nice evening.' Mrs Rupert shuffled out on her big slippers and closed the door to the panelled office behind her.

Smythe put several file folders in a stack then got up and pulled the blackout curtains part way across the windows. Blackout time was 9:50 today, but he wanted the meeting to feel confidential as well as to be so. He would close them later. He turned on the desk lamp and poured himself a cup of tea. Holding it against his tie, he walked slowly around the room and returned to his desk.

Now that France had surrendered so completely - surrendered all her stocks, equipment and territory - England faced a much steeper cliff face than it had before. She now had a frontier at her own door. Dunkirk was not so much a triumph as a tragedy. Things were becoming desperate for the country.

He put the cup and saucer down and tapped his fingers on the files. As he opened the top one again, he heard the front door open downstairs and voices preceded heavy footsteps up the stairs.

'As we are all here...,' Smythe cleared his throat and he and three other men seated themselves at the dark table at the back of the room. 'I don't know what you make of the news from France, but I must admit to being alarmed. Total surrender; men, stock, materiel, territory.' He shook his head slowly and drew in a slow breath. 'It is too soon.'

Edward Johnson, in a black suit and immaculate white shirt, leaned back in his chair and lit a cigarette. 'It's not good, I'll admit, but Churchill will prevail. He'll not allow any option of surrender.' There was a rumble of agreement from the other two men. 'The fighting will go on.'

'However,' Smythe looked around the table, 'It makes little difference to our tasks. We... and he... are ready for the next step.'

Neville Donaldson looked up in surprise. 'Already?'

'Yes,' Smythe continued, 'There is an opening at the language and cypher school at last which will suit. He can take the necessary radio training there too.' He straightened the papers in front of him and looked meaningfully at Johnson.

'Edward?'

Edward Johnson leaned on the table. 'Well done to you Neville for finding him. And to you Robert, for hiding him in the receiving station until the right time. That couldn't have been easy.'

Smythe nodded his gratitude for the unlikely praise. 'Thank you Edward. A few deals done, a few things bargained for.' He put his left arm carefully on the table top. 'His registration as a CO has also been taken care of.'

Arnold Carter put down his tea cup, knocking it lightly against the saucer in the silence that followed Smythe's statement. 'Is he robust enough? I confess to being a little concerned about his emotional health.'

Neville Donaldson snorted. 'Seemed to be fine to me when I saw him last with a certain young lady.'

Carter sighed. 'You know what I mean Neville. He's going to have a lot to deal with in a short time and he has been struggling with the position he has chosen to take. I know you are at the Foreign Office, Edward, but this will still be difficult. Especially for you.'

Smythe interrupted. 'Edward and I have the means to make this work. All Roy's weaknesses are to our advantage. I feel that he desperately wants to do the right thing – for the war effort, for king and country – but just not in the way that everyone else wants him to do. It is leverage that we can use if necessary.'

'I agree, but I also know that he is worried about, well, being found out, if you know what I mean.'

Johnson nodded. 'He wants to succeed – and he is also very, very good. He is the right man. I am sure of it. Could hardly believe the results of the Morse test when I checked it. Nearly 100%.' He leaned back in his chair. 'His insecurity is also to our advantage. I think he needed a focus for his energy but in such a way as not to compromise his principles. But if necessary…'

Smythe gathered them back to the issue. 'Shall we accept the assessment for now and plan for the next stage?' The others nodded. 'Edward? '

Johnson drew his bushy eyebrows together. 'The training will take him about 6 months I suspect. In that time, we have to – shall I say – create the place for him.'

10 June 1940: *I love this place. It is a large old estate with an eccentric mansion that looks like a piece was added onto it whenever anyone got a new idea. There are hundreds of people working here and the place has a fantastic buzz to it. It's wonderful. I am brushing up on my German, but what's more amazing is that I am learning Russian!*

Here there were passes, and military types who checked them, but there was little hierarchy and none of the saluting and stamping around among the people in uniform. They slouched about like everyone else. In fact most of the people were not in uniform at all and half or more of them were women.

When he arrived from his lodgings each morning, Roy was overtaken by an unusual chap on bicycle - like many others - but who wore a gas mask. Someone said he had hay fever. His jacket looked as if it had been slept in and he used a piece of string instead of a belt. Roy was impressed and concluded that with no doubt he was a genius at something who was unlikely to understand the concept of fashion or any critical observation of his appearance.

They could all be geniuses. Most of them had upper class accents and through conversation Roy found that many were university graduates or even lecturers in classics or mathematics before the war. Although he didn't ask and wasn't told, he was sure that many spoke other languages as well. But the eccentrics were the most fascinating. They were so lost in thought most of the time. One fellow walked around the lake in front of the mansion and at the far side would finish the tea he had brought with him and then throw the mug into the lake. There soon was a shortage of mugs.

Even with the weight of their tasks on them, and apart from the boffins who threw tea mugs into the lake or arrived with gas masks on, most people were sociable, had time for a laugh and there was a great camaraderie and a lot of fun to be had.

July 1940

Dear Mum and Dad,

I'm settled into both my lodgings and my work now. I spend most of my time in a school building where I am undergoing a lot of training. Just what the object of it all is, I am not yet allowed to know but it is an exciting place to be. There is an energy and 'positiveness' about the place that makes one believe that whatever is going on will solve all problems, make all things possible and be of unusual and important relevance.

I have lodgings in the town with two or three other men – I'm never sure because we all work different shifts and some of them seem to be gone for days, come back exhausted as if they had been awake the entire time. Then they pace up and down the floor boards, unable to give up on what is obviously troubling them. Then they will be gone again. My schedule is thankfully a day time shift at the moment. Perhaps when the training is finished things will be different. Perhaps I will not even be here.

Love for now,

Roy.

Having been pushed to his limits on Morse code and been subjected to hours of German conversation, Roy's training changed to Russian language both spoken and written. As autumn approached, there were weeks spent listening to Russian Morse transmissions. Naturally the transmissions could not be translated into Russian except for the odd word here and there and Roy did not have the skill or opportunity to find out just what all that jumble of Cyrillic letters really meant.

Then one day in September the instructor, Downing came in with a stack of papers which he handed around. The paper was well thumbed and crumbling at the corners as much from use as from the poor quality of the paper.

Roy looked at the slips he, John and Nick had been given. He turned them around and with a cold shock he recognised what lay on the table in front of him. It was headed 'Message Form' and below was a grid of rows and columns. Each box of every other row contained five unrelated Cyrillic letters ЫЦЙА ЬЮГВА ЙИДОН ЭЮ. At the top it was initialled by the operator and dated. It was the same form that Roy had spent weeks filling in from wireless transmissions received on the moors, albeit they were not in Cyrillic. At last he knew what happened to them. The motorcycle couriers brought them here.

Downing tapped the remaining slips into a neat stack. 'Now we can begin decoding. These are the messages taken down by listeners at the Y stations around the country. A message is usually written in cipher of some sort, but ciphers can be broken or understood. One only needs to understand the logic used.' He pulled on one trouser leg and sat on the edge of the table. 'So, if A has been allocated number 1, B number 2 and so on, or groups of logical words are reduced to a few letters or numbers then we have a cipher. It gets complicated further when a key is put to these numbers. This is where there is another process: the addition of a random number, or a random conversion of some sort, that complicates the letter or number further. The receiver has to have the key to understand the message. As we do not have it, we need to find it or discover it.'

Roy began to see what Downing meant: with a key and a cipher they would have an understanding of this disconnected mess of letters. What he was learning, he discovered, was cryptanalysis, code breaking or decoding, depending on who is doing the lecturing. Roy dare not think where this was leading.

Mr Downing began his usual walk around the room. 'Remember that keys themselves can be understood or guessed at, but it helps if there is a little plain or uncoded language somewhere. So look for that first. A simple 'Hello Alexei' helps enormously. And the transmission details at the beginning or end of a message are helpful even if they merely tell poor Niki that the next bit of the message is rubbish. Look for plain text. Real Russian words. They may just grumble about the weather or complain about supplies or the hint of lack of them. If by some miracle there is a plain word or message repeated in code - well, that's a gift to us.'

For the next month, they used all the logic they had to understand what was really being said and soon began to recognise the usual failures in the Russian cipher, the sloppy transmission mistakes: messages started, stopped and started again giving repeated phrases, the plain text they found in some sections and then applied the limited number of codes they had that they knew the Russians used. In a short time they were able to decipher most that came to them. And the Russian language training went on.

Sunday 8 Sept 1940 The news today is terrifying. Raids on London yesterday and during the night have left us all stunned. The docks are on fire and there are many people killed and injured. Raids began in daylight but then the bombers returned at night. The newspaper this morning happily tells us how many German fighters and bombers were shot down and the lesser number of RAF casualties, but I've written for a newspaper long enough to know that this is only one side of the story and that what is underneath will be much, much worse.

Monday 9 Sept 1940 It was worse, much worse. The raiders returned and this time it was the docks again and the City. A rumour circulating here, from goodness knows where it comes, is that the paving on the narrow streets in the dock area was made of tarred wooden blocks. Even the streets burned. God help them.

Sunday 29 Sept 1941

Dear Annie,

Thank you so much for your letters. You can have no idea how much I long for the envelope with your writing on it.

I am still in training. One course after another. I have no idea what any of it is for or when it will end. I don't know either when I might get to see you again. Everything about what I am doing is uncertain. The difference now is that I am enjoying what I am doing.

The news from London is grim and I fear for all those people. What have we come to Annie, what have we come to?

I can hardly believe what I hear on the wireless. Night after night of bombing, fires, death and terror. Is this Hitler's attempt to make us surrender? If so, he clearly doesn't know Londoners very well. A more stubborn lot would be hard to find. But even they must have a limit of endurance.

I miss you so much.

All my love,

Roy

4

October 1940

Friday 4 Oct '40 Worcester has been bombed!

Friday 4 October 1940

Dearest Annie,

We have just heard on the wireless that Worcester was bombed yesterday! Please, please tell me you are all right – all of you!

I shall go mad with waiting for news!

I love you.

Roy

London and now Worcester. What could they all expect now? Will it be as terrifying? Was it the start of another Blitz – of the county cities this time? Roy felt sick with imagining what Londoners were going through in spite of the brave stories in the press. He continued to read between the lines of the news reports. Searching for the truth; searching for the worst. From Worcester, no news. He felt as if there was a vacuum in his head.

'Roy!' He stopped as he was about to leave the gate. It was Alex, who shared his lodgings, running to catch him up. Gasping for breath he wheezed to a stop. 'Didn't you hear me? I've been shouting ever since you left the School.'

Roy smiled and apologised. Alex inhaled a huge lungful of air to calm his breathing. 'Off in your own little world again, old boy?'

'I expect I was. I'll try to be less consumed from now on.'

They walked by the guards who barely gave them a single look, never mind a second one. 'Is there any news from Worcester?'

'Yes, I had a note from Annie this morning.'

'And? What happened?'

'Annie says that it was a lone plane – her father said that it was a Junkers 88 and it dropped two bombs on the Mining Engineering Company Factory.'

'Was anyone killed?'

'Yes, she thinks seven. One landed in the canteen and clocking in area, but if it had been a little later the entire factory would have been queuing to clock off for lunch and it could have been a lot worse.'

'What time was all this?'

'Just after mid-day.'

'In broad day light?' Alex sounded amazed at this piece of news. Roy nodded. 'How brazen are they becoming? Why wasn't it shot down?'

'I don't know but I suspect that it just caught the city unawares; the weather was appalling, very low cloud and I suppose they just didn't see it coming.'

'Sorry, old boy, I didn't ask how Annie was?'

'She seemed OK, but I would be amazed if it hasn't severely shocked and upset them all. I mean, is this the start of the midlands Blitz? Will there be anything of Worcester to go home to?'

Alex put his hand on Roy's shoulder. 'Stay strong old boy.'

There was the sound of a bicycle bell behind them. They stepped aside as the odd man in the gas mask went past, coat flapping open in the cold autumn air.

The weather was getting colder and wetter. A winter like all the others in Roy's life. Regular and miserable. Was there no way he could be warm and dry ever again? To be fair this wasn't quite true. The training rooms were always hot, but with all the steaming clothing, it was just as uncomfortable. German training seemed to have stopped, but Russian translation went on, and the decoding was becoming more and more complicated.

On the 15th of November everyone arrived at the training rooms depressed and confused by the morning news on the wireless. Coventry had been bombed. Not just bombed but practically razed to the ground. A firestorm had destroyed a square mile of the city centre. More than 500 people had been killed.

Roy said nothing but was sure that it was more of the midlands bombing campaign that he feared; the one that would only now get worse and worse. Liverpool had already been bombed several times, Birmingham, too.

The room was silent as they all sat down and stared at the large tables where they worked. Mr Downing came in and distributed the morning's slips for decoding. He looked more tired than usual. As usual, he sat on the edge of the table at the front of the room and tapped the slips into a stack. 'We don't know what will happen to us in this war. The bombing seems to be getting closer and closer and heavier too. All we, here, can do is try to get the most information we can to the people who need it, as quickly as we can. Without that information we and they are blind. At the moment, Russia has a non-aggression pact with Germany. That means that we are very nearly at war with them as well as Hitler. We cannot relax. We cannot waste a minute or miss a single transmission. If we do, it may be the one that loses the war for us.' He began to distribute the slips.

'You will remember what I have said many times before: Russians, like other forces in this damn war, use a variety of codes. The poor human brain is forced to abandon known or suspected logic and look for the illogical. This is what the sender is counting on; that and the hope that our ability to think illogically is not greater than his. Well, I for one, knowing you and your abilities, will not be beaten by that assumption. We can think better than Boris can and fortunately Russian codes are not the most difficult ones we have to deal with.'

Roy leaned back in his chair, looked at the slip and started the process of decoding from the beginning in his mind. This was not a well-worn slip. This one was new! It was real. This time it was all for real. Roy felt a new thrill of enthusiasm. Their work was for a purpose. It really might end the war. He remembered very well the time he spent near Bridlington taking down all that gobbledy gook for hours on end. This was what it was for!

Roy and his colleagues were now responsible for getting these into Russian text that could be translated. With most systems, there was a way in and sometimes it took only a huge jump of logic or sometimes not even logic, just a good guess, to arrive at a solution. Much of it was based on experience of course and a memory of messages past. Somebody would remember that Ivan had let it slip that he was on leave for the next ten days, so that meant that someone else was transmitting his messages, and if they weren't as skilled as Ivan, then perhaps - and so it went on. Ivan's friend might ask about the weather. Josef might complain about his boots. It all helped to be able to make a guess at the keys used.

Reading the messages required some knowledge of Russian slang and profanity, but also abbreviations for military terms. Over time they became more conversant with these. In spite of all the problems, they had satisfactory success. And they moved from the school rooms to a Hut on the main site and they all went onto a three shift system; day time, evening and night shifts. It was all now very real. And the training continued.

Thursday 21 November, 1940 There was an almighty crash during the night shift. Everyone dived, through instinct rather than training, to the floor and crawled under the tables. My ears stung from the noise and I felt disoriented for a few seconds, probably from the shock blast. The air seemed to compress on one side of the room leaving the other side in a vacuum. The lights went out. It was over in seconds although there were other crashes in the distance.

As soon as there was some kind of silence, we went outside to try to find out what had happened and to see if anyone needed help. We were not able to see any damage but concluded that it must have been a bomb. Like everyone else here, none of us listened to the sound of aircraft overhead anymore, so no one could even remember hearing one.

On the way into work for the afternoon shift the next day, Alex caught up to Roy on the drive. 'Did you hear what happened yesterday?'

'I was in the Hut – we thought it must have been a bomb.'

Alex seemed pleased to have more information that Roy. 'It was three or maybe even more! Intended for the railway station I suspect or just some bomber wanting to jettison his bomb load on his way home. Hitting us was probably an accident. Naturally there will inquiries into whether any lights might have been showing and the Air Raid Wardens will be having a busy day!'

The bomb had hit the school where Roy had been only a short time before and the typists' room and telephone exchange were damaged. But there were no casualties. It also landed near the despatch riders' entrance and poor Hut 4, which housed the Naval types, had been shunted two feet off its base. Men were already working with winches and by the time the night shift arrived they had successfully dragged it back on its brick pillars and work continued inside with hardly a break. There were rumours of other bombs falling but not exploding. A lot of uniformed men where casting about in the shrubbery very carefully for several days.

The work went on in Roy's hut with not so much as a pause for breath. Their hut had not been affected so the slips kept coming. Sometimes they were able to decode them without help, but when they had no success, John, Nick and Roy worked on them together. Then they came to one that they could make no progress on in spite of working on it all day. When Roy took it back to Downing as the others left for the day, he apologised for not getting any results from it. The instructor sat on the edge of the table and tied a knot in his tie. 'This,' he flapped the fragile paper, 'is likely to be the product of a One Time Pad.'

'What is a One Time Pad?'

'We haven't discussed these in your training yet.' He smoothed the paper on the table. 'If that's what it is you won't be able to crack it. No one can, unless you have the corresponding codes to use. Next week when you are all back on a training shift I'll show you how it works.'

'Thank you sir. It sounds very interesting, but can I ask why you have tied a knot in your tie?'

He looked down. 'Oh that.' He undid the knot and then did it up again. 'It is my wife's birthday today and this is to remind me to take something home for her tonight. I do tend to forget things like this.'

28 November 1940 Our work goes on. What happens to our decipherings and translations and what use they are is completely unknown to us. We can only assume that if there was no benefit from knowing where troop movements might be taking place or where leaders are coming from or going to, what conditions Igor's boots were in or what Ivan's opinion of the Germans is, we would not be continuing to do what we do.

In the middle of the afternoon training shift Roy and the others were entertained by conversations in the duty officer's room. Several people inside were all seemingly talking at once. No one was actively shouting at anyone else so it must have been good news.

'Perhaps,' John suggested, 'one of us has decoded something vital. I wondered if we will ever find out.' But they did. The chaps from the Russian intelligence section came in and gathered everyone together around a large

43

table. With great ceremony, the chief laid a tiny book on the table. Was this what all the excitement was about? Well, yes it was.

'This,' he explained with great pride, 'this is a code book – and a fairly recent one – It was captured in Finland and passed to the Poles with whom they were working. The Poles have kindly sent it on to us.'

The little book had been well used – no doubt copied by Intelligence in every country that it had passed through. The covers were fraying cardboard and the pages inside were of roughly made paper covered with columns of Cyrillic text.

'It is a one time pad code book! For a while, we can crack the damn things!' The IO looked at it with reverence.

Downing then took over. 'Russians use very little machine coding, possibly because they do not have the machines. So, one time pads like this, are very effective.' He tucked the end of his tie in between the buttons of his shirt. Roy recognised this as a signal that what came next was going to be serious. 'These are almost impossible to crack without the book. The one time pads are codes used once only and then destroyed as the name suggests. A different one is used for the next transmission. The receiver has the same pad of codes and when decoded the page is destroyed at that end. When this is the kind of message we get, we have nothing to go on. However ...'

Seeing the little book brought the hair up on the back of Roy's neck. He pushed it back down, noting that he needed a haircut. At the same time, something from the dark side of his brain woke up, but there was no time to interrogate it until he got back to his room.

Here he stretched out on the bed and listed what he knew about Russia.

First: He knew where it was and it was huge. It was also on the other side of Germany, so not exactly a close neighbour then. But as it was enormous, there was a good chance it had a huge army and it was likely that its navy and air force were substantial too. Not exactly a force that England would want to take on just now. Then there was the so-called non-aggression pact that Russia had signed with Germany last summer. This was no doubt a worry to the English War Cabinet. On the face of it, it implied that Russia wouldn't invade Germany, but there was nothing to prevent her from invading anyone else if she felt like it. And that could mean Britain. When Germany and Russia carved up Poland in '39, Russia got the half with the oil; Germany got the half with the industry. All very neat. All very worrying. Russia invaded Finland a short time later. All right it wasn't a walk over and the Finns fought like tigers, but gave in by spring time. But the outcome was a very much larger Russian area of influence around the Baltic States. Where next?

The circle was beginning to close in Roy's brain. The British Government was very worried about Russia; probably saw it as unstable. And Stalin? He was a butcher and that fact alone would make the term 'unstable' equally applicable to him. But then perhaps the British government saw the Russian Government and Stalin as the same thing. So this is what it is all about. They, whoever 'they' are, needed people like Roy and the others to listen in on Russia – to see what was likely to happen next. The realisation, simplistic as it was, made his stomach suddenly cramp again. He, who had made it quite plain that he couldn't use a weapon, was using something else. Less deadly in his hands, but very deadly in the hands of someone else. How many people would die as a result of his work? How many would die needlessly if he got it wrong? How many if he got it right and 'they' got it wrong?

Roy got up and had a long drink of water and walked around the room until his guts and his head stopped rotating. What could he do? If he failed the work that he was set to do, deliberately or not, someone else would do it. No fewer people would die as a result. If he sabotaged the work or the results, even more people could die, he would be in prison and doing no good to anyone. He could resign pretending he was not coping and go to the tribunal and probably end up in prison anyway. Was Smythe likely to believe him? Not likely. Would they then send him off somewhere where he might have to use a gun after all? One by one, he saw all the possible ways out of this dilemma closing, darkly and firmly. He was trapped.

In the morning, he asked for leave.

Tuesday 10 December 1940 I've been given leave over Christmas. Sadly it is only for four days. Better than nothing and it is obvious that the work goes on here day and night without a break. Someone somewhere took pity on me. Maybe I am cracking up. Maybe I will get a visitation from Smythe and read something like the Riot Act and probably have to sign that as well. It would be no surprise. And I feel defeated already.

The news had become worse and worse throughout October and November. The bombings in London went on and on. There was no respite. Somehow Londoners carried on, but the Lord alone knew how they did it. According to the papers, 12,500 people had been killed and more than 20,000 injured since the raids started. More than 36,000 bombs had fallen. In all probability the numbers were actually higher than that, but no one wanted to give any succour to the enemy. As if these numbers weren't succour enough!

The Ark Royal was sunk; shipping on the Atlantic was falling to the bottom at a rate no one could comprehend. However codes were being broken and transmissions read on a more frequent basis. The Russian ones were now relatively easy and it was suggested in some whispers around Roy, that machines were being used to crack some of the German transmissions. Perhaps Roy and his colleagues were making progress. They would probably never know and could never say. The only news they got was the bad news.

It hardly seemed possible that it was a year ago that Roy was in Worcester at Christmas. It seemed to be a more than a lifetime ago. So much had happened in a year, but so much had happened to him that he felt as if he and Annie were becoming different people. The past was so unreal; or maybe it was the present that was bizarre. He walked from the station to Annie's house arriving about mid-day. The train times were so unpredictable that there was no point in anyone trying to meet him. There was a long halt somewhere along the line in the dark about 2 in the morning. They were there for over two hours. Finally when they started again, they heard, officially or unofficially that a troop train had been blocking the line when an engine broke down. It took several hours to get the old one off the track and a new one in its place. All in all, it was probably swiftly done, but it didn't seem that way when everyone trying to get home was left sitting in the dark in the middle of the country, cold, hungry and desperate for sleep.

Roy managed a wash and a cold water shave in the gents at the station and still felt exhausted but Annie was first at the door and he gathered her into his arms slowly. He wanted to savour every feeling of warmth, softness and sweetness that she gave him. He didn't want to end the kiss, and the feeling of her arms around his neck made all the tiredness and confusion in his soul drop away. Nothing mattered except her and the feeling of her body against his chest. It lasted only a few seconds, because Mr and Mrs Carter quickly arrived at the door to welcome him.

'Roy. It is wonderful to see you.' Mr Carter shook Roy's hand with both of his. 'Come in, come in. You must be exhausted.'

Did he really look that bad? Mrs Carter talked over his exclamation. 'There is a fire in the sitting room and I'll make some tea. We will have our lunch in an hour or so.'

'Nothing would be better Mrs Carter. Some tea … yes, some tea.' He still held Annie's hand and was reluctant to let it go, but she pulled it away and helped him out of his coat, stowed his bag in the hall and put his hat on the hall stand.

'Darling,' she whispered, 'I'm so glad to see you.' She hugged his arm. Roy felt what he could only describe as happiness rise in a wave from his feet. Something in the world was good.

In the sitting room, Christmas cards were hung on strings across the mirrors and small bunches of holly were tucked behind the pictures. It looked like Christmas without any enthusiasm. He hoped that they would not have to wear party hats at the lunch table.

In the living room, Mr Carter handed his tea cup to his wife who put it on the tray on the little table beside her. 'You will have to forgive Annie's mother and me as we will be out this evening. It was arranged before we knew you were coming I'm afraid and it's a special service at the chapel. We won't be long and you and Annie deserve a little time together.'

Roy didn't quite know what to say. To express sadness that they wouldn't be here all evening was definitely untrue, but to say thanks would imply that he had designs on their precious daughter. Fortunately Mrs Carter came to his rescue as she stacked the tray.

'What was your trip like Roy? The trains these days ...' Without really listening to his answer, she picked up the tray and turned to the kitchen. Where the tray had been were several newspapers. One was The Daily Worker – an obscure and very left wing publication. Many papers were routinely delivered to the newspaper office when Roy was there and he knew its distinctive flag.

Roy told what he knew which wasn't a great deal but reinforced the general attitude among people like the Carters that the country was rapidly on its way to hell in a hand basket. In due course lunch was served and conversation included the terrible events in London, the bomb on Worcester in October and general hardships. Rationing received mixed reviews, Mrs Carter grumbled that it was hard now to get enough tea, sugar and butter. Mr Carter pointed to the losses in the Atlantic, but Mrs Carter dismissed this as silly. After all tea came from India and we made our own butter surely.

Roy could see the conversation going nowhere and given what he did know about losses in the Atlantic, he groped for a safer topic of conversation. 'How are things at the bank, sir?'

'Well, we have lost numerous young men to the services of course and have had to replace them with women, but so far we notice little effect. Except for the shortages of course.'

'And the newspaper?' Roy wondered where The Daily Worker had gone.

47

'Much the same I think. But their difficulty now is getting paper for the printing.'

'Why is that dear?' Mrs Carter gathered up the lunch plates.

'Again, it's the Atlantic. Wood pulp and paper comes from America.'

'Well, well. The things I learn.' She disappeared into the kitchen and returned with the sweet. It was Christmas pudding.

'We would have had this with our Christmas lunch tomorrow but decided to have it while you are here.' Annie beamed. 'But tell us what you have been doing?' She put a slice on a plate and handed it to Roy. 'Custard?' He saw her father's head snap up to look at her. Then at Roy. 'Yes please.'

Roy said what he had been told to say: 'Just general administration – nothing very exciting at all I'm afraid.'

'Administration? Of what?' she persisted.

'Annie,' her father scolded. 'It is not wise to ask what someone is doing and Roy has, I'm sure, been cautioned about saying what he does.' He looked at Roy with some meaningful message on his face that Roy couldn't quite define.

'Sorry.' She grinned at Roy and lifted one eyebrow in a conspiratorial look of her own.

The Carters left about 6 in the evening saying that they would have their supper when they got back but that Roy and Annie were to go ahead if they were hungry. It was just a little cold meat and Annie could fry some potatoes if they wanted them.

By this time, he was almost too exhausted to stay awake, but when Annie snuggled up beside him on the settee, he felt happy and contented. He put his arm around her shoulders and pulled her as close as he could. Perhaps this would never end. Perhaps there would be a raid, right now, and they would die in each other's arms. Perfection.

'You can tell me now.' Annie's voice broke into his fantasy.

'Tell you what?'

'What you are really doing.'

Her innocence made Roy laugh. Would she understand if she knew? What difference would it make to her or their relationship if he told her? Would it solve the turmoil in his mind if he shared it?

'I told you Annie. Just dull old administration, typing, filing, running around.'

He kissed her forehead.

'But where are you doing this, this administration.'

'At the Foreign Office. You write to me there.'

'Yes, but you aren't in London are you?'

'Why do you say that?'

She snuggled closer and pulled a button on his jacket. 'Because you don't talk about the bombings or anything about the city, as if you were there.'

She was right of course and Roy laughed. 'No, I'm not in London.'

'Where then?'

He kissed her forehead and mumbled into her hair. 'I can't tell you.'

She pulled away and pouted. 'Well then, what is the office like? Who do you work with? What do you do all day? And what do you do in the evenings and on your days off?'

'I work six days and then I have a day off. We work in three shifts, days, afternoons and nights. I also get a long weekend once a month.'

'And what do you do when you aren't working?'

'There are four of us in the same lodgings, so sometimes, depending on who is off at the same time, we go to the pictures, if there is one. Or we go into the country – we have some bicycles – for walks. That sort of stuff. I read a lot.'

She picked up his hand from her shoulder and rubbed it on her face. Then she turned her face up to him. 'Roy, I want you to make love to me - before you go away again. I mean properly make love to me.'

He kissed her. He didn't know what to say. Finally, he managed to whisper, 'Are you sure?'

'Yes, very sure.'

'Will you be safe?'

'I've got one of those…,' she lowered her voice to a whisper, '… man things.' They both laughed and he helped her to her feet.

'Where?'

Her room was pretty. Full of frills and ruffles – on the cover on the single bed, the curtains and the lampshade. The dressing table was tidy and bottles of scent and lotions neatly arranged among the lipstick tubes and boxes of powder. Roy had no experience of female boudoirs, so made assumptions about most of the things. He took her into his arms and kissed her again. Her breasts felt soft and he wanted her very much. She drew him towards the bed and he began to undo the buttons on her blouse. She pulled down his tie. 'Are you sure? Quite sure?' He began to feel guilty for what had not yet happened.

'Yes. Quite sure.' She breathed into his neck.

Her blouse fell away and underneath she wore a lacy slip that revealed her lovely shoulders and smooth neck. Roy felt her slowly undoing the buttons on his shirt as he kissed her neck. They sat on the narrow bed; he kissed her shoulders and felt her breath in his hair and her fingers under his collar. He pulled lightly on the front of the slip and saw the rise of her breast.

'Don't stop,' he heard her whisper. He lifted one breast free of the lace and kissed it too. The nipple rose hard and vivid. They lay back on the bed.

And that is as far as it went. She lay rigid and straight, enjoying how far they had come but not really willing to let herself go any further. She would have done so if Roy had insisted, but he knew that would damage what they had built between them. Perhaps it was just too much too soon. They hadn't had time to get to know each other sufficiently to relax about this, and there wasn't enough time now. They had gone too far already.

'This isn't going to work, is it Annie?' He looked at her. She had terror on her face and tears in her eyes. 'It's not right for you and it's not right for me. And this is the sort of thing that should happen in marriage – that's what we've been taught isn't it? We can't be doing it if it's wrong can we?'

Roy felt her nod rather than saw it. Instead, he pulled his shirt back around his shoulders and picked up her blouse, now lying on the floor. He wanted somehow to tell her that it was all right; that it wouldn't destroy anything. That they still had time. She got up from the bed, put the blouse back on and turning her back to him, modestly did the buttons up again. He dressed too and she smoothed the bed covers. They did not look at each other. Downstairs again, they sat rigidly on the settee. 'You don't trust me, do you?' She spoke almost harshly.

'What do you mean not trust you? Did you mean what we almost did upstairs?'

'No. I mean about what you do - where you work - what's going on. I feel like I'm not part of your life anymore.'

'Darling. It's not about trust, it's just what we have to do.'

She turned her back and moved away from him on the settee. 'I think you put what you are doing ahead of what you feel for me.'

Roy couldn't answer. In a way it was true. She turned on the wireless and they sat waiting for Mr and Mrs Carter to come home. When the Carters returned, they were sitting in the living room with their tea things piled in the kitchen sink, no longer speaking to each other.

Roy caught the train to Aberaeron at 11 pm and a journey that should have taken a few hours, took, as was becoming the norm, all night. He could not avoid feeling that he was being judged during the trip. He was the only male of his age in the railway carriage not in uniform. People would have made judgements of that he had no doubt. The next time he had to travel this way, he decided to dress as if he were on official business and carry an attaché case. Maybe that will help. He doubted that any of his shirts would stand up to the scrutiny.

Mum and Dad were happy to see him. Haydn was somewhere in the machinery of the Army Infantry and could not be there. It occurred to Roy that this was a difficult time for families all over the land. Christmas was always the time to be together and it pushed the understanding of a great many older people who were not quite able to grasp the enormity of the country's situation. Surely for Christmas, some kind of arrangement could be made. It was impossible to explain. Roy's father understood of course. He had been here before, but as Roy wasn't in uniform he found it difficult to explain to other people except to try to make 'official war work' sound like, well, 'official war work.' Almost as soon as they got into the warm kitchen after chapel and Roy had a cup of tea in his hand, his mother handed him a letter. 'This came the day before yesterday but I'm amazed that anyone would know you were going to be here.'

Roy looked at the brown envelope and knew how they knew. It was another command from The Laundry and they knew everything. He opened it wondering what they wanted now. 'I need to be at Worcester for a meeting on the 27th.'

'With whom?' His mother was adopting her indignant role. 'Why?'

Roy put the letter back in its envelope and put it in the pocket of his shirt. 'I'm afraid I can't tell you the answer to the first question and I don't know the answer to the second.'

The next two days were full of tension covered with a blanket of faux normality. They wanted to know but couldn't ask, he wanted to tell them, but even if he were able to say what was going on, he wasn't sure he fully knew himself.

He spent a lot of time in the fields, among the animals, out in the rain. His

51

mind was in heavier weather than the countryside. God, who had always seemed to be so close to Roy at Christmas, was not where He should have been. The Chapel looked the same but the sound of the old hymns was hollow, unenthusiastic; the joy in the harmony was missing. The power of the last Amen disappeared with the last echo from the plastered walls. It felt as if it would be gone forever. In the fields, there was only grey murky rain, wind that spiralled around him, throwing heavy wet air and fine mist in his face, down his neck. The power of his faith was just out of reach and even Annie had moved a step away from him. He had never felt so alone.

PART TWO

5

February 1941

Wednesday 5 February 1941 Find myself in Moscow – at the British Embassy. The Embassy is on Sofiyskaya Embankment *. This is a street that runs along the side of the River Moskva in front of the building that the British acquired in 1931. It looks onto the activity of a busy river or it would be busy if it were not frozen over- and the Kremlin. Very much want to get out and SEE things.*

I haven't the faintest idea how I got here. There was a never ending series of boats, planes and trains and it felt as if I'd travelled far enough to be on the moon by now. There were quite a number of us making the trip, so it wasn't just for me that this was all laid on for. A lot of diplomats no doubt, the odd spy, and a business man and journalist or two, but no one admitted very much.

Now that I was here I was beginning to find my way around the building. It was a fine two storey classical mansion with arguably the best view of the Kremlin anywhere in Moscow. As well as whatever I was asked to do by the main Radio Man, Glen Hoffman, I could also write for the paper. All I had to do apparently was put my copy into an envelope, addressed to Worcester and drop it into the diplomatic mail. What happened to it after that – if it ever got to where it was supposed to - I have no idea. How strange it all was.

The cold was sensational – there were no words in English to describe it. I suspect there were quite a few Russian ones and I discovered several but the best descriptors were likely to be rude and I didn't know many of those yet.

The interview, if that's what it could be called, at The Laundry in Worcester was terrifying. Mr Smythe answered my knock on his office door with the usual brusque command. Thankfully, there was a small fire in the grate and I dared hope that the wet winter chill might begin to steam off my bones. I had the pack I'd carried to Wales and another of food that my mother insisted I bring back. I felt silly stacking them carefully against the wall so that the cake she packed for me stayed right side up. Smythe looked at me as if I were a fly pinned to a display board.

'Mothers,' I explained. He lifted one eyebrow in pitying sympathy.

The man who had taken my Morse code test paper, and who was now introduced to me as Mr Johnson came in before I could say anything else and we sat down in front of Smythe's desk. The lady with the huge slippers brought us tea, weak tea.

Smythe made a face when he poured it into his cup. 'Disgusting. I'm sure that she's used one spoon of tea to make the whole pot full.' He lifted the lid, looked inside and stirred the contents vigorously. He sighed, put the lid back and poured two more cups of light golden tea. 'Thomas, you've done a good job.'

'At what?' I was tempted to ask, but he talked over any squeak that I might have made and handed me the standard issue green tea cup. 'Your Morse transmission and receiving are second to none and you've managed to acquire a working knowledge of Russian in a short time. And your German is adequate. Now you've done the decrypting and coding and radio courses. Well done.'

I opened my mouth to express my surprise that my learning seemed now to be at an end. 'Why?' was all that I could manage to say. I accepted the tea, holding onto the cup with the other hand so it wouldn't rattle on the saucer.

'That will come.' He handed the second cup to Johnson. 'We are sending you to Russia.' Smythe stirred his tea while this sank in through the stunned shell of my brain. I really should have seen this coming but because I'm a stupid boy from the country, I hadn't. 'It is still quite an unknown entity to us and we need a man there who can help.'

We? Who was 'we'? The Government? The War Office?

Johnson accepted his tea and declined the milk. I presumed he might say something, but he still didn't speak. There was a short thick silence while I struggled for something to ask that wasn't too childish or made it blatantly obvious that I had no clue what was going on. Smythe continued, 'We need to discuss the job you will do and your cover.'

'My cover?'

Smythe looked exasperated and glanced at the ceiling. 'Thomas, we haven't been putting you through all this for your health or ours, you know.'

Stung by his words, I at last got myself together. 'Of course not. I am surprised by the idea of "cover" that's all.'

Johnson spoke at last. 'We have three jobs for you to do. You will be working first and foremost as one of the Ambassador's radio operators. There is a vacancy there. This means that you will transmit whatever he or others want to send to London and you will receive whatever comes the other way. There will be others doing the coding and decoding, so most of what you get will be ready to transmit. You may also be asked to do some clerical work. That is your cover.'

Smythe settled his cup in the saucer. 'And you will also work for us.' I blinked. 'There is someone in Moscow – he may be in the Embassy or even the Kremlin, or somewhere else altogether. We just don't know.' He paused and leaned forward, '…but whoever he is, he has been sending valuable information to us.'

I felt queasy again, but Smythe ploughed in – his voice a drone in my head. 'At present we are receiving this information via a rather dubious radio link which functions sporadically at best. Since we don't know who he is, we can't offer him the proper protection…and, here is where we need you.' He straightened up, leaned forward and stared at me, hard. 'Without doubt someone besides us will be trying to find him but they want to stop him. If they get to him, they will no doubt kill him.'

My mouth was too dry to speak. I could only stare back.

'Don't worry, we won't be asking you to give him protection. You will probably never know who he is,' interrupted Johnson. 'Your job will be to transmit what information he gives you.'

At last my mouth worked. 'But how…?'

'His reports will be encoded and you will probably receive them with all the other transmissions you will be there to do. He will arrange it so that they go only to you. You quietly take the paper and transmit it to us at an agreed time.'

There was a buzzing in my ears and I was beginning to feel light headed. I was about to become a spy for the British Government. But Johnson continued, penetrating my head clearly. 'You will recognise that they are not usual traffic because of the transmission frequency you will be given. You will know how important it is that he is not betrayed because it could result in his death and possibly that of others.'

Before I could ask, Smythe spoke again. 'He is not able to transmit directly – he does not have the skills, or a radio powerful enough to reach us here. And in any case, we need the information more quickly than having it couriered somewhere else for onward transmission. But what is most important at the moment, is that he is not betrayed.'

'But the Ambassador?'

Johnson shifted in his chair, which squeaked like it had a dry wooden peg in a tight hole. 'He won't know you are doing this but if there is anything we need you to tell him, we will advise and tell you how to do so. He will not know that you work for us. You will have a wireless for your own use. But it must be used in secret.'

'You must use it to check in with us once a week and use it for our man's transmissions. His reports are quite regular, but if they are late in arriving here or if there is something happening that we may wish to know about, we will advise you and tell you what to do about it. You may also be asked to report on something we have heard.'

I cleared my dry throat with a shaky sip of tea. 'We…may I assume that "we" is the secret service or SIS or …?'

Smythe gave me a withering look and flapped away the question with his hand. 'And lastly, you can continue to write for the Worcester paper on a regular basis. I am sure Neville Donaldson would be happy to have your thoughts. You are quite free to write about whatever you like, but we would encourage you to look at everyday life. It is bound to be very different from what is experienced here. It will be interesting to know how the Russian people are coping and reacting to world events. These reports will be of interest to us too.'

By 'us' he meant the British Government, surely.

Johnson put his tea on the tray. 'You must be very careful what you commit to paper and what happens to that which you do. You must also be careful what is heard and overheard. So take care with what you send for the paper. Your reports will help to give us a wider overview of life in the capital.'

I must have looked like a puppet on a string, mouth set in a rictus smile.

Smythe took pity on my shocked state. He shifted in his chair and it too squeaked loudly, but his was on metal springs. 'Write for the paper in any other way you like. Include what you see and hear. Anything at all except what you hear via radio or from our man. It will be too sensitive.'

Smythe gave up on his tea and put the cup and saucer on the tray on the desk. 'The Ambassador or his main radio operator will be the men you formally report to as one of his radio team. The Ambassador will have routines for you to use for his personal work but you will have codes that are for our use.' He looked at me as if trying to force the meaning of his words straight between my eyes and into my brain. 'As far as everyone else at the Embassy is concerned, you are one of the Ambassador's radio operators who does other clerical tasks and also writes for the papers at home and that is all.'

My mouth was incapable of speech.

Johnson delivered the next instruction. 'So long as you keep quiet about what you are doing, you will not be compromised. Transmit on Sunday at 0600 local time. The air will be quiet at that time and then check in again on Monday at the same time. If there is anything we need you to know we will let you know then. If you need to reach us at any other time, transmit as normal, we will have your frequency monitored at all times. Your journalism can be sent by telephone where telephones exist, teleprinter, if you get permission, or paper copy. You can use the diplomatic post. If there is anything urgent that we need you to do, a message will be sent to you during your shift on the Ambassador's signal in a code only you will know. We will then give you other instructions. So let us know as soon as you arrive, what your hours are and also if they should change.'

Instructions? Dear Heavens. What was I about to embark on?

'Back to the mansion to get you sorted out and to give you the rest of your instructions.' Johnson stood up and I wasn't sure but I think he actually smiled. 'Winter kit, equipment, paperwork, codebooks and so on.' But then he frowned again. 'Not a word to anyone.'

I was too stunned to even ask questions. He took the tea cup out of my hand and put it on the tray.

Monday 6 January 1941

Dearest Annie,

I am about to be sent off somewhere. They don't tell you much here, just hand you a pile of clothes, a few bits of information and a railway ticket. I'm off in the morning and will write when I get there. I have no idea when I will get home again.

I will miss you more than I have the words to express. This war can't go on forever and when it ends we can be together again. Without all the tiny specks of time that we try to pretend are normal. We can start again. This time apart is just a pause and we can be together in the future. And then life will unfold as it should. It won't last long.

Stay safe my darling.

All my desperate love

Roy

This city was amazing. It was a black and white city. White from the acres and mounds of snow and black from everything else in it. Machinery, clothing, all seemed to be dark and foreboding. Anything that might have been green was now dead, grey and leafless. Only St Basil's and some of the fine buildings presented any colour.

Foreigners here, even if Russian-speaking, were looked at with some suspicion - which was odd as there have been foreigners and visitors here since God was a lad. Perhaps it was because so many tribes wanted to conquer and take over this city and the country – and often did – that everyone visiting needed to be watched. When I went out of the Embassy I went with Adrian Richardson – his Russian was much better than mine – and he kept me out of trouble and places where it wasn't quite safe for me to go yet. Adrian was one of the Ambassador's assistants and a wonderful source of information. I came to find that he was a very private man, with rooms somewhere else in the city. He was also very clever, an Oxford graduate who spoke several languages, Russian, French and German and probably others.

The Embassy was a beautiful building. Built by a sugar beet magnate – a serf family who made a fortune before the Revolution by growing something that people wanted. Their name was Kharitonenko. When the Bolsheviks took over the government, the Kharitonenko family were turned out and probably had to make do with some other mansion somewhere. We, that is, the British, moved into it in 1931.

I didn't know much about architecture but I found it pleasing. It sat back from the railings on the edge of the street and had two storeys with additional rooms in the attic. It had a grand entrance, columns and pediments over the windows and was a lovely ochre colour. Inside, the rooms were very grand with dark panelling and there were numerous magnificent staircases. There was one room with an amazing painted ceiling and a very luxurious ballroom. The Ambassador had a suite on the first floor naturally and I worked in a little cubby hole in a large room now divided into offices. It used to be the formal dining room I was told. Everywhere there were office staff doing I know not what.

My little private room was at the back of the embassy in one of the many outbuildings, over a garage. It was about the size of a linen cupboard and was, by turns, very hot then very cold. The heating system was, according to Adrian, put in by Ivan the Terrible who did not, by all accounts, have much of a sense of humour. On the other hand perhaps he did. If I opened the little window in my room to let the heat out and then returned an hour later I'd find the heat had gone off and water in a glass by my bed was close to freezing. In spite of these minor problems, I looked out onto the gardens which were lovely, surrounded by hedges with shrubs and in due course if the weather ever improved, perhaps there would be flowers.

RUSSIA Moscow (Worcester Journal) Friday 7 February 1941
Winter in the Streets **by Royston Thomas**

Moscow would appear to be a winter city. Snow and cold sit so well on the city and daily life carries on perfectly normally. But then Muscovites have centuries of practice. This is what normal life is like here for a good part of the year. Spring does not arrive until it arrives apparently.

Snow and ice are scraped and hacked off the main streets by women with shovels and piled along the edges. Everywhere there are people pulling little sledges to take their children to school or do their shopping. Everyone is plump with woollen coats, long enough to cover the knees. These coats have large collars, usually of fur that they pull up to cover their necks and ears when the wind blows. Women wear either felt hats that they pull down to cover their ears or thick woollen scarves that cover their foreheads or sometimes they wear both. Everyone has thick boots of leather or felt with rubber soles.

Children are dressed similarly but are often to be found on skis that they use in a skate-like method to make great speed on the hard streets and snow covered pavements.

I also see wonderful men in uniform with brass buttons that run down the front in two rows from the shoulder to the waist. The coat skirts are long, to cover the knees, and they wear fur hats with ear flaps that they rarely use. They are clearly tougher than this correspondent.

On the first day I was introduced to the Ambassador's staff and was surprised to find that many of them were Russian. They were all hard working and cheerful and did the routine typing, filing, telephone work, cleaning, cooking, laundry, gardening – or this time of year, snow removal. All the English staff were fluent in Russian and Adrian, who seemed to have been given responsibility for me, was well liked by all of them. He was a very handsome small man about my age and was clearly adored by all the ladies. Once I got to know my way from the office to my room and then to the dining room, he took me to meet the Ambassador.

Sir Stafford Cripps was a lean man with a narrow face and rimless glasses. According to Adrian he had been a pacifist during the Great War but then had managed an armaments factory. My affinity for him, at once that of a kindred spirit, vanished within the space of a sentence. Adrian also said that the Ambassador was a Labour politician and a vegetarian. It was hard to know where to put my mind when he greeted me. But I needn't have worried, the interview was over in seconds and I was shunted along to something altogether more terrifying.

John Bull was a nom de plume or more accurately an adjective phrase given to John Pulmer, one of the Ambassador's personal assistants and the man in charge of personnel matters. He is the one who hires, fires and monitors all staff matters. Entering his office was a little like entering the green room before the gallows. He was tall, portly and about 45 years old. He wore a blue striped suit, blue tie, immaculate white shirt. Facing him was a great deal like seeing a hangman for the first time. His office was gloomy with brown thick cigarette smoke. There were several bent packs of cigarettes on the desk. They were an unknown brand to me, but the writing looked Arabic – the Turks made good cigarettes I seem to recall.

Here at least I was offered a chair, apparently no one sat in the presence of the Ambassador. Bull had a voice that matched his size and there was little that would be confidential if said by him. The entire office, even those outside, were able to hear all that went on. Adrian had disappeared and I was alone with the beast.

'Thomas,' he bellowed, 'glad you are here. The Ambassador has needed another radio man for a while. The last chap was sadly found dead in the back garden one day a month or so ago. So life in the radio room will be a lot easier with you on board. I'm sure that you've already been advised, but you will help the other two operators with regular transmissions.' He smiled – a rather nice smile. 'I'm afraid there are rather a lot of them these days.'

'Sir?'

'Times are uncertain at the moment, and we are treading a fine line here – needing information from Stalin, but never wishing to get to close to things – if you know what I mean.'

I didn't, but nodded anyway.

He leaned back in his big chair, 'Also, I hope that you will be able to find enough to write about for your newspaper. There is much here that is very unique and would be of interest to people back home. Naturally we will help in any way we can.' I had no idea what he was talking about and I could interpret it in any number of ways. My poor brain had not come to any stable thinking position in the weeks it took me to get here. I was still looking for shadows where perhaps none existed.

'I hope that you have everything you need, but if you do find something, then please just ask. My door is always open.' Somehow I didn't think so, but he seemed friendly enough. 'Any questions Thomas?'

I could only shake my head in total fear. I didn't dare, even if I knew what to ask.

'Well, Thomas that's all. Welcome aboard.'

I was out in the corridor in seconds.

The next day, Adrian and I went for a walk along the river after lunch. The sun was shining and the power of sunlight reflecting off the snow was almost blinding. We pulled our hats down and squinted into the glare. The sun rose at about 8 in the morning this time of year and set again at about 5:30 – so we had a short period of daylight. Embassy staff, such as Adrian, were required to spend most of the working day indoors. My hours were from 7 in the morning until 5 or 6 at night and then again when required. There had to be some flexibility in all this, but that wasn't going to be a difficulty for me. We took what sun we could get.

Glen Hoffman was the coder and head of the radio room; a thin, jumpy, grey looking man of about 30, who smoked evil Russian cigarettes more or less constantly. He worked an afternoon/evening shift, 'When London's awake,' he coughed in my direction when I shook hands with him. He had a room in the outbuildings somewhere and rumour had it that he liked a drink or two. But he spoke good Russian and had a certain charm... particularly to the ladies.

The other operator was Fred Jessop. He was short and thin, about my age, unfit for military duty he said, so took radio training and was totally surprised and terrified to be in Moscow working for the British Embassy. He came from Cornwall, so I found him difficult to understand until I got my ear in, so to speak. He did radio work for Bull but was usually on the night shift or when neither Glen nor I were available. Also, knowing the intricacies of this place, he may have other unknown duties. He seemed to be in terror of life so always looked surprised and guilty. He was probably as pure as the driven snow, but would be the first one I'd interrogate if there were a problem.

When Adrian could slip out he said he would take me around the city as far as we were able to go. Today he seemed troubled. 'You have found the embassy library?' he asked in Russian. We spoke Russian whenever we could. It was a way for me to improve, especially my deplorable accent.

'Yes, thank you. It has been a great source of information.'

'Good.' He paused. 'Good. I'm glad you are finding your way around the embassy. And are you getting to know people?'

I nodded. 'They have been very kind and for the most part very helpful.'

'Good.' He paused for a long second this time. 'How are you getting along with John Bull'

'I can't quite figure him out. He looks terrifying and sounds even more so...' I heard Adrian snort. 'But ...'

'He is exactly as you say. But don't let him intimidate you... he is a kind man and, I think, he genuinely cares about the staff. I've always found him helpful and if you ever have a problem don't be afraid to talk to him. He's a Cambridge man, good at languages, took his degree after the last war and has been with the diplomatic service since he came down.'

'Family?'

'None that I know of... I think his work is his family and that includes all of us.' His voice trailed off.

'Adrian, I feel a 'but' coming in here.' This I had to say in English because the Russian syntax defeated me.

Adrian smiled, 'No, not exactly, but I do have to tell you something.' I felt a cold chill somewhere between my knees and my navel.

'Let's stop here a minute.' He stopped by a parapet from where we looked over the river onto the absurdly beautiful front of the Kremlin and the gold covered onion domes of the Kremlin's myriad of churches and cathedrals now closed since the Revolution. He turned around and leaned his back against the parapet, tipping his hat and wishing '*Dobriy den*' to a couple passing by. The elderly man nodded in reply. In a low voice Adrian continued in English. 'We can talk here. We can see who comes and who might hear.'

'Why?'

'Roy, my dear friend. This country is very nearly at war with ours and it is a

64

dictatorship under the far-from-benevolent thumb of a ruthless man. We are under suspicion just by being here.' He took a small pack of cigarettes from his coat pocket, knocked one out and offered it to me. I shook my head.

'I just want to warn you to be very careful what you say. Speak to whoever you wish, but say nothing of interest; listen for more than you give away.' He lit his cigarette and blew the smoke up under the brim of his hat and tossed the match over the parapet and onto the snowy bank of the river. He looked at me and smiled. 'This is a very closed country. Foreigners come with a level of suspicion all of their own.'

'What could I possibly say that anyone might think was important?' I knew I was not being entirely truthful.

'You'd be surprised.' He inhaled deeply on the cigarette. 'I hope it hasn't escaped your notice that we are followed wherever we go. My advice is to assume that everyone on the street and everyone in the embassy is spying on you. Start with the Russian staff and do not stop until you reach the top.'

'Even our own people?' I felt sick. 'Are we followed now?'

'Even our own people. It will be good discipline for you and yes we are being followed.'

I stared at him, expecting him to look different after such a revelation. 'Even you?'

'Especially me, Roy. Especially me.' He grinned. 'You will have been briefed about the NKVD?'

'Secret police?'

'More than that. NKVD are the police, the regular police, traffic police, fire fighters, border guards, and Uncle Tom Cobbley and all.'

I began to feel a little weak. 'So I may have already met some of them – when we arrived here ...'

'Exactly. They will have a visual image of you already and now, having followed you they will have the beginnings of a file all about you.' Adrian turned to look straight at me, then rubbed his cigarette against the parapet in the snow. 'Make no assumptions about them. They are the ones who arrange the executions, disappearances and torture of anyone that the Russian hierarchy decides it has reason to distrust.' He flicked the dead ash off his cigarette onto the stone coping, felt the end and put it into his pocket. 'Anyone. They are not just uniformed police; they are everywhere – even in the Embassy.' Now I felt not just weak but sick as well. 'See the chap with the shovel? Behind me? Watch what happens when we turn to go back to work.' But it did not stop there. 'Also, it is not unlikely that some of the British staff are spying for our hosts.'

I choked. 'What?'

'I'm afraid so. It is also likely that some of our staff and others who use the Embassy – British businessmen, journalists, military attachés and a whole lot of others – may be spying for either us or for them.' He looked at my face which felt ashen to me and probably looked like it and laughed. 'Just be careful and trust no one.' He slapped me on the back. 'You will survive – most of us do.'

My conversation with Adrian troubled me more than I could say. Transmitting whatever the Ambassador wanted was easy. Decoding the erratic stuff sent from or to The Laundry was no problem. What I should call Smythe and Johnson was a ball of space in my mind. I presumed that they were part of the SIS since Smythe clearly had means to get clandestine things done and Johnson had the look of someone who had been in the diplomatic business a long time, but they hadn't confirmed anything. I had to assume that this was how bits of the secret service worked. No names, nothing to pin anywhere. I decided that the best nom-de-guerre was 'The Laundry' and that is what I used when I began transmitting information to them. They never objected. I was a spy I guess – so I tried to play the spy game without being too silly about it.

The idea of being spied on, however, was somewhat unsettling. I hadn't appreciated how closed a society this was. Sure there were things we didn't report on in England – one only had to think of the Mrs Simpson affair. But not being able to talk to ordinary people was disturbing. Not being able to trust people – anyone - was more so. I didn't think I was suspicious by nature, but now I felt that everyone I passed was about to plunge a knife between my shoulder blades.

The next time I went out alone, I bravely looked for an ironmonger's shop and was eventually directed to a dark little street. I took the chance that a visiting Englishman looking for an ironmonger wouldn't be suspicious enough to bring about an inquiry by the Kremlin.

Inside an equally dark little shop I struggled with my inadequate Russian to define a padlock, eventually through a few appropriate words, like 'close' and 'tight'. Then with some suitable miming, he understood enough and produced a selection. I chose two and also some clasps, screws and screw driver. He was delighted with the guessing game and presumably the pecuniary arrangement we eventually reached was satisfactory. I went back to the embassy, feeling that half of the Russian police and most of the population were following me.

Back in my room, I took the wireless that I had been given at the mansion from behind the loose wall panel where I had hidden it, put it into my trunk, and secured it with its padlock. Then I secured the new padlock to the bed side cabinet. It was merely a small attempt to confuse a thief. Then I sorted out the documents and other items that I carried with me at all times. I created a pocket to hang behind the back pocket of my trousers from a cotton handkerchief and sewed the papers and some paper money into it. It was a feeble attempt and would be of no use if I were ever searched, but it prevented it being stolen at least. My ID, I kept in a buttoned pocket inside my jacket. I sat for a long time on the bed with The Laundry's code books in my hand, unsure where I could put it to be safe. Should they always be with me, or secure somewhere in my room?

6

April 1941

Monday 21 April 1941: They tell me spring is coming. It is hard to tell. There is still snow, and more snow around the city. But I feel that the sun is stronger when it shines and there is a possibility that it might be strong enough to melt some of it soon. Flowers will be blooming at home now. I can't let myself get homesick. I haven't been here three months yet!

In spite of the darkness and lack of colour in this country it was obvious that some people lived very well. They clearly had money and rank – privilege if you like. They had the best clothes, women were fashionable and 'voices off' told of clubs, theatres and night life of some quality. It was silly of me to have assumed that this entire country was made up of penniless peasantry. I had been expecting to see bleak queues of starving people seeking a single loaf of bread. It was likely that in some parts of the country this was so, but here in Moscow, levels of life slid along beside each other as they did in other cities around the world. The distance between the rich and poor however was not a result of economics alone; it seemed to be based on meritocracy. Those who worked hard and did what was asked of them were rewarded. That is what we were being told of course.

I had little to report to The Laundry on my weekly sign-ins, so sent a short string of mundane observations, more to keep my skill at coding in good order as anything else and to let them know that I had some observational ability… I hoped I would never need to use it for real.

SA44 Moscow to BR10 The Laundry 27 April 1941 0609 133 Good quality of life and good night life here for many Fashion Opera Theatre Party and government officials have good apartments and cars No hostility obvious

Adrian and I went out on our usual – weather permitting of course - lunch time walk.

'Do you suppose that the NKVD is getting used to see us? I don't notice any obvious lurking wraith ...' I had to look the word up in my little Russian/English dictionary. '... following us today. We could be just out for a stroll.' We crunched our way over a mound of mushy snow scraped off the pavement but left across the path.

'Of course we are. We are also improving your education.' He stopped to sweep snow out of the cuff of his trousers. 'I have some news for you. The frequency you will be given this afternoon is an unusual one. It is not Russian but called Lucy.'

'Lucy? Some fancy lady transmitting gossip from the highest places?'

'No. All we know is that it originates in Lucerne.'

'The Swiss aren't spying on us all are they?'

'We have no idea who they are and naturally we don't want to know. But we do know that this outlet gives good information about German military activity. It has been active since 1939 and has as yet failed to give us something that didn't turn out to be true or of some use. At first we had trouble decoding it, but it now is being transmitted to the GRU and is in a different system. We get little bits of it.'

'If Russian Intelligence get it, does London receive it too?' Of course they did.

'Yes, but by the time they decode the transmissions, recode them for us, transmit again... well you get the picture.'

'And you want me to ...?' So I could now spy for two masters.

'That's what we do old chum. But this one is not for general information. Do what decoding you can. Jessop can probably help if you need it.'

'No pressure then.' I knew then that my duties here would get more and more intense.

The next morning when I checked in I got a coded message from Smythe.

BR10 The Laundry to SA44 Moscow 28 April 1941 0614 52 Excellent information Send more Good articles in Journal too

That meant they wanted more – what more could I tell them? It also meant that my articles were being published. I had no deep insights into what the Ambassador was saying to Stalin or what Stalin was saying to Mr Cripps. Radio transmissions from him or on his behalf were coded and not for my understanding, nor had anything I heard elsewhere contradict what I was able to overhear from other staff, Lucy or random signals I listened to. I was somewhat adrift.

So, as instructed, I sent my reports for the paper via the Embassy's mail bag. Apparently we had to trust that diplomatic bags weren't interfered with, but to be honest, any sensible person would have reason to doubt that. It would be foolish in the extreme not to admit that we would do exactly the same to them, given the chance.

I reduced my chances of saying the wrong thing by writing only what was legitimate journalistic copy for the paper. This would not prevent it from being dissected by those who look for coded messages, but it would prevent any secrets from being transmitted this way because there weren't any. I felt reluctant – given my status as a spy – to go into too much detail for the paper. It would look as if I were prying and analysing, so I stuck to observational material.

It helped that the post was delivered to the Swedish embassy in Moscow and sent on to Britain from there. How I had no idea. Sweden for the moment hadn't been taken over by the Nazis and in name at least was still neutral. Worryingly however, it allowed considerable numbers of transit movements from or to Germany with troops and provisions. The Swedish parliament claimed it did not damage their neutrality, but Sir Stafford was concerned. There was little he could say or do. But he was obviously worried. I had to make the assumption that, until told otherwise, it was still safe for my copy to be sent through diplomatic means but I was able to report to The Laundry about Cripps' concern.

I got out quite a lot, looking for things of interest to write about and tried to find people to talk to casually but this was difficult. People willing to talk were rare. The people in the streets did not smile and rarely spoke. They were all reluctant to chat. They wouldn't meet my eyes and replied only in single words as if giving directions to get somewhere. Clearly they were afraid that they might be overheard or seen to be too friendly and so reported, arrested, taken away with consequences I could not begin to imagine. The shadow of the NKVD was everywhere I was beginning to find. I had no desire to send some innocent person to prison or worse, because I engaged them in innocent conversation. So I listened. I would have loved to be able to speak to the man who happened to be sitting next to me on a bench but it was obvious that I was not Russian and I was always conscious of being watched and he probably knew it too.

When this wasn't giving me anything to write about or to report to Smythe, I found a great deal else to fill the obligation. Moscow was such an unusual city and so foreign to me, that almost anything was noteworthy; the weather, people and how they looked, the shops, such as they were, the Embassy and the people in it, within limits of course.

I was invited to Embassy functions, however low key they might be at the moment. We were in an unusual position, not at war with Russia, but not allied either. In fact the Non-Aggression Pact Stalin signed with Hitler in August 1939 still loomed over us all. Hitler signed a similar agreement with Estonia and Latvia in June 1939, then promptly invaded them. So without wishing to give advice to the great man, I should be very careful if I were Stalin just now.

I made conversation at these soirees and did my best to just be charming and a little thick. My lack of fluent Russian helped here and I was grateful that I could understand more than I let on. But I collected very little information of any importance either for The Laundry or for the paper. And Adrian kept an eye on me. I wished I knew just what his motives were. Like he said, trust no one. But I dearly wished there was someone I could trust. Through several social events I did hear a layer of disquiet among the people who attended. Some were party or government officials and for them, the universe was unfolding as it should. For the lesser mortals, like the waiting staff and employees of the embassy, or businessmen and military men, there were differing opinions, however lightly expressed, that all was not well with the world. But I recalled that people at home liked to grumble about their masters too. It was human nature after all.

During the day when I was 'just one of the Ambassador's radio men' I sat at my wireless set in the radio office, sending and receiving for Sir Stafford, or tuned to Lucy's frequency if there was nothing to do for him, and if that too was quiet, I listened in to any Russian frequency that I could find especially if it was in code. I wanted to keep my hand in as far as I could.

Not all of them were in code, but if they were in plain text they concerned everyday needs, wants and grumbles and were not worth too much investment on my part. If I were analysing traffic or trying to assess where Igor was complaining from today as opposed to yesterday, and why he had moved, there might be something in it, but that was beyond my abilities. I looked for the transmissions that didn't make sense to anyone else. Then, if I could, I worked out what the code was and what they were actually saying. The senders seemed to have the idea that they were the only ones smart enough to do this. Anything I found of interest from these random frequencies or from Lucy I forwarded to

Smythe when I'd analysed it. What happened to it next I had no idea, but I was probably not meant to know.

At other times, I was getting to know people by sight at least in and around the Embassy and we had gentle conversations about nothing in particular. Everything was wrapped in layers of wool. One morning, I went to the radio room for my shift, and found Fred asleep or dozing in his chair. He had his ear phones on, but suddenly woke and jumped for the key. He responded with a few key strokes and was about to settle back when he saw me and jumped again, looking characteristically guilty.

'Were you asleep?' I asked.

He pulled one ear phone off and yawned. 'Only a little,' he grinned. 'I can wake up if I get a signal that I need to reply to. Try it.'

It was the way he did things and it seemed to work. So, more often than not, unless there was a particularly busy night, I found him dozing. While it was quiet and before the reports for the day landed on me, we chatted. He was a great gossip.

'You will have to keep an eye on Glen,' he told me one day early on. 'Quite fond of a drink, so you may have to cover for him now and then.'

'I'll be prepared. But how does he keep his job if he has a problem like that.'

'He's so good at it that he can do it even if he's half pissed.'

'What if he's totally... pissed.'

Fred grinned again. 'That's when you cover for him. Put him in the back of the radio room – there's a pile of boxes and stuff there. He can sleep it off.'

'Surely someone will notice that he's not here when he should be.'

'Just so long as the work gets done, and there's no international incident, no one seems to care much.'

James, Cripps' secretary, came in at that moment with a sheaf of work, and we both put our headphones on and began the long trudge of transmitting indecipherable gibberish.

28 April, 1941

Dearest Annie,

I think about you every day and wish I could be close enough to telephone or see you. The photograph you sent is the one joy I have at the moment and I carry it everywhere with me. The winter seems to go on forever and I long for spring flowers and a walk along the river with you on my arm.

Please keep writing to me – tell me the everyday things you do and the people you see. I want very much to be able to spend time with you and if this is how I must to it, then that will be my one consolation.

Sorry to be so gloomy – it is snowing again.

All my love,

Roy

RUSSIA Moscow (Worcester Journal) Friday 2 May 1941 *St Basil's in Red Square* **by Royston Thomas.**

This colourful church is such a bright sight in the grey streets and Red Square seems to be illuminated by it. It was built in the middle of the 16th century to commemorate a military victory by Ivan the Terrible. It has a collection of irregular and brightly coloured onion domes, all different and seemingly added for no other reason that joy. Its proper name is Cathedral of Intercession of Theotokos on the Moat, but St Basil's is easier for the English tongue.

In contrast to the huge cathedrals as we understand them, this is made up of eight individual side chapels built around a ninth - each filled with icons and highly decorated walls in soft colours. The chapels are connected by narrow corridors and winding stair cases. Added onto one side in 1588 is the tomb of the so called holy fool Basil the Blessed for whom the cathedral is colloquially named.

Basil is thought to have died in 1552 and been a prophet who correctly predicted a fire in the city in 1547. He was born about 1468 in Yelokhovo, now a part of Moscow to a poor family. He lived to a very ripe old age for the times and became well known in adulthood as an eccentric who shamed people into helping the poor. He even went so far as to rebuke Ivan the Terrible for his violence.

Astonishingly, when he died Ivan the Terrible acted as one of the pall bearers who carried him to his final burial place at the cathedral. He was canonised in 1580.

His family was extraordinary and not only were his mother and father canonised but four of his nine siblings also.

This church, like most others in Russia, was secularised in 1929 and has been a branch of the State Historical

Museum ever since, but it remains a stunning icon in its own right. Regardless of the gloom of winter around, it is guaranteed to give a lift to one's feelings.

I tuned to the frequency that the Laundry gave me at 0600 every Sunday morning and from time to time got messages back the next morning that told me they were monitoring what I wrote and to carry on. Carry on what? I felt like a blind mouse in a field trying to find the burrow that I belong to. Every time I sent copy I felt as if I had mistakenly wandered into the open and was about to be swept up by a large bird with an appetite. I sent situational observations that I translated from Russian transmissions which were appalling and simplistic – they made my soul raw from the understanding of them. The poor man on the ground had no idea he was in the shadow of the eagle from the west.

The paper on the other hand wanted general information – everyday stuff for the readers of middle England. And that's all I could write. No one here said anything unusual. No one had any concrete opinion. Everyone was consumed by the war, or fear, or food, but no one had anything to say about any of them. No one wanted to comment. It was like living in two worlds at once – two worlds that were not quite matched to each other – there was a huge gap in between that everyone was ignoring.

The material I decoded was pretty boring stuff. Maybe it had more significance to minds more militarily acute than mine. I wondered what good I was doing. At least I wasn't shooting people.

And the 'spy' transmissions that I received regularly were meaningless.

RUSSIA Moscow (Worcester Journal) Wednesday 21 May 1941
Babushka **by Royston Thomas**

Babushka is a lovely word. It is what English speakers here call the colourful headscarf worn by most women. It is a large square of cloth folded corner to corner worn over the head and tied under the chin. It is the same as worn in England.

For the Russians however, babushka means more than a headscarf. In Russian babushka means grandmother. So it is easy to see how a term for one thing can mean another and be transposed to a visible symbol one sees every day.

Most women wear the headscarf and during the winter it comes as no surprise that some kind of head covering is necessary. If made of wool as many of them are, they will

74

be warm and provide protection for head, ears and neck. In summer they may be of lighter wool or other material and may be worn tied at the back of the neck. Then they may serve only to keep their hair tidy and out of the way, in the same way that women in England wear turbans.

Its origins may be in religious modesty of times gone by but is not in any way unique to Russia. Eastern European, Muslim and even Christian women have worn a head covering for centuries. They have other names of course, like wimple or rousari. They may have been symbols of fashion or social status. Only here has it become allied to the real or honorary title of a family member.

They have in times past, been identifiers of status or purpose. During the Russian Revolution red headscarves were symbols of female commissars or others who wished to show loyalty to the revolution.

Today we see babushkas everywhere. They adorn women doing their shopping, young girls going to school or the women who sweep the streets. It is a leveller that promotes every woman to that of family member.

Soon I was getting tired of trying to find things of interest to write about. This had to be one of the most tedious I had yet sent.

Intel for months had been about a pending German invasion. It came from Lucy, transmissions we made that I could read, conversations in the office, dropped hints, gossip and a thousand other places. Dates varied widely, statistics about the scale of an invasion varied. The only common element was that an invasion would come. In spite of this, no preparations seemed to be in place, no increase in military activity, either in radio traffic or boots on the streets. There seemed to be no change in factory output, but that perhaps was beyond my ability to know. No instructions or warnings had been given to ordinary people, on how to stay safe, how to prepare or what to expect. No ditches had been dug, no guns rolled into place. No one seemed to be taking any notice.

I got to the radio room early one morning. Fred was asleep as usual and I flicked through the pile of transmission slips that he would send to the young lad in the office later for delivery around the Embassy. I began to put them in order. Clearly Fred was listening to Lucy in his quiet moments too because last night she had given up a terrible secret – a date. I took the terrifying slip and left. Fred hadn't moved.

Back in my room, I sat down and wrote a short message. I took out my conversion tables and converted all the letters to numbers according to our agreed cyphering system. Then I turned to sheet 76270 - the next one in the code book -and added the numbers I had created to the numbers in the five digit blocks on the sheet. The resulting sums were then converted back into random letters via the cyphering system. These I would transmit. In plain text I wrote my sending call sign, the receiving destination, date, time and number of letters and then the horrifying message. I used the emergency frequency.

SA44 Moscow to BR10 The Laundry 20 May 1941 0710 115 Very firm intel that Germany planning to invade Russia in late June probably around 20 German planning well underway and firm No prep here

I went to the window again. In spite of what I now knew, the world looked just the same. I didn't want to think what it was going to take to change all this.

I went back to the bed, collected the used page from the code pad, my plain text and coded transmission slips and burned them in a large ashtray on my bedroom table. Then I leaned on the window frame and put my forehead on the cold glass. It was surely about to begin.

Minutes later, I was at my desk in the main office again, headphones around my neck and the incriminating message from Lucy mixed with the others from overnight. Fred was awake. 'You're late this morning.'

I handed the stack to the runner. Stalin must know this. Lucy knew this. The Laundry knew this. Surely the Ambassador already knew this too. Why was I the only one to be horrified?

Saturday 21 June 1941 It is necessary to keep everything looking normal at the Embassy so Adrian has organised an evening event tonight. We did not speak of what we know. As it is midsummer's eve the sun doesn't set totally. There is a kind of dusk after about 11 pm that blends into dawn and it never truly gets dark. I don't know if he has planned an evening of bacchanalia but I expect that some decorum will exist and thankfully we aren't expected to arrive in some silly costume. As usual, most of the guests will be embassy staff, business people of both British and Russian-British interests, journalists from the English speaking papers and a few others. I probably will never know why they have been invited.

I get little info to The Laundry these days. There is little to say having already given them the damning news from Lucy. Nothing is being done here; there is nothing to report. Even the spy is quiet.

Bull was delighted with the idea of a party and arrived early in what must have been his best suit. He slapped me on the shoulder as I passed him with an empty tray. Even I had been pressed into helping set up the tables. 'Lovely evening! What a lovely time to have a party!' All I could do was agree but I felt as if I were waiting for the other shoe to drop.

The party was a great success and the weather was nice, although it had been raining in the days before. We spent most of evening on the embassy lawn. There were lights in the trees, long tables covered with the best linen and plenty of food and drink. Bull was having a wonderful time, laughing and joking with anyone who would listen. He really was a different person when he was enjoying himself. Adrian, too, was in his element. He was born to entertain like this and it was a pleasure to watch his confidence in meeting, greeting and introducing people to each other. He dragged me in front of a young woman who seemed to be alone or abandoned and forced me to 'look after her' as he put it. She was called Lana and she looked to be about 18. She had little English and so we conversed in my halting Russian which caused her great amusement. The party had started late because of the late evening and by about 10:30 my little guest had disappeared into the company of an older woman who took her home. But I had enjoyed her company. I excused myself about 1 in the morning and went to check the radio. Even I was entitled to a night off and away from my little claustrophobic wireless station. But given what I knew I felt I needed to check and see if there was any further information. The 20th had now come and gone. I had done this every day since we got the original news but all had been quiet. It was still quiet so I tumbled into bed and was annoyed when my alarm woke me before 6. It was only much, much later that I discovered that Lana was Svetlana, daughter of JS himself! She particularly like the British and so, heavily chaperoned, was allowed to attend occasional parties. I doubt if it ever happened again.

I undid the locks on my trunk, took out the set and opened it on the bed. I put the cable for the headphones into the socket, plugged in the key and aerial. I selected the crystal and plugged it in, then clipped the aerial to the bed springs. This was just my usual Sunday morning check-in. I could let them know I was still alive with nothing to report in a few key strokes. Then I could go back to bed if the world was still a quiet place and use my day off to sleep.

The headphones were heavy and when I yawned the action of my jaws pushed the things into my skull. I turned the set on and the resulting noise made me wrench the headphones off my head. I was sure that the sound would be heard in the next room. The frequency that I normally used was active and I frantically tried to tune to another but every frequency was equally busy.

Then I listened. The noise was in plain language – Russian language. And language in panic. Stunned I sat on the floor and searched other frequencies. All the transmissions were fractured, broken, pieces of language, demanding information, reporting damage, seeking help or direction. All in plain text!

I tuned one frequency at random as finely as I could and listened. Stations and military sites somewhere in the west were under fire. Hundreds of them. No doubt it was the Germans - the Poles and most of the Baltic states were already under occupation and could hardly have raised a platoon of rifleman according to what I'd been told. It had to be the German invasion. The very big German invasion that we had been warned about and knew was coming.

I leaned on the wall beside the table. My stomach was like a rock, my legs like water. I hugged my knees and leaned my head on them. I knew what this meant, but my mind was not prepared to accept it. It meant all the things that I hated most in life were now rampaging towards me. Would I have to escape or would I be overrun? Did I run or...? I stowed the radio and its parts, dressed as quickly as I could, went to Bull's room, and told him I had been listening downstairs... a lie, but did it really matter? Clearly Jessop wasn't on duty or he would have raised the alarm long ago. Even if he were asleep, he couldn't have missed this.

A second later, Bull was running down the corridor in his dressing gown and slippers banging on the doors and bellowing as he went. 'Get up! There's been an invasion!' 'The Germans are here!' 'Come to the main office!'

The office was never a place where order reigned: messages coming in from other Consuls all over the country, telephone calls from other Embassies, checking information, asking questions, business people and people in trade in the city seeking clarification of any number of disparate rumours on which this city seemed to thrive, or passing on information. But usually there was a sort of control. Today there was only energy.

Within a few minutes, all the English residential staff in various states of dress and undress were rushing in looking for the right thing to do. The large wireless set from one of the private rooms had been wheeled in and someone I'd never seen before was trying to keep it tuned to the BBC Overseas Service. The window was open and he was shouting to someone out of sight, with instructions on what to do with a cable. Fred and someone I had seen only now and again were hunched over other receivers, trying to hear on headphones through the noise in the back ground; there was no sign of Hoffman. Clerks were on the telephone, calling in other staff; typists were busy apparently transcribing messages. A few Russian staff had arrived in response to telephone calls and were stunned to find out what had happened. It was Sunday and the need for them to come in had to be very unusual indeed. There was no word on the streets. I was sent directly to the radio.

Out of the corner of my eye I saw the Ambassador's private secretary, James run – actually run – to the other side of the room as the Ambassador came in. The Ambassador alone among the rest of us was dressed properly and had had a shave. Hoffman slid into a chair beside me, looking very dishevelled. We all stood up. This was an historic moment – we all knew it. James called for quiet and the din receded. The Ambassador, immaculate and controlled, stepped forward.

'I regret that I have to tell you that Germany has invaded Russia. At about 2:30 this morning, over 100 divisions began crossing the border.' There was a collective gasp at this news. A hundred divisions sounded like a lot and I looked at Adrian beside me. He seemed to read my mind. 'One or two million,' he whispered. I felt weak and my head seemed light. I looked for a desk to lean on.

The Ambassador was still speaking. 'And at 5:30 this morning, Germany formally declared war on Russia. There has so far been no comment from the Kremlin and we do not know what Stalin proposes to do. Neither do we know what the German objectives are. We only know what we have heard from the sources you see around you. We don't know what we here in the Embassy will be expected to do or what will be required of us. Although it is likely that Russia will join the war on the side of the Allies.' There was a brief sign of relief around the room. '... or alternatively it will be overrun. I urge you all to stay calm and remember that we are here to serve the King and do whatever is requested by His Majesty's Government. I thank you for your loyalty and can only say that adversity will come our way. How we respond to it will be a mark of British resolve in the face of that adversity. We will all do our best.' There was a second of silence and then someone shouted 'Three cheers for the King!' and the cheers lifted our spirits and enclosed us all in the same task.

I put the headphones back on and re-connected to the big radio set. Jessop looked as if he had seen a ghost; Glen Hoffman was in the other corner did not even look up. The messages that were being bayonetted into my ears were incomplete, garbled and full of military jargon that I didn't understand, but the message was the same. 'We are being over-run!' I handed the scribblings to a young typist. He continued work without acknowledging them.

I worked for several hours – the messages coming as fast as I could write them down. The slips disappeared as I stacked them in the tray beside me. When I looked up the next time they were collected I asked, 'These,' I shook the pile of slips, 'are all coming from the front. Why are there no replies?' He shrugged and shook his head. An hour later I took a message in code, replying to an incoming message. It was a simple one and I unpicked it in a few minutes. It read, 'You are insane. Transmit in code.'

For the rest of the day I scribbled until I thought that my finger joints and wrist would soon fail to work at all. I will remember the messages until I die: 'We are under fire. What shall we do?' 'We are being overrun. Help us.' 'No officers left. Send instructions.' 'Aircraft destroyed on the ground. None got into the air.' 'Division destroyed. Equipment, men destroyed.' 'Bridge gone.' 'All dead.'

SA44 Moscow to BR10 The Laundry 22 June 1941 2146 176 Details uncertain TX received show Soviet field in disarray No orders returned No counter authorised No comment from Kremlin German front advancing very rapidly Germany declared war 5:30 am Will report daily

The next day in a few minutes snatched in the fresh air, Adrian and I saw that people were buying what they could and apparently withdrawing their savings from banks. There were queues outside. The streets were busy; people were focussed, not speaking. Many had packed up what they could transport and were leaving the city. Where they went was largely unknown and not many people cared. We saw shops shut and houses with curtains and shutters firmly closed. Would they ever come back? What would the city be like when they did, if they ever did? Stalin said that the invasion was just a rumour. I no longer cared what day it was, in fact I wasn't at all sure; I transmitted to The Laundry with what little I knew.

SA44 Moscow to BR10 The Laundry 23 June 1941 0558 115 Banks closed no cash left People leaving Some activity in defence of city Announcement from Molotov on 22 June probably written by Stalin

SA44 Moscow to BR10 The Laundry 24 June 1941 0618 154 Front now Barents to Black Sea 2000 aircraft destroyed Rychagov arrested for cowardice and conspiracy Also others Few leaders of experience left Orders to front line too late or wrong

SA44 Moscow to BR10 The Laundry 25 June 1941 0610 42 Everyone in Embassy exhausted No news from Stalin

SA44 Moscow to BR10 The Laundry 26 June 1941 0551 162 Embassy works to gauge public opinion, no firm news from Kremlin Some queues for food Bakers conscripted, bread gone. Some criticism of government silence Public believe war can be won in weeks

7

July 1941

Thurs 3 July 1941 Stalin has at last spoken. He has been silent since the invasion. One suspects that he did not believe it possible and did not wish to believe it when it was put in front of him. But today, he broke his silence with a rousing address exhorting all citizens to 'put all production on a war footing,' and for 'partisan units to be formed' across the country. But more horrifying, he demanded that the earth be scorched and not a loaf of bread or pint of oil be left to be of assistance to the enemy.

We worked as long as we could stand up, slept at our desks or caught a few hours on a sofa where there was one without a body already on it.

Everyone worked all hours possible. As usual I was sending and receiving for the Ambassador and when I could I listened for Lucy and Russian transmissions through the day and most of the night and then caught a few hours sleep in the early morning before starting all over again. I had not seen my bed for a week, except for brief transmissions to The Laundry. After two weeks of frenetic activity when I, like most others who had worked straight through without a break were all about to collapse, Bull called me into his office.

Smolensk? Bull wanted me to go to Smolensk? The Ambassador was worried about the staff, Adrian said. He had sent some Russian staff home for a few days to rest and banned other residential staff from working more than 10 hours. For some reason Bull had decided I needed a few days away.

I went to the embassy library and took the huge atlas of Russia from the desk where it was kept. The pages were well thumbed. Clearly I was not the only one without a good grip on Russian geography. According to the atlas Smolensk was not quite half way to Poland – I should be safe. The German front line was a long way to the west.

Bull handed me an envelope. Inside were numerous papers giving authority to me from the British Ambassador to deliver papers to some people whose names I could barely pronounce, the papers themselves, travel passes and a scrappy piece of rough paper signed by some Russian authority at the NKVD, some money and a train ticket inside. The ticket was for tomorrow. On top was a list of names and addresses.

He looked tired, harassed and spoke uncharacteristically quietly. 'Be prepared to stay a week. Boarding house behind station. Deliver the papers from Cripps and find people whose names are on this list; insist they leave immediately and help them get out. It is very important that they leave and leave immediately. As far as anyone else here is concerned, you are on special duties for me... and me alone.' He then shoved a bundle across the desk. It contained clothes and some very worn boots.

I was not so naive as to think that the day would never come when The Embassy would ask me to do something for it. But I was just a radio operator as far as they were concerned. What did they really want? Why was it so important for people to get out of the Smolensk area? Stay a week? Would it take that long to find these people and convince them to leave?

SA44 Moscow to BR10 The Laundry 3 July 1941 0615 202 Germans at Baranovichi 100 miles in 4 days Also at Molodechno by 25 June 150 miles Railways in chaos Wounded returning Troops outbound with no orders just a destination Few adequately armed Rumours of heavy surrenders and many encirclements

SA44 Moscow to BR10 The Laundry 3 July 1941 1905 318 Am being sent to Smolensk Will be gone a week Rumours that German Panzer Divisions have captured Minsk on 28 Thousands of Red Army lost or captured Sources report no radio communication to the Red Army front lines Flags and hand signals only Leadership is poor or non-existent Orders are old fragmented and frequently contradicted Arms are late Mass evacuations from western cities

I looked long and hard at the suitcase that contained my radio set. If found in my room I would be charged with more offenses than I could imagine. The loose wall panel was too insecure. If I took the heavy thing with me, I would have to bury it in my pack and again, if caught with it... In the end I put it in my small trunk, covered it with clothes, padlocked the trunk and prayed.

RUSSIA Smolensk (Worcester Journal) Friday 7 July 1941
Smolensk by Royston Thomas

It is a peculiar feeling to be on a street in a small
Russian town on a beautiful summer evening. The weather is
fine and the days long, but life is tense and uncertain.
There are rumours that an invasion from the west is
possible. German forces have been reported advancing in
this direction and many people are worried. However the Red
Army is enormous and several divisions are advancing
towards the area for its protection.

People take comfort in the huge reserves of the Red Army
and are sure that the German Forces will be beaten back if
they advance too close to the city. Faith is an important
thing in Russian life and faith in the strength of the Army
and the land of Russia will see this city survive.

I wrote and committed it to memory rather than paper – most of it was lies
anyway. In the white shirt that was no longer white, trousers that were rough and
too large, flat cap and broken boots, I was able to pass as a person from
Smolensk. I spoke as little as I could and feigned a bad head cold to cover up my
accent a little. The travel pass and NKVD paperwork helped and no one
questioned me.

Over the next few days I found the people I had been sent to find. They were
all British nationals who moved to Russia, either because of political belief in
communism after the Great War or for reasons of greed. They wanted to make
money here. Almost certainly they were of other uses to the British Government,
but no one made a gift of that information to me.

There was so much activity in the city that I passed largely unnoticed. At least
I hoped so. Adrian's coaching in how to recognise the NKVD (impossible) or to
notice if I was being followed (a little easier) was invaluable. I adopted the
panicked look that everyone else had and like all the others, I kept my gaze
down and did not speak to anyone.

I found the boarding house and my landlady helped me find the addresses,
with a map drawn on a piece of rough newspaper. I delivered the papers and
sought the people I had come to see. The first people were non-committal. They
operated a small draper's shop on a narrow street of shops. Like all others, it
was small, dark and had a limited range of goods on offer. It probably had few
customers, but somehow struggled on. The old man behind the large dark
counter looked up in alarm as I came in. He quickly sent a small girl through
curtains that hung over a door into the back of the shop. The flash I got of the

interior was one of brightness and colour. Fabrics, furniture, lamps and wall hangings. It was a complete contrast to the gloom and the old man.

The next shop was a gunsmith. Like the drapers, it too was dark with a single hanging light. It was larger but only because the front counter was part of the workshop. Two young men were bent over work benches with pieces of silver and brass that were being tooled. They were intricately inscribed and the results would be magnificent – if you liked that sort of thing. As soon as I entered, they draped their work with oily cloths and I caught only a glimpse. Ostentation like this was obviously not meant to be visible. Perfectly understandable I thought in this country, where no one was meant to have anything of value.

The last on my list was a professional man – a doctor. His little office was sparse with only a small table and two chairs. Presumably he did not treat patients in the front of his premises, but I could only guess.

Like everyone else in this country, they were all afraid to talk. I spoke in English; tried to tell them who had sent me and that our information about the future of the city was bleak. I had the confidence of ignorance that they would not betray me, but I could not know if they understood what the Embassy needed them to do. Perhaps they believed that Stalin was right and nothing would happen to them; perhaps they did not wish to believe someone who looked and sounded like I did. But I delivered the messages, told them where to go to be helped out of the city and encouraged them to do it tomorrow or the next day at the latest. I told them to look at the chaos in the city if they did not believe me.

In each place, the response was the same. I went back every day and after two or three days, I began to see small signs that they might be taking me seriously and that perhaps packing was going on in the backs of these shops. I wondered if they were Jews, more used to dramatic upheaval that I was. It is entirely possible of course that the muffled sound of guns in the west or the constant rumours had more effect that I did.

In the meantime I cultivated an acquaintance at the boarding house. He was a soldier of old wars who limped from an injury, walked with a stick and maintained a keen interest in military matters. After our evening meal he asked me to help him take a walk to provide his weak leg with some necessary exercise. And so arm in arm we would wander slowly down the dusty street to an open space and then once around. When he was safely out of hearing distance from the boarding house and anyone around, he told me much. Perhaps he accepted the story that I came from the south east and therefore was not Russian. It may have given him confidence to speak; perhaps he saw through me from the beginning.

In spite of the heat he wore a large felt hat and long coat. 'I knew this invasion would come,' he snorted as he clutched my arm '... it is just our stupid leaders who did not.'

'Papa ...' I said in a whisper, '... be careful of what you say.'

He snorted again. 'What do I care? I am as good as dead anyway so I can say what I like. I am an old man, I am ill and I will not live long. So you can turn me over to the NKVD if you want to. It won't matter. Let me have my say.

'We knew they would come.' I could not tell him that our intelligence knew the same and told Stalin so in May. 'I go for a drink every day to hear the conversations there – my old friends from the last war – they tell me much.'

He stopped momentarily to catch his breath. 'There are two large German Armies advancing toward Smolensk. There are also several Red Armies gathering to the south. We have many, many more men than they do. The German supply lines by now will be so stretched...' He drew in a wheezy breath. 'Their insane rush to defeat us will be their downfall. How can horse drawn ammunition wagons, trucks that break down. How can they supply two – two! - whole armies?' He wheezed again. 'Through the rain! For once the terrible roads they have given us have will be our one defence...our only defence.'

He stopped at a wooden fence that would have fallen over but for the weeds and grasses holding it up. Here he let go of my arm, drew a single black cigarette from his coat pocket and struck a match with his thumbnail to light it. He drew on it and exhaled evil smelling smoke in my direction. 'The only one she allows me,' he cackled. 'She' presumably was our land lady. 'She can always smell it if I try to have more than one.'

No wonder, I was tempted to say, choking back a cough, and was ready to walk on, but he caught my arm. 'Hitler doesn't want our big cities. There are too many mouths to feed and too much risk from the people. So he will encircle them and starve them. Smaller cities like Smolensk, he wants.' He drew in the disgusting cigarette again. 'He wants the railway and the roads. He doesn't want the people. So he will kill us all.'

'But, the Red Army ...'

'Pah! You might think we can win, but we won't.' I must have looked surprised because he laughed hoarsely again and then coughed on the smoke. When the spasm finished, he spat into the grass. 'No, we will be overrun. There are no military leaders who can take us to victory. Stalin has killed them all.'

I knew some of this history but was anxious to hear it from his point of view, so I pretended not to know. 'Why?'

But he was shrewder than I had given him credit for. 'You will have heard of the purges no doubt?' I had to nod. 'Insane. To kill all the brains of your army. To kill every bit of experience. And at a time when the world is in turmoil. Stupid. Stupid.'

We turned back to the boarding house. 'Now we have no one except Stalin to lead us. Heaven help us all. Death will be total.' He stopped and wheezed again. 'But you must know about Katyn. You must listen and then tell. Damn Beria to hell.' Lavrentiy Pavlovich Beria: feared and fearful head of the NKVD.

He then told me a story that I could not comprehend. My mind failed to visualise it or to understand it. I failed the old man. I could not speak of it.

July 9 I look around me at the people in Smolensk and am afraid for them. What will be left of them? Who will be the destroyers: the Germans or the Red Army? But surely they will all be destroyed.

Smolensk

Wednesday 9 July 1941

Dear Mam and Da,

I've had a quiet few days near Smolensk. Quiet but tense. We know that the German advance is close, and there is no intelligence to indicate what their intentions are. However it would be stupid not to expect the inevitable. But the word around here is that nothing will happen for a week or two.

The advance has been incredibly quick and brutal so far, but it seems to have halted. Whether that was due to the need for supplies to catch up to the troops or the incredible rain storms earlier we may never know. The rain has turned the dirt roads, such as there are, into streaming rivers of mud and the German heavy guns will be immobile until it dries.

In the meantime, those who live here and who can, will get out and those troops of the Red Army that can be moved up will be brought forward. I'm in the middle trying to find out what is going on and apart from confusion and chaos I'm able to report little.

As soon as the roads dry a little and the trains begin again, I will return to Moscow. There is little I can do here now. But when I leave, I will be moving with a large evacuation.

With love from

Roy.

Friday 11 July 1941 It was dark and the heat was oppressive when the train arrived at Belorusskaya Rail Terminal in Moscow. It was early morning, but my sense of time had evaporated in the chaos and heat. I didn't look back. I walked to the embassy and sat on the step until the guard opened the doors in the morning. I didn't have the strength to knock. Someone took me in, relieved me of my blood stained clothes and put me to bed.

At Smolensk, I heard the bombers come and the dust from the Panzers was visible in the west as the inevitable approached. The Germans wanted this place very badly and enough of the mud had dried to dust. Its rail line led directly to Moscow like the old man said. They shelled the town and all that we could do was duck our heads, run for shelter and pray. The shelling had no perceivable discrimination from our point of view. The pilots did not care what was hit, only that something or someone went up in fire and smoke, and there was as much hell and damnation as possible. The reverberations and concussions from the guns seemed constant. Planes came from the sun just over the treetops. In the noise from explosion after explosion, a few defending guns, and terrified people, we could not hear them coming. Just a dark blurred shape and a trail of exploding buildings, sprayed fragments of concrete or rubble and timber and another one in its wake.

Prayer was all I had as I ran for the train station. I prayed that there would be a train leaving; I prayed that I would live to get on it and I prayed that it would leave before we all died. Behind me, the shells continued to crash without discrimination; buildings, people, animals, streets disappeared in volcanoes of concrete, wood, bricks, blood and flesh. Then more shells did it all over again.

Those of us who could ran for the train; I could see firemen shovelling anything that would burn into the firebox to get the steam up as quickly as possible. I could see the wheels begin to tense and grind against the steel rails as I and others grabbed any part of the carriage that would get us onto the train. My pack on my back crashed against my spine as I landed face down on the platform between two cars. Someone else landed on my back. As I extricated myself, I found it to be a wounded soldier who had been thrown on board. His right arm was missing and a wad of clothing had been tied crudely against it and strapped to his chest, presumably to stem the bleeding. His eyes were closed and he was barely breathing. One leg trembled.

As the train moved, men were digging against the rails with shovels. I dragged the bleeding body into the carriage. Someone at the other end of the carriage was ripping up wooden seats. Every space between those that were left and down the central aisle was occupied by bleeding, moaning and weeping people. Many of them soldiers but all of them physically damaged. A man who I took to be a doctor and a young woman, who I assumed was a nurse, were doing what they could to administer first aid. They looked at me with derision and I realised that I was the only unwounded person in the carriage, apart from them and it was easy to see how they assumed that I was a coward, fleeing a dangerous situation without regard for the situation that had created all this blood on the floor. They would have been right.

The young woman looked at the man I had dragged in and motioned to two large and only moderately injured men behind her. They took the wounded man from me and threw him off the train.

I shouted something at them – I don't know if it was in English or Russian. She looked at me with utter contempt. 'We deal with those who live, not those who are dead.'

I clutched the seat beside me and swallowed the instinct to throw up. There was enough vomit and blood already on the floor. 'How can I help?' I heard myself say. A second later a rush of air pressure and a loud whoomp enveloped the train from the rear. Everything including the air was thrown forward. The train took the thrust and lurched ahead. The men digging the tracks had blown them up. There would be no trains following us to give any assistance to the Germans. There was probably no succour to be had in Smolensk for friend or foe. I wondered about the old man with whom I had been philosophising such a short time ago.

With every crash of bombs near or far and with every mile we travelled away from the carnage, I prayed in thanks. Every crash might have been our last, but had it been, we would not have heard it.

For a few days, in the safety of the Embassy, I felt immune to the bombing I'd witnessed. I seemed to be safe, sane and more or less unaffected by what had happened to me. Until the Germans started bombing Moscow. We had been warned by Bull and his staff and told how to quickly get to shelters. But we had no warning. The first we knew was when several bombers began their run on the Kremlin. Being so close it sounded to us that they were flying straight into the Embassy. The building shook, windows rattled, books and clothes fell off the shelves, plaster cracked and ceilings buckled. All this was accompanied by the sound of more planes coming in overhead and of bombs exploding in, on and around us. Explosions that rammed air and noise into my ears so that I thought my head was going to implode. Why was the world tipping sideways? Why was I so dizzy? Where was everyone else? Sounds all around, but I couldn't hear any of them. My radio, what if it uncovered my radio. Get out, just get out. Dig the radio out later.

SA44 Moscow to BR10 The Laundry Tues 22 July 1941 0607 221 City bombed last night Embassy hit 3 firebombs Roof fires took 6 hours to bring under control Considerable damage but no injuries Some resistants many fires in the city in the city Food warehour and ammunitieeen train dama. EEEEEEE error

I was making errors on the key. My hands were shaking. My brain wouldn't connect properly with the coded letters I had in front of me. My mind was grey. My aerial was lightly damaged but still seemed to function. Closet broken and slightly burned in the fire. A few clothes damaged and everything thick with smoke. Roof timbers continued to smoulder and the room at the end of our block was open to the sky

SA44 Moscow to BR10 The Laundry 23 July 1941 0604 215 Raid again last night 195 bombers Estimated 46000 incendiaries dropp 300 in Kremlin. Peopl in panic Running with what they carry We EEEEEEE error I can't Stop

Again, I had to stop transmitting before I reached the end. The shakes were getting worse and the coded message became a jumble of letters. Was this shell shock or some other kind of breakdown? I was jammed in a corner of my room with my aerial hanging out of the back window. BR10 assured me that this somehow worked but they noted the errors and kindly assumed it was a transmission problem.

SA44 Moscow to BR10 The Laundry 24 July 1941 0616 151 Another night of bombing Report of 325 civilians wounded 31 killed Everyone in shock Embassy staff in panic or not at work We live in basements People in metro I can't EEEEEEE

RUSSIA Moscow (Worcester Journal) 24 July 1941 3:50 pm (GMT) *Night Raids on Moscow* by Royston Thomas

Moscow has continued to suffer almost nightly air raids. The British Embassy has itself been hit, but like so many great buildings, it was not seriously damaged in spite of fires in the roof. The fire services responded quickly and it was put out in a short time. The routine work of the Embassy staff goes on with barely a pause.

89

The work done here is important now that England and Russia signed a pact of mutual support on 12 July. The people who work here are dedicated and keep in contact with the Foreign Ministry in Moscow. The deputy Foreign Minister, Andrei Vyshinski keeps us informed of the Soviet Government's plans for the city and also the war. From him, we hear that the city is safe and secure and that the Red Armies are making good progress in holding back and even forcing retreat of the advancing German Panzer Divisions.

The nightly bombings are of course disconcerting, as anyone who has experienced them will know. But people are safe in shelters or in the Metro and no matter what damages are wrought, there are willing hands to re-build or to repair and everyone goes back to work in a matter of hours. It is clear that if Hitler intended to defeat this enormous country in a few weeks he will by now have revised his opinion.

It took hours to write the report; I could not get my brain to think with any logic. Mistakes and crossings out and wasted paper and what a load of rubbish it was. Lies, lies, lies. If we choose to believe Vyshinski, we must also believe that Stalin should be sanctified. But there is no way that the truth would ever be printed. No one would believe what was really happening here. No one would print the real facts except the enemy who want only to demoralise. We would soon be demoralised anyway – or dead. I just want to write the truth.

The ambassador was constantly back and forth over the river between the Kremlin and the Embassy. He seemed to have the weight of the war on his shoulders added to the responsibility of all of us and those who had their families with them. At the same time, he had to stay in close proximity to Stalin and Vyshinski. I didn't envy him. If I tried to imagine how it was for him, the weight of responsibility would be too much for me. How could I get out of here? This was not what I came here for. It was not what I wanted to do in this war. It was not what I could do best – not what I could do that was right.

26 July 1941

Dear Mum and Dad,

The biggest air raid so far in the war took place last night. There has been no official announcement yet of the size of the raid, nor the scale of the damage resulting. When we emerge from our shelters however, damage is obvious. Magnificent architecture that took my breath away yesterday is now lying in the street in huge piles of brick and stone.

Perfect plasterwork that once graced the street fronts of these buildings are now smashed beyond recognition. Skeletons of structures sliced in half show their innards – front walls are gone and curtains flap in eyeless windows; furniture teeters on sloping floors and timbers that many years ago promised to hold the buildings strong forever are broken and burned, sticking out of the huge piles of bricks blocking the streets. This goes on street after street. By climbing up the church towers that are left, one can see that this same destruction has spread over a wide area. We have no idea how many people were killed, but solitary souls climb over the destruction seeking anything that may be recognizable. They try to locate where they lived or worked and anyone who may still be alive.

We, on the other hand, cling on at the Embassy. Nightly we wait in the shelters for the bomb that will destroy it all. Then we climb out in the morning and try to carry on. I am trying to do the same. But being in the middle of this – the real centre of things – where real bombs fall and real people die - it's not how I would have chosen to live. Nor is it how I would have chosen to take part in a war. But now that I am here, I too, will just have to carry on, no matter the state of my nerves!

Much love, Roy.

PS And now Smolensk is being overrun. How long do we have?

We all moved into the library downstairs and slept among the furniture with a few screens and book cases here and there. I banked my wireless and a bag of personal things with the others in a chaotic pile at the end of the room. I would have to listen and transmit coded messages to the Laundry in the open office in the dining room on the main set. To be honest, I no longer cared who knew what I was doing. The 'spy' was thankfully quiet.

Then Bull called me into the remains of his office. There was a deep crack in the plaster of the ceiling and a thick layer of dust everywhere, except on the desk top and the cigarette packs. He closed the door behind me.

'Roy?' He had never called me by my first name before. I felt that he was getting close to me in a way that I was not sure about. He settled at his desk with his elbows nestled among the papers, and frowned at me. 'I'm a little worried about you.'

'I'm sorry sir...' he wafted away whatever I might have been able to think to say next.

'I think that I gave you too dangerous an undertaking by sending you to

91

Smolensk. I'm sorry.'

'It's all right, sir. You could not have known how it would be.' I struggled to believe what I was hearing...Bull apologising to me!

'The first time under fire is not a pleasant one and will be something you'll never forget. ' He inhaled deeply on the brown cigarette. 'I remember my first time. I was at Vimy, supporting the Canadians. I didn't think I would ever be the same again. But...' he blew a plume of smoke towards the ceiling. '...I don't want to worry you. We all cope in our own ways and you will too.' he tapped the black ash dangling from his cigarette onto a pile of butts in a large ashtray. 'Selfishly, your work is crucial to us ... as are the other two operators. Without you, we are blind. How we can help you overcome that shock, is for us to offer and something we must do.' Where was this leading? 'So, I have arranged for some leave for you – for a week or so.'

I opened my mouth to ask where I was to go and what I was to do, but he got there first. 'A little restful place where you can relax, and perhaps even write if you want to...a little R&R, if you like.'

Sunday 3 August, 1941

Dear Mum and Dad,

I have been away for a week or so. Recovering. The Embassy has use of a small dacha or summer residence a safe distance out of the city and I and a few others have been there enjoying some quiet and peaceful few days.

When I returned from Smolensk, I was not well. I had seen too much and felt too much. I expect I sounded quite irrational when I got back to Moscow and Mr Pulmer quickly sent me off with a sort of nurse and a cook. He probably needed to get me out of the way of the Ambassador. The dacha is by a small lake – just a small wooden house with a veranda in front from which it is possible to sit and look onto the water. There are trees around and all was very peaceful.

Don't worry, I was not injured, but what I saw of Smolensk was a shock that I found difficult to think of as real. The bombing was continual and the damage to people and buildings, businesses and families was fatal as far as the eye could see. It was a miracle that I survived, but I have no such hope for anyone else left behind. I got on the last train to leave – a hospital train, do I need to say more? But when the bombing started in Moscow, I guess I must have been in worse shape than I knew.

But now, a week at the dacha with gentle conversation with Serge, the nurse and good food prepared by Misha, the cook, have restored me to a kind of normality.

I find it very difficult to believe that human kind can do to itself what I saw but Serge tells me that I must believe it and once I do that I will be all right again. When I said to him that I did believe, but could not accept, he said I was ready to return to Moscow.

All my love,

Roy.

RUSSIA Moscow (Worcester Journal) Monday 11 August 1941
Moscow Raids **by Royston Thomas**

Moscow is experiencing what London has endured: air raids almost every night since 21 July.

In the first raid on 21 July, 195 bombers were counted and 6 or 7 were shot down but 46,000 incendiaries were dropped along with over 100 tons of high explosive, according to officials. Miraculously fires were started on only 1900 sites, but one was a food warehouse and another was a munitions train, hit while it was in the station. Three hundred incendiaries and 15 high explosives were dropped in the Kremlin alone, but little damage resulted.

Last night there was a major raid again and two aircraft factories were damaged. The government is asking everyone to stay calm. Measures will be taken to ensure the safety of everyone and the defeat of the German forces.

It is likely that people here are reacting in the same way as Londoners; many are leaving the city with what they can carry for the safety of the country. Those choosing to remain are seeking safety in the underground, known as Metro here. They take small beds into the tunnels every night and stay safe there 15 meters below the city until morning, when they emerge and return to work or to clear the damage of the night before. But there are others who meet the bombers by manning the anti-aircraft guns around the city or fight the fires that the incendiaries create. Further heroic activity is done by men and women who wait on roof tops and collect the incendiaries before they have time to set the buildings alight and throw them into the street where they are doused or cause little damage. This is a more heroic task than it might at first seem to be. The buildings here are largely wooden, and once alight the fires are hard to control. The men and women on the roofs are the first and finest line of defence of the city.

Thursday, 14 August 1941

Dear Mum and Dad,

I wish there was some way to describe my feelings now and some way to get this past the Embassy censors, but I feel like I have to try.

At the time of the bombings – what am I saying - the bombings of the city are still going on – almost every day. At the time of the early bombings and under the anguish that I brought back with me from Smolensk, my mind clawed itself into a tiny space in my head. It could take no more. Mr Pulmer arranged some peace for me as I mentioned in my last letter – I suspect that the Ambassador's staff wanted shot of me – I was probably a serious liability at that moment, probably blabbing all the wrong things.

Wish I could say that I feel better now. Calmer yes, but no less disturbed by what I saw and heard. Every bomb that lands within my hearing brings the promise of my death and the death of thousands of others – horrible deaths, burnings, mutilations, pain, pain, pain and death.

Will write again, when I have some good news.

Love from Roy

BR10 The Laundry to SA44 Moscow 23 Aug 1941 0601 15 Info re factories

SA44 Moscow to BR10 The Laundry 24 August 0621 329 Vyshinki cannot be found Cripps goes daily to the Kremlin begging for information and an opinion as to possible evacuation Do we stay or do we go Ambassador cannot lose contact with the Kremlin and yet we are being bombed into oblivion German troops continue to advance on the city with other troops being diverted to the north and south We don't know what the objectives are Probable encirclement

I took my hand off the Morse key. We were in a state of nothingness and what the hell did I know about factories? Are they stupid or choosing to ignore everything I tell them?

In the city there were shortages, shops shut and looting in places. The Russian internal police, NKVD, were harsher than even we could understand. We knew that they were an organisation not to be confronted even in the calmest of times. They were probably in their element now.

I was put back onto the radio – working for Cripps and listening to coded

94

Russian transmissions. There were more now, but there seemed to be no effort made to strengthen the codes used. Transmission was sloppy and relatively easy to understand. The Germans were no doubt reading the messages as easily as I did. I continued to give the sigint to Adrian who sighed heavily and passed it on to John Bull who no longer even spoke, loudly or otherwise.

This afternoon, as we took a break in the garden, Adrian looked exhausted and told me on the QT that the Russians have little faith in any radio sigint, preferring to intercept and decipher written communications. So it has been extremely difficult for the British Ambassador to pass on any information that might be of use to Stalin. He was suspicious of everything that comes by radio.

More worrying of course was the lack of security. Anything, written or received by our other sources, passed to Stalin by any means, was probably copied or cracked, confused or refused, so we had to assume that anything we sent would be known to the Germans too. Added to this of course, Stalin refused to see anyone, including the British Ambassador these days. To some degree we knew what was about to happen, but he probably did not.

There was no news from the spy for me to transmit for some weeks, but I continued to check in at the usual times, when I was able.

BR10 The Laundry to SA44 Moscow 25 Aug 1941 0605 48 Can you identify JS financial advisors in Kremlin Urgent

SA44 Moscow to BR10 The Laundry 26 Aug 1941 0604 23 Stalin picks who he chooses

BR10 The Laundry to SA44 Moscow 27 Aug 1941 0600 51 Info needed on productivity Factories War materiel and so on

BR10 The Laundry to SA44 Moscow 29 Aug 1941 0602 16 Factories Finance

SA44 Moscow to BR10 The Laundry 28 Aug 1941 0604 120 No info on productivity Munitions arriving at front for wrong rifles or wrong rifles for bullets or no rifles at all No uniforms Looting for food

SA44 Moscow to BR10 The Laundry 30 Aug 1941 0559 67 Factories moved to the Urals Productivity improving Quality quantity unknown

What the bloody hell did they mean? And what did they think I could do about getting it in the midst of this chaos? Hadn't they been reading what I'd sent them?

8

September 1941

Sept 1, 1941 We still don't know where we will be. The nightly bombing continues – railway yards, factories, civilian areas, schools, hospitals, everything. Cripps wants out. Stalin ignores everything.

Bull asked for a few minutes of my time – as if I had a choice in the matter. I should have guessed what was coming. Please go to Kiev. The Ambassador wanted information taken and handed over to certain individuals in the city.

'These people are important to us, Roy. We have to get them out.'

'Like before?'

Bull smiled. Of course he couldn't say. 'Things will get bad in Kiev and they will be in danger. But they are Jews with businesses and it may be hard to shift them. They need to receive the demand face to face. You have to tell them that the city will be overrun in the next few weeks. They must believe you and then they must be made to leave as soon as they can. They can come to Moscow. To us. Here. You must insist that they come out.'

'Are you sure you want them to come here? They may be in more danger in Moscow.'

Bull just shrugged. 'We will send them elsewhere as soon as they get here. It will be quiet in Kiev for a while yet. The front is some distance to the west and our information is that Hitler has abandoned his drive to Kiev in preference for renewed attacks on Moscow. Decrypted intel says he again wants the capital above all else. So you will be safe, but we don't have an infinite amount of time, particularly at this end.' He smoothed his hair above one ear. It was always short

– I wondered who his barber was – and immaculate.

'I hope you don't mind going. I think it is something you can do and we will have someone meet you and give you a place to stay. He will also help you find these people. You will need only a day or so.'

What could I say? Just how bad was the situation in Kiev? It could be nothing like Smolensk. How important were these people? How many were there? What could I say that would convince them?

He handed me the usual envelope with addresses in Kiev, the usual fold of roubles and the official and, probably spurious, passes. My story according to Bull was that I was a courier for the British Embassy. However I had nothing to deliver. Just how creative could I be if I were stopped and questioned? There was the usual pile of worn clothing on my bed and another pair of old boots.

Kiev: What did I know about Kiev except that it was south and west of Moscow? According to the thumbed atlas, dusty with plaster from the ceiling, it was at the eastern end of the Prip'yet Marshes and on a railway route from here. I was aware that there was a Ukrainian language – would my spoken Russian be enough for me to get whatever is needed? Hopefully, the someone I was to meet, would help with the language?

SA44 Moscow to BR10 The Laundry 7 Sept 0609 85 Am being sent to Kiev to deliver warning to certain people in the city May be out of contact Will take set

BR10 The Laundry to SA44 Moscow 8 Sept 0558 84 Report on the situation on your return Important Who are they What is Ambassadors role vis factories

Oh, bugger off. I have no idea.

I met a man on the train. He was huge, taller than me by nearly a foot and took up most of the seat beside me. Wavy hair, a grey black in colour although he was no more than 30, flopped over his forehead. A wide face, dark blue eyes, and straight eyebrows made him a handsome man. His size made him intimidating, but, I hoped, a friendly bear sort of man.

He was Ukrainian he said and happily told me all about the state in perfect Russian. I was not surprised to find that he was a blacksmith who spent most of his time in the countryside looking after the equestrian requirements of large land owners. I did not need to have it confirmed that the peasants on the huge collective farms were not in need of his services. They made their own arrangements no doubt. But he talked cheerfully about the last estate he had visited – a government official – something in the military structure but he did not go into details. But I did hear a lot about his horses – beautiful things, great hunters and racing stock. He went on at length. I could offer little about horses in the way of conversation as I have had no luck with either end of the animals. He did not seem concerned.

When we arrived at the central railway station after a seemingly long trip over many bridges, and left the huge building, my companion's voice boomed down on the top of my head. 'Where are you going now?'

'Someone is to meet me here.' I looked around me. No one seemed to be the slightest bit interested in me and certainly no one was coming up to me with open arms and a friendly smile.

A voice trickled softly down from above. 'Come with me.' I barely heard him, but when I looked up, he was looking at me knowingly and gave me a grin showing a wide row of small but perfect teeth. I had little choice but to lift my bag onto my shoulder and follow.

He led me through a busy part of the city to his small house in the old part on the west bank of the Dnieper that he shared with his mother. Here were woody hills, ravines and small rivers with the house tucked in among them. From the advantage of a little height, I looked onto part of the city ablaze with golden onion domes of countless churches. In the summer evening, the slanting sun lit them like a holy bonfire.

Kostya's mother was short and round and I was curious to know about his father and what genes produced such a mountain of a man. She was only concerned that we had enough to eat, urging plate after plate towards me with halting Russian, 'Darlink, darlink, eat, eat, you are too skinny.' I did my best.

When it was almost fully dark, we sat in the garden. Kostya offered me a glass of something clearly alcoholic. 'Malynivka,' he explained, 'a favourite drink of mine.'

'I'm sorry but I don't drink.' He looked at me vacantly and I felt obliged to continue. 'We are Methodists.' That had no effect on him whatsoever. He pushed the glass towards me and poured a glass for himself. I decided I could at least hold the glass out of politeness. I picked it up and looked through the glossy liquid. 'It is beautiful, what is it made from?'

Kostya rolled a mouthful around his teeth, swallowed it with pleasure. 'Raspberries.'

I looked again at the liquid. 'But it is not red like I would expect raspberry liqueur to be?

Kostya leaned his head onto the back of the chair. 'It is because my mother puts the bottles on the roof in the sun to bleach it.' I must have looked surprised. 'No I don't know why either. Drink. Is beautiful.' I saw that I could not offend, so decided to commit my soul to the devil, and took a sip. The fire went from my throat to my stomach without touching anything in between.

After he had finished his first glass and I had taken several sips from mine, Kostya leaned forward on his knees. 'Royston Petrovitch, there is much I must tell you.'

I blinked as well as I could; my eyelids were becoming very sticky and I tried to look sober. It was evident from the moment he sat down beside me, that Kostya was my contact and what he had to tell me would determine how I was to find the people I needed and more importantly what I was to tell them.

He leaned forward with his forearms on his knees. 'Germans are already at rivers 20 kilometres from city.'

'Twenty?' I hadn't heard him correctly surely. It wasn't what Bull had led me to believe.

'Our forces are holding them. They make no advance for some weeks.' I must have relaxed into my chair, because Kostya drew himself up. 'We cannot defeat them. They are dug into holes. They bring up re-enforcements and supplies. We see them again soon. They will use roads. Now that they are dry. They will come.' He put his head down.

I felt a sudden rush of sympathy in the face of his helplessness. I felt exempt from the destruction about to descend. 'How long do you have?'

He lifted his head and reached for his glass of pretty drink. 'Days? Weeks? Hours? No one knows.'

'What do you think will happen?

'They will capture the city and we will all die.'

'Why don't you get out? You are not in the Army?'

'Red Army takes who it wants.' For some reason, it had not wanted him, yet.

'What about your mother?'

'I send her to Moscow tomorrow.' He smiled showing his lovely teeth. 'Tomorrow night we cook for ourselves.' At that he laughed.

Kostya drained the last drops from his glass and refilled it. 'Red Army is huge – millions, but no officers. No, is untrue. There are officers, but none experienced or trained well. Stalin killed them all.' I nodded. The old man in Smolensk had

99

told me this. 'So we will be slaughtered. We have many Jews here and Hitler has said Ukrainians are even lower life than Jews and must be killed.'

'So why don't you all just get out.'

He looked at me with amusement that was close to mockery. 'Because we will be shot anyway.'

'But if the Germans aren't here yet ...'

He interrupted. 'Not by Germans.' He inhaled a good portion of the second glass of burning liquor. 'Stalin.'

'Stalin!'

'He has guards at rear of Red Army. Anyone who deserts – anyone who retreats – even a meter – is shot.'

I could hardly speak for disbelief. 'Not even to regroup and fight a better battle?' What was I saying...!

He shook his head.

'So, so - you will be trapped. From both sides.'

'I do not even know if my mother will get out. Perhaps there is still time.' He leaned back in the chair again and the wooden joints crackled. 'You...' he looked at me and his eyes were dark. 'You might be also trapped. They did not tell you this?'

My mouth felt suddenly very dry. 'No. They didn't tell me that – do they know?' I sucked in a great lungful of dry air and tried get my scattered thoughts together in a logical string.

'This is what I must tell you.' His face brightened momentarily. 'You must tell this to London, not to Moscow, but to London. You operate their radio – you can reach London. You tell them what Red Army is doing. How it is failing, how soldiers feel about Stalin. How he is being defeated by Germans. How we will be killed and how this country will be defeated unless British and America help.'

I thought I might faint.

'But why you ... what are you ...?

He waved the question aside. 'I am sent to get you to where you need to be and to translate for you and to get you out when it is necessary. That is all.' He grinned with those fine and perfect teeth. They fascinated me. 'You have ways to tell them.' I felt sick. The alcohol sat in a thick layer across my stomach. 'While you do this, we will also seek the people you were sent to find.' This did not

100

make me feel better. It was a kind of blackmail again.

Kostya looked serious again. 'Kiev will fall very soon. It will be blown to tiny, tiny pieces and Ukrainians will be also.' He threw the remaining drink down his throat. 'But come. We must rest. Tomorrow I take you to the front. The people you need to meet there are not combatants. They find good business opportunities for themselves.' He snorted with derision and a kind of humour. 'They are the ones who supply our troops with guns, food, ammunition. Stalin can't find these things for us. These people make good money, if they ever get paid. Our sad Army seems only able to shoot big guns and make big noise.'

The time had come for me to put an end to the wool around what I was here for. There wasn't time to wait and see how things unfolded. I would have to act quickly. 'Who do I see first?'

9 Sept 1941

Dear Mum and Dad,

Incredibly I am at the front line. Thankfully it is quiet. A runner is going back to the city, so I will send this with him as I mustn't have too many personal papers on me.

The Russian troops here are a motley assortment of men, some trained and professional, others men and boys from the fields. They are all determined if terrified. They all know that they are likely to die.

I will write more when I am able.

Love Roy.

9 Sept 1941

Dearest Annie,

I have time only for a few lines as someone is waiting to take this back for posting.

I am well and the summer sun is welcome. Take care of yourself too my darling. I miss you more and more every day.

Dearest love,

Roy.

10 Sept The weather is incredibly hot and it is dry all around us. We are well dug in and the enemy is a few miles in front of us. For some reason they make no attempt to charge and we speculate about the reason for this. There are astonishing clouds of dust a long distance behind them and my companion speculates that they are bringing up supplies. They are not using the railways as the gauge is wider than their trains so they are being very possessive about the roads while they are dry. The dust however must be a huge problem in its own right. I need to see what these men do and find out how they feel about the situation they face. Is Kostya right? Will they all die? Me among them? I am here to find a group of people who need to be got out of here.

I set up the radio and flung the aerial up onto a smoking spar of a shattered tree.

SA44 Kiev to BR10 The Laundry 14 Sept 1941 0612 111 Red Army Troops are dug in Food arrives most days Weapons varied Ammo scarce Enemy makes no advance May be re-enforcing and supplying

SA44 Kiev to BR10 The Laundry 15 Sept 1941 0558 157 Runner reports Germans re-enforcing but held up by mud and dust Russian troops give strong resistance to any attempts on their lines Shortages acute Counter-attacks halt Germans for now

15 Sept 1941 Kostya has taken me back to the city. We have located several of the people we need to see and tried desperately to get them to move, to run, to hide. But they are reluctant. Either they know what is about to befall them and are resigned or they don't want to believe. Or perhaps they don't want to leave such rich, if dangerous, business opportunities. Don't know how I will be able to tell Bull that I've failed utterly.

SA44 Kiev to BR10 The Laundry 15 Sept 1941 0603 169 Rumour Budenny asks to evacuate Kiev Refused Troops know this is the end They fight to die Rumours of Germans beginning encirclement but still some distance Desperate for Allied help Wait instructions

BR10 The Laundry to SA44 Kiev 15 Sept 0610 67 No possibility of assistance Info that Red Army very successful Why assistance

SA44 Kiev to BR10 The Laundry 15 Sept 0618 64 Troops badly equipped not trained no leadership Will be shot if they retreat

16 Sept 1941 I think I may have succeeded with one or two of my contacts. I am worried about turning up in the trenches too often. It might look suspicious,

especially if I have Kostya in tow. He is fairly unmistakable and not exactly
subtle. I think he may have got his mother to Moscow. There has been no reply
from the Laundry to my last transmission.

SA44 Kiev to BR10 The Laundry 16 Sept 1941 0615 167 West bank of lower
Dnieper in German hands Russian troops ordered not to surrender or retreat
Alternative is to be shot by Red Army Troops fatalistic but not angry Discipline
not panic Morale resigned

I lost weight. My clothing was loose, filthy and torn. But I was in better shape
than many of the men in the dug outs. They knew their fate and so the condition
of their clothing, or themselves for that matter, was of little consequence. Some
planned to live until winter, so took better care and scrounged what they could
for when it was needed. Others were resigned and did not plan even for
tomorrow. They didn't care if they ate, washed or shaved. They scrounged only
ammunition or weapons if their supplier could not provide. Later in the week
Kostya took me back along the front lines to speak to the men. I was rarely
challenged. Kostya was so large a presence that few even wanted to, it would
seem. Most of the troops were suspicious of me to start with, but Kostya always
managed to produce some vodka or other noxious drink and soon we were all
friends. And they talked. I heard what Kostya has brought me here to hear. A few
of them would perhaps save themselves, if only for a time. But the rest were all
dead men.

A man went out over the top of the dug out this morning, in broad daylight to
relieve a festering corpse of its weapon and ammunition. When I asked if he had
brought back the man's identification he looked completely puzzled. Why? He
asked. So that his commander and his family could be notified. The man
exploded in laughter. Why would anyone want to know that man's fate? He
gestured to the decomposing corpse. I had to admit he was right. Some things
were better not to know.

Most of our time in the trenches was spent in discomfort, hunger and
boredom. Meals if and when they arrived were largely inedible and almost
always cold. Those who delivered them received the brunt of everyone's
frustration. They were usually men or boys who were not, or not yet, fit for other
duty and had a dangerous task to get what they could to us.

In spite of our status among these men, they were generous with what they
had. Kostya told them quietly that I was there to send out information to Britain
and even though I was a non-combatant, they were helpful and good
companions. I did not feel able to make demands on their resources, but rations

were fairly divided. They had good hearts. There were no commanders or commissars here to read the words of Papa Stalin or to threaten them with death. They were amazingly cheerful and free with their information and it confirmed over and over again, all the terrible things I had heard before and from other sources.

But maybe this was how all armies and wars worked. Maybe death was all there was to be certain about. Even victory or pride or enthusiasm or fighting for what you believed to be right were doomed as soon as a soldier came face to face with the realities of war. Did they not even wish to fight for their lives? But the lives of these men were cheap.

One rumour among all the thousands of apocalyptic ones was that an officer might be arriving. This rumour had been wandering around for a couple of days, but so far no one in a smart uniform had been seen. Naturally there was much speculation and a little worry. As Yurgi explained it might actually make things harder for the men in the trenches and behind the barricades. Yurgi was a recruit from a workers' battalion. These units were cobbled together from field, farm and city workers and had little training. I could see that he might be intimidated by having to obey orders in military fashion without knowing how or even why.

Yurgi snorted at this suggestion. 'None of us knows how to be smart soldiers. We only know how to shoot guns.' He grinned and then he leaned closer to me conspiratorially. 'It will be harder for us to get away if he comes.'

'Desert? But I thought all of you loved Papa Stalin and would fight to the end?'

He snorted again. 'We love Papa Stalin of course. He gives us our bread and our shirts. We will do whatever he asks.'

'Because you will be shot if you don't?'

He nodded and then grinned again. 'Or maybe I will run away.' If an officer arrives it will be time for Kostya and me to run away as well. Maybe I was wrong about self-preservation. But run away? To where?

I reported all this to the Laundry. All they asked was for more, but facts only. They did not want anecdotes. Just how I'm meant to get battle tactics and strategic facts when I am in a hole beside the Dnieper, I'm not quite sure. They didn't seem to believe me.

The runner brought me a note this morning – I don't know how he found me as I was just one face among thousands. It was from Adrian who was still at the embassy and it told me that a major bombardment of Leningrad had begun. More alarmingly he said that the Germans were now very close to Moscow. I was beginning to feel my exits closing on me one by one. It must be time to leave Kiev, but I had one more family in one more business to convince. They were in the city. We would go back to the city in the morning.

17 Sept. Kostya wakes me early this morning. The dew is still on my ragged clothes. He speaks quietly obviously not wanting to wake the others. 'The Germans have put bridgeheads across the Dnieper. They are now on the east side.'

I was instantly awake 'What does this mean?'

'They can now encircle Kiev. Perhaps it is time for you to go.'

Perhaps! What the hell did he mean, perhaps? I began rolling up my blanket. 'But we are still firm on the Irpen and the Weta?' The Red Army had held these two rivers secure on the way into Kiev for two months. It seemed inconceivable that they should be taken too.

As usual, Kostya knew more than I did. 'It does not matter. They will come from the west and probably the north. Come.'

Just how I got out was a memory that came to me later in black and white flashes like photographs – two dimensional and silent.

I know that the bombings started a few seconds after Kostya spoke. I remember a huge artillery assault and dive bombers. I also remember Kostya pulling me along by the shoulder of my jacket. We ran bent double under the brush and over the heaving ground into a small defile leading to a stream. I remember feeling safe here and being annoyed with Kostya for dragging me onwards. We stumbled along the stream until it emptied into the Dnieper. He pushed me into the water until it was up to my knees and we splashed towards a large clump of grass and branches. Wet, terrified, he pulled me into the weeds.

Breathing heavily, he stopped and swore. 'Shit. I wasn't expecting that the bastards!'

'That's the advantage of surprise, old boy.'

He grinned with those perfect teeth and nodded up the river. 'A little further.'

Somehow over the next few hours, we kept ahead of the German assault. Sometimes only just ahead as big shells exploded overhead and beside us. We kept close to the river and once in the city, we joined the throng of confused and desperate people who were rushing in all directions or none. Trams, horse drawn carts, a large assortment of motorised vehicles were flooding out of the city through any exit or route not yet bombed to vapour.

We uncovered a different rumour from everyone we spoke to, but gradually, the opinion seemed to be that von Bock was closing from the north and von Rundstedt from the south. We and everyone would have to go east or stay behind. Kostya deposited me in a town square with instructions not to move unless under attack and then disappeared. I tried to be invisible, but that clearly was not a sensible option, so I set about helping people and their belongings onto whatever transport was available. It felt good to be helpful, but it also helped make me invisible.

After a couple of hours when I had set several hundred people on their way, and there were more people than ever in the square, Kostya returned. 'Come.'

'Can we get out?'

Kostya just shook his head. 'Budenny has again asked to evacuate Kiev. Stalin has refused again. Kiev is to be surrounded and shot to death.' We went back to the river and this time there was a floating mass of grass, weeds and branches against the bank. He pushed me into it and onto a small boat hidden underneath.

'Now,' he grunted as he pushed off with a short pole, 'we must make this island float against the current.'

We floated forward and across the river and back again, both of us using poles, through the slow pools along one of the many branches of the water way. In the darkness of the second day we moored - if you can call tying a floating island to a bunch of reeds, a mooring. There was an unusual silence and in the morning, we risked looking out of our reed and weed nest. The air had the appearance of fog but the stab of smoke struck the back of my throat. The land, what we could see of it, was waste. Not a building was left standing nor an animal left alive. The smoke was not fresh; it had the smell of smouldering wood, burning flesh, grass and green vegetation for as far as we could see. The fields that would have provided the Ukraine and the rest of Russia with bread were gone. So were the people who would have harvested it. There was nothing that could be used by the Germans to be sure, but there was nothing for anyone else either.

'Where is everybody?' I asked.

'Driven out. Dead.' Kostya looked exhausted. 'The Red Army makes sure there is nothing left.'

'This was done by the Russians? The bastards.' I was not surprised to hear myself swear. It seemed to be an appropriate descriptive noun.

He nodded clenching his jaw in sorrow and anger. 'Stalin orders that nothing be left to help the Germans. Now we must continue, past the lines.'

'German or Russian?'

'Both.'

We picked up the poles to our boat again. For days, I could not estimate the miles, under darkness, daylight, guns, and bridges we floated our nest further and further upstream. At times, the current threatened to undo a day's stealth in minutes, but Kostya with his strength and me with my panic, kept us moving forward.

Eventually we turned west into a large tributary and were very soon being shot at by wild looking men.

9

September 1941

10 October. It has begun to snow. We don't expect it to last but we know that it will come again and again and one day it will stay. The leaves have all but gone from the trees and we feel more exposed than ever. While all of this is unnerving, I am most worried by what will happen next. No one wants to guess.

The river we turned into became a slowly moving stream and Kostya poled our little craft deeper and deeper into forest and marsh. Huge areas of shallow water cut by low dykes of grass and weeds, thin trees, areas of low bushes, falling leaves, streams within streams. And there was a light misty rain. It all created an uncomfortable and eerily silent picture until the men came out of the bushes beside the water.

It took not a little energy and Kostya's quiet diplomacy for them not to shoot us both. They held us both at gun point for several days. I was tied to a tree in the open. The heavy dew soaked my clothes each night and I was sure that pneumonia would be the last intimate companion of my life. Every morning, I choked on panic that I would be left here for the rest of my short and miserable life. But if the sun shone it dried everything and life returned to my body. If it continued to rain…

My wireless didn't help the situation of course. Neither did the fact that I spoke Russian with a peculiar accent. Either of these compromising facts must have made me seem more like a spy than I really was; and the possibility that I was a hostile spy was a natural nervous conclusion.

The wireless was of great interest of course since these men clearly did not have the use of one. I suspect that they presumed I was some high ranking type or at least was attached to a big tank or infantry division. But why I was carrying a wireless without Russian lettering confused the issue considerably. Eventually someone finally accepted what Kostya said; that the radio and my Embassy papers were English. Suddenly I looked quite different to them. I was probably a real find and possibly worth something. Just what use they thought I'd be was not made clear, but as none of the others could use the set I was valuable for barter, for ransom or perhaps even for their own use.

After a few uncomfortable days, they gathered around us, assorted and evil looking guns pointing at our very vulnerable bodies. Carefully they untied me from the tree fully expecting me to burst into flame and rocket into the sky by the look on their faces. A lean looking man in wrinkled jacket, trousers that seemed too large for him and a flat cap, gave me my instructions.

'They want me to send messages to some invisible source that might provide them with arms or food. Just who am I supposed to send them to?' They obviously had no real idea what the set was able to do and more importantly, not able to do. 'Kostya, please try to explain to them that if I give away our location, we will be found out. Try to make them understand that there is always someone listening.'

'They may think it is worth the risk.'

'I doubt it. The Germans have very big planes and long range ones. They have direction finders. Even if I can change the frequencies regularly... or we move every time I transmit... Besides I don't think they are that far away.' He looked thoughtful and a little troubled. 'I can transmit anything to just about anywhere, but I need to find out who, where and what they want and even then, I am sure we will be overheard.'

'Can you put their requests into code?'

'I could if there was a code to use – one that could be decoded at the other end.' I tapped the top of the wireless set. 'I have to say that even then, Russian codes are not difficult to crack.' He looked surprised. 'I've done it myself.'

'Can you find some of these coded transmissions?' He nodded at the wireless set. 'Find out where they come from and send message back?'

'Kostya, I don't want to ...'

He frowned. It was as close to anger on his face as I'd ever seen. 'Roy. I'm trying to keep you alive.'

'Alive?' I felt cold suddenly

'They can shoot you if they want to. At any moment. You need to be useful to them or ...' He left the rest unsaid.

I had to swallow a large chunk of my precious principles. 'If you can find some way for me to re-charge the battery and find a frequency that isn't a German one for me to transmit to....'

He nodded apparently deep in thought. Then got up and walked to the leader, presumably to report. My immediate future hung on what he would believe.

I tried to find a source of information for my hosts. The trees act like aerials in this boggy place to some degree, so I pinned mine into the wood, and listened to what transmissions I could. I did not yet transmit as I had no confidence that there weren't direction locators listening to the whole huge area. I searched for a suitable source to contact. I tried to identify where the transmissions were coming from, Moscow, Stalingrad, Warsaw, Berlin... I listened to the frequency that the British Embassy used and by decoding the little I could, I was able to confirm my suspicions. The Germans were not far away and were probably encircling us as we sat there. I kept myself and Kostya alive, by reporting what I heard in Russian, German, Ukrainian – if Kostya could translate my scribblings.

But the batteries were fading. I demanded whatever batteries they had or could steal. A 6 volt battery of dubious usefulness arrived. They were very proud of their efforts and I realised that it was probably acquired at some risk. After a week or two, while we were still subject to occasional observation flights and bombs, they became noticeably fewer. Perhaps the Germans didn't seem to care that we were here and so bothered us little. Our limited information was that the Germans had by-passed us and gone on to more lucrative targets. We were probably surrounded, but this was an enormous place and we felt somewhat safe. From what little I knew or overheard, it seemed that the German practice of encirclement was succeeding. Whoever was encircled was about to be starved to death, and so provide little problem for the advancing troops.

A day or two later, I was brave enough to contact the Embassy. The Germans did not, as I feared, send a squadron to bomb our precise location, so I continued. I had so miserably failed in what it sent me to Kiev to do, that I felt as if I were hiding here if I were honest with myself. I couldn't yet face what may have happened to the ones I could not convince to seek shelter closer to Moscow. Not that Moscow was any safer than many other places. The Germans were at the gates.

The Embassy was kind; glad I was still alive, stay in contact, try to get back and not a lot else. I led them to believe that I was using an old Russian radio of uncertain abilities. They could not know that I had a perfectly good wireless of my own.

As time went on I got to know more about this collection of men. The group was made up of men from defeated Red Army units, stragglers, men trying to escape factories or towns that the Germans had taken over, or just men who could not accept the destruction of the doctrine they had come to accept. They all took the chance that they would be welcome here. They came with remnants of uniforms or pieces stolen from dead or wounded comrades or the enemy, washing lines or each other. They had few if any weapons and even less ammunition, but they were fanatical to a man. They would do whatever they felt necessary to harass the Germans. Somewhere the Russian 5th Army was still in nominal control of the area, but it had little if any impact on the 20 or so men in this group.

I was able to gather more and more information for them. It came from plain language transmissions, in either German or Russian, which I chanced upon. I learned which frequencies were most likely to give up secrets through bad transmission. At last my rudimentary German had a use. The German transmissions which we dearly needed to understand were coded and impossible for me to crack quickly if at all. Perhaps my colleagues at the mansion would have more success if they received them and were the slightest bit interested. I had no way to contact them.

The Russian transmissions that I was able to de-code were almost always hysterical requests about defeat and shrieking screams for men, machinery, munitions, winter clothing, boots. How and where this booty was to be sent was unknown. I hoped that the call signs would indicate to someone, somewhere, other than me, the locations of these desperate men. But that was information to which I was not privy and there was nothing I could do. The message was still the same. Help! I made tentative requests in plain language on similar frequencies, but we were largely ignored. I reported regularly to the group and they sat with me when I was listening or transmitting, eager for any tiny scrap of information and fascinated by the magic of the radio. It told us too, about where the Red Army was... or where it thought it was and what battles it was undertaking. There was no mistake in thinking that the Germans were listening in just as I was.

Within the group one or two of the men seemed to organise the others, but I would hesitate to say that they were leaders in any real sense of the word. People arrived and were fed with what little there was available. Then they talked. They told us about the German supply lines, their types of transport, the roads they used, the telephone lines they laid. They talked about the railways that run in this inhospitable place. They talked and talked.

When the battery began, again, to fail, I said that I needed electric or telephone cable and a magnet. With the copper wire, I could make a small generator to charge it. They were delighted with the challenge and came back from heaven knows where they went at night, with rolls of the stuff. They also proudly presented me with a bag of broken bits from an aircraft compass with German lettering, and its integral magnets. I had all I needed. It took days to strip the cable and retrieve the copper wire inside but Misha trusted me with his pocket knife.

Now it was snowing in earnest. Huge wet flakes that melted on whatever they touched. It did not take long before we were all wet through. Kostya found a huge woollen great coat for me and a quilted one for himself and they offered some protection. But it continued to snow faster and faster, wetter and wetter.

Kostya brought me a cup of hot water, or maybe it was tea. It was so weak it was hard to tell the difference, but it was welcome. I was cutting a hole with Misha's knife in one side of a small wooden box I had made.

'They talk,' he confided, 'of the damage they can do. But they plan. They are great planners, and scroungers.'

I blew some cuttings out of the hole. 'Is that where they go at night?'

'They go to see what they can, to find where the Germans are, to get information from others they know…and to get you your compass and whatever food or materials they can.'

'Will they be able to damage the Germans do you think?' I pushed a heavy wire through the box and tested that it was loose. I did not want to hear the answer.

'Not without some means to do it with. They have no way of knowing if they have any effect. They need to contact others and work together, but that is difficult.'

'Why is it difficult?' I fitted the magnets securely onto the wire and checked that they and the wire spun easily.

'Because no one knows where the others are – or if they are friendly or not. No one can really trust anyone else.'

'What will they do?'

Kosty grinned. 'Tonight, they rob a supply dump beside the railway and then blow up the line.'

'With what? There are no explosives here. What will they use?'

He nodded in the direction of the forest. 'They have a pile of it; they have been stealing for some weeks. They have argued enough about what to use and where. Now they are ready to act.' He looked at the little box I had made, that I was now wrapping with copper wire. 'Will that work when you are finished?'

'I hope so.'

At night fall, most of them disappeared. Even Kostya was gone for several hours. I felt that I should have been with them, but had no skills to offer – I was wise enough to know that I would have been only a liability.

In the early hours of the morning, they made a noisy return.

Kostya slumped into my bivouac beside me. He was still excited with the thrill of what he had just seen. 'The rail line they choose was on other side of thick forest. He wiped his nose on his sleeve, '... and at a bend in the line.' He demonstrated with a sweep of his arm. 'They dig in wooden boxes of explosives with pressure fuses. The next time a train goes over them ...' He raised his hands in the air. I could well imagine what happened next. 'Other devices they set into the switching points so when man who pulls levers ...' His hands went up again. Kostya was clearly delighted. 'So simple,' he kept saying, 'simple.' I put my hands over my ears. I had heard enough. It was too much like what I had experienced in Smolensk.

It cannot be said that this rag-tag bunch of terrorists was about to rest or even consolidate. We were then constantly on the move, seemingly from one major explosion to the next which was just as well, as it made finding us via our radio transmissions more difficult. I listened on the wireless when I could. When I found something involving a group known to them, they let me study the maps they had or simple ones they drew themselves and we tried to locate them. From time to time I decoded a Russian transmission and passed the information to the leaders. What they do with it I had no idea. Usually it was about troop movements or request for air cover.

Occasionally when I was not observed, I attempted a rapid communication to BR10. Just a call sign, no message. I received no replies. I had to assume that my outgoing messages were not received and that to them I was lost. All I had left was a redundant one time pad. I wanted to apologise for not being able to send on their spy's reports. I had failed badly – him, whoever he was, the Laundry, the British Government, everyone.

I tried to reach Moscow, but the frequencies I knew seemed no longer to be monitored and I felt that I could say little. I tried all that I could remember or that might have connected, without success.

Other situations and movements of the Germans were relayed to us. These came from runners and messengers who worked for the Germans and were therefore able to go through the German lines as civilians and pass the information on and on. Through this means details about supply trains, troop movements and changes in troop concentrations were relayed. And still it snowed.

Kostya continued to look after me, if one could call it that. I had no doubt that he defused situations in which I was seen to be either a traitorous spy or a useless additional mouth to feed.

'They need you to come with us on the next raid.'

A rocket of fear shot through my chest. 'Why?'

'I convinced them that you are a brave British spy and that you need to see what happens, in order to get England to send us what we need.'

I stared at him in disbelief. They still thought I was some kind of liability and needed me to prove my worth. 'What you need? Just what good will my going along do to prove such an impossible situation? What on earth can I possibly.... I can't get you what you need.'

'Maybe not, but it will keep you alive.'

I grabbed his arm and snarled at him between my teeth. 'Kostya. What are you not telling me?'

He relaxed on his tree stump. 'They know you are British.'

'They have my papers; of course they know I'm British.'

'... and that Britain and Russia now fight together. They also know that Britain has resources ...'

'Most of them are being bombed to the bottom of the Atlantic.'

'... and that they are being sent to Russia through Arkhangelsk and probably Murmansk. They want more and they want them sent here.'

I looked at the trees around us. 'I have been trying to get supplies from Moscow and I can't do it. I can't even make a connection! Just how do they propose I can get supplies from England to us here?'

He looked at the sky visible through the branches and put his finger in the air. 'By air. Can you do it?'

'Don't be ridiculous. Why do I need to go with you? It won't make any difference to what I transmit.'

Kostya just shrugged.

As if the British Government would listen to me. I couldn't even get a reply to my transmissions to The Embassy. 'I need a higher place to transmit. I also need a better battery or at least a better recharge. I make no promises. Not even one.' I felt another of my dearly held principles fall into the snow. No active help to make the war worse...useless now.

My first night time sortie was a simple one. Five men – and me – were taken to the railway line. It seemed to be about 20 miles away but was probably not more than five. Here, two of the men were sent in one direction up the line to warn if anything was approaching and two the other way. I was put in the middle to watch for a lighted signal from either end. I was to give the warning to my colleague who was behind me, sawing through a telegraph pole. When the saw was through, he carefully withdrew and flashing a light to the others, we all crept back the way we had come. A few meters into the forest I heard the soft thud of a pole falling across the railway tracks into the snow and a sharp snap as the line broke.

'What about the tracks we have left in the snow and mud?' I asked Nazar, the tall gaunt man who sawed the pole. Nazar was one of those eager young men who needed to be kept from exploding himself some times. His enthusiasm often outran his thoughts. They gave him jobs which he felt were important, but that they could control.

'They will not want to be too far into the forest on such a small errand. It makes them targets for anyone behind a tree.' He cackled with the pleasure of it.

True enough, during the rest of the night we returned to the camp, gathered our things and walked on. Later in the day we set up a new camp in another densely forested part of the marsh. We built bivouacs of pine brush and rested. I tried to sleep but my mind was asking me a great many difficult questions to do with my conscience. Did I contribute to anyone being hurt by bringing a telegraph pole down across the railway line? This was a war, of course people set out to hurt other people. But was I now one of them? I concentrated on the cable. A loss of communication wasn't such a bad deed was it?'

In the evening, I was woken by Kostya. 'Come,' he whispered.

The entire camp was awake this time and silently we walked again through the forest. I was given a large empty canvas bag to carry and everyone else was likewise burdened. By about three in the morning, we stopped to rest. Aleks disappeared with a couple of others and was gone for an hour or so. I had met men like him before. Men with a wide streak of adventure. They had huge egos that replaced normal fear, caution and apprehension that hold the rest of us in reality. They were the ones who read the reconnaissance, heard the reports and knew what was needed next.

The snow by now had fallen to a depth of several inches. It was still wet and our tracks softened into muddy holes. Anything we trod on or sat on turned to wet slush. But it continued to snow.

When Aleks returned, we followed him to an open site just in the shelter of the scrubby trees. I could make out a compound filled with barrels, boxes and mounds covered with tarpaulin. Two bored guards wandered around the perimeter stopping to smoke and chat. Several of our group silently slid back into the forest and disappeared. A short time later, the guards separated and continued on their patrol. Only our men came back.

Quite in the open this time, they signalled us forward. En route around the edge of the supplies, I tripped on something on the ground. Looking back, I saw one of the guards – a huge red slash across his throat and blood pumping from his severed artery into the grey mushy snow. His eyes focussed dimly on my face and he made an attempt to speak. Kostya pulled me forward to the compound; its wire fence now torn open, and packed my canvas bag with an unknown assortment of heavy boxes, then helped me hoist the weight onto my back and pushed me back towards the forest. Again I passed the man on the ground and again I looked at him. My stomach began to heave, my mouth felt dry and my head full of light. Kostya hissed into my ear and pulled hard on my sleeve. 'Keep moving. Don't stop.'

I made it nearly a mile back into the forest, before I threw up. 'Why in hell did you bring me with you? I am useless to you.'

I discussed these raids with Kostya. I told him again and again that I was not a combatant and couldn't take part in killing people. He spoke close to my ear. 'If you want to live, you will do whatever these men tell you to do. If not they will kill you. The wireless will keep you alive, only until they find someone else to do it.'

It couldn't have been clearer; I wanted to stay alive and this was the price I had to pay to earn my keep. That was the stark reality. The radio was not enough.

I brought Kostya tea this time. We sat on a pile of cut boughs and leaned on some small trees. ' Kostya?' I swilled the tea around to make a little vortex in the tin mug. 'Are you all right?'

Kostya exhaled a long breath through his nose. 'I failed.'

'Failed at what?'

'To get you out of Kiev safely.'

'But you did. I'm alive aren't I?'

'I was to get you back to Moscow.'

I turned to look at him; eye to eye. 'Then why in God's name was I sent there in the first place? The Germans were practically opening the gates to Kiev when I got there. It could have all gone up at any moment.'

'But it didn't. Moscow and your embassy knew that they wouldn't invade for a little time.'

'How did they know that?' I knew the answer to that question before I'd asked it. Lucy or the mansion at work again but it didn't alter my situation. 'And so what? What did I do there that was so important?'

He grinned and his bearded face produced wrinkles by his eyes. 'Everyone has their spies. You did what you were supposed to – you told Moscow what it needed to hear and helped to get those people out. That was important.'

'That seemed to be such a small thing.' For their sakes, I had to try to reach London again.

He seemed to make a decision to speak. 'I am not big enough in the world of spies to know how successful you were. Others I have looked after were successful in Russian society. They live and work here for years like everyone does. They are called on when needed. They are put to use. They did not have to get out of anywhere – not so quickly.'

So he, too, was a spy. For whom? The British? At the Embassy? 'Others?'

'Yes, others. Those in Smolensk ... and the others in Kiev... and elsewhere.'

Of course it began to make some sense. 'But what now? What do I do now?'

'What we all do. We wait and do as we are told. That way we will stay alive, perhaps.'

My transmissions achieved little initially. Among the material we 'liberated' from the German supply dumps periodically were small car batteries. My little generator was of limited use, but helped charge the old battery when we had no other means. I went into the forest a short distance where there were fewer trees, but more importantly, I was alone. In the dark dawn, I tried again. Eventually, the atmospherics were good enough.

SA44 Marshes to BR10 The Laundry 23 November 1941 0618 272 Am with a group of Russian partisans in the interior marsh land They undertake small raids of incredible daring against large German installations railways supply dumps But are not well led and have few guns and little ammunition Desperately need both Require air drops Can you help I will listen at this time each day for reply

The next morning I went back with the set to see if there was a reply.

BT10 Laundry to SA44 Marshes 23 November 1941 0607 98 Glad you are alive Can do little to help May be able to do so later Report in as you can Go back to Moscow as soon as possible

I reported all except the last part to Kostya and the others. Reactions were mixed. 'Why can't the British help us right now?' I doubt that many of them knew where Britain was. 'They have not said no, perhaps we can hope.' 'When will they send aid?'

RUSSIA North-western Front (Worcester Journal) 29 November 1941 *A Moment of Quiet* by Royston Thomas

I am in the countryside and winter is here. Snow has been falling for over a month now. The cold is deepening and the snow continues to fall every day. Trees branches are piled high with it and bend under the weight. Everything is grey or white; the trees, grasses and people. We have snow on our clothes, our hats and our eyebrows. Even the air is coloured by snow. The days are noticeably short and the light is weak and low in the sky. It is difficult to see

117

very far into the distance and clouds and snow fill all the space. Even under this greyness, the snow sparkles with diamond-like crystals. Sound is muffled and people near to me speak softly so as not to disturb the peace around us.

In the midst of a terrible war, there are a few minutes of peace, colourless but beautiful peace.

Yet another article that would remain in my notebook, unpublished, unread, unknown.

30 Nov 1941 We were pushed back so quickly it was stunning. What we may have heard or invented about the term 'blitzkrieg', could in no way have been true in view of what we experienced. I am the only non-combatant in the group, but the aircraft killing everyone wouldn't have known that. We looked all the same from a safe bombing height. We ran for our lives – those of us with legs still attached to our bodies. The wounded left behind were lost and we knew it. So did they. We had to close our minds to the horror of it.

No one can be prepared for the noise of machines, the noise of arms, large and small, the screams of men and horses. None of us was ready for the smell of gunpowder, blood and burned flesh.

10

December 1941

19 December 1941. I feel lost. There has been no further communication from the Laundry and of course no post. I wonder how Annie is – I miss her in ways I cannot explain and would give anything for a note from her, however small. I long for a newspaper and I long for news of my mother and father. Without something that anchors me to my family and home, I am lost.

Somehow we survived the bombing. A few killed or died later, but it was over in seconds and thankfully, the bombers did not come back. We moved on anyway. I cannot let my mind return to what I saw.

The weather was terrible and the cold beyond my ability to describe. The others felt it too and it was the only thing we talked about. We lit fires under the shelter of thick trees and used dry wood where we could find it. Rodya, the boy in charge was under a deep threat if smoke was seen to be rising. He kept the fire low during the day and only let it up at night. There was not a great risk of over flying planes seeing the flames since few of them flew at night and if they did see it, we would have it doused by the time they came back and dropped anything in our area. Day time smoke was another matter. But it meant that we were cold during both the day and the night. Desperation would surely breed indifference to the danger eventually.

Our raids on supply dumps have provided us with padded clothes, boots and an odd assortment of hats, and we continued to scrounge whatever we could. Petr took great pleasure in taking all the German insignia off and condemning them to the flames with huge ceremony. Although I haven't been informed directly, I suspect that some of the raids were on civilians who lived in the marshes and who were intimidated into giving us food, fuel, fodder for the horses and clothes for our backs. When the alternative was to die of cold, it was easy not to think too deeply about it. In other cases, the incredible people brought us food and clothes, even money sometimes and did so willingly. They were as desperate as we were. Anything to put an end to what we were all living through. I was beginning to like these men. They were generous, fanatical, desperate, but had a greater understanding of the danger we were in than anyone else in this bloody war.

We ate whatever could be found: potatoes, cabbage, sometimes frozen and meat of dubious sources. I feared for those who were left without.

A leader had emerged from within the group. His name was Zoya. He was gaunt like everyone else, with small ears and a goatee beard. He wore compilation of uniform pieces held together by a belt with a star on the buckle and a Sam Browne belt over his right shoulder. He usually had a huge dark blanket over his shoulders and a flat cap like the kind Lenin wore. He was softy spoken, but had great plans for us. He talked eloquently about derailing whole trains, destroying electricity stations, blowing up German headquarters, about setting up farms for our use, schools and hospitals and an underground printing and delivery system. Maybe there will be a role for a journalist after all! I would not go so far as to say that he was fanatical, but he was certainly enthusiastic! Kostya told me that he had been a farmer and village elder at the edge of the forest before the war but lost his family in the advance of the Germans. He escaped to the marshes like so many others.

In the meantime we had those who stole what we needed, Rodya who cooked what he could and various people who appeared and then disappeared. And I asked myself why they needed me to listen on a wireless set that said little if anything. All I could tell them was what little the Embassy could report or what the Russians were saying and they were in such disarray that there was little to report except continual chaos. But they seemed satisfied with what crumbs I could give them. It seemed as if they were resolved that they would have to act alone if they were to act at all. But details, crumbs around them told them that they were not alone.

Yesterday there were two women at the campfire. They were young, muffled in heavy coats, and deep fur hats, with long rifles slung over their backs. While I may have been amazed, the others were not. They were partisans like all the others. By afternoon, they had gone. Apparently they went to find another group. Zoya said that there are several other groups in the marshes – none he knows too much about except that they exist.

Today another boy appeared. He was wearing a coat several sizes too large for him and a flat cap. He looked ill fed, anaemic and had a terrible cough. He sat by the fire and ate what our cook could afford. Then he collected a canvas bag from Zoya and disappeared again.

'Courier,' advised Kostya. 'He takes things past the Germans and brings back information.'

By mid-December, everyone not engaged in something else – like planning what disruption to engage in next – was sent out to find wood. Something in the quality of the air today reminded me of home. Home never had snow like this, nor cold, but the air was still and there was a light mist on the ground. With imagination, I could have been in Wales. I could imagine the men going out to check the sheep in the fields; someone coming down the track bringing a lady to visit my mother. I could hear the clatter of hooves on the stones and the clinking of harness and the hot breath of the horses. Someone bringing wood into the kitchen for the fires; my father heaving his big coat onto his shoulders as he walked from the house to the cattle shed. I could feel the dampness on my face and saw it glisten on my coat. For a second I was at home... in the valley... at home.

Homesickness was not something I had ever felt before – not to put a name on it at least. Today I wished more than anything in life that I could see green again. I no longer wanted to feel that there was so much urgency to my life; that every moment was pressured and critical; that every second was full of menace or danger; that every word I uttered could be the wrong thing to say or that I would be seen to be the spy that I wasn't – or maybe that I was. Every moment in each day was a battle to stay sane and alive. There was no possibility of staying calm – that had been dealt with long ago. We were in a perennial state of crisis, dependence, displacement and subsistence. It was a miracle that we weren't killing each other. The mist coated me like a blanket, soft, cool, safe.

I wanted to feel the heat of the fire in my mother's kitchen; I wanted to smell wet wool from my coat in the chapel, the bread from the oven; I wanted to sing the old hymns of my youth. The words came to my throat and I sang. I sang of forgiveness of hope; I sang the songs from the mines, the joy from simple lives and from the love of God. The trees were my only companions in this chapel – the only ones who would hear my Amen. On my knees in the snow, I sang the Amen – the great Amen.

In the quiet, deeper now than when I started, I got to my feet, gathered up the wood and returned to the camp site.

The tears I had almost shed were dry on my eyelids by the time I got back. I put the wood on the pile as Sydir dropped his broken branches by the fire. 'Can you teach us to sing?' he asked quietly.

It may or may not have been Christmas, but I hummed the tunes and the others tried to remember and hum them too. Amen they understood even if it was a word they didn't use in this nominally secular society. Communists were not meant to be practicing Christians but many quietly still did so. Some remembered the religion from older members of their families and so understood the celebrations that were taking place in ordinary lives at this time of year in the rest of the western world. Eventually they sang - in Welsh and in English, the Christian songs of life.

In honour of the occasion Zoya sent out some men to steal something we could have for a festive meal - I didn't want to guess what it was likely to be – and declared that we will have a moratorium on our raids for a few days after. The songs and hymns we sang awoke something in all of us – even if small. I hoped that perhaps we might learn to pray too and then perhaps we could call that part of us that had shrivelled, a soul again.

RUSSIA North Western Front (Worcester Journal) 2 January 1942 *Men of the Snows,* **by Royston Thomas**

These men are an unusual collection. Some were left behind when the Red Army fell under the wheels of the German advance. By some miracle they escaped with their lives. Others have left villages aware before the German advance could swallow them up. In some cases it already had. Others have come in the full knowledge that they could not continue the lives they had before or the work or businesses they had before. They have all given up lives as they had lived them and drifted into the marsh and forests. They have collected together in small groups where they do what damage they can. There are farmers, soldiers, shop keepers, school teachers, factory workers, foresters, or civil servants. Anyone disaffected or displaced or who has a chip on their shoulder is here. Increasingly there are women too, young boys and old men.

Even those whose intellect or disposition would have kept them from violence are now behind a gun or carrying explosives. They came here to escape but have found an outlet for their anger. They have become partisans with the same objective: to inflict what they can on an enemy many times their size. They know that their own lives will

probably be short. They know that they will die in the
attempt.

RT19 British Embassy to SA44 Marshes 4 Jan 1942 1809 134 Information
received concerning large German troop movement south of your position
possibly near co-ordinates following Advise numbers direction 6587420

SA44 Marshes to RT19 British Embassy 5 January 1942 1806 81 Confirm
movements Possible consolidation of divisions Panzers Personnel by rail Tanks
by road

We went along the railway line again. This time I was given a heavy roll of
wire to carry. The Germans had repaired the damages we and the others had
created and so our tasks began again.

The explosives were laid as usual, but this time we did not retreat before the
train arrived. From only a safe distance, we saw the train approach and the blast
lifted the front of the engine off the tracks and its own momentum sent it toppling
into the snow. We felt the blast through the fabric of our clothes and it thumped
into our ears. The train ploughed an explosion of snow, dirt, roots, steel and
timber sleepers in front of it. Other cars followed and disappeared into the
expanding eruption of sound, snow and trees. The second and third explosions
further back on the line sent other carriages up into near vertical leaps off the
rails; the following carriages rammed up and onto the roofs of the ones ahead.
They tumbled over and into each other into the forest – breaking wood from the
carriages, glass, dirt and snow – into the darkness. The concussion rammed into
my ears through my hands and heavy mitts and replaced normal sound with a
buzz of pain. In the flash of light from the window of a carriage I saw that it was a
hospital train.

Horror caught in my throat and choked me so I could make no sound. 'Stop!' I
wanted to shout, but someone advanced with a flame thrower and in minutes the
carriages that were not folded and broken beyond recognition were all on fire.
'No!' Then it began to rain – pieces of the train and all it held began to fall.

I was barely able to move. Someone, I expect it was Kostya, dragged me by
the shoulder to a safe distance. The bile in my stomach stopped words escaping
from my mouth.

In the camp, I sat on the ground against a tree and wept. Kostya pushed me
roughly into the tree. 'Roy,' he shoved a mug of something hot into my hands.
'This is real. Grow up and drink that.' There was a fire in his face that I had not
seen before and some things almost began to make sense. I had done that –

that killing, that terrible end for vulnerable people. It was at my doing. But I now realised this is what I was here for. I was here to condemn other people to death. I was not here to do it myself; I was just the vehicle that caused them to die.

'Why do you think we take you? So that you see what we fight for. It is not just to carry the wire.'

'But that was a hospital train.'

'Do you think they do not do the same, or worse to ours?'

I shrugged. I had no answer.

'Drink it.'

'It' was a brew of hot alcohol. Hot in all senses of the word. It burned my lip and then burned all the way to my stomach. I drank all of it. Then I fell asleep in the snow.

We found the courier later that week. He had been caught and tortured. We found him hanging from a tree – not a neat and tidy hanging, but naked and hanging by one foot with a long pole rammed into his rectum. His death was not a quick one, nor was it painless. His face told us that. I wrote the picture. The act of pushing it out of my brain through my hand to the page of my notebook made it less real. It also made it two dimensional. I could exclude myself. I could pretend it was in my imagining. Not real, not real in any way. But I thanked God that I had not asked him to take letters for me…this was not my fault…I was not to blame.

They buried him in the snow. There was no way to dig into the earth while it was as hard as iron. 'The wild animals will make use of his remains.' As always Kostya was pragmatic.

I had passively contributed to the death of hundreds in that train. I tried to excuse myself in all the ways I could think of. None of them absolved me of the reality of the part I played. In the long night in which I slept little, I spoke to myself in the darkness. The sky was black and the stars were within touching distance. I did not feel worthy of their beauty. I had contributed to all those deaths on the hospital train but not the courier. Blame and guilt are not warm blankets. But the cold wakefulness nudged me to a decision. I now had a reason. I had to do more to get this story out – to Smythe and his ilk but also to the papers. They had to know what was going on here. I had to get these men the supplies they needed to stop this happening. This brutality and sickening barbarism was from the time of the Mongul hoards – it was not for a so called civilised nation to do. I was here to witness this and to speak and to stop it if I could.

SA44 Marshes to BR10 The Laundry..... How do I begin to relate the atrocities I have seen. Where are the words for this?

BR10 The Laundry to SA44 Marshes 28 Jan 0604 53 Need details of battle successes Report on morale among troops

What was the Laundry asking? What successes? We dealt with limiting the possibility of our own deaths here. Not grand military successes. Morale? Desperation would be a more accurate word. I don't know what to tell the Laundry. I don't know what to tell Moscow. How do I speak this?

2 February 1942: *The cold is indescribable. My hands are stiff in spite of being wrapped in strips of cloth and covered by mitts I've made from a torn canvas bag. I cannot understand how those with responsibility for weapons manage to load and fire frozen metal with hands nearly as cold as the frozen steel. I am in pain from using a simple radio key. Normally I can feel the kickback from the key, but no longer. I have not been asked to carry a weapon of any kind for which I am thankful. I am not sure if they know my feelings on the matter or just doubt my ability to be safe with one. I just get to haul this radio.*

But we are in an unoccupied part of the forest, far from the edges of the marsh. Perhaps it will be safe and quiet here for a little while.

I pulled the white hood over my head and leaned around the tree stump. Through binoculars I saw our next object of attack. It was a large railway siding with several runs of track and service buildings along side. Huge and dark they loomed over locomotive engines and rail cars. Sergei nudged me and pointed to an open sided building a bit further down the track. We wiggled further down the embankment nearer to the building. 'I love railways,' he confessed in a whisper. I focussed the heavy binoculars and saw several men on top of a locomotive pulling overhead hoses in preparation for filling up the water tanks. Muffled through the hood, I heard distant German voices through the clear, still air discussing someone else who had caused great amusement when he was found in an apparently compromising position with another young man. *Poor chap,* I thought, *how does one live that down?* There was a huge gush of water and I was not to know the outcome of poor Fritz's dilemma. Sergei and I looked the building over carefully, noting where it might be possible to enter; where it might be possible to get up onto the trains and where the source of the water might be. He was a good scout; he observed and noted the importance of things that I surely would miss. But I was glad to do what I could if it meant I did not have to carry a rifle. After an hour, the locomotive engine had taken on all it needed and was slowly shunted out from underneath the booms. Along with all the other engines on the site, it remained firing. The boilers would freeze in a short time, if they were ever allowed to go out. Anyone found to be responsible for a cracked boiler would surely have a short career in military maintenance.

When the sun gradually produced long shadows in our direction, we slithered back into the trees and went back to the camp to make our report.

Two nights later, we returned. As usual, I was given a huge roll of wire to carry. By now I had no illusions about what it was for and what the potential of its use might be. People would die. It was quite well known that I couldn't manage a weapon (perhaps they didn't realise that I wouldn't do so), but my lack of skill meant that I did not have to explain. However it didn't stop them from using me as a pack horse.

The explosion was spectacular. From our position, a good distance back in the trees, the light was greater than day light. We could see the huge water tower with all its hoses and booms open like a lotus flower and then collapse onto the engine in the shed beneath. The machine rocked on the tracks when another blast twisted the rails underneath it. Water exploded into the air for a brief moment and then flooded in waves over metal, timber and snow. It would freeze in minutes in this temperature and the railway, its sidings, its machinery and its men would be of no use for months. With no water, the locomotives could not move and in time they would freeze and their boilers break. The line would be unusable until spring at least.

In spite of the chaos and damage, I felt good. We had succeeded and a simple task had huge implications. Few men were killed so far as I could tell, but many more would be needed to undertake the repairs. They at least would not be in the front lines or the occupied areas doing the damage they were there to do. I went back to the camp and to my radio. To earn my keep, I reported in detail up the chain of command, what the outcome had been. This was the kind of war I could just about manage. I could earn my keep.

BR10 The Laundry to SA44 Marshes 10 Feb 0601 40 Info on troop numbers organisation leadership

I pretended I hadn't got the message and made no reply. It was impossible for me to answer even if I'd wanted to.

A plane went over very low today. As usual, we ran for the trees as soon as we heard it. But this time, there was great excitement because it was a Russian plane. I couldn't tell one kind from another, but my colleagues were positive that we would now get help and supplies and that it was all down to me. There was much back slapping and libations for everyone.

There had been rumours of such flights from other groups in the marshy forests but this was the first one seen here. Everyone willed it to come back. Instead, we received more people on foot. This time they were men with military skills. The three men who came to us were regular Red Army soldiers sent to co-ordinate our group and others into a more effective force.

I was introduced as the group's radio operator. This was good news as far as they were concerned and I let Kostya do most of the talking. He let it be known that the wireless had been stolen months ago and had no idea why it was labelled in English. The others nodded in conspiratorial agreement. He said that I had been trained in a little radio work before the war and he and I had escaped from Kiev and quite by accident got the set from a dead German en route. Thankfully, they accepted most of this and asked me few questions. The next few weeks were busy ones for me and I was given transmissions to make to rear Red Army units for everything from airplanes to first aid kits.

Kostya had been right, and as I knew, few of the rear Red Army units had wireless, relying on primitive means of communication, but higher up the chain of command radio equipment existed and it was to these that our repeated requests were made. There was a certain amount of surprise in the replies we received but eventually more planes came over and this time supplies were dropped. It felt like we alone had won the war!

I dearly wished I could find a way to get the copy I had been hoarding, out of here.

RUSSIA, North-western Front (Worcester Journal) 12 February 1942 *Life in the Forest* **by Royston Thomas**

There is an unusual stillness in the air today. No wind trembles a twig or dead leaf. Even the air has stopped breathing. Arseni, who always prefers to see the dark side of any situation, tells me that it means a huge storm is approaching. He may be right but for now the sky is clear and the only sound is the occasional clink of the horse harnesses and the crunch of our feet on new snow. But he is always pessimistic.

It seems odd that when the sky is clear and the sun is out, it is the coldest. There is no cloud cover to keep whatever meagre heat this part of the planet generates, near to the earth and the frozen living beings who try to survive on it.

The light hurts the eyes where it reflects from the snow and the blackness of the trees in shadow is darker than ever. The contrast with the blazing whiteness of the snow makes one wonder where all colour has gone. No colour exists among the men in this group; their clothing is a collection of anything that will provide some protection from the cold; coats of all description, boots, mitts and hats likewise - none of it with any colour except grey or black. This is not intentional. Clothing has been cached in the forests and we retrieve what we need and most of it has come from the people of the area. Some of it has been purchased, some donated and probably a little stolen. But at this temperature, we are all glad to have anything.

The men with whom I live in this harsh environment are sturdy, stoic and inventive. We are fed, sheltered and looked after by their wits and amazing ingenuity. Their knowledge of the wider world and its larger war may be limited, but their understanding of this world is superb. Perhaps it will snow tomorrow.

'Look at this!' Sergei came rushing up to me as I was listening to a scrambled German transmission. I pulled the headphones off my head and he thrust a newspaper under my nose.

'Where did this come from?' I asked. It was a single page, folded in half. The top was clearly German but the text was written in Russian Cyrillic text.

'Courier brought it. He says that they are all over the towns. What is it all about?' I didn't realise that Sergei couldn't read and so as gently as I could I scanned the main article. 'It is about how good the Germans want to be to anyone who voluntarily gives himself up.' Sergei snorted and laughed out loud. I continued. 'They are promising decent treatment, jobs and land. And if you are a former Red Army deserter, they may even give you cash for surrendering to them.'

'Really?' Sergei was clearly alert to the word 'cash'.

'Sergei.' I folded the paper and gave it back to him. 'Do you honestly think that they would?'

'Is it a trap?' I nodded. He looked crushed.

'I'm afraid so. We are all much better off here than working for the Germans.

Do you think that they would really trust someone who was a deserter in the first place and then surrendered in the second?'

Sergei tore the paper into tiny pieces and dropped them in the fire. I talked to Kostya when he squatted down beside me later in the morning. 'Sergei needs to be assured that what he is doing is right.' I told him what we had seen. 'He needs to be looked after. And don't let them do anything harsh to him or I won't tell them anything else I find out.'

Kostya nodded. 'We haven't had many deserters from this group.' He punched my shoulder and grinned. 'They are too charmed by you and your radio.' I snorted and he continued in a more serious voice. 'Deserters are a problem. We don't know where they go usually and more worrying is that we don't know what they say. They can be dangerous. That is one reason why we keep moving. Any information they may give to the Germans will be old by the time they get it.' He got up. 'I will speak to him...' He looked back at me. '...gently.'

BR10 The Laundry to SA44 Marshes 18 Feb 0600 27 Details of military leadership

I have no idea what they are asking. What does my little backwater in the wild marshes of western Russia have to do with their British spy? Can't he tell them? Military leadership here isn't...isn't even... There is nothing to tell. I pretend I am out of range and do not get their transmissions.

20 February 1942 Today we met a group of the enemy in the forest. They were on horseback. They looked like men who were last seen in pursuit of Napoleon. Great heavy coats, huge boots, gauntlets and fur hats and long ancient rifles slung over their shoulders.

We came across them by accident and they took us all by surprise. No orders were given by anyone – the charge and the firing began immediately and bodies of men and horses fell in action that lasted no more than a few minutes.

We all ran when the charge began. Everyone knew there was nothing we could do except run for our lives. As I ran, I saw Sergei fall – the back of his skull seemed to be detached from his head and something splashed onto my arm and my neck. I could not stop. He was not the only one to die. Others too fell into the snow. Many others. I don't know what became of so many of them.

Undated winter 1942. I asked, but no one could answer: why was this nation fighting an ultra-modern armed force with 19ᵗʰ century tactics and equipment. It was lunacy – insanity in its highest form. They were Cossacks, but fighters who opposed Stalin and fought with the Germans.

We were all changed men, but we ran because our lives depended on it and even then, more died.

I spent the night separated from the others. When they found me, I was still conscious enough to recognise who they were and to know that I had not been captured. But that was all.

11

Mid March 1942 There is a warmth in the air today and the sunlight is a different colour.

21 March 1942 I am able to stand today and walk a few steps. I assume this is a kind of recovery.

24 March 1942

Dearest Annie,

The last six months will have been very hard for you not hearing from me for so long. I am recovering well now from a serious illness of some kind – no one is saying just what it was, but it has had me in hospital near the British Embassy for a month.

I was evacuated from my posting outside Moscow by air and brought to the Embassy.

Please don't worry my darling, I am being very well looked after and will be able to write to you more often now that I am better. Thank you for all the letters. They were waiting for me when I got here and have helped much to make me feel a great lot better.

Much love
Roy.

Although I was aware of very little, my illness, something like pneumonia I think, had the men in the forest very worried for me. I'm told now that Kostya discovered that the Russian forces had created a few air strips in the forest and got me evacuated on a flight.

The flight was through the *Surazhskie vorota* – the Shurazh Gates, a gap in the front line in the Vitebsk District. Moscow was all but surrounded by Germans, it was a miracle that we – the plane, the other wounded and I – made it out at all. But I knew little about it.

The Embassy had moved in October from Moscow to Kuibyshev where they and much of the Russian Government were now located and I was sent here by hospital train. I was treated here and it became a little warmer at last. Finally I began to feel that I was recovering - although slowly. Being on a hospital train was somewhat unnerving – knowing what we had done to one, but I had the benefit of little consciousness during the trip.

I had lost nearly everything, arriving with only the clothes I was wearing. The wireless is another missing item. I recall a paper flapping on my chest, so perhaps I had an address label. I am sure I have Kostya to thank for that, but everything else; the wireless, note book, the little generator and my ID papers were all left behind. I suspect that my colleagues have put them all to good use by now. I truly hope so.

Russia Kuibyshev (Worcester Journal) 31 March 1942 *The New Embassy* by Royston Thomas

Life is calmer here out of the danger zone. The Embassy has moved from Moscow and all the families and staff are now safe. The trek to get here was a worrying episode as it was decided and executed in very short order. A special train was promised for staff, families and foreigners. Everyone due to leave – a total of 89 people – gathered at Kazan Station by 10 pm on the evening of 15 October. Sleet was falling and huge bags of diplomatic correspondence not burned at the Embassy were dragged to the station with all personal belongings. The city was a bit like the outskirts of Hades with all manner of people in a state of heightened anxiety trying to flee by any means possible. Everyone, including the Embassy staff was of a single opinion that this was the end of the end.

After some delay, the train departed about midday the next day and it took four days of short distances broken by long stops to reach their new destination. The major problem during the trip seems to have been lack of food. In Kuibyshev the new facility was a building known as Pioneers' Palace, but in reality it was little more than a dirty barracks. But being what British people are, everyone took on the work of ridding it of infestation and creating a suitable place for all.

From that day, work continued as if nothing untoward had

happened. Everyone found lodging, inside or outside the so called Palace and Ambassador Cripps still in suit and tie continued to maintain his links with the Russian Government. It was another example of British grit. We all suspect that much more of that will be needed again and again before this war is over.

Since then Sir Stafford has returned to England and we are under the direction of a new Ambassador, Sir Archibald Kerr.

Naturally I was debriefed by Bull. He roared into his office where I waited, like a steam train on a downhill run. He frightened the staff in his outer office and I was left alone with his intimidating self. 'Good to see you Thomas,' he blared. 'You had us worried.'

'I radioed the Embassy ...old Russian set.'

He waved a meaty hand. 'Yes, yes, we know all that. Must have been a tricky time.' I was only able to nod as the barrage went on. 'Doctor tells me it was a lung infection, so I mustn't trouble you too much.' Too late for that, I thought. 'Start at Kiev. Need to know all about what happened to you. Stop if it troubles you.' He stopped abruptly and the silence pulled me in. I started to talk – slowly and with a lot of deliberate breathing.

As soon as I mentioned Kostya, he interrupted. 'Yes, yes, I know Wozniak. Go on.' So Bull has done this before!

He seemed concerned about my health and once I had assured him that whatever it was I had nearly died of was over, he relaxed and asked the questions I expected. How many were in this group? And the other groups? Where were they? What were there activities? Here I was able to give details.

I tried to put all that I wanted to say into a logical order. 'Here,' Bull stood up. 'Come let's sit in more comfortable chairs.' He opened a door in the panelling I had not noticed and led me into a tiny comfortable room with two soft chairs, a low table, lamps and shelves of books. It was dark, very tidy and supremely comfortable. He waved me to one of the chairs. 'Whisky?' he asked opening a cabinet door, 'or sherry.' In shock, I think I asked for whisky. And that is what I got. He sat in the other chair and putting his elbows on his knees, leaned towards me. 'Go on, Roy. What are they doing?'

'Anything. Anything at all that will disrupt the Germans.' I took a small sip of the whisky and just managed not to choke as it went down. 'I can only speak for the group I was with; there are others as you know, but organisation between them is not good.' Bull nodded urging me on. 'I saw them blow up rail lines, time and again, rail yards, and they broke into storage dumps as often as they could. The raids were well reconnoitred, quickly done and almost always successful. Although the Germans quickly repair and then they do it all over again…if they can.'

'I'll want details as specific as you can make them. Put them in a written report later.'

I nodded. 'But sir…' This was my chance, perhaps my only chance. 'They are desperate for help, men who can organise, materiel especially armaments, food, clothing, guns, information, money, boots, radios, training, coding, maps…' I ran out of breath, my damaged lungs could produce no more. 'They need help sir. If there is the possibility of transport out, such as they sent me on, then surely help can be got in…sir.'

Bull looked at me for a few long seconds. 'It surprises me to hear you talk about guns and armaments, Roy, knowing you as I do.'

I had no idea what he knew about me but should not have been so naive as to think he did not know about the moral stand I had chosen to take. 'In the circumstances in which I found myself, sir, I could do little but try to help them. Without help, sir, they are all dead men, as are all the villages and towns and farms where their families and friends live. The Germans will kill them all.'

He tossed back the remains of his whisky and I drank what I could. 'Give me your report as soon as you can and I will speak to the Ambassador. He will report as he thinks best; be that to London, or to the Kremlin. But I can't promise them salvation.'

In all the chaos of the move to Kuibyshev, they had not replaced me on the radio and so as I got stronger, I was able to resume a short shift usually first thing in the morning.

And I made a quick transmission to The Laundry from the main radio. I needed to know where I was in relation to the job that they needed me to do. After a few weeks with no information, I received by post a book of Worcestershire history. It had been posted in Worcester and I knew what it really contained. I carefully peeled the paper off the inside covers and found the OTP codes I needed.

BR10 The Laundry to SA44 Kuibyshev April 5 0605 89 Have another operator sending info we require Act as Embassy operator for now Will advise if needs change.

Another operator? It could only be Glen or Fred... or perhaps someone else hiding in a dark cupboard in another building. I was in danger of becoming surplus to requirements.

With the beginning of April, I was allowed out now and again. Getting out in the fresh air was a kind of therapy of its own. I began to write copy and send it to Worcester again. The diplomatic bags disappeared as always in the direction of the Swedish Embassy I think and then onward. Did the copy every arrive? I wouldn't know until I had some reply from Mr Donaldson.

8 April 1942

Dear Mum & Dad,

My last letter was of necessity short and to the point and I am sorry that there was so little information. I haven't been well since I was evacuated from the Marshes where I had taken refuge after my time in Kiev. Once there, it was almost impossible to get out but eventually I was able at last to get some messages to Moscow. I hope that they were passed on to you so that you knew I was at least alive.

I am now at the British Embassy in Kuibyshev, recovering and being given small jobs to do. It all helps with my recovery and I am getting stronger each day. Today I have spent several happy hours if you can call them that, peeling potatoes for dinner before I spend a few hours on the radio.

Food is basic here, as supplies are limited especially in the winter, but for some reason there are lots of potatoes. Our cook has made everything with them that it is possible to make.

The weather might improve now according to people here who should know and I will be ready for whatever assignment I am presented with next.

In the meantime, I peel potatoes, do typing jobs, a little radio work and give some lessons to the Embassy children.

Love to you both,

Roy

While peeling potatoes and other light radio work, I had time to reflect. I did not wish to dwell – in my mind at least – on the horrifying details of what I had seen and done. But the stories and pictures came to me uninvited. In my quiet hours or solemn moments, they were vivid and bright. I saw the explosions, heard the screams and felt the snow sting on my neck and hands. I just didn't know when or how I would be able to live normally again without these horrors that were such a part of my soul just now. Nights were the worst times; there was no other noise or activity to blot them out. There was nothing to stop them coming. I tried to put a blanket over them – to give me some kind of distance and to make them into scenes I merely observed and did not have a part in. But it didn't work for long and I spent many night time hours awake sitting up in bed with my head on my knees. Maybe there would be no escape from these visions – ever.

In the daylight I tried to turn my mind to other things. The mud was amazing. With no paved road surfaces, melt water made mud of every surface. This had the effect of slowing everything down as if it were in treacle which in a way it was. Motor vehicles were stuck and horses too if they were used to pull them out. We walked on board walks through the town and ventured off them at our peril.

RUSSIA, Kuibyshev (Worcester Journal) 29 April 1942, *The New Capital of Russia* **by Royston Thomas**

Kuibyshev is now the capital of Russia. The Communist Party, the government officials, diplomatic missions and a great deal of Moscow's cultural institutions have been evacuated here. Although Moscow is nearly surrounded, the people have dug in and are prepared for any assault. It has not yet been defeated.

The new capital is on east bank of the Volga River where it is joined by the Samara River, about 200 miles north east of Stalingrad. North of the city are the Sokolyi Hills and the famous Steppes are to the south and east. Until the war took it over, it was famous for bread and flour making – a bread basket of the Union.

Kuibyshev is now given over to heavy industry in common with much of the rest of Russia's cities. It produces aircraft, firearms, ammunition, spare parts and the factories and foundries operate 24 hours a day. Their output is phenomenal.

But Kuibyshev is also a cultural city and the ballet is often performed at the Bolshoi Theatre. Shostakovich's Seventh Symphony was performed here on 5 March to very high acclaim.

As we have come to expect from these resilient people, they can turn from riveting tanks together in exhausting emergency conditions to being enraptured by a performance

of beautiful music. Surely this resilient stubbornness will
not be defeated and a sensitive heart will be the stuff of
ultimate victory.

I firmly doubted that this one would ever be published. The powers that be would probably decide that it gave too much information to the enemy. To be honest I didn't care. There was too little to write about here except the war and how hard the people worked to turn the tide in our favour. I hoped that I could get out and about. Perhaps I could find something else to write about. The paper wanted it sanitised anyway.

15 May 1942

Dearest Annie,

I was overjoyed to get your letter of 23 December. It was the first one I'd received since I got here and I hope that you have not had to wait so long for mine. The post is of necessity very precarious and with sinkings, winter and loss of personnel it is not surprising. Through means I don't know and could not hope to understand, someone, somewhere forwards most of our personal mail, but even then, we have no control over how or when or in what order it arrives. Please don't think badly of me if you don't hear from me often!

I am almost fully recovered now and will be out and about soon. I have been given some work in the Embassy that is not too taxing and which helps me regain my health. With the summer coming, I will be fine.

Please give my love to your mother and father and reserve a very large piece for yourself. I promise with all my heart that we will be together again one day. God alone knows how much we want it and surely He will see that it is so.

All my love, always,

Roy.

Then at the beginning of June, Glen was discovered dead in the street.

5 June 1942 The weather is beautiful. Summer weather, almost hot, lies over the city and we are taking full advantage of the warmth and light. Some vegetable gardens have sprung up in various Embassy sites and in some flowers are also beginning to bloom. I am sure that the British are becoming known for

137

eccentricity: flowers can't be eaten after all. The mystery of Glen's sudden death has created rumours of every hue and the ensuing chaos has affected us all.

One evening a week later, Fred came into the radio room early. 'I'm bored,' he announced as if it were the cricket score. 'So I've come down to annoy you for a while.' I had to smile but before I could reply, he added, 'You've heard the latest about Glen?'

'What happened to him anyway? This place has been in turmoil ever since. But there's only the rumours of course. I know he liked a drink.'

Fred put his head phones around his neck and pulled up a chair. 'And he was a ladies' man. He was seeing a woman - one of our secretaries in the city somewhere - who is no longer a secretary by the way. Also, there was a lot of drink involved. I know John Bull was worried that he might have been a bit loose with his pillow talk. Anyway, the latest is that...,' he put his elbows on the table and put his fists under his nose, '...he disappeared that weekend, which was not all that unusual, but then he was found in a little side street... and he had been shot...through the head.' He obviously liked a dramatic finish. He leaned back and looked at me from under his eyebrows. I knew some of this...rumours being what they are, there were several stories making the rounds. But we hadn't been told how he had died. I felt unusual, uncertain, shocked – something else, I'm not sure what – a soup of emotions. I was sure that I had lost the colour in my face as well.

But Fred wasn't finished. He leaned forward again, closer this time. 'And,' he added with dramatic flourish, 'when they cleared out his room here, they found a small wireless!' He whispered, '...he was spying...no one knows who for. It was all kept very quiet. I only know because I had to code the messages for London. And then...,' he looked around the room, trying to be nonchalant, but seeking anyone too close, '... they took his room apart – floor up, wall panels off, ceiling down, then they did the same to her lodgings – to see if there was anything else.'

I swallowed hard – and attempted to say something – anything. 'And did they?'

'They aren't saying.' But Fred bowled on. 'Bull was... well, like someone I'd never seen before.' He wiggled forward on his chair a little as if confiding to me. 'He was red in the face and shouting, louder if possible than he usually does. We thought he was going to have a stroke. He was more than just a little upset by it all, I can tell you! We didn't know what they were going to take apart next. You must have been in the kitchens if you missed all that.'

I could feel my eyes getting wider and wider. Not in surprise as Fred no doubt thought, but in horror. Thank God I had taken the little wireless with me to Kiev. I felt a chill down my back. And thank goodness I'd left it there.

I couldn't speak. '…that's not all.' Fred whispered. 'Glen's fate was nearly the same as the chap you replaced.'

I must have flinched because Fred grinned, clearly pleased with the reaction his comment had generated. 'Except,' he went on, 'I think Orville was strangled.' He leaned closer. 'I'd be careful if I were you. I know I watch my back.'

So suddenly, I was back at my desk on a full shift. In Kuibyshev the Embassy staff working accommodations were considerably more crowded, so I shared the desk with Fred who worked the late shift. Fred now did the coding and decoding for the Ambassador and occasionally, when urgent, he did some transmission, but usually it was left for me in the morning.

It was liberating in a way, not to have a radio locked in a cupboard in my little room. I now shared it with Fred, so it was a relief to be free of the terror of being caught. Until, the evening when I returned to my room after handing over to Fred and there was a knock on the door. The woman who did our laundry stood there with my shirts, trousers and underwear in a large paper bundle. She handed it over and I nearly dropped it. It weighed three times what I expected. When I untied it, there was a small radio set wrapped in my trousers. As I expected, a set of crystals were hidden in its innards and an OTP, to supplement the ones from the book lining, in the pocket of the trousers. I felt as if I had been shot by a secret that I thought I had hidden too well to be found. I let the sickness of guilt and terror slowly slide over me until it disappeared somewhere beneath my feet. I was trapped yet again even though I had hoped against hope that it was all over. And who and where had this come from? That was perhaps more terrifying than the work I knew I was about to do again. And the horrifying fact that someone out there was still watching me.

Carefully I checked in on Sunday morning, while Fred was still on duty and just before my shift started. I locked the bedroom door. Then the radio went back into a little locker that contained everything I owned, but which thankfully had a lock. Not that it would stop Bull on a purge, if he chose. I had to find somewhere else more secure.

The searches has been thorough, so where was safe? Surely whoever arranged for me to have the thing would not want me to be caught with it. Maybe the purge was over.

Within a day or two the 'spy' reports came trickling across my desk again. Because the Embassy was short of staff now, I had the job of sorting the newspapers in the morning and the first reports fell out of a Russian paper when I cut the string that tied it into a roll. I looked very hard to see something positive in all this, but could only note without enthusiasm that they, so far, had not made any further requests for information I had no hope of getting.

Reports from our 'spy' came about once a week and never on a regular day or time. As I could not transmit until Sunday morning, I had to hide not only the radio but the report. I took a panel off the ceiling of the bedroom closet, to hide it among the dust and mouse droppings, then pushed it along the floor joist, so as not to disturb the dust too much, to a place under a tank over the toilet next door. If it were discovered, I could deny I knew anything about it, but I could still get to it through the bedroom when I needed it. I knew it was futile, but it was all I could think of.

The renewed weight of my betrayal of all that I valued brought me close to fainting. I was trapped in this country, in this building, in this job, in all these lies. I had no choice but to do everything I was asked to do. Somewhere out there was someone in a lot more danger than I was, doing God knew what, sending information, desperately needed, for the British Government, and it was up to me to get it there. I steadied my breathing. He had no choice but to trust me and I had no choice but to do what I was sent here to do. But there was someone here who knew both of us and we were both being watched. It was never going to end until one or more of us died.

I stretched my back from the typing that I had been given by the Ambassador's secretary – a long report on just where Stalin was or wasn't and when, and why he had not come to Kuibyshev. He was clearly an elusive character. At the moment he was denying that anything was going on at all, in spite of reports that he had already lost 170,000 men, 258 tanks and 1138 guns at a single battle between the Black Sea and the Sea of Azov on 20 May. He had made no comment on the 214,000 prisoners taken at Izyum on the 28th and the 1246 tanks destroyed along with a further 2026 guns.

Ambassador Kerr was clearly frustrated by the unreality of the Government in Moscow or wherever it actually was these days. He was far too diplomatic to say so of course, but because we knew the sound of his voice, we also recognised its sound in the words of this report. However, he had a good relationship with Stalin – as good as it was possible to have given the volatile nature of the beast

SA44 Kuibyshev to BR10 The Laundry 14 June 0602 42 Duties changed Will report in at 0530 local time

BR10The Laundry to SA44 Kuibyshev 15 June 0531 54 Has ambassador

140

commented on Russian heavy industry in your area

What? It was starting again.

Adrian clapped a hand on my shoulder. 'Great to see you old boy. What busy lives we lead these days eh?' I hadn't seen Adrian for a couple of months. He was off on some errand for the Ambassador I was told and our paths hadn't crossed.

I suppressed an inclination to hit him and then saw the twinkle in his eyes and remembered his warning about the staff around us. I followed his lead. 'Shall we compare notes over lunch?'

'Glad to see you more or less recovered. Nasty business.' Adrian took a chunk of dark bread from a paper bag and handed it to me. We sat in an open space that might have been a park once, but was now covered by sheds and makeshift housing. We had a little corner in the sun.

'It wasn't the finest time I've ever had.' A slice of cured meat followed and I laid it over the bread. 'What about you?' I still didn't want to talk about my time in the wilderness. I was more interested in his and hoped that he might have some information about what 'they' wanted me to do next or when I might be allowed to go home. I knew very well that this kind of information was not in Adrian's gift and getting home before the end of the war or maybe not even after it was a faint hope. But I could live a long time with hope.

'I've spent the last two months battling my way back and forth to Moscow. Got back last night. The trains are pretty well the only way to get around these days – although occasionally there's a plane. But I usually get bumped off when there is some large chest of medals wanting my seat.'

I bit into the mound in my hand and Adrian delicately folded meat onto his bread. 'Stalin has been difficult to pin down. I know that Cripps had to shout at Vyshinski more than once about where the government actually was and on which day – probably why he was replaced by Kerr, but nothing much has changed. We still don't know who we are meant to deal with or where on God's good earth they are. Hence my constant travel.'

'And Kleist and Hoth continue a stampede to the Caucasus.'

'And Paulus to Stalingrad. Take heart, their supply lines are already stretched beyond the breaking point. They will all starve to death sooner or later, or run out of machines and supplies.' He pointed his mound of bread at me. 'Mark my words, the state of the Russian roads will be their undoing.' He meant it in jest,

141

but I had seen those roads. There was some truth in what he said. 'But what about you?'

Did I want to tell him or not? Some of what I had seen and, dear God, what I had done were lodged in places in my brain where I did not really want to go. 'A lot of radio work and Kerr's secretary has me typing up anything he can find and so for the moment that's sufficient. I've sent a few pieces to the paper, but there isn't much more I can tell them unless I can get out and about. At the moment there doesn't seem to be the ways or means to do it.'

Adrian dusted his fingers and digging back into the bag, produced two spice cakes. 'Well I'm happy to share some of my travelling about.'

Adrian was full of enthusiasm although I told him little. He grinned at me. There were times, not many admittedly, when I saw tiredness in Adrian's face. He seemed to have no other life than what he did for the Embassy. Now that there were no grand balls and soirees for him to organise, his skills were used elsewhere. Elsewhere appeared to be with the new Ambassador. I had no idea what Adrian did in his few hours off work. He had rooms elsewhere in the city, but I was never invited there. He did not discuss what he did.

'I've always wanted to see the eastern steppes. Did you know ...?' he charged on before I could remind him that we were located on the edge of them, '... the grassland covers an area from the Ukraine to China. Imagine a journey through that! The old chaps on the Silk Road must have thought they would never reach the end. Amazing. And ...' he rushed on '... did you know that the temperature in the summer can go up to over 100 degrees and to 40 below in the winter.' He shook his head. 'One has to wonder how people survive it.'

'What use is it, the steppes? What do they do there?'

Adrian rubbed his hands together. 'Well, as it is grass, they farm it, raise cattle and feed the nation. Can you imagine the scale of it? Astonishing. And so romantic too. It's where the Cossacks lived.'

Something turned over in my stomach. 'Really?'

'They were very well organised in Tsarist times – had good administration, good schools and were quite wealthy. Many of them gave military service to the Tsar for something like 20 years at a time.'

'Twenty years!'

'Yes, but they were well paid – in land usually. Then they either farmed it – or the rest of the family did - or they leased it for farming or for the mining rights. But then the Revolution divided them into supporting the Red Army or the White and

142

afterwards the whole issue of land ownership went into disarray and it was divided among other people. They were quite cruelly repressed.'

That feeling of sadness that I so often felt for this country frothed through me again. 'Where are they now? Are they still around?' I knew the answer.

'Oh yes. Some of them have gone to fight for the Germans. I suspect they see it as a way of getting their own back on the Bolsheviks. Ever heard of Ivan Kononov?

'The 436th regiment?'

'That's the one. Defected on the first day of the war. Now seems to be guarding communications for the Germans against the Soviet partisans.' He looked up at me.

A chill covered me in spite of the heat. 'Little horses, big hats, fight like ghosts?'

'I think you have met them already.'

All I could do was nod. The memory of men charging towards me, screaming like they had just been released from the mouth of hell. Oh yes, I'd met them.

BR10 The Laundry to SA44 Kuibyshev 16 Aug 0530 18 status of Stalingrad

SA44 Kuibyshev to BR10 The Laundry 17 Aug 0532 79 Paulus ordered attack on 15 Aug Stalin takes personal control of battle to south Troops pour in

Why ...why? Because that was what I was here to do, that's why. I had little choice and I knew it. The Laundry knew I was back the minute I arrived...they knew from any number of sources I was not privy to and once they knew...it was life as usual.

BR10 The Laundry to SA44 Kuibyshev 30 Aug 0534 50 Has Stalin financial reserves for big battle at Stalingrad

Just how in the hell of this place, miles from Moscow, in the depths of a world war, in an Embassy not privy to any Soviet secrets, from the lowly position in which I worked, was I supposed to assess the financial reserves of a nation as unstable as this one?

I sat back on my chair, heart pounding, stomach rolling. The emotional lead weight under which I functioned pressed harder. I had done work that the Embassy knew nothing about; I, too, had a small wireless hidden in my room, likely to be found at any minute. I was a known conscientious objector. If I refused – or failed – I was ... the consequences and deadly options piled one on

143

top of the next, reached infinity. I was probably a dead man, too. I now had to spy from the Embassy of my own country.

SA44 Kuibyshev to BR10 The Laundry 6 Sept 57 Losses very high Men Materiel Sgrad and elsewhere Numbers not known

12

September 1942

16 Sept, 1942 It is raining again.

Occasionally, the Ambassador, Bull or Adrian asked me to code or transmit something to Britain about our situation here but usually that responsibility fell to Fred who had now taken over Glen's role. Usually the transmission sought clarification. The Government here was still uncertain. We knew who was supposed to be doing what, but one could never be sure that the person in charge hadn't been arrested and sent to some dark and dismal place for interrogation or killed in an unexplained car crash. It must only have been the power mad who took on these jobs. Any sane person would find some excuse not to.

The work was often dull; transmitting, receiving, typing and then the same for the next message. I began to look for silly words in the coded messages or for the decoded words – anything to make the routine more interesting. The coded messages from the 'spy' were the worst, some short, some long that I had to break into pieces, all unintelligible. My game of seeking words in English, Russian, German, Welsh or any other possible language got me through a great many boring hours. I found parts of words in most languages, some silly, some obscene; some were abbreviations for other longer, but well known phrases and even occasionally there were some Russian words in plain text. It was just careless coding, but amusing all the same. This continued for weeks, until one day when I was nearly asleep I found *parti yatov ara*. Put together as regular Russian it was *partiya tovara*. It meant a shipment, a consignment or parcel. I finished the transmission and found two other references to a package. Elsewhere there was schifrovka which meant dispatch. Why these words were

145

not coded I could not begin to guess.

BR10 The Laundry to SA44 Kuibyshev 18 Oct 0530 44 Info good Comment on recent battle successes please

SA44 Kuibyshev to BR10 Laundry 18 Oct 0610 120 Russians in Sgrad supplied by boats across Volga Industrial areas of city captured by Paulus Von Kleist stopped 50 miles from Grozny Oil Fields

RUSSIA Kuibyshev (Worcester Journal) Saturday 28 Nov 1942
Stalingrad by Royston Thomas

We have heard today that tide of the terrible battles in Stalingrad may be turning at last. A Russian assault began in mid-November involving over a million men, 13,500 guns, nearly 900 tanks and over 1000 aircraft. Because the weather has been poor the Germans were not able to fly their planes and so did not have good reconnaissance to withstand the attack.

Naturally the Germans counterattacked and met Russian tanks in snowy conditions. The Germans were forced to withdraw to avoid being trapped and the Russian troops over ran at least one German headquarters.

By the 22nd, Paulus and his German Armies were encircled in the city of Stalingrad where they were now trapped. Although it has not been confirmed, it seems as if Paulus and his troops are short of supplies and in spite of this has been ordered by Hitler to hold on at all costs.

What a dilemma for any military commander who has troops to look after and a war to fight but with fewer and fewer resources to do so.

There was so much more I want to say in these reports. Like the loss of life, the loss of limbs, the loss of liberty for prisoners and troops alike. Neither Germans nor Russians had the better situation. Both were freezing in the cold, ill clothed, ill fed and probably badly led; the Germans from the top, the Russians from the top, bottom and middle.

As for my research into the financial affairs of the Russian Government, I realised I was far out of my depth. But I scanned the official newspapers, *Pravda*, the voice of the Communist Party and *Isvestia*, containing the sainted words of the Government. They were never going to provide me with the truth, but reports would at least show that I was doing the Laundry's bidding.

I quietly looked at the attachés – those people attached to the Embassy with special expertise, hence military attachés, legal, cultural, scientific, commercial and so on. They came and went and I looked for one who might have any insight. I would probably have to start with the commercial attaché, since they had hopes, I guessed, of assisting western businesses to develop here if the war ever ended and if it ended in Russia's favour. Since I rarely saw him, it was difficult for a lowly radio operator to establish any kind of rapport with any of them. I offered to do their coding and transmission.

BR10 The Laundry to SA44 Kuibyshev 29 Nov 0530 20 German loss statistics

SA44 Kuibyshev to BR10 Laundry 29 Nov 0550 56 Much loss on both sides All in poor condition Low morale

Surely they knew all this. Why did I have to tell them what they surely could get, with much more detail from their official sources? Why me?

1 Dec 1942

Dear Roy,

I write to say that Dad died on Wednesday. He had been ill for some time.

We will bury him tomorrow at the chapel and I will see about being able to come home and run the farm.

Haydn

PS I will arrange for a memorial stone for him later

It was the first letter I had from Haydn since I left Wales.

24 January 1943. I have lost my father. The letter arrived today from Haydn, short and to the point. No additional news, no emotion, no sympathy for me. But I am being selfish and not very Christian about it. My father. The person who has always been in my life. The one who was kind to me, helped me to get an education and a job. The one who taught me how to read and send Morse code. The one who got me into this place where I am now and helped to save me from active military duty.

Haydn will take over the farm. That is no shock to me, it was always known that is how it would be and I do not feel bitter about it. How he will manage to get out of the Army I don't know, but perhaps it can be arranged, if not he will do so after the war – if he survives.

I had a wobbly moment when I considered what would happen if he didn't survive and I did. What do I know about farming? Nothing of any use. It was presumed from the day I was born that I wouldn't need to know. I pushed the idea out of my thoughts. It was still far more possible that I would be the one not to go home.

Here I was, more or less trapped in Russia – near a huge, bloody, busy war with no real part to play in it. A war that could consume us all in a heartbeat and was still likely to show me things that I would never have chosen to witness.

I must write to my mother.

I went for a long walk at lunch time. Kuibyshev is a small city and strange to most British refugees. It seems odd that I should think of them as refugees, but they, like probably millions of Russians around this great country, are displaced, finding refuge and trying to create a kind of normal life away from what they came to know. The city doubled in size when it became the temporary capital of Russia, so there are hastily constructed offices and housing everywhere. With or without the Russian government there are people from everywhere so the mix of people is unusual to say the least.

The wide straight streets seemed to have a different quality today. Time went by more slowly although activity around me was going on as normal. Colours seemed brighter. Sounds on the snow were stronger. Did this mean that God was nearer? I hoped so as I dearly needed Him to be so. I wanted to understand what this meant. I needed to find the new distance between me and my father. I needed to talk to God.

The little Russian Church was foreign to me. It was down a narrow street away from the main part of the town and I stumbled across it accidentally in my random rambling. It was tiny, with a single small onion dome; dull on the outside as if hiding from the world. The Bolsheviks had not been kind to the Christian churches but more survived than might have been expected. Inside it was empty and dusty. There was a pile of timber along one end. It was being used as a store, but still held the faith of life. I went in quietly and listened to the silence of the tiny holy space. The few remaining icons glowed through the dust in the wonderful light that this space seemed to generate all by itself. The fabrics, faded though they were, had been made by loving hands and received with gratitude by the Church. All its parts fit together with a sense of loving belonging. I let the warmth of the light calm my thoughts and then focussed on the front of the church; the altar, clear and clean, its cross on the wall with the double horizontal arms and oblique arm at the bottom, the silent censer.

A small priest came in. He was dressed plainly and it was his bearing rather than his clothes that marked his as a priest. He too tried not to catch the eye of the State. I stammered an apology although my throat was constricted with emotion. He touched my arm. 'Sit.' He led me to a small collection of mended chairs. 'You may talk,' he whispered kindly. But my throat was too full and all I could do was shake my head and touch my throat.

'I think you are not a regular attender here?'

I shook my head again. They still had regular services?

'Nor are you Orthodox Christian?'

By now I had a small voice. 'Methodist.'

'Ah,' he relaxed and put his arm on my sleeve. 'I see you study our cross. Do you know it?' His breath made a thin white cloud in the cold.

'No, I ...'

'Then let me....' He pointed to the crucifix. 'Do you see the top bar? That is where the proclamation by Pilate was nailed in mockery of Christ. But we have cleverly converted that to a proclamation about Christ a King in Glory.' He smiled and shifted a little on his chair.

'The second bar is the one to which our Christ is nailed. At his right hand you see the sun and at his left the moon?'

I was beginning to focus. 'Yes,' I whispered and pulled my coat closer around myself.

'It is a quotation from Joel. *"The sun hid its light, and the moon turned to blood."* And behind his body you see the lance that pierced His side and the sponge on a cane that gave Him vinegar to drink. There are also inscriptions to His glory. But the bottom bar is slanted and is the brace for His feet. Can you see?'

I nodded although my voice had returned.

'His feet are nailed with two nails and the bar slants. Do you see? This is because the two thieves on either side of him had different fates. The one on his right was saved. See, the bar points upwards on that side – to heaven, but the one on his left....' He spread his hands.

Then he touched my arm again. 'Look at our Lord again. See that He is not in agony. He is in repose. With dignity, with calmness. He wears no crown of thorns. He is at peace. Do not be in pain my son. Death is not agony, death is peace.'

149

I put my head down and wept. When I looked up again, I was alone.

26 January 1943

Dear Mum,

I have just received Haydn's letter. I do not know what to write. By the time you receive this two months or more will have gone by but I am as sad now as it would be possible to be had I been there.

When you are able please tell me what happened. Haydn's letter did not say.

I will write again when I can prepare my thoughts better,

Roy

Winter was a time in Russia when many of us wished we were somewhere else. It was a time when I felt particularly depressed. How I wished I could see colour in the landscape. How I wished there was a time when I could feel that every second of every day was not spent dealing with emergencies – continual emergencies. Everything seemed to be a crisis or the frustration of waiting for an emergency we knew was coming. My thoughts were particularly confused as I tried to make real the news that my father was dead.

I recalled time on the farm when spring meant the machinery and shire horses were on the land again. When there were new lambs, new chickens, new plants in the greenhouses and the walled garden was dug and planted with new fruit and vegetables. How I wished. But then I remembered that it was unlikely that I would ever enjoy it again as it was.

So I turned my thoughts to Annie. I received letters periodically from her although the order was sometimes confused. I suspected too, that some of them have been opened, but the censors would be curious about mail these days so that was no surprise. What would the future be for us? We hardly knew each other. We had spent more time corresponding with each other than we ever did together. How would the war have changed us when we met again? Can we really expect to pick up where we left off? Did we love each other enough to do that? Would we be two different people by then? Would we be changed too much?

24 March 1943

Dearest Annie,

I have been in Kuibyshev almost a year now and it would seem that spring is beginning at last although I have been told that we can expect at least a month of snow and cold yet. But on the other hand, the severity of the wind has been less of late and the snow is retreating. We can hope.

I fondly think of spring where you are and the daffodils that will by now be blooming along with the spring trees. I fondly think of you too in your spring dress and little hat. How I wish I could see you as I imagine you to be.

With love and longing,

Roy

BR10 The Laundry to SA44 Kuibyshev 21 Mar 43 0530 13 General morale

SA44 Kuibyshev to BR10 Laundry 21 Mar 43 0540 54 Desperate then euphoric Soviets forced from Kharkov by Germans

BR10 Laundry to SA44 Kuibyshev 28 Mar 43 0532 9 Successes

I had no idea what they wanted. They wanted me to discover, by means I did not have, what the economic status of the Russian Government was and then in the next transmission wanted to know about morale, but only after a successful attack on something about which I had no knowledge. Increasingly, I felt that they had no connection to the reality of this place. I had hoped that they actually read my newspaper reports, but clearly I was wrong. Donaldson seemed to print only the articles with uplifting reports of success and the moral resistance and fortitude of the poor people being bombed, shot, betrayed. How was I ever to answer these increasingly stupid requests? They made no sense. But the requests went on and on. Increasingly asking for the impossible. Comment on communist rhetoric in articles in *Pravda*? If they have access to *Pravda* they can work it out for themselves surely.

28 April 1943 Went out to buy some new trousers today. The two pairs I had arrived with were long gone and I had replaced them with padded, confiscated things in the marsh winter and then I was given others while I convalesced. But now, a year on, I needed something that didn't look quite so badly fitting and would be suitable while I sat in the Embassy listening to Russian radio signals and waiting for the 'spy' to speak. Thought of having the seat reinforced.

I found a little tailor after a wife of one of the clerks gave me directions. He was thrilled with yet another customer and I realised that all the foreign embassies that had relocated here had been a boon to businesses like his. He probably had never had so much custom in his life. And as per instructions, I returned three days later to be handed a brown paper parcel which I traded for the requisite number of kopeks and walked back to the Embassy.

As I let the door close behind me, a voice called over the clatter of the office, 'Thomas.' It was John Bull and I wondered if the trousers would be enough for what was about to happen next.

'Thomas,' he began in his huge voice. Would nothing he uttered could ever be confidential? Again he surprised me. 'The Embassy will be moving back to Moscow in the summer. The situation there has stabilized. It can all go wrong of course, but since Stalin refuses to leave Moscow, the Ambassador needs to be near. We can't go on with this shuttling back and forth. So as you speak good Russian now, we want you to go to Moscow and get the Embassy building cleared and ready.'

I must have blinked in amazement. 'Hire the repairs you need and any other staff. Adrian will pop in and out and help you with recruiting. We want to be back and working by July.'

'But...' I flapped my hand towards the office outside, '... what about the families and ...'

'They can come later. They will be safe here. For now, get to Moscow and see what needs to be done. Come back with a list of work. Fred can manage the radio work and we can get someone one from the office staff to fill in if we need.' Then he added a little more quietly, 'I don't want to send you on any more dangerous missions, so I thought this would suit you.'

The idea of that elegant mansion being given to me for renovation made me blanch – who was I to decide how the lovely building should be repaired. I knew that it had been built in the late 1800's and just saved from being destroyed by post revolutionaries in 1919. It was a joy; eclectic, elegant and built by a sensitive man who had installed the amazing carvings and wall panels. Who was I to know how to preserve them as they deserved to be?

It was its position that made it critical – opposite the Kremlin and its shadowy world of power, hate and intrigue, where the its almost invisible tyrant-in-charge directed not only the war – that bit of it that he believed to be real – but the lives and welfare of millions. Millions who were still starving, but who still loved him. No wonder Kerr was desperate to get back there. Any little scrap of information about Stalin and what he was or wasn't doing, was important and was nearly impossible to discover or analyse from the edge of the Volga where we were. It was all a bit like my relationship with the Laundry.

SA44 Kuibyshev to BR10 Laundry. 18 April 0530 57 Stop or reroute all reports
Am being sent to Moscow Will report later

So here I was on a train to Moscow, wearing my new trousers and with the other new pair in my bag on top of my new little wireless.

The building on Sofievskaya Quay stood more or less as we had left it – thoroughly looted naturally - but sound and with most of its fine interior still in place. Someone had torn down some of the wood panelling and tried to light a fire in the entrance hall but that was all the damage I found, apart from the roof – not adequately repaired after the 1941 fire bombing. My old room was just about habitable, dry at least and my unused OTPs were still safe behind the wall panel. I put the radio in with them, so I could continue using it when I got back next time. Selfishly I wanted to have some time away from the spy business and the Laundry would have to believe that I was not able to communicate. The reasons, they could make up themselves. This time, I tacked the panel back in place with some sturdy pins. If another bomb was going to hit the place, I rather hoped it would destroy it all and not merely knock the panels out and give up my guilty secret. Moscow had been relatively quiet of late; the bombing all but stopped in January. The Germans seemed much more interested in the terrifying siege they had laid on Leningrad. They must also have been looking over their shoulders while the RAF bombed Berlin.

I charted the basic repairs necessary for ambassadorial staff to live here and to work, then the works necessary for the rest of us to do the same.

John Bull stood up and walked around his chair as he read my report. 'How long will this take Roy?.'

'Three weeks or so for the first part to be finished, sir, and then a month or six weeks for the rest.'

He nodded and rubbed one hand inside his jacket pocket. 'Labour?'

'Adrian has been looking into it. There is plenty of labour around – it's the skills that may be short, but he's sure we can manage, sir.'

He wafted the page at me. 'Off you go then. Get it done.'

And I was on yet another train on the way back to Moscow with no real idea how I was supposed to get the British Embassy ready for occupation. What do I know about timber or plaster?

The lengthening daylight hours of June would make the work easier and today the light was dragging itself slowly toward the western horizon. The huge train snuffled its methodical way through farmland, forests, ravines and over rivers and tributaries. Little pockets of snow remained, tucked into shady places under over-hanging rocks or behind trees. Our compartment got steadily hotter as the day dragged on. I was wedged in with two other people from the Swedish Embassy, their bags and cases, but also with an interpreter from the American Embassy on his way back to Moscow. As usual, the train made stops where we expected it would and many more where we didn't.

This one was not only unexpected but sudden, as we were run suddenly onto what appeared to be a siding in an area of thin trees and heavy low growing brush, and slammed to a screaming halt on the rails. Moments later a heaving and dirty engine pulling a line of old carriages slowly drew along our right side. There seemed to be considerable activity on board.

The train carriages were full of men on their feet, pushing shoving, swearing and throwing punches at each other. They were poorly dressed, some with uniform tunics and hats some without. There was little doubt from the language that came through the broken windows in their carriages and the open ones in ours and the fighting going on that the troops were hugely dissatisfied about something. The train eventually came to a halt beside us and the shouting clearly told us that there was a near mutiny going on.

In seconds, they became aware of us and their anger engulfed us too. Officers disembarked and in the narrow passage between the trains were trying with orders, threats and pistol shots to quiet things again. But the men inside didn't or wouldn't listen and the heaving mass became more and more threatening. Then they were spilling from the train windows, cursing us and asking what we had ever done for the Revolution. Why were we so privileged that we could travel in such comfort, while they were massed into rudimentary carriages without food or sanitation? I began to wonder for our safety and realised that this was about to become very difficult. My companions, in western tradition, largely ignored what was happening or moved to other compartments. But this inflamed the men even more.

Suddenly, we can feel our carriage lurch and it was obvious that some of the men had boarded the train. I heard people on the roof of the carriage. At the same moment, a young woman dressed in a long shirt belted at the waist and loose trousers tucked into boots, slammed the door of our compartment open.

'Get out! Vychodite!' She shouted. 'Get off the train. For your own safety. Srochno evakuirovat'poezd! Srochno!! Quickly!' I didn't need to be told twice. I grabbed my bag, hoisted it over my shoulder and bolted for the passage over the poor soul with whom I had been sharing a seat. The young woman was just ahead of me, shouting into the compartments and banging on the doors, 'Vychodite!! Get out, get out!' Other passengers were following behind me and I heard women screaming, doors slamming, bags and cases falling, people shouting, a baby crying.

The young woman sharply rammed open the door at the end of the carriage, hitting a body with a meaty whack. As I crashed through behind her, I saw a young soldier fall off the platform between the cars. I jumped off the platform opposite the troop train and followed the young woman as we ran and stumbled down the bank. I didn't know if there was anyone behind me. I fell on the dry grassy bank and slid down on my back to the bottom. I didn't look back as I ran after her. She was crashing through brush and small trees into the darkness of the forest and into the setting sun.

Eventually, I could run no more and collapsed against a tree, my breath crashing into my damaged lungs which would seem to be able to take no more air, but at the same time needed even more than I could give them. I slid down the tree to sit on the long grass until I could hear again over my gasping breath, and the pounding need for oxygen subsided. All around was silent; then I heard the distant sound of rifle fire.

Flickers of reality began to infiltrate my pounding brain. I was alone. The extension of that thought was even more unpleasant. Alone – with no plan, nowhere to go that I can be safe, no understanding, no nothing at all. It all seemed like too much to take in. I couldn't get one thought to follow another. I had to just stop, calm myself and then I might be able to think. I put my head down on my knees.

A voice from inside my head, instructed me to get up and keep moving, and as I did so, I saw the young woman. Perhaps it was she who spoke. She turned and walked further into the forest and I followed. We walked without speaking until complete nightfall.

The night was silent except for the rustling of small birds somewhere above us. We stopped in the forest with small saplings around us. Above were larger trees that nearly covered the sky. It was still quite warm and we sat leaning against the trees. I was so tired that the strength to lift my head was more than I can summon.

'Here. Eat.' Her Russian was abrupt, forthright – almost commanding. She squatted in front of me and handed me a wedge of dark bread from the pack she had on her shoulder. She was short and slim, tiny even, with strong eyebrows and long hair pulled back and covered with a headscarf tied behind her head.

155

There was a long plait of blond hair down her back. Her face was wide and strong and she looked at me as if she were capable of pinning me to the tree with a stare.

'Thank you.' I slid my pack across my back and located inside the slightly mashed remains of bread and cheese that the Embassy had given me. I offered it to her. 'Keep it, we may need it tomorrow.' Her boots were crumpled and the leather worn on the toes. Her hands were dirty.

With some of the bread inside me, I eventually was able to speak. 'Where are we?'

She shrugged. 'They have burned the trains.'

I felt cold very suddenly. 'Both of them? The people?'

'Probably the people too. I saw the fire when I climbed the tree.' She gestured over her shoulder.

'What do we do now?'

'We must keep going. The soldiers who mutinied will be running also. We must keep ahead of them.'

'Why? If they are Red Army?'

'They are not Red Army. They are prisoner battalion.'

I could see some of her face in the summer evening light. There was a smudge down one side of it and she looked pale and tired. 'Prisoner battalion?'

'Where on earth have you been? Don't you know what they are?'

I gestured at my clothes. 'Do I look like I should know?'

She crawled towards me and glared at my face. 'Who are you? Your accent is strange. Where do you come from?'

'I am from the British Embassy. I was on my way to Moscow to do some work in the building we have there.'

'British.' She spat the word. 'British.'

I was probably over tired and over wrought, but her tone offended me. 'Yes, British.' I spat it back. 'The ones who are on your side in this stupid war.' She sat back on her heels.

'Get some sleep. We will walk again in one hour.' With that, she leaned on the pack she had carried on her back and fell asleep.

She must trust me a little, I thought. I could have slit her throat. She obviously

156

knew I wasn't capable. I leaned back on my pack and slept too.

We walked most of the night and daylight was just rising as we continued through the trees, now becoming thinner and smaller. 'All right, treat me like dirt if you want, but at least you could speak to me.' She shot me a glance that could have killed. 'What is your name?' I panted.

'You want to know my name?'

'Is that so strange?'

She hesitated for a second. 'Yeva Vilenovna.'

'And your family name?'

'Lavrentyev'

I grinned. 'Now that wasn't so difficult was it?'

She stopped suddenly and turned smartly in front of me with her face in my chest. 'Don't patronise me or I shoot you.'

'I don't think you have a gun do you?'

'All right, I will strangle you while you sleep.'

That made me smile. 'I am Royston Thomas.'

'Thomas what?'

'Just Thomas – that is my family name.'

'Then what is your father's name?'

'Peter.'

'Royston?' She rolled the strange English sound around her mouth. 'So you are Royston Petrovich Thomaseev. Unless we make you Ukrainian, then you are Thomasenko. No I think Thomaseev is better.' I thanked Adrian silently for coaching me in the minefield of Russian patronymics. I think that got a tiny smile from her. But it was only fleeting if it existed at all.

'What is a penal battalion?'

We stopped by a small stream to drink and wash. 'You have heard of Order 227?' I shook my head, the water running down my neck. 'The order for no retreat, no surrender, not one step back?'

I remembered transmissions about something like this and nodded, '…about a year ago?'

'And the barrier troops?'

'The ones at the rear of the regular battalions to stop retreat or desertion?'

'But you have not heard about the ones at the front?'

'No.'

'These are prisoners or convicts given a choice of dying by a shot to back of head, or a shot in the front.' She sneered. 'Those men and boys,' she nodded in the direction, from which we had just come, '...are sent in front of the fighting battalions, to set off land mines, to draw the fire of Germans. They are not armed until they get there. The shots you heard were the guards. I hope some of them got away.'

'How are they expected to set off land mines?' I regretted the question as soon as I asked it.

She stamped her foot. 'By stepping on them.' She grinned and I could not believe my own naivety. 'Come. We must go on.'

'Where are we going?'

'I don't know yet.'

'Don't you have any idea? Where are we? '

But she just walked on. I followed her watching the long blond plait bouncing on the back of her shirt.

At what might have been mid-day, we stopped and squatted down at the edge of the forest. A large plain stretched away to the west. It was all sown to grain and cereal crops but there was a track or roadway in the distance. 'Ah, great. Civilisation at last.' I shrugged my pack onto my shoulder and stood up. 'Come on.'

She grabbed me by the shoulder and rolled me over her leg and onto the ground. 'Idiot!'

'What? There is a road there, we can get help, find out where we are.'

'Stop being stupid.' She slid down in the long grass at the edge of the trees. 'I can't ... you can't ...'

I gathered my disarranged clothes and sat down to face her. I tried to speak with more sympathy than I felt. 'Can't what? What is the matter?'

'What will we do? Because I left that train I am now AWOL from my unit. That is a death sentence. Didn't you hear anything I said earlier about the barrier battalions?'

'Well, yes, but can't you just explain??

She sighed heavily and pushed the heels of her hands into her eyes. 'You don't explain. You are guilty here. There is no explaining.'

'But ...'

'I would be shot.' My mouth gaped. I felt like a fish thrown on the bank. 'And you. What am I going to do with you?'

'Me?'

'I am running around the countryside with someone in a suit! I could get shot for that too – after they shot you of course.'

'But we are all on the same side.'

'Only because Stalin says so. It has nothing to do with us, me or you.'

'So what do we do?'

She got up and pulled her pack across her shoulders again. 'Wait here.'

13

June 43

I had little choice but to wait. I had nowhere to go; I didn't even know where I was. Travelling north-west towards Moscow was one possibility but I had no compass or map and no way of knowing what I would encounter between here and there. Also it was hundreds of miles away. And if, as she said, I would be shot for being alone in the countryside in a suit.

This was the stuff of desperation. All I could do was wait.

Yeva arrived back just before dark. She hurriedly took off her pack, opened it up and produced four small carrots still with the tops attached and a dead rabbit. 'We eat tonight! Come.'

We retreated some distance back into the forest and built a small fire in a hollow she dug in the ground with a stick. 'Where did you get these?' I asked.

She jerked her head in the direction we had come. 'I passed a source.' She offered me the rabbit or the carrots and I took the latter. She skinned the rabbit and showed me how to put it on a spit over the fire. I cleaned the carrots as best I could and she wrapped them in leaves and placed in the coals. Her face was set in deep concentration, long eyebrows almost meeting in the middle of her forehead. She was thinking hard and I didn't doubt that I had a large part in her consideration. What was she going to do with me? But source or theft, carrots and rabbit was the most fantastic meal I had eaten since I was a boy.

As we ate, we talked. Or rather I asked questions and she told me as much as she wanted me to know.

'Do you know where we are going?'

'I think so – if we go to the west, we will find our troops somewhere.'

'But that's where the Germans are. And the front line!'

She shrugged. 'That's what I need. And they need me.'

'I thought they would shoot you if they found you?'

'Probably.'

'And I hesitate to mention it, but what about me?'

'I try to find you a nice farm where I can leave you.'

'Look. I really need to get back to Moscow.' She didn't reply. 'We are going to go back to the Embassy building there.' I had probably said too much already. 'And it's my job to get the building ready.'

'Moscow.' She spat the word with contempt. '... and you told me this already.'

'What's wrong with Moscow?' She did not reply. I was getting annoyed now. We were getting nowhere. 'Look. I can't go on like this.'

'So go, just go.' Her skin was pink and stretched over her wide cheek bones. Thin clumps of short blond hair stuck to her forehead.

'I need to have a plan. I need to get back to Moscow. I have work to do.'

'Pha! Work in this chaos? What work can we do? Now or ever?'

'I can't predict the future, but I know that I'm here for a reason and you are too I suspect, but I have no idea what you are meant to be doing. Somehow we have to stay alive, even if all the rest of this country kills itself and each other.' She didn't answer back, so I carried on. 'I want to go home again. I want to sing in my church, I want to go back to my real job, I want ...'

She interrupted. Her voice was a little kinder. 'What was your real job?'

'I worked for a newspaper. I write articles on news events for them.'

'What are you doing here?'

That was too long a story to tell. 'I still write articles for my newspaper. I live and work at the Embassy.' That should just about cover it without lying. She draped her arms over her knees. 'What do you do when you are not ... not ... whatever you are now. What are you now?' I asked.

She took a deep breath. 'I am ... I was with the ... I was taught how to fire a rifle. Then I went out to shoot Germans.'

'And did you? Shoot Germans I mean?'

'Yes, of course.'

'Why aren't you shooting them now? Why were you on the train?'

'I was injured. You may have noticed I have no rifle. I was going back to my unit.'

'Where are they?'

She shrugged. 'I don't know. I was going to be told when I got ... Go to sleep.'

A deep rumble in the air woke us with the sunrise and a clutch of airplanes went over at low altitude. Yeva shaded her eyes to look into the brightening sky. 'Yak.'

'What?'

'Yak.' She squinted up at them again. 'Yak 7. They are fighters. Flying south west.' She gathered up her things. 'Good fighters. Now we have fighters with radios and stronger undercarriage. Now they don't crash land so much. And fuel gauges! Come, we have a long way to go.'

'So you do know where we are going.'

'Moscow – I can hide there and you can go back to work.'

'I thought you hated Moscow. Are we going to walk all the way?'

'I do. But we have to go somewhere. So unless you have a travel pass for yourself and a spare one for me, we walk.'

'Well, can we get a lift or something?'

She looked me up and down. 'No.'

We walked for several days in what I hoped was the right direction, but to be honest, I had to trust her judgement. I had no idea where I was or how to get anywhere. We saw no one, and passed no roadways or major routes – only simple track ways. Sometimes we used them, but Yeva was always cautious.

Occasionally we found small settlements or farms. We would retreat into the forest and wait until dark, then go down to the small vegetable patches where we would steal vegetables, perhaps eggs. If there was a dog or a restless person about, we walked on and went hungry.

I wanted to leave a little money for what we stole, but Yeva prevented it. 'We do not take much – they will not miss it. We may need your money later for serious things.'

'Serious? Like what?'

'We may need to bribe someone or buy some silence.'

162

Given so much time together, we did have the opportunity to talk – or at least I took it as an opportunity. I felt piqued. She was being condescending.

'I'm glad you have decided that I am not sub human at least.'

'Why?'

'Because I am now at least able to walk beside you and not behind, like a servant.'

'Everyone is equal in Russia.'

I bit off the 'some more equal than others' remark that wanted very badly to slip off my tongue. 'But some people have higher rank than others.'

She sighed in exasperation. 'Promotion and status are earned not given. Citizens like me are expected to serve the Revolution for life and can have promotion when we have earned it. It is based on merit.'

I could see several flaws in this argument. 'Merit? Like what kind of merit?'

'Service to the state is expected and if we are dedicated to that and do not avoid our duties, we can expect reward.' She seemed to warm to the subject or perhaps she felt that I badly needed educating. 'Dedication is part of all aspects of Russian life.'

'Even for the women?' I began to feel that the situation was becoming objectionable.

'Women have equal rights to men in all aspects; culture, politics, government, education, pay and even the armed forces.'

'Armed forces?'

'Of course – women like me and women who fly planes.'

'Pilots?'

'Have you never heard of our women's regiments?' I had heard something about them. A sort of terrifying blast from the night sky that no one knew when to expect. I nodded. 'There are many all women regiments. They fight in active combat and they terrify the Germans at night, by flying low over them and keeping them awake.'

I didn't really know what to say to this revelation. It sounded a little precarious and somehow not a suitable thing for women or anyone to be doing. 'But there are no women generals.'

'We have not always been equal – until Stalin we were expected to be at home making babies. Now we have added responsibilities.' She turned away and walked quickly to get in front of me again.

In the days that followed, we watched as more planes went overhead.

Smythe closed the door to his office and sat down at the small board table, pulling the chair towards him. Its legs scraped on the thin carpet. He looked at the other three men around the table.

'Our man appears to have gone missing.'

'Missing!'

'Again?'

'He didn't arrive in Moscow on Tuesday.'

There was a silence until Carter spoke. 'Do we need to worry?'

Johnson lifted the flap on his ancient brief case, looked inside and closed it again. 'According to official sources in the Kremlin, and confirmed by the Embassy, the train Roy was on was delayed. But it has now been three days since we last knew where he was.' He stretched his back and leaned on the table once more. 'So we have resorted to other sources and find that the train he was on was attacked and burned by a band of renegades of some sort.'

There was a moment of silence. Donaldson, who had his head in his hands, spoke first, 'I fear the worst.'

Johnson looked at him pityingly.

Smythe got up and went to the window. 'We can only hope. And if he really is lost, we must look again at our plan. I've had to stop the reports.'

Carter looked at his hands on the table. 'But how do we start again? He was perfect for our purposes; he couldn't refuse what we wanted, he was unlikely to find himself in the front line being shot at and killed; he had good skills at finding out information thanks to his work at the paper and his transmission ... That's why we went to such trouble to get him back into his post.'

'Yes, yes. We all know that.' Johnson sounded short tempered.

Donaldson pulled a large handkerchief from his pocket and wiped his face. 'Let's not panic. Roy is resourceful.'

Smythe glared at him. 'We've lost our link again. Do we recruit yet again? If we find Roy and then end up with two operators doing this work, what happens? Do we have to deal with one of them again?'

Johnson was nodding slowly, looking at the clip on his briefcase. 'Perhaps...,' he rubbed his hands through his sparse hair, '…perhaps he will be lost for good this time. Perhaps we should hope he is. It will make all things easier.'

Carter looked pale. 'Why does Pulmer keep sending him off on these wild sorties? What is he trying to do?'

Seven days after we left the train, we heard a roar that did not gain altitude and fly over us. It started at first light and as we walked, it got louder and we were drawn to it. At about 5 o'clock in the afternoon, we crawled to the top of a rise and looked into a wide flat plain. There were columns of military vehicles on the plain about a mile away. I knew by now not to stand against the sky line and we lay down in the grass and shrubs at the top.

In the strong light of a summer evening, we saw thousands of tanks throwing columns of sand into the air from their tracks covering the plain. Amongst the tanks, there were cars, trucks full of troops, covered trucks pulling wagons or weapons, and a huge array of other tracked vehicles that I could not name. Dust obscured the horizon and whatever followed.

'What does this mean?' I asked.

'It means that we can't get across this way for a long time.' She looked down the convoy. There was no end to be seen. 'It means something very big is happening. I should be there. I should be involved, doing my duty.' She slammed her hand into the dirt. 'Chert proberi!!! Damn, damn, damn!'

I watched as she wiped her face with the ends of her headscarf. But whether there were tears, I couldn't tell.

'What do we do?'

'Wait.'

She reached out, pulled on my sleeve and we retreated a few miles into the low scrubby trees. When we settled in a thick group of bush she shrugged off her pack and took out the bread we had saved. 'We cannot have a fire tonight. There will be scouts around this and we must not be caught.' I ate the bread with little saliva in my mouth to make it soft enough to swallow. We took turns standing up and leaning against a small tree during the night to listen for anything that might mean our discovery.

The roar of the machines continued throughout the night and most of the next day. Then about 4 in the afternoon, it abruptly stopped. The last vehicle disappeared into the afternoon sun and we slept in our little brushy holes for another night.

A few days later, the trees that had been sheltering us as we walked, grew smaller and eventually they gave way to pockets of open grazing land although there were no animals in them. We did however find a small wooded valley with a quickly flowing stream. After a week and more in the same clothes, I was desperate for a decent wash, some clean clothes and a proper shave. I insisted that we stop.

'I don't care if I am arrested without a stitch on. I need to clean myself and at least my underwear.' I saw her lift one beautifully arched eyebrow and look away. She quickly walked up the bank and disappeared into the brush. I didn't care if she sat there with binoculars and watched, I took off everything I was wearing, walked into the cold water that took my breath way, dragged my clothes in after me and cleaning myself with a branch of juniper, I squeezed and thrashed the clothes until I felt they were clean. The shirt was still grey around the collar. The cuffs were the same with added patches of grime and they were beginning to fray. I was tempted to let the pants float out of my life, but knowing that I had only one other pair in my pack, I washed them as I had the other clothes and then I did it all over again and threw them on the bank.

Then I lie back where the water was shallow and let it carry away everything.

As I was spreading my shirt on a bush to dry, she returned. I had put on my second pair of trousers, underwear and socks and had shaved and cleaned my hair and teeth. I felt a lot more civilised.

She took off her pack and leaned it against a tree. 'Now it is my turn.' I picked up my clean shirt and jacket and started to walk up the bank. 'No.' Her voice had the sharp sound of near panic. 'Please. Stay here. Just turn around and don't look.'

I sat on the grass, my back to the stream, with my jacket across my knees and tried to brush the dirty patches and stains out of the woollen fabric. I could hear soft splashing in the stream. I wondered what she looked like. I had no desire to be voyeuristic about it, but I was curious. So I let my imagination do the looking. She would have taken off her clothes as I had done, scrubbed the worst of the grime from them and then she would lie back in the water as I did and let her long blond hair float and float …

On the morning of the next day, we began to notice a thick worsening smell on the air. There was little wind so it was difficult to tell where it was coming from, but it got more and more disgusting as we walked. It was the smell of dead animals.

In the late afternoon, we got to the edge of the woods which we had been using as cover. In front of us was a large open area adjacent to what might have been a village or settlement of some kind. It was littered with mounds of broken machinery, twisted and stripped sheets of metal, gun barrels, wheels detached from cart or gun carriage, mounds of broken earth and trees, pieces of canvas, metal boxes spilling their unknown contents into the dust and dirt. There were also hundreds of dead men.

15 June 1943: When you walk on a battlefield, you walk on the hearts and souls of the dead. We came to a battlefield today and the only thing to be seen was the dead. Dead men, animals with bloated bodies, limbs sticking into the air at obscene angles; broken machinery, damaged wagons, vehicles, armaments; but the men – all dead. We tied what we could around our faces to reduce the smell and walked towards the carnage.

There were many hundreds of them – all from one Red Army regiment according to Yeva who knows these things. We were many miles from any kind of front line. My companion stood among the bodies for a long time. Then she walked to the top of the slope looking at the ground as she walked. When she came back she spoke. They were killed by the Red Army she decided. How did she know this? The shell casings left at the top of the slope where the firing came from were all 7.62 x 54 mm calibre. Only the Red Army uses it.

But why kill their own men? She shook her head. 'Who knows in this crazy war', she said.

We looked around us; they were young men all with lives to live; now they had only past, there was no future. Few of them had rifles. They may not have been able to defend themselves. I cannot ever remember being so upset. We were walking on the hearts and souls of the dead.

I had to look at the scene as I would have as a reporter – not unaffected but a step removed. I would not have been able take in what I saw if I allowed personal natural normal emotion into my own head. The ground was torn and exposed. Earth was embedded with pieces of weapons, vehicles, bodies. There were not just bodies, but body parts, limbs, faces, hands, gore, boots, clothing long separated from their owners. Bodies had no chests, heads; internal organs spilled onto the ground. Now they were drying in the sun and the birds and flies were feasting. I felt my stomach knot and begin to turn. I could not add to the desecration I saw here and I ran to an unadulterated place. Here I crashed to my knees and did desecrate the grass.

Yeva put her hand on my back. 'Poor Royston Petrovich. Sit for a moment.' She pushed me onto the grass. 'Look at me.' She sat in front of me, pulled her headscarf from her face. 'Now close your eyes.' I did as she instructed and felt the bile in my stomach gradually stop frothing and my mouth begin to dry. When I opened my eyes again, she was still looking at my face. Her eyes were dark and hollow. Her face was pale and there were bright blotches on her cheeks. She had not been unaffected either. I reached for her and pulled her head onto my shoulder. We leaned on each other.

'I'm sorry. So very sorry.' I whispered into her hair.

'Why sorry? What do you apologise for?'

'For not being a man.'

I saw her smile – a smile of sympathy, not the smile of derision that I deserved. She got up and held out her hand. 'Come, we have work to do.' She pulled me upright, and put the scarf back over her nose. I followed her into the carnage again. She tipped over boxes, opened personal packs. 'What are you looking for?'

She flicked open an ID card and looked at it. 'Here, this looks like it might be you.' She tipped the pack upside down. 'Pay book!' She opened it up and squinted at me and then at the photograph then at me again. 'You are 21, yes?'

'No, I'm ...'

'Yes, Gleb Alekseev Rozhkov, you are 21.' She handed me the book. I looked at the photograph. A young man in life. From Smolensk. I choked. I felt as if I knew him.

When I looked up she was tipping out pack after pack from what had obviously been a supply wagon, until she had assembled a uniform to fit me: a tunic and belt with pouches of ammunition, a shovel in another pouch, bed roll, a pack for my back into which I shoved most of what little I had with me, wide baggy trousers that narrowed below the knee, ankle boots and puttees, wedge cap and a helmet with a red star on the front. The star felt like a bull's-eye. I saw her relieve some of the packs of other bits of kit, but it was the boots that bothered me the most. Dead man's boots. She seemed pleased that I was now a rifleman. What the hell was I doing? I wanted to scream and throw up all over again.

We worked our way across the desecrated vision of hell. We collected water bottles, a compass, mess tins. And a rifle. This was for me to carry of course and I slung it on my shoulder with a feeling that I was getting closer and closer to the horror. She took the bayonet off the end and shoved it in a scabbard on my belt.

She found a pistol and stuffed it deep in her bag; then another rifle and ammunition. As the sun began to slide to the horizon, the shadows showed the carnage in a new way. The bodies had shifted position, as if trying to come with us. Arms lifted in salutation and supplication. I could do nothing.

As I turned to follow Yeva a long thin shadow crossed my feet. I followed it to its source and cried to Yeva to stop. On my knees between a decapitated body and a sheet of twisted metal splattered with material I could not give a name to, I began to dig out a radio set. The shadow of an aerial showed me where to dig.

We sat away from the edge of the battlefield as the sun went down. By now we were somewhat used to the smell, but the shock of actual death, real war kept me breathing from the top of my lungs. The tension in my neck and stomach made my muscles ache. I looked at my feet. Lord alone knew what was on the soles of my boots. Lord alone.

'Come.' As Yeva got to her feet I saw her stagger, but she quickly recovered and hoisting the now very heavy pack onto her shoulder turned her back on the rotting remains. 'We must find shelter. I think it will rain tonight.'

I got up, looked over the battlefield, my legs only just able to keep my torso upright. 'Lord, give them all peace. Give peace to those who did this and give the land the right to claim them.' I followed Yeva into the forest.

Deep in the woodland, we cut boughs from the pine trees and made a rudimentary shelter under a thick canopy of oak and birch. Although we had some of the rations from the battlefield, neither of us could eat. We sat in front of our little shelter and stared into the tiny layer of brightness in the west gradually disappearing into a dark foam bank of clouds. I felt rather than saw that she was crying. All her strength was not enough. I shuffled inelegantly closer to her and put my arm across her shoulders. She leaned against my chest and sobbed. The first sob of emotion was enough to release all the tension, fear and horror in my emotional store and I wept with her. She put her arms around me and I put mine around her and we cried until neither of us had strength left.

'Here, use my handkerchief.' I pulled it from my pocket and she blew her nose and wiped her eyes.

'*Spasibo*. Thank you.' She handed it back and leaned against me again, her head warm and heavy on my shoulder.

'I admire your courage.' I spoke into her hair and she looked up at me in surprise. 'You were amazing. You didn't collapse like I did; you used that massacre as an opportunity to help me when you needn't have and yet you didn't desecrate what was there or triumph in what we found and took. You had great respect.'

She leaned on me again. 'I'm sorry that radio didn't work.'

'So am I. I might have been able to do something to help. I don't know what, but...' We were quiet for a few minutes and I listened to her breathing against me. 'What happened there? Why where they all killed?'

She sat up, shuffled in front of me, crossed her legs like a yogi and took my hands. 'You British have soldiers who walk into the mouths of death when they are told to. They fight until they are all dead if they are asked to; because they have confidence that their officers and leaders know when to fight, when to retreat and when to surrender. They have faith.'

'But them?' I inclined my head towards the battle field.

'Our soldiers have no faith. Our officers are not good ones; they are made into officers through merit – not training or experience. Many of them don't know what they are doing. Not like your British officers.'

'But if they have merit?'

She spoke more sharply. 'Merit does not mean skill or understanding. Sometimes it means only that you are good Stalinist or have place in the Party. Sometimes, it doesn't work.' Her grip on my hands tightened. 'I think that this was an accident made by an officer who didn't know what he was doing. And then I think they all ran when they realised what they had done.' I felt the tremors in her again and pulled her towards me. She leaned against me and in the darkness I felt her kiss my neck. She pulled my head to hers and I kissed her.

I pushed the scarf from her hair and let the thick braided plait slip between my fingers all the way down her back. As she leaned against me again, I felt her breasts firm and yet soft on my chest and we both lay back on the boughs we had cut for the bottom of our shelter. I undid the belt that held her shirt around her waist and she pulled the it off over her head. There was just enough light for me to see the slim undershirt that fitted tightly around her. She picked up my hand and put it on her breast, pressing my fingers around the nipple that rose hard under the fabric. I pushed the shirt up and over her head and she pulled my head down to her breasts again. I could smell the warm scent of her skin and feel the smoothness of her breast against my nose and lips. The feel of her nipple in my mouth made me want her in ways that no words could describe. I felt her back arch and she made a small noise in her throat. 'I've never done this before.' I confessed. 'Please show me what to do.'

She laughed gently. 'A virgin?' She took my face in her hands and kissed me.

170

Her tongue slipped across my lips. 'Yes, I will show you.'

She undressed me, slowly and ran her fingers over my body, exploring it all and then she took my hand helped me trace it over her chest and legs.

In the dark, it was a sort of worship – a kind of celebration of human kind, human spirit and survival. I didn't ask if she would be safe. Selfishly, I didn't even think about it. There was so much between us and it was so fragile.

We slept that night under a pile of clothing.

14

June 1943

In the morning, I was embarrassed by what we had done. She was fragile, in spite of her bravura and incredible skills and stamina. I should never have done what I did. It was my fault... had I no ability to resist temptation? It would seem that I no longer had strength to be a good Christian. I felt ill – I had committed yet another of the deadly sins.

I looked at her sleeping, plait undone and her hair swept up above her head, body covered with my new tunic and her feet still in their socks. It was hard to describe to myself what my emotions felt – never mind my morals. Underneath the heavy layer of my own guilt, there was a kind of exhilaration? Triumph? Only in the sense that I had conquered my own reluctance. Or had I merely let my emotions overcome my sense of honour? I took a long breath to slow my heart and calm my head. To be honest with myself, I didn't care. But it was a sin of the largest order. What was happening to me? I had talked to God at that battlefield then I had forgotten Him entirely. This was not what I had been brought up to do. This was not what I wanted for myself. It was just wrong. Sinful, lustful and wrong. But in my heart, I knew that she wanted it as much as I did. I did not do this alone but it was no excuse.

I sat up and looked out of our little shelter. The sun was just rising and it was already becoming warm. In spite of Yeva's predictions, it had not rained. The ground was dry and the sun shone into the forest in deep spears and through the roof of our shelter. Dust rose in the shafts of light and the tiny particles shimmered and flickered. The smell of the pine, crushed by our bodies, cleared my nose, throat and head. I felt different. I was now someone else. Perhaps I really had become Gleb Alexseev.

She moved and woke beside me and I looked down at her. The tunic had

172

slipped off her stomach and she snatched at it to pull it back over her. But I had seen what I seen. For a second I did not know what to do. She had not wanted me to see it; she had not taken my hand over her stomach last night. But now I saw the marks. Large scars of dark, red skin and wounds now healed.

I looked at her face. She was staring at me in horror. 'You didn't want me to see that did you? You didn't trust me – or you thought that I would be horrified or not want you, or ...' I stopped myself from ranting. I was becoming illogical. I lifted the edge of the tunic again. She pushed it back. 'Don't.' But I held her hand and lifted it again. The scars were down both sides of her stomach and across the front. Healed but still red and raw. There was evidence of stitches. I bent over and kissed them. 'Tell me. Tell me what happened to you.'

She reached for her undershirt, sat up and pulled it over her head. She pulled up her knees and rocked slowly back and forth. 'I was pregnant.' She hugged herself and bent over her arms. 'At Stalingrad ...we ...' I saw her eyes close and lines of tension crease her forehead. Some pieces of short blonde hair fell across her face. 'We were caught by some Germans. We were trying to get away when they caught us.' She pulled the front of her shirt between her legs. 'They kicked me until I aborted...' Her voice had almost disappeared. '... then left me at the side of the road. Now you are satisfied? Happy that you asked?'

I felt like screaming but could make no sound. My voice had vanished into my head. All the sound in the world had gone. I could only shake my head. I saw her disappointment and realised that it must have looked like I blamed her. Finally I was able to whisper. 'I believe you, I - I just can't take it in. I can't understand why. How can anyone... so cruel, so insane? Did you not think that I would see that ... ever?'

She wiped her eyes with her fingers, smearing tears down her cheeks and left the question unanswered. 'I am a sniper - at Stalingrad. Against orders I married a man I met while we served together. By the time we were sent to Stalingrad, I was pregnant but I couldn't say anything about it or I would have been dismissed and my husband sent to a work camp or something. So, we decided that I should hide it as long as I could, then desert and get home. There was so much chaos in Stalingrad then that my absence wouldn't be noticed for some time. When the baby was born I would come back. Somehow.' I must have looked shocked. 'I know it was stupid, impractical. A stupid idea, but what else could I do?'

'How far along were you?' I coughed. This was hardly the kind of conversation I wanted to have with a woman.

'Six months.' She smiled. 'Baggy clothing.' She picked up her long over shirt.

'It helps.' Then she took an uneven breath and her voice shook. 'I was in civilian clothes when we were captured. They beat us both and shot my husband.'

'But you got away. Even after all ....' I touched her scarred flesh. '... this.'

'No, they just left me there, bleeding in the ditch. Someone else found me, I don't know who and I was eventually treated somewhere.' She paused for a very long breath. 'But the doctor said I would never have children again.' There were more tears in her eyes now and they were beginning to overflow. I wiped them with my thumb. She caught my wrist. 'I do not want children now. How can anyone want to bring children into this? It must never happen.'

I hugged her and rocked her while she cried again. I felt the tears on my bare chest and I felt something in my heart that I cannot hope to name. It was a combination of anger, pity, horror and concern and the need for revenge at any level but preferably personal. Above all there was compassion.

'Why have you come back? To all this? To all the killing and blood? Why again?'

She looked up and I saw her eyes darken. 'To kill the bastards – as many as I can.' She wiped her eyes with end of her shirt.

'You are not alone then. I will help.' I couldn't believe I said that. What was happening to me? I took a deep breath. Not only would I help, I would protect her. I would try to stop her - or would I? I would ...

She smiled at me as if I were a child. 'I had no choice. Once I was able to leave hospital, I was sent back to my unit. That is why I was on the train.' She turned over some of our clothes and found her underwear, boots and belt. 'But I had time to think and I think I want to kill Germans.' She pulled the long shirt over her head, wrenched the belt around her waist and stood up.

I handed her the trousers.

---

10 July 1943 Now that I am in a uniform we can be braver about where we are seen. We stay away from large groups and towns of course, but in the smaller ones we are not remarked upon and Yeva has some story ready about special work we are doing, or that we are in transit or something else equally possible. We have not yet been challenged for papers. If we had, I'm sure Yeva would have shot them.

We also are beginning to get information about a huge tank battle at Kursk. I had heard rumours of this from Lucy. The network had told me some months ago about a build-up of Russian forces. It even speculated that Kursk would be the location. The Germans would have been very foolish if they had ignored what they surely also knew. It could only be the battle to end all battles. How many dead this time? How much death and destruction? How much more? But we are too far away and going in the wrong direction to take part or to find out much more.

One evening as we sat in our little camp eating the bread and cheese we had purchased from a farm in the morning, I emptied my pockets and laid my meagre resources on the pack in front of me. 'I don't know about you, but my money is running out. We will need to get somewhere soon, so that I can contact Moscow – or get to Moscow or something.'

She sniffed. 'I am not doing a good job – I am not getting you to Moscow fast enough? Are you wanting to be rid of me?'

I most certainly was not. 'Of course not.' I sounded as put out as she did. 'I'm just saying that we will not be able to buy food or whatever we need soon. I don't like the idea of stealing it.'

'Why are you so, so, reluctant to steal? Everyone does it.'

'Maybe they do, but I was brought up to believe it was wrong and I don't feel good about doing it.'

'You are a funny man.' She took what money she had out of her pocket and laid it with mine. 'You are right; we will have to do something. Even with stealing, this won't last long.'

'Perhaps we can get onto a train or a truck or ...' I saw that this worried her. 'Why not? I look more respectable now.'

'There will be questions. Questions that neither of us can answer and we will be split up and, we have no travel papers. Well, I have but I am going in the wrong direction so they will be of no use... worse than no use. And yours...' She left the rest unsaid then she smiled. 'I have an idea, but you must tell me everything about you. I cannot protect you if there are secrets.'

'Secrets? I have no ...' I saw the Secrets Act I had signed. Somehow it all seemed so long ago and so far away. Surely it didn't matter anymore – or perhaps it did not matter as much as it might have done a life time ago. 'I told you the truth before. I work for the British Embassy. I am a radio operator. I send and receive Morse code messages.' I looked at her face. Her eyebrows were lifted in encouragement. I had to carry on but I was sure my face told her that I was not telling all the truth. 'I also ... and I do other odd jobs, typing and things.' I was repeating myself, but perhaps she would not know. 'I ...'

'What are these messages?' she interrupted.

'Usually they are reports from the Embassy, sometimes from German sources sent to us from London. They have been decoded and then recoded for us. Sometimes, I have to decode them myself.' I didn't tell her that usually these were the Russian ones. 'They tell us what the Germans are planning.'

'That is why you were so happy to find that radio at the battlefield.'

'Yes, it would have allowed me to contact Moscow and tell them that I was alive.'

'And?'

'And what?'

'I know there is more. I can tell by the look on your face.'

I would make a lousy spy. If captured I would sing for my supper without any problem at all. I trusted her; that made it easier.

'I listen to other transmissions not authorised by the Embassy, but needed by London. I report what I hear.' That was the easiest way to describe what Lucy was all about.

She grinned and I saw her small lovely teeth alive in a face, for once, not frowning with worry. 'So you are a spy.' She rolled back on the grass and laughed again until she choked and we made love again under the trees, in the evening air.

We shared the last of the hard bread and even harder cheese. 'I have decided what we must do.' She broke the last piece of black bread in half and handed a piece to me. 'We must find the partisans.'

'What?' The vision of those mad men of the forest, blowing things up clogged the lines of thought in my brain. 'The...?'

She did not appear to have seen the horror on my face. I was sure that the blood had disappeared from my skin. It had certainly gone from my brain. She carried on as if I had made no sound at all. Perhaps I hadn't. Perhaps it was too dark to see the horror on my face. 'They will be glad of our skills so we are not likely to be shot when we find them. We just have to be sure that they find out what we have before they decide to kill us.'

A cold wash down my back prevented my voice from functioning. 'And ...' she smiled that perfect smile again, '... we can be together.'

The last sentence put everything right. The first comment had no effect once she had uttered the last. We could stay together. That was all that mattered.

28 August 1943 It took us almost 2 months of hiding, crawling, stealing and keeping our heads down. We walked miles, caught lifts with sympathetic peasants who gave us food and information about the German positions but we kept going to the west and deep into the forests. Somehow we got through whatever front line there was and nearer to the marshes.

We met the group on the roadway. Now that we were near to the marshes it was raining. It took only one glance at their collection of uniforms, if one could call them that, their odd arms and lack of any kind of strict military organisation, for me to know that this was a partisan group. This time however, they looked battle hardened, more disciplined and had what seemed to be leaders.

In spite of what Yeva had said about military officers, these did not presume to be officers at all, but seemed to be men who had seen active service, perhaps in other ways. The other men with them – and women, there were several – listened and obeyed. This was a different situation than I had known before and they did not care that Yeva and I were obviously close. All they seemed to want was people with rifles, the skill to use them and a will to win the war.

The leader was dark, short and probably had been a bear of a man in a past life. Now he was thin but upright and still a commanding presence. He wore a belted tunic that came almost to his knees, a flat cap with a wide crown now wet and soft from the rain, and tall boots. A strap across his chest supported a pack at his hip and he held a very long rifle on top of his shoulder. 'Where are you going?'

Yeva did the talking. I still wasn't entirely sure that my accent wouldn't raise questions I would rather not have to answer immediately. 'I am trying to get to my regiment – we were train wrecked at Kasovko.' Train wreck? I thought. Mutiny more like.

Another man, taller perhaps a second in command was sceptical. 'Train wreck?' He looked over his shoulder at the others. 'Has anyone else heard of this train wreck?' Then looking hard at Yeva, 'When was it? Why are you here?'

But the leader interrupted. 'What is your regiment?'

'The 1077th AA.'

I saw the leader's eyebrows lift – in an expressionless face, it said much. The others around suddenly looked less menacing and listened more closely. 'The

1077th?'

'Yes,' Yeva spoke softly, but there was not a sound to contradict what she said. 'At Stalingrad.'

'Were you on the guns?'

'No, none of them survived. I was a sniper – outside the city.'

That seemed to be enough for the leader. He turned to me. 'And you?' I drew breath to present my best accent but Yeva interrupted my efforts. 'He is my husband, Gleb Alexseev Rozhkov...' Husband? Bloody hell! No one so much as blinked except me. '...and he is a radio operator and he knows codes and code breaking.'

My breath caught in my throat. Just how on earth was I going to make this work? The Embassy was hardly going to give me the codes and tools to break the German transmissions; nor even the British ones. They would have no idea if I was who I said I was, nor even which side I was aiding. They wouldn't trust me to tell them the time. They couldn't get code books for me – nor could they tell me what transmissions to monitor. All this with no radio. It was impossible.

They took us - not exactly at gun point because they did not relieve us of ours – but had one of us reached for it, we would not have been treated kindly. There were 10 of them; two walked in front of us, two beside and the rest behind. There was a little conversation mainly with Yeva. I said as little as possible so as not to give too much away too early until I had the opportunity to explain myself to the commander whoever he might be.

The forest changed as we walked and we passed farms with open fields, small collections of buildings and what might have been called villages. Some were just a few houses with an occasional official building, others were larger with seemingly organised structure; a market, buildings for community use. Some villages had been attacked as a message no doubt, but it was the homeland of the Partisans so they abandoned them or repaired them. Life went on. They had little choice. I was back in the marshes which the Germans continued to ignore as being of no value and a waste of their manpower to take over - except for an occasional strafing raid or bomb or reprisal on an easy target if they felt they needed to make a statement or take some revenge.

By evening, we approached their camp, as one of the followers gleefully told me. It wasn't a camp at all. It was a village in a thin forest. In contrast to my experience with the partisans last time, this was progress indeed.

Animals had pasture and housing; gardens were looked after; vegetables growing and being harvested. Fields as we approached were being cut as fodder and bedding for animals and to provide bread for the people. There were carts and ploughs, farming tools and horses.

The village contained about 200 people at a guess, including women and children. There was accommodation; apparently men separated from women, in what looked like bunk houses but others, possibly married couples, had separate wooden shelters. I could hardly call them houses.

Two men in a little shelter seemed to be refilling cartridge shells. Women were doing laundry in cut-down wooden barrels and clothing was drying over bushes and railings. Children ran around in great excitement; one little boy rushed up to one of our guards clearly very glad to see him. The man whipped the lad up in his arms and hugged him. A little girl peeked around a large butt of water under the corner of a small building. The sound of a baby crying and a woman soothing it came through the open door. This was a self-sufficient collective enterprise. It was amazing and there was mud everywhere.

We were first taken low roofed log building. It had benches and was a kind of assembly area and also, amazingly I discovered later, where children went to school. There was also a place set aside as a kind of infirmary; a blacksmith in a shelter with his forge who probably doubled as weapons repairer.

After a lengthy discussion – I would hesitate to call in an interrogation – in which I let Yeva do most of the talking, they seemed satisfied that we might be of some use and put Yeva and I together in a small shack. I can describe it no less than a grain store; a wooden building skidded into position on the logs on which it was built. It was leaning against another wooden building and was covered with overlapping slabs of timber with some bark still attached cut from the sides of logs. The roof was made of smaller slabs, lapped like shingles. The door was made of sturdier planks with a string latch. A large tin container with a pipe through the roof sat glumly in the corner and suggested that it might act as a stove and heater sometime soon. The floor was made of timber planks with gaps to the earth beneath. There was probably no permanent intent for its use. I felt that we could be ordered out of here and into hell in a heartbeat.

Before the sun has set completely, I was called to an interview with the leader and his committee. Maybe it was not a Committee – maybe they were just curious hangers-on. Maybe they were Party leaders. Maybe they would see through my thin veneer and into my inadequacy.

I asked to speak to the leader alone. His name was Leonid Savarov. There was nothing to be gained and everything to lose by ignoring my accent and deplorable Russian.

We sat on log benches facing each other. I handed him my British papers. I don't know if he recognised them as being British, but as they were clearly not German, he merely raised his eyebrows in a command to speak.

'I am British and work for the British Embassy. I was sent to Moscow to start repairs to the building damaged in the air raids on the city. Yeva has told you what happened to the train and how we came to be here.'

'What do you do for the British?'

'A little radio work – I know Morse code in English and Russian – and quite a lot of administration work, typing, filing… that sort of thing.'

He nodded at my tunic and his gaze took in the rest of my assorted uniform. I told him the battlefield story and felt my face change as I talked. He said little else, but continued to look at me – in my uniform I must have presented a mixture of pictures…but then so did all of them. 'I can help,' I heard myself offer. 'Do you have a radio? I can help …'

I presume that it tallied with what Yeva had told him because he stood up and beckoning me to follow, took me to see an ancient radio set with German labelling, and watched closely while I assembled it. It was old but seemed to have all the parts necessary. I had to make up a connection to a dubious battery, whilst silently praying that the power from it would not be too great and blow the whole thing up in my face. Or conversely that it would have enough to actually work. They had me transmit a fictitious weather report. I have no idea where it went if anywhere, but have a vision of some German interceptor trying to understand what it was all about and assuming some massive code implications. Perhaps it would keep them busy for a while. Neither did I know if anyone among them could check that what I sent was actually what they asked. An hour later a reply came asking who we were. Savarov was delighted. I dearly wanted to transmit to the Embassy to say that I was safe but did not want to push the boundaries of our safety too far too soon.

Savarov looked at me closely. 'You are a radio operator,' he confirmed as if to himself. His grin showed tobacco stained teeth, but he relaxed. 'We need you, Gleb Alekseev.'

I too relaxed and looked again at the great chunk of equipment in front of me. It was dusty, uncared for and it did not look like it had been used in a long time. It was clear that they had no operator and probably had never had one. I also realised that perhaps I would be safe here and of some use. I grinned back. 'What do you want me to do?' I had a contact with Moscow and the British Embassy at last if and when I was brave enough to do so.

'What did he say? Did he believe you?' Yeva swept a pile of dust out of the cabin door with a handful of small branches.

I smiled at her worried expression. 'Do you mean; did they send me off or shoot me or something equally nasty?'

She threw the sticks onto the ground. 'Durak. Stupid.' Then she saw the grin on my face. 'Yes, you are stupid. You make me worry.'

I went into the cabin after her and caught her in my arms. 'Yes. But would you have it any other way.' She put her face against my chest and either wiped her nose on my tunic or shook her head. It was hard to tell.

We sat on the step and I told her what had happened.

'How is this going to work?' Yeva frowned. 'Contacting the British Embassy, listening in to radio transmissions, the Germans, the Russians, the, the ...' She spluttered. 'This is durak stupid, just stupid. You will get us both shot.'

'They want me to listen in to Russian transmissions to find out what is going on. Russian codes are not hard to crack. The Germans and we do it all the time.'

She looked shocked. 'So what is point?'

'Because in time, the partisans could be part of a co-ordinated effort – with other groups – with leaders – with headquarters.'

'Durak. Stupid. It is just stupid.'

'Is that your word for today?'

She ignored me. Perhaps everything around us was stupid including both of us. 'Was that big man with the smart hat there?'

'Yes, why?'

'I think he is called Simonvic Rytin. Please be very careful of him.' She looked around quickly and began to whisper. 'He is a Commissar.'

'And so...'

'So, you stupid man. Do you not know about the Commissars?'

'Not a great deal.' She looked at me as if I were a dense pupil.

'He is dangerous. Because...' I had opened my mouth to ask why. '...he is sent by Party to be sure we are being good Communists.'

'But you are aren't you?'

'Not everyone is a good Communist and in the war we don't need untrained and stupid men from the Party, contradicting what the military leaders want. It is just stupid. We would be better off without them.'

'Why? What do they do?'

She turned on the step and looked at me. 'You have nice eyebrows.' She ran her finger along one of them.

I caught her hand and kissed her fingers. 'The Commissars?'

'They have equal rank to the military leader whoever he is. They can countermand his orders – Rytin has the military authority to do that.'

'That's... stupid, as you say. But why do you think I should be wary of him?'

'Because, their interference was eliminated last year, so I don't know why he is still here.'

'Do you think he still has his authority – over Savarov I mean?'

'Perhaps the Partisans were exempt from the order. Perhaps he is in hiding.' Her voice rose with increasing excitement. 'Perhaps he is a spy... like you.'

'Shhh!'

She whispered again. 'Whatever he is doing here, we must watch him and be very careful what we say or do when he is watching or listening.'

'I am sure that you can scare him enough to keep him quiet.'

'I can do that too. But I need them to give me a decent rifle. Then maybe I can shoot him.'

SA44 Western Russia to RT19 British Embassy 1 Sept 43 Plain text 1006 (Russian Standard Time) 87 Survived train mutiny at Kasovko Am safe with Partisans but have no codes Escape unlikely Instructions

RT19 British Embassy to SA44 Western Russia 2 Sept 1029 (RST) 14 Glad you are safe

SA44 Western Russia to RT19 British Embassy 3 Sept 1048 (RST) 22 James was a king of England

And so we agreed on a numbers code, simple, but unless someone had the same book it would be hard to crack for a while at least. Adrian knew which Bible I had, he'd seen it and somehow he would get a copy the same as mine. We could communicate by reference to page line word. Cumbersome but effective. Easy. Just how I was to communicate with the Laundry was a completely different problem. And to be honest I didn't care if I ever heard from them again.

It was very late when Smythe slipped a transmission slip into the top drawer of his desk, closed it and locked it.

Today he had received a coded message from Kuibyshev.

He put the little key in his waist coat pocket, and wondered if there was another reason for Roy's disappearance. Had they put too much pressure on him? Had he discovered something?

15

September 1943

10 Sept The Battle at Kursk was all that was discussed during July and August. The scale of it, no doubt exaggerated by the telling and re-telling, was nearly incomprehensible. Four thousand tanks under Russian command, 50,000 guns, anti-tank guns and rocket launchers and more importantly the Red Army at last took the advantage given to them through intelligence. This time they believed and listened. Maybe the war will turn to our advantage now. But my heart still aches for those who will never have a known grave and all those who continue to beat huge chunks of iron into tanks in the factories on the steppes.

After Stalingrad, this was another defeat for the Germans in this war. They were driven back, defeated utterly according to the Russian sources I decoded. But the British Embassy said it was probably more like a battle to a standstill and the German retreat, if it existed, was a slow one.

Now, however, the Red Army was advancing towards Smolensk and Kiev was again in turmoil. I thought again about the old man who had first warned me about the state of the Soviet forces. I thought about Kostya and prayed that he was safe somewhere in these same marshes as me. Perhaps one day I would know his fate. In the meantime I prayed for the people who would be destroyed in the freeing. I prayed in the morning, in the forest, in the silence. I prayed for the old man.

SA44 Western Russia to RT19 British Embassy 10 Sept 959 (RST) 58
German air attacks on villages Many casualties Survivors scattered

Our little shack was a sort of home. All it contained were our few possessions, my Bible, and English/Russian dictionary, Yeva's spare clothes and my two pair of trousers, new once, our weapons and our paillasses; blankets of a sort, roughly stitched together and stuffed with grass and straw, but a refuge for our two hearts. No one commented on our relationship; that we are together was not remarked upon; we were left to be what we were.

I undid her long plait and brushed the cascade of her hair. The same hair I had imagined floating in the river. It was not gold, nor was it white like Germanic blond. It was like warm wheat straw. It lay on her back like a cape almost to her waist. I slid my forefinger from the bump of one vertebra on her spine to the next – over the soft smooth pale skin of her back and into the curve of her waist. She caught my hand and brought it up to her breast; soft and warm, soft and magical.

We made love silently whenever the night was quiet and the settlement was asleep. We made love slowly, touching and learning about each other. We slept without clothes or blankets when it was warm. We seldom spoke. Our urgency was gone now that we had time for each other. Later we talked. Then we went to sleep her hand in mine.

SA44 Western Russia to RT19 British Embassy 11 Sept 1005 (RST) 58
Russian air drop yesterday Army demolition specialist Training now

As I uncovered the bulky radio in the morning Yeva came into the shelter. Sitting on a chopped log she handed me a mug of tea. I touched her hands as I took it and smiled. She always made me smile. Her straight mouth softened and her face became light and happy. If it were possible to do so, she became more beautiful.

'I will go out tonight.' She said it matter-of-factly, like she was telling me the price of a cabbage.

A lump of fear exploded in my heart. 'Where? When?' I cleared my throat of the black terror. 'What for?' She smiled a wicked smile and I knew. 'You are going out to kill Germans aren't you?' I knew this would happen the afternoon she came back with a new rifle. She called it a Mosin. It was hideous.

Her smile widened. 'Of course! That's what I'm here for.' She wiggled closer and spoke softly as if sharing a conspiracy. 'We will go out once it is dark. We go to attack a railway. There will be a co-ordinated attack on a long front. Several hundred verst.' She looked away. 'I may be gone some days.'

'Some days?' I threw the canvas radio cover onto the floor. 'You could be dead and it would take days for me to find out.'

She smiled at me as if I were a child. 'Why do you think I will be dead? No

185

one shoots like I do.'

I could not argue with that. I had seen her practice. Not a shot missed the tiny target. 'Why bother? The Germans just repair it all, so why?'

'Because it uses men, materials and time to fix it all. These cannot be used elsewhere.'

Sometimes I was ashamed of my own naivety. but I felt the loss of her even before she had gone.

SA44 Western Russia to RT19 British Embassy 15 Sept 1114 (RST) 50
Confirm report 400 plus demolitions RR blocked S of Bryansk

RT19 British Embassy to SA44 Western Russia 16 Sept 1019 (RST) 124
Confirmed Also over 1000 attacks to date on RR 350 plus locos damaged 1200 plus carriages and trucks out of action Lines blocked total 2600 plus hours

While she was away, I concentrated on the radio. By now, there were codes to use. Runners arrived with reports for me to send up the chain to HQ and they then took back orders received from our commanders. The scene created in my head was one of insane demolitions on areas of railway behind the German front. Bridges burned, blown up; sections of track dug out. Snipers? Oh yes, snipers.

I tried not to colour the picture too vividly in my mind but some parts of it were so simple that it was impossible not to. I focussed on the Morse key in front of me and waited for her to come back.

When there was no radio work to do, the women found other jobs for me to do. I began to feel like a pet. They giggled, teased and fed me the best of whatever they made. I tried to refuse, but up against these formidable ladies, it was hopeless. In return I begged to be allowed to help. So I was sent out to collect wood, dig ditches, peel potatoes or cut cabbages. I also began to give lessons to the children. They were keen and eager, so it was a pleasure. They even learned to sing…albeit in Welsh. It amused me to think that in the future, someone would wonder how these people had come to learn Welsh music.

Yeva's skin looked translucent; her eyes were wide and she could hardly sit still; she was vivid in all kinds of ways. I tried to understand but felt that she had changed - she was no longer the person I knew.

'The train,' she rubbed the barrel of her rifle harder and harder. 'It leapt off the tracks, high into the air and then it tumbled, like a toy train down the slope. It was like photographs – one after the other. The trucks - one by one. over the top of the engine, over the coal, over each other. Pieces flying high into the air. Smoke. Fire. Dust.' I squatted beside her and she put down the rifle.

'We pulled a section of track away just as the train was about to go over it. Some of the men pulled it away with ropes and wires.' She demonstrated. 'The sand truck went first. It was the heaviest and pulled ...'

I interrupted. 'Sand truck?'

'Yes.' She was more excited now. 'They send a sand truck ahead of the locomotive to set off land mines and save the train. But,' she laughed, '...it didn't work this time. The weight of the sand truck pulled the rest of the train down the long slope to the river. Every car was pulled off the line. Faster and faster.' She demonstrated a tumbling action with her hands and rolled back onto the ground, laughing. When she caught her breath again, she continued. 'Then it was my turn.' I wasn't sure I wanted to hear this part. I knew what was coming, but I didn't want to see it through her eyes. 'I was on the bank. I had a good position and I saw everything. I shot many of them. If they survived the crash, I got them.' She demonstrated with an imaginary rifle. 'Through the head, the chest, they did not survive.'

I put my head into my hands. How was *I* ever going to survive this? The reality of what happened every day in this war was heavy bread indeed. But we needed bread to stay alive. And air. If I just kept breathing – just breathing.

Later when I had finished sending the reports – words I did not want to let through my brain. I pushed them from the paper to my fingers on the key without letting them go through my consciousness. I found her behind our shelter, sitting in a nest of tall grass, leaning against the wall with her head on her knees. Her shoulders were trembling. I knelt beside her and pulled her against my chest. Her head fitted under my chin and I could feel the sobs as they rose through her body. Great deep gulps and huge tears. I held her until my shirt was soaked and when the tears were finished, I gave her my torn handkerchief. It began to rain – a light pattering on our wooden roof.

'What is it milaya, my darling?' I whispered over her head. 'What has done this to you?' I knew the answer but I wanted her to say it. I wanted her to say that what she had been asked to do was wrong and that she would never do it again.

She wiped her face on her sleeve. 'I'm all right now.' She sneezed and blew her nose. 'I'm OK. I don't know what happened to me. It wasn't like this last time. Last time, I ... '

I pulled her back to me. I didn't want to hear about last time. 'Don't. Don't.'

'Gleb.' She gave me back the handkerchief. 'I suddenly felt so sad for the baby I lost. Not because I lost it. That was the right thing to have happened.'

'But darling, a baby?' I didn't understand her. 'The right thing?'

'How could I bring a child into this? How could anyone? What would have happened to it?' She sat up straighter and took a long breath. 'I have a job to do, and I will do it. I will do it. By all the saints in your religion I will do it. I will die doing it if necessary. It is the only thing I can do for my baby. The only thing.' I lifted her into my arms and took her inside out of the rain.

In our little shelter, Yeva had at last gone to sleep. I got up, put my trousers on and stood at the door. The night was warm, and the sky through the shelter of the trees around it was very black, but the starlight made the world grey. For once it was not raining but the snow would come soon. I had no idea what time it was, but knew that it was very late. A few birds rustled in the trees and I could hear a horse in the field next to us ripping grass and snorting through its nostrils. There was a light breeze that kept the mosquitoes on the move. I shut the door behind me to stop them from invading the stillness of the room behind me.

Such silence; such peace; such a normal moment. There was no terror; no hate; no blood; no killing. I leaned back against the door. What would happen to us? If by some miracle, the war ended in our favour tomorrow, what would happen to us? To Yeva and me? I thought of the sleeping figure behind me. Like a coating of sweet butter icing, a realisation descended over me. I realised that I loved her, more than my own life. Neither politics, nor this bloody war would change that. I wanted her for the rest of my life. But I had seen the bruises on her shoulder from the Mosin and I knew that there would be more. Many, many more, and I wanted to be beside her to make them better… if only there was a way.

I went back in and looked at her in the moonlight. I had seen her as hard as flint, never forgiving, never giving in, totally focussed and completely consumed. But tonight, I saw softness around her. The soft velvet centre that I knew was there was usually covered by a coating of determined revenge. Tonight her face was relaxed and beautiful, with a depth that I would probably never get to see the bottom of if I lived with her for a thousand years.

The weeks that followed continued in the same way: Yeva went out at night and came back a day or two later, completely consumed by what had happened. She was one of the men. One of a cohort that I could never be part of. They went over their success in never ending detail. The bloody details were just the bloody details to me, but to them they were battle honours. Thankfully, no one kept a tally on the number of Germans they killed; a number that would have become meaningless anyway; a number of living people, whose life ended probably before they heard the shot. Most, I prayed, ended without shock or pain. Ended without them knowing how or even why. They were conscripted with no knowledge of the bigger picture. They were just flesh, bone and blood sent out to stop steel. And they did, time and time again. Numbers. They were only numbers without name or a life story. Their names and bodies now rotting on Russian soil. I could not make it any easier in my own mind. My principles as they related to this war were intact; I just needed to find a way to continue without compromising them further. I contributed to this carnage. I could not escape or excuse that fact. How many other compromises would I be forced to make to keep myself and her alive. I was in a double life.

Early one cold morning, I felt her come back from her assigned assassinations, wiggle into bed and press her herself against my back. Cold flesh and warm breath, she was giggling and pinching my arm.

'What?' I rolled over. 'What has got into you?' Her giggle was infectious and the Lord alone knew much we all needed to laugh now and again.

'I have brought you something.' She made it sound like she had just been shopping.

'What? How?' I sat up. What was she talking about? She lit a candle and opened the pack she always took with her. She handed me a heavy box.

I undid the clip and took the lid off. It was a tiny portable typewriter. 'What?' I was beginning to realise that this was all I seemed capable of saying.

'Look,' she wiggled closer to me. 'Look at the keys.' She lifted the candle higher.

The keys were not in Cyrillic but in Arabic. It was an amazing find. Not just because these machines were rare, but because she knew how I longed to write and how much this simple gift would mean to me. I found it hard to speak and pulled her head to my chest. I kissed her hair. 'My darling, I don't know what to say.'

'Do you like it?'

'Do I like it?' It's ... it is ... perfect ... incredible.' I struggled to find Russian words. 'I ... I ...' I felt emotional. It was like a gift to the centre of my soul. 'My milaya ... you are perfect ... just perfect.'

She blew the candle out. 'Now we have to find you some paper.'

Her smile was more of a gift than the typewriter. I didn't know that I could love so much. I loved the way she laughed until she no longer could make any sound; the way she opened one eye before the other when she woke up; the way her hair covered her back when she brushed it; the way she drew pictures on my chest with her finger while we talked in the night and the way she put her socks on before her trousers in the morning. There were a thousand things I loved in her – there were a thousand reasons why my life was perfect. And now...

Savarov came to me quietly one morning carrying his rifle on his back. I had just finished the daily report to the Partisan HQ or whatever it was. The chain of command was not explained to me – I just knew that we were at the bottom.

'We are bringing some prisoners in to interrogate. We pass them on as soon as we take them, but this time there is no one who can take them right away. They will have to stay with us for a day or so.'

I was tempted to ask where they went, but just as quickly decided I didn't really want to know. Savarov hefted his rifle higher on his shoulder. 'Do you speak German?'

The few weeks I spent at the mansion updating my school boy German were hardly going to be sufficient for whatever he had in mind. 'Only a little. I doubt that it would be up to the task you will have to deal with.'

'I just need you to listen to them. They are mainly officers and so they may try to communicate in English. Or they may use German.' I nodded. 'Good. I will put you as a guard and all you have to do is listen. Don't speak to them in English or any other language except Russian.' He handed me the rifle. 'They will be here in one hour.'

There were 10 of them and Savarov was right. Most of them were German officers or at least NCOs. They were put into a shed with a small open space surrounded by wire fence and left there. The cook, Anna Kolynova was allowed into give them some thin soup but that's all the communication they were permitted. By late afternoon, they were getting restless and after several hours of mutterings among themselves they began to want some attention.

One, who would appear to be the highest ranking, the insignia were lost on me, began to rattle the compound wire. Rurik and I patrolled outside and occasionally banged the wire with our rifle butts to shut him up. After an hour or so, I affected boredom with this and stopped to stand at the wire watching them but without looking interested. The officer asked in a calm voice in German, if I spoke the language. I affected a blank stare and shrugged my shoulders. I told him in Russian that I didn't understand. He repeated the question louder and louder until I had to hit the wire with the rifle butt again. He calmed down and this time asked if anyone spoke English. Again I managed the blank stare, shrug and hoped that my eyes didn't give too much away. He too shrugged and went back to the others.

They spoke in a combination of languages: English, French, German and probably slang and profane versions of all three that I could not understand. The English and some of the German conversations I reported to Savarov. The prisoners discussed the big battle at Kursk and their retreat, which they did not call a retreat, when they were captured. The details made little sense to me, but caused a certain amount of excitement among Savarov and the rest. Apparently there were details of troop movements the Russians did not know about that HQ found very interesting. So my low level spying had some function. I was sent straight back to the radio.

Five or six days later, when their fine uniforms were beginning to look dusty, wrinkled and a lot less intimidating than they were meant to, a new collection of prisoners was brought in. There were 5 of them and they seemed to be of no particular army at all. They had bits of clothing that appeared to have been robbed from peasants, prisoners, and most armies in the conflict. One was wearing a leather flight jacket. It bore no insignia. It was interesting because it was a warm October day and not yet cold enough to need it in the day time. But the prisoner refused to take it off. He also refused to speak.

Savarov did not seem particularly interested as they were put in with the Germans. 'They will all go to HQ next week where the real interrogation will begin. They will have no secrets left then!' He laughed whistling through the gap in his top teeth.

I continued my patrol trying to look as bored as I felt and noticed that the German prisoners now spoke only in German if at all. They kept their distance from the new ones. On a round when I'd heard nothing for several hours of interest in German or even in English, I hear a moan from one young man who was leaning on the fence with his head on his knees. Beside him was the leather jacket. 'Fuck it Ryley. We're done for.' The accent was American.

'No. No.' Savarov leaned back in his creaking kitchen chair. 'They are prisoners. They go for interrogation. No exceptions.'

'But, Savarov, they are American. They are on our side. If they go to a POW camp they'll be lost forever – of no use to anyone.'

'So? It is not our affair.' He picked up his rifle and pushed past me. Our interview was at an end.

I had heard what happens to POWs. The Russians are not a forgiving race and this was not a time to find what little compassion they might have had. In the radio hut, I tuned to the Embassy frequency. As the word American does not feature in the King James Version, I transmitted in plain. No one else understood Morse, so if necessary I just said I was replying to Russian transmissions from HQ.

SA44 Western Russia to RT19 British Embassy 15 Oct 1405 (RMT) 85 Five American prisoners here S41V will not release Instructions please Due to transport in a few days

As usual a plane over flew us the next morning. This happened more frequently now. We listened for the characteristic drone of the German planes and if necessary ran for our dug out shelters. More often it was a Russian supply drop or some kind of reconnaissance the purpose of which we would never know. The plane disappeared and we waited to see if a drop would follow when it returned. It did not come back.

Several hours later, three of the guards arrived in the camp as the sun was lowering behind the tree line. They had yet another prisoner with them. His hands were tied behind his back. Two of the guards held him by the arms and a third was almost consumed by a large pile of parachute silk.

There was a rush of people who wanted to see the parachute. The prisoner was of no consequence, but the silk was of huge interest. We received few drops of supplies and the parachutes used were not as coveted by every female in the camp as this clearly was. It was also hugely valuable. It would be traded and sold for a great deal of useful material.

I went up to the prisoner. 'Hello Adrian.' He smiled as if his face would split. 'Hello old man. Good to see you.' By the time he was untied and reunited with his bag Savarov arrived and the questioning began.

'The Ambassador sends his compliments.' Adrian began. This was lost on Savarov who merely scowled and went directly to the heart of the issue without preamble. 'Why do you want my prisoners?'

Adrian settled more comfortably on the log he had been assigned. He was wearing a sort of boiler suit with a single breasted jacket over it and a pair of very scuffed boots. The knees of the suit were covered in mud. He must have fallen when he landed. 'They are valuable to us – and to you – in winning this war.' Savarov said nothing and Adrian continued. 'They are highly trained as airmen, their skills are critical. It takes a lot of time and money to train men to their degree and we cannot afford to lose them. We must put them back to work.'

'We have work here. They can work for us here.'

Adrian leaned forward putting his elbows on his knees. 'I doubt that they would be much use to you Savarov. Their skills ...'

'Pah! Skills? They need only shoot a weapon or lay a mine to be useful to us.' He looked up at me. 'Or use a radio.'

'They may be able to use a radio, but I doubt that they have much training in coding or decoding, or weaponry and none about laying mines.'

'What? Are they not trained at all?'

'They are highly trained, but not as infantry. They are airmen.' For a moment I wondered who had taken possession of the parachute silk they had landed with.

'American airmen are only trained to be airmen? What if they need to do something else?'

Adrian put up his hands in a gesture of defeat. 'The Americans want them back please.'

The Commissar Rytin who had been quiet to this point spoke suddenly with his wet guttural voice. 'Do they want to go? They can be very happy and do good things for us too. Why would they want to go back to America?'

I spoke then. 'Because they are comfortable with the American way Rytin.'

Rytin was genuinely puzzled. 'But our way? Why would they not want to...?

'I am sorry to say,' I continued, 'but Americans are not happy with the idea of Communism. It is something that they do not understand and to be honest, I doubt that very many of them even know what it is or where it is.'

Savarov had a smirk of surprise creased into his weathered face. I pressed the advantage. 'They would need to be trained to do what you want. They do not speak a word of any language except English and they do not want to be here. They are of no use to you, but they are of great value to Russia's allies. They would cost you much in terms of housing, food, and clothing while you dealt with them. I suspect that the others would complain.'

Adrian dealt the final blow. 'The British and American governments will pay for their return. It will be helpful to your cause.'

'Have you spoken to them?' I asked Adrian, as the airmen were loaded onto a cart. 'Do they know that you are on their side?'

'They do now. I had to tell them some quite uncomfortable truths about Russian POW camps before they chose to listen to our alternatives.'

'Even the alternative is not without its perils.' I suggested.

'Walk with me.' We walked away from the others into the tree cover. 'We need you to stay here.' I opened my mouth to explain that I had no intention of leaving but he spoke over any breath of opposition I might have made. 'Now that we know where you are, we will direct other escapees and evaders to you. You will make arrangements for them to be held here until we can evacuate them. I think that for the right price, Savarov will co-operate now that we have made an initial payment.'

'We? Adrian, what is going on?'

'You won't have heard of MI9. Our role is evacuation of prisoners, or others who have evaded capture or escaped. It is part of Military Intelligence. It's what I have been doing since the war started. All the arguments that I used with Savarov are true. But he will not know that we are organised in the movement of people like poor Ryley here and his chums. Poor Ryley and his chums won't either. As you will have seen, we have the added complication of getting people out of the clutches of the Russians as well as the Germans. There are many chains for the transferral of these people. It is dangerous work and our lines are not always secure. No one must know more than they need to know. Most lines and most people in the chain work under code names. These people will now bring evacuees here. This camp will be important as a collecting point until an evacuation can be made. You will let us know when there is a batch ready.'

I felt a bit stunned, but Adrian did not appear to have noticed. 'I've told Savarov that we will be responsible for allied prisoners; he can do what he likes with all the others.'

There was a sort of chill in the air. Adrian shifted his bag higher on his shoulder and grinned. 'Naturally any intelligence you can get in the meantime from the prisoners or the radio, we would be pleased to hear about it.'

'Such as?'

'Kursk was decisive but there will be lots of stragglers. Although there does not seem to be a clear victor in the battle, it has stopped the Germans and given them pause for thought. Things may well change now. Any military traffic among the partisans for example or any stray Russian transmissions – some smaller units still transmit in plain – anything that you can give us; troop movements, German re-enforcements, movements, evacuations – that sort of stuff. It will all be valuable, and of course, anything that the prisoners let slip.' He clapped me on the back. 'It means you will have your work cut out.'

He stopped and held out his hand. 'It was great to find you again Roy. I expect that we will see each other again when you have a new batch for me to retrieve. ' He dug into his pack and handed me a canvas bundle. 'This might help. You can explain it to Savarov however you like. Until next time...'

It contained a radio, smaller and new. Hidden in its innards was a tiny One Time Pad to use with the Embassy. A smaller package in the bag contained letters. Letters from home! It was months since I last heard from mother and her handwriting in English on the envelope was joy beyond words. I tore it open wanting more news from home, from my mother, from some point of sanity in the world.

19 May 1943

Dear Roy,

It has been so long since we heard from you, but we hope that news will come soon.

Haydn was home on leave for a weekend last month and hopes to have harvest leave in the autumn. The tenants have all been marvellous since your father's death and help out on the farm in every possible way. I also have some POW's to help. Germans mainly but also one or two Italians. We are managing.

I hope that they are feeding you well and not working you too hard. Write when you can.

Much love,

Mother.

PS. I enclose some clippings from the Journal – thought they might interest you.

Write when I can? How was I going to write? What could I say? What would make sense?

Then, another letter.

16

October 1943

10 June 1943

Dearest Darling Roy,

I haven't had a letter from you for months and months. Where are you darling? I miss you so much. I continue to write once a week and send the letters off into the wilderness. I have no idea if you have received anything. Please write and let me know how you are. I hope against hope that you have not forgotten me.

Please darling. Write anything. Just write so that I know you still love me?

All my love,

Annie.

A coldness started at my feet and slowly rose to my stomach. Annie. Dearest Annie. I hadn't thought about her for weeks. Not seriously thought about her. Not considered how she was, what she was doing this very minute. I'd stopped wondering if she was seeing the same stars and moon as I did; was she awake or asleep, at work or with friends. I had disconnected from her almost completely. The lines between us had become slack and suddenly a simple letter had snapped them taut again. I hadn't been so unfeeling as not to have considered her at all in the past weeks and months, but I had been unfeeling enough to have pushed her to the periphery of my emotions. How could I let her go? How did I tell her what had happened to me – what had happened to my heart?

What I had to tell her depended very much on what my heart would honestly allow me to say. And what would my heart say? I realised that I had never thought of Annie in the same block of time or place as I thought of Yeva. The two women had never coincided in my mind – or my heart for that matter. They lived in two completely different sections of my life. Annie could no more live in this world than Yeva could in Annie's given the demands the war made on us and the situation we now lived in. Somehow I had to close the section of my soul where Annie lived. I had to find the feelings I might have had for her, take hold of them and then let them go. I had to let Annie go.

Annie had been lovely and fun. She was also naïve and uncomplicated. She would never be anything like the challenging, opinionated, pig headed and cold-blooded killer that Yeva was. Yeva was wise, educated in life at its worst, able to overcome horrors that most people would never be able to even imagine and sex with her was incredible, full of fun and joy. Annie was so much unknown, so much untested and so immature. Perhaps the war had changed her too. Perhaps she had grown up. Perhaps she was not the same person she had been three years ago. On the face of it, and given what kind of a person I had been - simple, pacifist and unskilled at the things that mattered, Annie should be the perfect companion for the rest of my life. But I also knew that she would bore me to suicide. Yeva on the other hand would probably drive me to murder. But there was no contest really.

How to write a letter that might never get there? Send a message via Adrian? How unfeeling that was? Would she believe me? How truthful could I be? What would I say? Did I say anything? Should I wait until I got home?

What was I thinking? I was never going home – not even if offered the opportunity.

I had my conscience to settle. How many things had I done and how many were yet to fall to my responsibility that conflicted with everything I believed? I lived the life of a dead man, indulged in profanity – most of it in Russian, but never the less..., drank intoxicating liquor, I hated a great deal of the human race and contributed actively to their deaths in hideous ways, I lived with and had sex with a woman to whom I was not married. Was there any sin left that I had not committed? Neither had I sought forgiveness for my sins or done anything to stop my participation in them. I could not recognise who I had become. I didn't even know myself any longer.

Yeva found me at old the radio set; headphones on but nearly asleep on my hand.

'Gleb?' She pulled on the wire to the headphones and I woke with a snort. 'I wasn't asleep. Not really.' I pulled one of the headphones off my ear.

She laughed and the sunlight that it put in my heart made all the decisions for me and gave me all the forgiveness I required. She was a place of peace in my heart. In this chaotic crazy world in which I now lived, she pushed aside all the guilt that my thinning morals continually dropped in front of me. She gave me space to be myself without all the religious and social rules of my previous life. With her there was a place where I could rest and find no need to justify what I had compromised or what I had done. I could set it all aside and be what I wanted to be – Gleb Alekseev.

And I knew what I had to do. I would write to Annie regularly with reducing attestations of my affections, wait for them to be collected by Adrian and hope that they arrived in some sort of order. Perhaps I could let her down gently. Then, when it seemed appropriate, I would confess what had happened.

'Did you get letters? Who from? Was it good news? You do not look like it was good news.'

'Yes, it was good news. A letter from my mother. All is well there. They are safe. The Germans so far haven't found any need to bomb mid Wales.' Did I love her enough to tell her about the other letter?

'Then what is wrong? You don't look happy.'

How much to say? 'I guess ... I guess I miss my family.' Tiny flakes of snow floated through the air, floating left and right with no direction from the wind. They tumbled slowly over themselves.

She disappeared and came back with tea in a tall glass. She handed me the tea. 'These are the snowflakes that we would try to catch on our tongues when we were children. But when we catch them they are so tiny and soft that you can't taste them or even feel them.' She was right because we tried.

'Why do you miss your family? Are they not busy doing the same thing as you? Defeating the Nazis? Are you not proud of what they are doing to save your country?' Yeva lay on my arm with her head on my shoulder. I traced random shapes on the warm skin of her back with my fingers.

How simplistic it all was for her. I pulled the blanket up over her shoulder. 'My father is dead, my mother is trying to run the farm without him and my brother is somewhere doing whatever the Army wants of him.'

'Well then. What is there to be sad about?'

'It is hard for my mother to manage such a large farm without my father and brother. There are not many men to help now. They are all off fighting. It is difficult to produce enough to keep the farm viable and do what the government needs of it.'

'Viable? What is viable?'

I had used the English word, so lit a candle and looked it up in my little dictionary. It was a huge word and its pronunciation rocketed around my head. 'It means that the farm has to pay its way. It has to make money.'

'That's silly. What good is the money? Surely it is better to make food to feed the people.'

'That is what farms are for. They produce food. Our country is not able to make enough food to feed everyone, so a lot has to be imported. Much of that is being lost to the German U-boats in the Atlantic. So farms are working as hard as they can. If they make money as well, then the owners and everyone else including the government, knows that they are making as much food as they can and it provides incentive for them to maximise...'

'But don't people want to save the motherland; to do what they can to feed the people. Is that not enough? And what does your mother do with this money that she makes? Does it not belong to the workers?'

'Men who work on the farms are paid well and have houses on the estate. They use the land at their houses for themselves.'

'But,' she frowned, 'that means your mother is bourgeoisie - we have destroyed the bourgeoisie – what will happen to your mother when the revolution comes to your country? Who will save the bourgeoisie when working people rise up?'

How to explain the class system, the role of the landed gentry or tenant farmers, land owning classes like us in a way that made sense to someone who had seen it all destroyed and replaced with famine and destruction but still believed that the Revolution had been a complete success?

'At the moment, we are not looking for a revolution. We just want to beat Hitler.' How I loved the puzzled look on her face. I felt puzzled myself.

16 October 1943

Dear Mum,

I received your letter of 19 May via Moscow. I am in a camp in Western Russia and communication has not been easy. For a long time I had no way of getting letters out of here, but now I do and so will be able to write regularly, but you may not receive them all, or indeed any of them.

The paper on which I write is made in our camp. Some of the women here are very good at it and although it is rough and wouldn't do to get wet, it serves very well. However I shall be conservative in its use all the same. As you see I now also have a typewriter!

The summer has been relatively calm in the camp after Kursk, but we still go out regularly to watch what the enemy is doing and occasionally to destroy some of his posts. This I find most difficult, given my attitudes to death and war in the first place. There is a lot of killing – and a lot of almost killing which leaves many dying slowly and in great pain. Although I know it happens, because I have seen it, I am not able to make it real. It is all some kind of horrible fiction. A terrifying film. But a film with smell, taste and air around it. Air that moves with screams and terror.

We all know here that if we are ever injured or captured we will be tortured and then killed. We have seen the results of this many times and everyone here accepts the possibility without questions. Perhaps they have their own personal horrors; I just know that I do – often.

Love from Roy

As I shut the envelope I prayed that Adrian would get it directly to the mail bag without too many eyes reading too much into what I had written.

Mid October The moon lights the path; twigs, roots and broken branches are all safely illuminated for us to find our way. Trees reach up to catch the moonbeams, sway and stretch never quite reaching high enough. The moon is safe for now.

She walks beside me, her rifle clicking against her webbing. Her Russian blond hair is plaited down her neck, wet with the sweat of our long march. It is still hot and the cool evening air does not penetrate this far into the forest. We march while we can under cover of the darkness and the slightly lowered temperatures. It is still dry and the tinder underfoot is dangerous. There will be no hot meal when we are done. Cold rations, as many as we still have left, and cold tea.

200

I was still quarrelling with my conscience. I was carrying the radio Adrian had brought on his last visit. Savarov was delighted – a new, better radio and the fact that the British Embassy saw fit to send it directly to me raised my kudos no end. I was also carrying a rifle. I knew it would come to this. Somewhere in the bottom of my soul I knew it would come to this. The last time I carried a rifle it was a cover to make people think I was real – a real Red Army rifleman. But now they knew I was not. Somehow, that made no difference and it was assumed that I would just do as I was told and that this silly idea that I didn't really want to kill anyone was not given so much as a thought. If I opened my mouth to complain about it, I would probably have been beaten to a bloody pulp at best, shot at worse. And because I was a devout coward, I chose to keep my mouth shut. Yeva said nothing but I think she would have intervened had I broken the taboo. I soothed my heaving conscience by promising myself that I would never fire the thing. I didn't know how and couldn't hit the broad side of a bus, so that would keep my soul safe. The men and women around me could not and would not understand that I didn't know how to do these basic things. They grew up knowing this. Why didn't I? It was incomprehensible to them…and to me.

It took us two moonlit nights and two sweating days to get here. We walked by night and rested – it would be foolish to say that we slept – by day. We were safer at night, less likely to be observed. The march has been planned in meticulous detail, over difficult terrain, using pathways, tracks, road and river crossings in remote areas where observation was unlikely from over-flying German planes. Borya Ilyavitch Sobolev had gone ahead and left subtle clues behind us to guide others who followed: a pile of stones, a twist of grass, a broken branch. Everyone in the group had studied the maps over and over again. I had not for a second considered that I might be going with them, so paid little attention. I had no idea where we were or how to get back again. But everyone else knew exactly where they were and how to escape if it all went wrong.

As daylight on the last day approached, Savarov stopped us under cover of the forest and came to ask me to set up the radio and get the orders. As I worked with the coded messages, many other people arrived. All partisans by the look of them.

The messages which I handed directly to Savarov were instructions to advance on and take a village where the Germans had set up a training camp for Russian civilians they had captured and hoped to turn to their side and advantage. The partisans were to take the main administrative and command centre and hold it until the arrival of the Red Army. Simple, I thought, nothing to it. Dear God what was I doing here?

Savarov called the leaders together, his own and the leaders of the other groups that had now joined us. He outlined the process which meant nothing to me. Someone drew a plan of the village in the dust and marked the defended positions with twigs he stuck in the dirt. Savarov then took over and outlined what would happen and who would do what. I listened with half an ear. Once they were all dismissed to get some rest before the planned attack at dawn, he pulled me aside. 'You will go with Yeva and her group. She is in command and you will do as she orders. Just as the others. Leave the radio here to collect when we are done.'

A cold fist hit my stomach. I was not prepared. What would she ask me to do? Savarov knew full well that I would be useless to the Germans as I had no idea where I was or where the partisans were likely to be. No wonder he had not worried when I did not pay attention. Was it part of his plan? To be rid of me?? Other groups now had radios. Perhaps I was becoming a liability and could easily be made redundant.

Diary entry, undated. The deprivation in our lives exists on top of emergency. We live in a constant state of reactionary terror. We can react to anything; we do react to everything but may die in doing so. Even in the state in which we exist, love fills my heart. Even now when all is wrong, I can live with joy – if I choose. If I love enough, nothing can hurt us.

The noise of the shooting when it began was more than terrifying. It shook all parts of my body and ground on which I lay. Yeva, I and several others had crawled in the dark with as much silence as I could achieve to the shadow of a water tower. From there we had a good view of the rear entrance to the concrete block that was the command centre for the village and the barracks beside it. We had cut our way through the poorly erected wire and the guards were silently dispatched elsewhere. Sheltered by the mounds of rubbish thrown behind the tower we waited.

At a signal I missed, a great noise began and large bits of ordnance crashed into the building and the barracks. The noise of the shelling completely covered the screams and shouts of the men inside but within seconds, men were streaming from all the buildings. Some wore only their underpants; many had helmets and weapons; some not even underpants.

It mattered not, Yeva and the others began firing and men fell as fast as the rifles could be fired. In less than a few seconds the poor bastards stopped trying to get out and the doors were slammed shut. Communicating with hand signals, some the men from our group settled down beside us to keep watch along their rifle sites. Yeva tugged on my tunic. We wiggled our way back into some low brush and putting her mouth close to my ear, she shouted over the shelling, 'Come. We go around the other side.' We ducked and ran. The heavy rifle banged into my back and shoulder. What the hell was I going to do with it? We slid into a trench with a heavy pipe at the bottom, Yeva pushed me down. Bullets crashed into the dirt behind us and the brush beyond that.

'Keep still,' she ordered. I was too terrified to do anything else. 'You will load for me.' I must have looked blank. 'Here.' She pulled the evil thing off my shoulder, instructed me as she loaded it, handed me the empty one and wiggled up into the soft dirt. Clumsily, with my hands shaking, I pushed the cold brass and lead into the clip and then into rifle as she showed me. Above me, she pushed the barrel up over the edge of the hole, fired rapidly then ducked down when there was answering fire. Again and again, she emptied the rifles and again and again I loaded them for her. The screams, groans and calls for help from the victims could be heard in the tiny pauses in the on-going chaos. I did not need to see what was happening to know what the ground out there looked like. Maybe I imagined the screams. Maybe it ended in silence. Maybe the screams were mine.

I still had not gone to any of the Laundry frequencies; the number I knew so well. As terrible as our lives were, I was afraid to add more. It was a deep place in my past and I did not want to go there.

The days were getting visibly shorter. The leaves on the fruit bearing trees and bushes showed vivid colours now. The bright red and purple were alive among the dark greens of the timber trees. Alone among them were the yellow gold of a beech-like shrub. There was a heavy frost last week and that seemed to be a shot fired that halted all work in the trees and began the about-turn into slumber. The little flakes of snow we had seen earlier had not stayed, or affected the trees, and they had not yet returned. But they would, along with all their cousins.

Yeva and I sat at the edge of the field. Overhead was a large oak and in front of us the long field where we had been raking the last hay cut from it this year. It was a second cut and inferior to earlier hay but adequate enough to supplement winter feed and important for the animals' welfare and therefore our own. I opened the bag we had put in the shade that morning and took out the parcel wrapped in a cloth that Anna Kolynova handed us as we left the village. It contained some of her wonderful blinys and we fell on these as though starving.

'Do you have blinys in England?' Yeva asked wiping crumbs from her lower lip. She obviously noted the enthusiasm with which I devoured these little buckwheat pancakes.

'Not exactly, but we do have pancakes, especially at Easter. In fact, we have pancake races.'

'Races? Who wins?'

'The woman who can flip a pancake out of a fry pan and catch it three times, over a given distance and get to the end first.'

This had her in fits of laughter and nearly choking on her bliny. 'Why do you race with a fry pan?'

I then had to describe Lent and the tradition of Pancake Tuesday and the old church requirement to use up eggs and milk before Lent. 'Why then,' she looked sober, 'do you think that our ways are hard ones? Surely denying food to the poorest people is not right.' Knowing what I did about Stalin's plan to starve millions in the 1930s I was lost at the first step of another argument I did not wish to have.

'Fortunately we don't treat Lent with quite so much enforcement as we used to.'

'Do you miss England?'

I leaned back on one elbow, wiped my mouth of the last crumbs of the bliny and reached for the jug of kvass. 'I do sometimes. I miss my family and my mother's puddings.' I handed her the jug – kvass was a fermented drink made from dark rye bread – not very alcoholic, but refreshing. 'I miss my old room and my books. And I miss my father ...'

She rubbed my arm. 'Poor Roy.' She did not often use my real name. It was a gesture of sympathy and love. She took a long drink from the jug and handed it back. 'If you and I are ever separated, I will look for you in your old room, among your books, eating your mother's puddings.'

'And where shall I look for you? Not that I intend to be anywhere except beside you for the rest of my life.'

She pulled up her knees and wrapped her arms around them. 'I don't know.'

'Don't you have a family home, where your parents are? Or where your grandmother lived or where you went for your summer vacation?'

'My parents were denounced when I was away at Stalingrad. I knew nothing about it until I left the hospital. I escaped the questioning only because I had

204

been so injured. I would probably have been interrogated when I returned but the train was stopped and ...'

I put my arms around her. 'No wonder you were so worried. But I still don't understand why you wanted to get back to your regiment so badly. You might have been killed there.'

She put her head down on her knees. 'I guess I wanted to tell them that I knew nothing about what my parents were doing. I wanted to be safe from them.'

'But did they really do anything that caused them to be arrested?' I knew how this worked. Somebody said something to someone else and eventually it reached the party big shots and the next thing you knew someone was banging on your door during the night.

'Probably not.'

'Don't you want to know?'

'No. If I begin to ask, I too will be suspect. My father would not expect me to condemn myself in that way. He would expect me to look after myself.'

I stroked her hair. 'And where would you go if you needed to be alone, to be safe.'

She lifted her head. 'I don't know where I could go to be safe. My parents' apartment will now belong to someone else if they have not returned. I had no home with my husband. My grandparents are now dead.' She sighed and looked into the tree branches. 'I guess I would see if their little cottage was still there, if it is not occupied, if it is safe.'

'What is it like and where is it?' I pulled her closer and kissed her. 'I will come there and rescue you, no matter what happens.'

Russia North Western Front (Worcester Journal) Friday 22 October 1943 *Partisans* **by Royston Thomas**

After a long period in which I was not able to report, I am now with a group of partisans who live in the western forests of this great country. This group of men and women live in a village with local people. And the timelessness of rural Russian life continues as it has for centuries. Families live in wooden houses, cultivate vegetable gardens near the house where they get the best sunshine and plant

and harvest cereal crops in the surrounding fields. They
use horses to plough and till the soil and raise pigs and
chickens for food. Everyone works where there is a need for
labour. A Committee plans what is to be done. This is, in
effect, a working kolkhoz, a collective farm. It survives
under unusual and sometimes terrifying conditions. There is
a war going on in the far distance around it. It could be
bombed or overrun at any time. No wonder then that the men
and women who tend to the crops and animals carry weapons
to the fields with them.

Yeva was rubbing the barrel of one of her rifles when I got back to our small hut
after a morning in the radio hut. She was sitting in the doorway and had pieces of
the hideous Mosin spread across the step. The sun was warm. There had been
days of wet snow, but also days when the sun, like today, melted it all and it
made me question if winter really was near. The sun, lower in its orbit now, drew
long shadows from the trees across the paths and across the step where she
sat.

It took hours of her time to clean the weapons and although it seemed
macabre to me that she should devote so much care and attention to such an
instrument of killing, I know that it also gave her time. It was time in which she
went over what happened, putting the events to rest on her personal list of
revenges. Her emotional moods were less extreme now and I knew that it was
because she was leaving the reality of what she did further behind her. It was
becoming more and more of a mechanical exercise.

I picked up her pile of cleaning rags, recognising among them, a piece of her
undershirt, now relegated to more important duties. I sat down beside her and
put the pile of rags down between us.

'You seem cheerful this morning?' I asked it more as a question than a
statement.

She blew something invisible from the innards of the weapon. 'It was a
successful night.'

I looked away. 'I am not sure I want to hear the details.'

She laid the rifle over her knees; its business end pointed over my legs.
'Gleb. Why are you like this?' She frowned at me.

'Like what?' I knew what she would say.

'Like you are in a different place – a different time zone – with a different
sense of ... of ...'

It was a conversation we had started many times, but this time I wanted us to get to the end of it. 'I can't do what you do.' She drew in a long breath on which to place all her arguments. I got there first. 'I have objected to this war from the beginning. I came here because I could not be a full combatant.'

She choked on laughter. 'You! Not a combatant!'

'I have not killed anyone.'

'You have helped all the rest of us to kill them.'

I couldn't argue with that. 'Yeva. I was sent here because I made it be known in England that I was not going to fight. People like me are called conscientious objectors. We object to fighting and killing on conscience grounds.'

'Conscience?' Her voice was getting louder and angrier. 'What conscience? When the bastard Germans are killing us, our women, children and old men in the most hideous ways! You object because it hurts your conscience? That is ridiculous.'

'To you perhaps it is. To me, it is not.'

'So what would you have us do? Put down on our weapons and kill ourselves so they don't have to do it?'

'I cannot justify what I believe in the face of the reality as it has become. But I know that my Christian faith will put it right in the end. It will not need me committing more crimes to do so. I have other roles to play in beating the bastard Germans as you call them.'

She thought for several minutes, absently stroking the barrel of the Mosin. 'I don't understand why you are not angry.' Her voice was now cold. 'Like the rest of us. So angry you would kill with your bare hands. Why not?'

'Because I can't. I know it has to be done. But I have to let others do it.' She breathed in to expel her objections but I stopped her. 'I know it is a double standard. I believe one thing, but know that another is equally real.'

'That is silly.'

'Not everyone hates as much as you do. Your commanders are dispassionate. They lay their morals on one side of the line and then plan, carefully, without emotion, what they need to do. I am a little like that, except that I can't send men and women to do what they send you to do.'

'So?'

'So, I do what I can. I gather the intelligence. I send the messages, I get the orders, I listen and report. I don't make the decisions. I can't. It would be wrong, morally wrong. I can only go so far.'

She rammed some steel bits back into the dreaded Mosin and smiled at me. 'It's OK. You will get over it.'

Get over it! I tried to speak, but she was already getting up to lean the Mosin against the wall of the hut. 'You will be like us one day. You will see.'

17

October 1943

30 October 43

Dear Annie,

I received your letter of 25 May at last. I have no idea where it has been or indeed where any of the others are. But it was good to hear from you.

I am fine, although in an out of the way place, with little means of getting a letter to you. I will write through a contact in the Embassy who I see now and then. He will direct the letters through various channels and if these are successful and the ships on which they get to you are not sunk in the Arctic, you will receive this.

So many uncertainties in life these days.

I did not know what else to write. I had come to the end of my emotion for Annie. I felt a sickness inside. It was over. I felt Yeva's hands on my shoulders. It was over, except for the guilt.

'Who are you writing to now? Is it your mother again?'

Did I tell her? Did I risk her feelings for me by confessing that there was someone else? Would she understand? Never mind understanding, would she forgive me for living another kind of double life? Or would she just shoot me? 'Yes. Yes, it is.' Now I could add lying to my list of sins.

In the evening gloom in our hut, the sickness from my guilt relaxed in my heaving stomach and I felt my soul shed some of the spikes I had driven into it. She stood behind me and I leaned back against her. Her hands slid down my chest and I felt her cheek on my head. I turned on the block of wood on which I sat and pulled her onto my lap. I kissed her neck, her chin, her lips. She put her hand in my hair and pulled my head hard against her shoulder. For a few brief seconds, I was in another place – a place where there was light and colour and pretty flowers and lovely dresses and her – Yeva in a place where we were safe and the only emotion around us was love. All we owned was the need to be together. I touched her breast. She slipped the shirt over her head and taking me by the hand led me to our bed. A tiny place where we were safe, alone and all that was wrong with the world went away. I put my lips on her breast. The dark nipple grew hard and she arched her back. 'I love you.' I don't know who spoke the words. I only knew they were true.

As we lay quietly, I tucked some stray golden hairs back from her face and kissed her ear. 'What will happen to us when the war is over?'

She rolled over until we were face to face and put her forehead against mine. 'If the Germans don't kill us and if the Red Army doesn't kill us and if Stalin's mob don't kill us you mean?'

I chuckled at the thought of the black scenario. 'Yes, in spite of all that.'

She breathed deeply before she answered. 'I don't know.' She put her fingers into the hair on my chest. 'I don't know if we will still be alive, or still together. I don't know how we can ever have a normal life again.' She rolled onto her stomach and looked at me. 'Look at us – look what we do every day… how can we stop all this one day and do something entirely different the next. I don't know how a person can do this.'

'Both ideas frighten me.'

'Why?'

'Because life with you now is terrifying enough… every day you go out or we go out together I don't know if I will see you again. One or the other of us could be dead. Or we could be separated forever. If the war stops, we could be quite different people in a different world. Maybe we would no longer be together in a new world. Maybe we wouldn't love each other in that kind of world.'

In the silence that said everything and nothing, I let my worst fears take on life. 'I don't know what I would do if you died and I was left alone. I don't know how I would stay alive. I don't know how I could still be a human being.'

She wiggled her head onto my shoulder and I felt her breath on my neck. 'I would live forever on your grave. I would never move until I died and went into it with you.'

We lay quietly together and then she whispered. 'If we don't die, let's not change things. Let's stay here when the war ends. Let's become farmers and peasants. You can teach and I can farm. We can be happy and quiet – right here.'

I turned to her and brushed her face with my lips. 'Will you marry me?'

She lifted herself on one elbow and looked at me in the darkness. She put her hand on my throat. 'Yes.'

SA44 Western Russia to RT19 British Embassy 31 Oct 0815 (RST) 87 New Commissar arrived Political views now more cautious Communists now more confident Change awaited

5 Nov 1943

Dear Mum,

We have just returned from another period away from the camp. It was our longest one yet and we were away for two weeks.

These partisans are amazing people. Nothing seems to distract them from what they are here to do. There was a time when they made their own plans about what that was, with the result that their effectiveness was fragmented. Now they have a leader in the military hierarchy Moscow, responsible for all activity and their work is now better focussed and co-ordinated.

What they have to do is beyond belief and I am forced to watch so much that I dearly wish I could forget or not have to witness at all. There is a lot of killing, torture, much ugly violence. They will justify it of course, but it is cruelty to me. Not just to Germans, but to a great many of their own people. They suspect, rightly or wrongly, that these individuals – or groups – are collaborating with the Germans and so they are summarily executed or interrogated (and I leave it to you to imagine what that is) and then executed.

We come to more villages razed to the ground, full of the dead, than we find intact and functioning. It seems as if more of the population is dead than alive. Those who are alive are just barely so. We take what we need and leave them with nothing.

And I am helpless in it all.

But in happier news, I have met a wonderful woman and we were married several days ago. It meant a long trek to a large centre where there is a bureau that does this. But I wanted to do it properly and although I had to use a Russian name, it has now been done. I have never been happier than I am now – even in the midst of all this horror.

I will tell Annie when I write next. Please tell no one until I have told her.

Roy

SA44 Western Russia to RT19 British Embassy 7 Nov 0825 (RST) 150 New commissar is a zealot Previous had power to countermand commander This one subordinate But he intends to ensure everyone is good Communist and Party member Commander unhappy

A group of Partisans arrived in the late afternoon yesterday. With them were regular Red Army soldiers and a few others who I could not identify but were probably prisoners of some high quality. Savarov came to me immediately. 'These must be sent to Moscow... you will radio?'

Adrian would arrange and I could send my copy and my letters again. I had yet to write to Annie. I had to let her go. She needed to find someone else who would love her, keep her warm, safe and happy. I did not want her to wait for me – I was not the person she fell in love with – not in any way was I the person she knew.

RUSSIA North Western Front (Worcester Journal) 8 November 1943 *Facing the Enemy* **by Royston Thomas**

The sergeant was hit earlier today and we are now under continuous fire. The forest is steadily being destroyed as the Germans pass the boundary edges of the marsh. We have no sight of them yet, but the heavy guns are an unwelcome complication and the explosions are getting closer. We have only small arms and rifles with which to reply. There are none of our troops in the area so far as we know and no air support that we can call down at this time of night. If the Germans can't find us they will take reprisals on villages nearby.

A lad has dug a hole beside me and is siting down a rifle longer than he is tall, but it is too dark to see what might be advancing. I tap the Morse key with a hand barely able to function. Perhaps we will see daylight, perhaps not.

28 November 1943 Boredom is our greater enemy these past few weeks. Men are showing stress. They are becoming fractious. They want action. Our commanders want intelligence. Nothing happens.

Oleksandr shows me how to play card games – incomprehensible to anyone not Russian – have lost every time, but then I don't know what I'm doing. He laughs at me.

The Germans were in retreat, although they wouldn't call it that of course. But we knew from reports via radio and runners that there were fewer of them surrounding us now although we were still behind the German line. Our tasks had not changed in terms of action or sabotage, but reconnaissance had now been added. What had changed also was that we now had a lorry and a big gun. I say 'big'. It was a Maxim 1910 machine gun – or so I was told. It was only a yard and a half long but needed two men to lift it. Fortunately it had little wheels so a single person could pull it along - if the terrain permitted – which around here it didn't. But it now lived in the back of our lorry. Vasili, our troop leader, was delighted with it, telling me that it fired so quickly that it could not be cooled by the air around it, so was water cooled. That accounted for the big housing around the barrel I assumed.

'What about the winter?' I naively asked.

'Ah', Fedya grinned, showing his few remaining teeth. 'We fill it with snow! Or we pee on it.'

We had not yet had need to fire it or fill it with snow or pee on it.

I reached up and stuck the binoculars onto the crest of a frozen wave of fresh snow. The lip of the wave shone in the weak sunshine and a light wind blew finger flicks of fine snow off the rim. A short burly human being in a padded coat beckoned me up with an overstuffed arm. It was Vasili. I pushed myself up until the rim of my hood cleared the binoculars. I blinked into the whiteness beyond.

The entire horizon and the unending plain in front were entirely empty; so empty it was barren of colour, detail and even distance. 'They'll come,' I thought, 'they'll come.'

Our waiting position was a good one – the trees at the edge of the plain where we sheltered were large and encouraged feelings of security. Their evergreen canopy provided some protection from air recognizance and the pine boughs above dissipated the slow puffs of smoke from the engine of our truck left on the iced track behind us in the trees – shut it off and it would never start again. No engine and we could not move our one big gun. No big gun and - my imagination could not fill in the 'what if....' In time I would know.

I wiggled my elbows into the hard snow – two sockets of support – and crossed the long horizon again with the glasses. The Germans would come; the intelligence I had from the radio said so. It did not say when, or how big the force would be, but we were used to that. We were accustomed to living in snow banks for weeks on end.

Raking the indistinct grey line between sky and plain, tiny dots of darker grey appeared just left of the centre of the horizon. I shut my eyes hard and looked again. I was sure they were still there. I glanced at the bear-like mound beside me; had he seen them too? The heap gave no indication of positivity in any form. I poked him and pointed to the site of the grey specs – arms flung wide I brought them together to indicate half way and then pointed 5 degrees or so to the left. It was easier than trying to describe in his colloquial Russian. The fellow looked long and hard then, looking back at me with small black eyes almost hidden by eyebrows white with chunks of his own breath, he grinned, the deep creases in his face disappearing into his icy beard. He touched his temple with a fat woollen finger and made little circles beside his head. Imagination? I looked back at my specs. They were gone. It happened often in featureless landscapes. Imagination was stronger than reality. It often happened.

I rolled onto my back and slid a few feet down the bank. If my candle held out tonight in my show hole, I might be able to write something again. My little typewriter would probably function if I had brought it, but there was nowhere to send the copy and the tiny repeated snap of the keys on the platen would sound like so many distant rifle shots to the highly strung, poorly trained and badly equipped men around me. A pencil and my notebook would be safer and quieter.

Anyway, how do I describe unending waiting, interminable monotony, days short and cheerless, nights long and more cheerless. Mix all this latent potency with low-level fear and the certain knowledge that when the waiting is over they would all dearly wish it weren't and then try to write it down so a British public in front of their little fires could understand. The newspaper wanted realism and no matter how I wrote this it would seem like fiction, fictional fantasy.

Three weeks ago before I found myself in this particular part of the wilderness, there was a world to communicate with – things going on and things I could understand. Communication within Russia was fractured but command structure was good now and somehow the orders arrived; somewhere there was a strategy, a plan. This group was very protective of me; I was one of the few radio operators in small units like this. They weren't about to let me go. In that I found some comfort that they weren't likely to let me get captured or injured either. They would shoot me first. But it really wasn't up to me. So when Savarov told us I was to go with this small band of ragged fanatics, my only thought was that I might be separated from Yeva. But she seemed not to even consider the possibility. She was already sorting her few clothes and packing her ammunition into her pack.

I stoked her hair. She looked up and laughed. I could not resist a kiss. 'Thank you.'

'What for?' She rammed the woollen socks she had been mending into the pack.

'For coming with us – for not letting Savarov separate us.'

Had I not loved her laugh so much, I might have been offended. She pulled the draw string on the pack savagely. 'Not you so much. I need to kill some more German bastards.' She stood up and put her hands on my shoulders. 'Well, maybe you, yes, just a little.' She winked.

They were kind in their bear-like ways – giving me enough gear to keep me from freezing to death if I used it intelligently – and more importantly, giving me details that surprised me. Perhaps they had come to trust me after all. I was never sure of my place in the pattern of the Partisans. I suspected that they had not ever trusted me completely; I was not Russian, I was not even a soldier and couldn't even fire a rifle. But they admired Yeva – I dearly hoped that some of that worship might have fallen in my direction. More likely they were just being friendly as they always were and probably didn't care that they knew less about the plan and strategy than I did. I had the luxury of the radio intelligence. Much I could not tell them.

I wiggled back up the bank, kicking the toes of my compressed felt boots into the hard snow. There was still nothing to see, but the sun was beginning its slow arc to the west and throwing shallow indistinct shadows in the snow. Patterns of waves like crescents of beach sand deepened but did not move. They remained solid, frozen and immobile. Fragile though they appeared, they were almost hard enough to drive our one small lorry over. In spite of the distance and early warning we would have, there was no security in the depth of snow. It was like cement, whipped hard by the unending wind, but you just never knew where you might fall through.

The wind today came from the north – it would bring bad weather. This was helpful to us in that it kept the Germans dug into their snow holes, but it also blew directly into our faces.

I felt someone crawl beside me. 'Gleb Alekseev, I bring tea.' Vitya handed me a tin mug of tea, by now lukewarm from the wind. The little man, something over 50 I guessed, should have been anywhere but frozen into a forest's edge. His language was a colloquial version of Russian with some other words thrown in delivered through a mouth full of broken teeth. It was well beyond my ability to understand much of it. There were limits to his English but he liked to use what he knew and through a conspiracy that I actually needed a translator, we were able to keep the poor man away from some of the active combat and on reconnaissance instead. Some of the interpretations were laughable at best and hysterically funny at worst. But we both kept faces that showed only total comprehension. So, the little man also served as a sort of batman, bringing tea.

'In morn vee ghost,' he reported happily.

'Where? Where do we go?'

The little man looked puzzled. 'Here.' He pointed at the ground. 'We ghost from here.'

I tucked a smile behind my cheeks. 'Yes, from here.' I pointed to the ground, 'to… where?' I pointed north, east, south and shrugged my shoulders, spreading my hands in ignorance. The little man shrugged too and wiggled back the way he'd come.

It was hard to determine the level of intelligence in someone with whom you can't communicate, I thought. Where there was no link of conversation, no questions and answers, how does one know whether one's companion is an idiot or a philosopher? Pulling one glove off with my teeth, I reached inside my jacket for the tiny notebook in the top pocket of my tunic. That would be the next article for the paper. It would be easier to write than anything else about interminable boredom.

The bulk on my right suddenly became excited and shouted for Travkin, the Red Army Sergeant, or whatever he was called. The ranks and titles in the military changed so frequently we were never sure what was in use. I clawed back up to the top of the bank and rammed my face back into my binoculars. There were more dots, but they were black this time and they were in the west. That was bad news - it meant fresh Germans – or at least Germans who were not yet likely to be in inglorious retreat. Numerous, insidious, grievous black dots.

The wait was over … or were the dots just in all our collective imaginations.

Whatever they were, there were a great many of them. They crossed the plain recklessly knowing that they were superior in numbers and that our ordnance would not cause them much damage. They were right. We drew back into the forest. The lorry was quickly driven off and we also drew back. But we had something they would not know we possessed. We had a map reference. I was drawn back first and Vitya carried the radio. We set it up and I sent the numbers back into the white sky. When the others arrived, we went deeper into the forest. A short time later, we heard the aircraft and the bombs. We had no way of knowing who had fired what. It was just too far away.

Russia North Western Front (Worcester Journal) Friday 10 December 1943 *Waiting Game* by Royston Thomas

After two weeks dug into the snow, the only thing that has changed for the men here is the amount of snow they have to dig. Each day there has been six or eight inches more of it to move, but for the last two days, there has been little. Today there has been none and the sky is clear.

The men feel some security in not being able to see through the falling snow - knowing that neither can the enemy. The Germans will not attack if they don't know our Russian unit is here. But today things may change.

On the first day that we camped here, everyone was alert and waiting. Every day since then the monotony has become deeper. Today we just wait. Those whose turn it is to be alert, look over the edges of the dug outs to the open space in front of us. Even though it is clear they are in danger of not being able to see if they stay too long. The danger this time is snow blindness.

Such blindness comes from staring into bright sun or glare for hours at a time. The sentries are particularly vulnerable and one is often seen rubbing his eyes as if there is something in them. Some suffer from headaches. The sentry will usually save himself from permanent damage because his vision becomes hazy and he stands down. He will recover in a day or two - if there is time and he is not called back to stand and stare. It is a kind of sunburn of the retina and can be permanent if the eyes are not cared for. Even those whose duties do not require continual scrutiny of the glaring snow plain will be found squinting with faces that hurt from the continual muscle tension. After weeks of grey snow and greyer skies, the brightness is all the more dangerous.

But the sun concentrates every mind to the potential for

a much more devastating kind of damage. One that also comes from the horizon – also out of the sun.

I folded my notebook shut, stuck the pencil between the pages and tucked them into my tunic pocket. We continued to wait – and wait. Each man's personal objective was to get through the next few hours or days, keep warm and not go mad. The men who were so far not psychologically or physically affected played card games that were impossible for me to understand. I was sure there were some cards missing and anyone who got to know which ones had a better chance of winning. A group of five or six men threw sticks, carefully measured so that they were all exactly the same, into a packed snow circle eight feet away. The winning stick was the one closest to the stake in the centre. It reminded me of the game of horseshoes. Hand grenades they called it. Vasili told me that it was a stupid game. 'Close, is good enough with hand grenades,' he grumbled.

Josef sat in his little snow hole carving faces on sticks. He told me that they were all Hitler and he'd modelled them on shadows in the snow that had a likeness. No one will get to judge the likeness because he burned them all, one by one, on his tiny fire.

I could find no one who could tell me why the unit was here. Vasili just shrugged when asked. 'We've got to stop the German bombs with something and there is plenty of Russian blood to make ice in the snow.' He grinned. 'But they don't know we are here!' he cackled slapping me on the back, 'Yet.'

I leaned back against the snow, in a depression now faintly shaped like my body. It was surprisingly comfortable. I looked down the bank. Yeva was doing her look out duty, leaning into the snow, binoculars partially hidden by the big scarf around her head, her rifle carefully balanced on the rim, within reach in a heartbeat. Her breath rose in slow tiny clouds. My hood fell forward onto my forehead. I watched the hairs on the front of my furry hat under it ripple as I exhaled – once, twice, once a little harder, then almost nothing when I breathed out slowly through my nose. As I inhaled I felt the tiny hairs inside my nostrils stung as they tugged in frozen clumps. One more breath, two. Perhaps if I blew my breath down, the hairs would not move – once more, and again –

The frozen earth beneath our position lifted in a huge plate before the noise of the shell and the flying snow hit us. More by instinct for self-preservation than training, everyone around me drew himself into a foetal shaped lump – except for Vasili who scrambled to the top. Orders and reports came from all sides as men recovered their equilibrium and scrambled for weapons and kit. Travkin waved everyone down below the parapet. Vasili grinned at me, 'three verst' - two miles. He gestured to the right of our position.

Before he can slide down from the top of the bank again, another huge quake and following crump with flying snow and branches erupted on our left. I felt sick. I knew they were ranging their guns – measuring the distance and position in which the shells would fall. Vasili slid down to crouch beside me. This time he was not smiling. He slowly raised one finger, two fingers and then three. He shook his head. I nodded, one left, one right and the third…where would it land?

Russia North Western Front (Worcester Journal) December 31, 1943 *Reporting Gets Harder* **by Royston Thomas**

Yeva shot him. She is our sniper. I did not know he was there until he fell into the snow with a whump and disappeared into the soft billows at the bottom of the tree. This left my companions with another problem of course since he may not be dead and any advancement on the hole would be a dangerous one. The NCO settled it with a well-placed grenade and body and tree combined in a slush of flesh and pine branches. The ensuing silence was bigger than the space it filled and we waited for responding fire. None arrived so we wiggled to the sloppy mound to see what we could find out. Surviving fragments of man and clothing identified him as a partisan – trigger-happy obviously, but on our side.

The time we spent back in the camp was as cold as it was when we were out on the patrols. The only advantage was that we could build fires in our little huts, huddle together and try to keep warm. The village looked like it was part of the snow. Deep slabs of it lay over all the buildings in softly undulating lumps. There were deep paths between them, cut deeper every time it snowed. They were hard packed and shiny where our feet had compressed the snow into solid surfaces and the children had polished them to a gloss by sliding on them. They were hardy little souls and played outside much of the time; cutting caves in the hard snow and making ramps for sliding on – usually on their boots at increasingly terrifying speed. They pulled each other along by their scarves and fought for anything that took their fancy with huge mitts that had no effect at all on their thick coats and hoods. It seemed difficult to get them to come in and they were outside all day, only disappearing inside when it snowed heavily. Even in the moonlight, there was still shrieking and laughter. Occasionally, the adults were happy to join in and, although I had further to fall and took a harder landing than they did, the joy of flying across packed snow was fun for everyone. Yurgi, Micha's son had a sled and the best run for the sled was from the roof of his house down the snow packed under the eaves and then a slight slope into the trees. Miraculously there were few accidents although the speed that it achieved by the time it crossed the path was frightening. Anyone on the path had the responsibility to be nimble because the sled could not be stopped once it was launched. Children here, like children anywhere had the ability to make fun with nothing and in spite of the terror that their fathers and mothers witnessed, created and took part in, their childhood was still one of joy – if only for a short time.

I had made no communication with the Laundry since I was in Kuibyshev. The freedom from the responsibility and guilt of that relationship were heavy coats to wear. I left the fear of discovery, the guilt of betrayal in a small radio set hidden in the wall panel in Moscow. I had replaced it with a bisected world in which Gleb Alekseev lugged a radio everywhere he went, reported on and received instructions every day that sent the men and women like Yeva, and poor Gleb off into a war from which there might be no return. And then there was Roy who found himself living in all that he hated, blood, death, fighting with the most savage methods known. He was a fugitive from sanity; a criminal living in holes; hiding from everything that was normal and compassionate. The ideals with which I had been gifted as a child and the stand that I had taken were all now impossible, irrelevant and one by one being lost anyway. I had no idea who I was any longer. But one person anchored me to her so strongly that she was all that mattered. Today, this moment and this picture of her were all that mattered. One moment, one day at a time. Tomorrow it might all be gone.

Coming back to our hut early one morning after another bland transmission to our higher ups, I stopped to feel the place in which I stood. The cathedral arches of trees made me stop and listen. There was only silent air – not the silence of a vacuum, but the silence of time. The air did not move, but the trees, although dormant, lived and breathed. The snow settled molecule by molecule. A little sloping sunlight, chased diamond flashes from the snow crystals as they lay in soft piles on the ground in the eternal winter. Moisture that froze in the air flickered in the sunlight. A lump of snow falling from a tall branch landed with the sound of an explosion. No birds moved, no animals travelled, no air moved. It was the silence of eternity. A silence of snow in time.

I scavenged as many boards and slabs from sawn trees as I could and lined the inside of our little hut. They covered many of the gaps in the outer ones and cut down on the swirling wind that blew snow across the floor and onto our bed. Then I stuffed the space between inner and outer with whatever sawdust, shavings, tree boughs, pine needles, anything I could find. It made a huge difference and when we had a good fire in the tin heater, we were able to take off some layers of clothing.

We had wood that we collected all summer just to keep us warm in the winter, but extra was always useful. In digging out some broken branches, I pulled a metal trough out of the snow. It was a cattle trough. I remembered it from the summer, but right now, to me it said 'bath' and I promised myself that I would bring it back when the cattle were again put out. I filled it with wood and branches and dragged it back to the hut like a sledge. I cleaned it up and then took it inside. I looked at the relative sizes of the tank and the little tin heater. I tried to balance the tank on it and saw the impracticalities of keeping it stable once full of snow.

18

January 1944

The alternative was to melt buckets of snow one at a time. By the time the second one melted, the water from the first would already be cold. The job had to be done on the top of the stove. I went out to source more wood.

When Yeva came in she saw a trough about four feet long and two feet wide precariously balanced on our little tin heater, propped with sticks of wood so as not to fall over. 'What is this for?' she gulped between hoots of laughter.

'This is my bath. I long for a bath – a soak in hot water.'

'A bath! In this weather? You are so, so… English.'

'No, I'm Welsh… but we have baths too.' I had to defend my nationality.

She hooted again, snorting with glee.

In the end, she participated with enthusiasm and when the water was nearly boiling, we struggled to get it off the stove and the props and onto the floor without flooding the entire hut. Then we put more buckets on the stove and around it to provide more hot water when we needed it. We added snow to cool down what we had and then I got in. Yeva giggling as I did so. It was bliss. The sides were straight and there was a lip around the edge so I couldn't lay back but I felt all the muscles in my legs and lower back relax. I pulled up my legs, 'Come in, there's room for you too. Bring some vodka. Hot bath water needs vodka.'

Still giggling, she handed me the crock of vodka, got out of her clothes and delicately put one foot, then the other into the water. Then she lowered herself into the other end. I saw her face dissolve into relaxation. We sat there for some time, one of us getting out from time to time taking out cool bath water, adding some more warm water from the bucket on the stove and putting more on to re heat. And we talked. And we drank rather a lot – a great deal in fact.

Being in a tub with a friend, I decided was one of the most companionable places to be. It took away all the outside influences of clothing and with it went the pretence of time and place. We were who we were, no more, no less and it was honest and above all it was warm.

As we sat there with the cold air on our shoulders and warm water steaming lightly around us, we relaxed. We talked about spring, about being a child and being who we were. In that hour or more, I learned about being alive, being happy and I learned about being in love. Not only did I want to stay forever in this hot bath, but I wanted to stay close to this woman for the rest of my life. I did not allow the reality of this present tiny situation or larger world wide politics to put so much as a ripple on the feelings I had for her. If our lives never became better, or easier or longer or softer I didn't care. It was now and here and her that mattered. It was happiness like I had never hoped to feel. A shiver of the future breathed across my bare back. I had so much to lose – so much could happen – so much could disappear forever.

Darkness was falling, but neither of us wanted to get up and light the candle. Yeva was wringing out her long braid, just as there was a terrifying banging on the door. 'Yeva Vilenovna! Gleb Alekseev! Are you there? I have come to visit!'

With the first bang on the door, Yeva dived half out of the tank with a large wave of water that swamped the floor and grabbed for the Mosin. It was never far away from her hand. Then she slid back into the water to cover herself.

It was Maks. He was a committed partisan, if a little slow and not the brightest button in the box. He saw us as some sort of place of safety. We encouraged him to talk and sort out his jumbled thoughts. We tried not to ridicule or tease him. He liked to come to our hut. We fed him and warmed him up at our little stove. But there were times when we found him to be more than we wanted to take on.

'Go away!' I shouted. 'We are not having visitors tonight.'

There was a pause on the other side of the door. 'Are you sure?'

'Yes!' we called in unison.

'Not even me?'

'No!'

There were a few seconds silence and then we heard Maks giggling. 'Right! Right!' The giggle turned to a snicker and then we heard him crunching over the packed snow back where he had come from. 'I will tell the others not to disturb.'

223

There was more laughter.

Yeva took the vodka from my hand, raised the earthenware bottle in a toast. 'Naked but right. Naked but warm.' Then she had a long drink and closed her eyes.

Russia North Western Front (Worcester Journal) 10 January 1944 *Snow Bound on the Russian Plain* by Royston Thomas

In deepening weather, our lorry has become stuck in snow as hard as concrete; the tracked wheels are jammed solid. As soon as we dig a wheel free, the wind packs it full again. It is threatening to overturn. We had managed to keep it moving but it has dug itself deeper and deeper into the unknown depths of white. Still we dig. Maks has lapsed into a layer of language that I can no longer understand.

The canvas covers had been spread to provide some shelter for the men, and the NCO who dug beside them. The process was hopeless and we all knew it, but the exercise was the only means by which we could keep warm. Although that term was perhaps relative as hands were freezing in wet gloves and mitts, ears were white from wind sucking under the flaps of our scarves and hats. Feet mercifully stayed dry; the snow was too cold to melt unless it was ground between shovel handle and leather. The sentries were the ones to be pitied; staring into the white air where no definition meant no depth perception. Anything advancing, were it foolish enough to do so, could be half a mile or five miles away; it was all the same. Still we dug.

By mid-afternoon, it was too dark to see but thankfully the wind dropped a little. We gave up on the trucks and dug a deeper hole in the snow, pulled the tarpaulin over, lit a fire and doubled the sentries. Maybe we would survive until morning when we could expect to be sitting ducks if the weather cleared.

Days later we were in a new position, under the edge of a forest. Vitya said we were to wait here and watch. 'For Germans,' he grinned. 'Bloody Germans.' His English improved with the swear words he picked up from me. The moon was a bronze smudge just above the distant tree line. It looked as if it was too timid to show its face tonight, skulking behind thin clouds. It was hard to believe that this same moon shone on the rest of the world; places where it was warm, where there were camels and sand, where there were people in tents, singing or storytelling, places where there was no terror, no danger, places where there was peace, places where there were people moving in its romantic light.

We were making progress more or less in the direction our orders had commanded. We had replaced our damaged compass and maps, but the new ones were years older than the ones we had in the first place, so we felt confident only when we visually confirmed what we found on the torn and dirty papers we did our meticulous planning on.

'There is a time and a place.' Romas rammed the weapon back into his enormous leather belt. He cackled through his missing teeth and shot a gob of phlegm into the soft snow where it slowly sank out of sight.

Watching as it disappeared and then looking again at the dark smooth wooden object I felt somewhat queasy. There was something about seeing the bloody means of murder up close that gave finality to what we were here to do.

I'd seen German after German fall under Yeva's sniper rifle and knew that they had been dead instantly and that somehow put distance between the act and the reality. This object had no name, but it was loved by its owner. He'd polished it smooth with sweat and fat. It glowed under his love and attention. He had created it, loved it and cared for it.

He'd also put it to lethal use – up close where you could smell a man's sweat.

I turned away and saw Yeva polishing the stock of her rifle.

15 January44 It is dark now. We have moved back into the forest as far as we can push the vehiclse and stopped where we feel safe. The engines has been drained of water, so that we do not need to run them all night. If we have time in the morning, we will melt snow and refill the radiators before we try to start them again. Vasili is not above lighting fires underneath them if necessary. He says he doesn't care if they burs up. He rubs his hands and grins.

We thawed out our rations and brewed tea over tiny gas stoves. It was an improvement on many night time stops I can remember when we ate nothing and had no heat or comfort from a fire at all. We slept in the snow under whatever shelter we could create from brush, canvas, blankets or coats. Vitya curled into a shell of snow and slept happily in whatever he was wearing. He never suffered from the cold he told me – at least I think that was what he said.

In the morning, I panicked when Yeva disappeared. Shells were falling everywhere. Tent, bivouacs, stores blown up. Vasili ordered us to the lorries – by now we had two to keep from freezing solid. I raced around screaming until I found her dragging the small stove, mess tins and weapons out of the canvas bivouac as if it were the last act that would win the war. She told me angrily that I had to care for myself not her. I don't understand Russian soldiers especially women soldiers. We were the last aboard the lorry. I was angry. So was she.

The Germans doing the firing were a crew with a lone gun – lost probably and retreating in front of us – and startled by finding us. A few of our shells finished them but we moved on quickly as the commotion might bring others with bigger guns than ours.

We did not stop to see if they were all dead or to offer any assistance if they weren't. I have witnessed this time and time again and by now I have learned to control my panic at the possibility of wounded men dying without some kind of compassionate help. I know very well that the practicalities are beyond us. For every prisoner, two or three men must be taken out of active work to guard them. It was the same for wounded prisoners, but with the addition of first aid or medical skill and yet more manpower to care for them. We did not have enough people to do this. They had to remain in the snow and die. It was something my heart could not relax with. It would never sit well with my soul. It was something I would have to carry in my heart, quietly and alone, forever.

When we returned to our village again I felt as if I'd returned from hell. The normality and calmness of the place was a sauce that covered the cinders of what I knew and had seen. I felt that, perhaps, I could get some of my own self back from the abyss.

For some days we had little to do. So we mended our kit and cleaned the weapons. I sent messages one after the other, reports on what we had done, where we had been and what death and destruction we had achieved. I also gave some English lessons to the children. Some of the men and women also came, to watch their children they said, but in reality to learn as well. It was so little I could do and it would never be of any practical benefit, but the experience of learning was exciting for them.

In the evenings, we gathered in the meeting room/school room. It was one room we could keep warm with our collective body heat and a little tin stove in the middle. Sometimes they talked and I listened. I felt invisible at times like these; there was so little that I could contribute. They asked me about England from time to time – Wales was too difficult for them to place, so I used England to mean both. It was hard to describe our politics and the theory of one person one vote ever amounting to government that achieved anything, was a broad one to understand. I think perhaps they were just being polite.

Other nights there was music and sometime dancing. It went past the heart and straight to the spirit; the dancing terrifying. Men rarely danced with women and even if I knew how, I would have been crushed in the attempt. It was all very energetic with a lot of deep knee bends, waving and shouting. Far too much for a feeble Methodist to take on but I tried and provided great fun for everyone else.

The music on the other hand could tear the soul from my body. It was wind in the trees, the grass swaying on the steppes and sleighs on the snow. It was produced by a balalaika; a four stringed triangular instrument with a long neck played something like a guitar. But the sound of it immediately took us all away from the here and now. The player of this lute with the magic power to transport was Bogdan. He was a slight young man and I wondered why he was here – he was no political fanatic and had no skills that might have come from military training. Perhaps he was an artist or musical student, cut adrift in the maelstrom of life in Russia in this Great Patriotic War. But his right hand plucking the strings and his left on the frets called up memories in everyone – child or adult, Russian or Welsh alike. It was taste of true magic. Yeva leaned against me and I pulled her towards my heart so that we were transported together. In the gloom of the room, I saw Makar reach for his wife's hand and Stepan rock the child on his lap. These were men like me, men with families and love to give. They had other terrible tasks to perform and maybe their lives to surrender, but they were not in-human. They had souls.

That night I watched Yeva as she sat on the edge of our mattress and brushed her hair with a brush that had lost its handle. She pulled it over her shoulder and brushed the knots from the ends. It glowed in the candle light and she saw me looking at her. I smiled – how could I not? The light showed the planes of her face; thinner now than when we met; skin like the petals from my mother's irises; eyebrows that could say so much from a scream of derision for something stupid I'd said or done, to a line of love and concern that made the moment into eternity.

'What?' She began to braid it again. 'What is so fascinating?'

I took her hands away and combed out the braid with my fingers. It felt like cream from the milk churn, the silk of my mother's scarf. 'This. This is like white gold.' She leaned towards me and kissed me. I held her in my arms and we lay back together. 'If I were to die tomorrow, the picture of you brushing your hair will be the last thing I see in my mind.'

'And if I die first?'

'Then, the picture will be here.' I put her hand over my heart. 'Forever.' I rubbed her fingers. 'If I ever lose you, the picture will here and so will you.'

The row made me break off transmission. The others witnessing it did not intervene.

Savarov had been left under a cloud as far as HQ was concerned by the disappearance of the Commissar Simonvic Rytin some months ago. There was speculation about his fate, of course, but no one formed a strong opinion. Most of us were glad he had gone, wherever it was. Theother one who was like a wraith had been recalled to no one's disappointment. None of us liked either of them. Pavel Nikolayevich puffed himself up to defend the Commissar and in so doing made comments about the Party in general and Stalin in particular. He talked about the evil man being a saint and father of the country. Savarov had seen much in his life and something snapped in him. He'd had enough.

'How many people have disappeared, you idiot?' he shouted. 'Disappeared, denounced, sent to prison for the rest of their lives, for what? For doing what? For saying what?' He leaned toward Pavel, his face uncharacteristically flushed.

Pavel Nikolayevich shouted back. 'For talking against the Party, for being traitors! Don't be sentimental about them! They deserve to die!'

'Did 3 million people deserve to starve to death in the 1930's? Because of Stalin's order? Did they deserve to be sent off their land, to die where they fell?'

'Lies! Lies! You deserve to be denounced yourself!'

'You stupid young zealot! What do you know? Do you know anyone who was denounced and never heard of again? Do you know what happened to them? Do you know what kind of torture they had to endure? Do you know how gruesome their death? Don't condemn me until you know what happens to people!' Something about the emotion with which Savarov spoke told me he knew much.

'I know of no one, because there is no one! No one has been sent to the prisons or the gulags unless they deserve it. They are guilty.'

'Guilty? Of course they are guilty. How can they not be guilty? No one speaks in their defence! The only ones to be heard are the ones who denounce them and lie to preserve their own lives. That is where the lies are!'

I looked desperately for Yeva. This was a story she did not want to hear. But I saw her, pale and small behind the group. She had heard every word. But then, Pavel Nikolayevich made a lunge for Savarov but was hauled back by the others. Everyone was breathing hard and staring in horror at the two of them. Savarov flicked his head, 'Take him away from my sight. I never want to see him again. *Ublyudok!* Bastard!' Pavel Nikolayevich was forced away by two large fellows. I wondered if I would ever see him again. It was the Russian way I was beginning to realise.

Later, Savarov had calmed himself and brought some vodka to sit with me in the radio hut. 'Is this true Savarov?' I asked.

He looked at me pityingly. 'Of course it is true. It is the way of this country now.' He leaned towards me. 'You must get the information out. You must tell England what happens here. You must survive this war and tell.'

'What do you want me to tell? Please speak plainly. I can reach England. I can tell them now.' If I tried hard, if I could remember the frequencies, if I dared.

He poured two large vodkas. I hoped I would remain sober enough to remember what he was going to tell me. 'No one is safe in this country. Even now that we may be winning this war, we are in danger. The only people who will survive both the war and the peace are those who do nothing, say nothing, have no aspirations, give nothing, take nothing, are nobodies or those who climb quickly enough without mistake and become like Stalin himself – or worse. *Sukin syn Son of a bitch.*' He drank the vodka down in one gulp, coughed as it hit his throat and poured another. 'They however have a slipperier path to climb.' He got out his tobacco pouch and rolled an ugly, oily cigarette.

'Why is that?'

He smiled around the cigarette as he put it between his lips to light. 'Because Stalin knows who they are.'

'And you?'

'Stalin does not know who I am – yet – but others do. I will not survive long.'

'And Pavel Nikolayevich?' But Savarov just shrugged and got up. 'Tell England.'

The one person I could not tell was Yeva. It was all too close to her own story. I could not make it worse for her. But she had heard the argument. The camp was alive with it and she would hear the gossip too.

SA44 Western Russia to RT19 British Embassy 28 Jan 1012 219 Information that Stalin's campaigns of death caused death by starvation of 3 million plus in 1930s Many now are sent to jail or death because of false or incomplete accusations of others Rules by terror and intimidation Has probably caused more death that Hitler

SA44 Western Russia to RT19 British Embassy 31 Jan 0947 253 Commander in row with Commissar HQ sent warning of his behaviour with possible demotion All partisans support him Do not expect any retribution by Russian government But he may disappear like others Shot or died in prison No defence no justice No promotion by merit here Submission by intimidation fear

In my heart, I knew that the Embassy, Britain and probably most of the world knew this already, but could do nothing.

.'Yes, I know. My parents knew too.' Yeva and I sat on a log soft with moss in a boggy part of the forest now frozen beneath the water and deep into the ground. There were many of these places, marshy in summer, full of water, grasses, fallen trees. Little pathways wound through them on higher and slightly drier ground. Now we kicked the snow aside and made our own path. I paraphrased Savarov's feelings on the failings of Stalin's communism.

'They were there one day doing their everyday work – my father was a school teacher, my mother managed a children's nursery. Then late one night there is a banging on the door – the police ... that is the last anyone knows.' Even her iron clad exterior showed thin places and I could feel an emotion in her voice.

'Don't.' But she put her finger on my lips. 'I can only tell you what I know – I can't tell you what I think or what I suppose. Only what I know.' I nodded and she continued. 'My father's sister wrote to me while I was at the hospital. It came through the mail system – somehow it got to me – she did not sign the note, but I knew it was from her. She told me in a coded way where to look for the rest of the message and so I knew it was not good news. I went to my grandmother's old cottage and found what else she had written. She had hidden it in a stone wall. It was not far from Moscow. Clandestine? Yes? We could not speak openly and if I went to see her, it would mean the arrest of both of us.'

I could not interrupt what she was feeling and I did not want to stop her and miss what I wanted desperately to know.

'My parents were taken away at night. They took nothing with them of value. Their neighbour went into their apartment to clean after they had been missing for a few months. She found that much had been searched. She did not know what might have been taken.'

'Could there have been anything incriminating?'

'Probably. Who knows. They may have been traitors. They would not have told me would they?' I reached for her hand, put it on my thigh and pressed it hard against my leg. 'My aunt said what she had heard – she could not ask directly – and even she was interrogated, but they did not charge her – she knew nothing. She heard that they had been sent to Lubyanka, to be interrogated.' Here her voice failed for a second and she squeezed my leg muscles as if wanting to find courage in them. 'I do not know what interrogation means, but some have survived it and they speak little about it. Any imagination ...'

She looked to the sky and shut her eyes tightly, then opened them again. 'They say that Lubyanka is the tallest building in Moscow, since from its basement you can see Siberia.' Her laugh was bitter and shrill.

I let go of her hand and put my arm around her. She leaned on my shoulder. 'They were found guilty of being enemies of the state or something else equally stupid and then sentenced. We don't know where they were sent. If they were sent together or separated or even if they are still alive.'

'How do you know? Can you find out more?'

She sat up straighter and wiped her eyes with the back of her hand. 'My aunt gave me that information from our neighbour who knows someone who works at the court, but that is all. They have disappeared.'

'Can we find them?' She looked up sharply. 'When the war is over, I mean.'

'No!'

'But why not? Don't you want to know and maybe, I don't know, see them or...'

She smiled at me sadly. 'You don't understand do you? They are enemies of the state.'

'But if they are not guilty?'

They have been arrested and sentenced.' She spoke sharply. 'So they are guilty. Even if they did nothing, they are guilty. And if I try to find them or communicate, or argue, I am guilty too. They are gone – forever.' She pulled away from me. 'Maybe they really are guilty.'

This is the terror, the fear of denouncement. The fear of disappearing or being found out whether rightly or wrongly. This is the terror that keeps people from even imagining a revolt or uprising. Even in their most private thoughts.

21 Feb 1944 At home it will be spring. Here it gets colder, the air gets harder. Feels as if a shell could not crack it.

Today the site we sought was on the horizon just ahead and I went ahead with a small party to determine if it would be adequate for our reconnaissance. We needed a place where we could watch and report on any German movements, their size and direction. Partisans all over the marsh and its environs were watching the retreat, harassing it and catching stragglers. The place designated to us was in a forested area with piles of high rocks and if it was the place from which we could watch, I was to signal to the rest. All was quiet and there was no sign in the snow of human activity. I was therefore unprepared for the shot when it came.

The wound on my right arm was only a flesh one the Sergeant informed me as they bound it up. He sounded impatient and I was reminded that he probably didn't want me along in the first place. But it made transmitting my report up the chain of command a problem. I prayed that it arrived at the other end in an encryption still intact.

Russia North Western Front (Worcester Journal) Friday 18 February 1944 *Fighter Attack* **by Royston Thomas**

Is smoke rising from the hut or not? It is an important debate but from a mile away, our binoculars cannot make us sure. To call it a hut is only a term in lieu of anything more accurate. In truth it is just a mound in the snow; but there may be smoke rising from it and that makes it a dangerous mound.

Temperatures that rose and cloud cover that did not were our salvation from the storm. The snow softened and we were able to dig ourselves out, but it meant being wet through. A young lad suffered from frozen toes on one foot and Vitya was ordered to open his jacket and shirt to warm them again. The pain of returning circulation is unbearable for all of us. He may lose his toes; he may not. We hope we can save them as frostbite is a disciplinary offence in the Red Army.

Two small white clad figures are crawling over the open space between us and the hut; their breath making clouds larger than that which they are sent to investigate. This may be a German forward base; it may be a peasant stubborn and refusing to leave; it may be spumes of snow blowing from a cusp of snowdrift. We wait buried in our individual shallow snowy graves spread across half a mile of plain, eyes burning in the whiteness. The horizon blends into the sky and the tiny white figures ahead are lost in the space between land and air. The wind blows towards us, creating its own sound and taking our body heat away as it passes.

It is probably the reason why we don't hear the plane. It rises from behind our truck on the glassy roadway, sends it into fireballs that glare painful and red on our seared retinas. The pilot drives the plane forward and over us, guns splattering ordnance into the snow towards and past us. Then he pulls straight up into the sky, turns over and disappears.

It is probably to our benefit that we have no chance to fire back. He may not have even seen us, but merely leaned on his firing button a second too long, shedding rounds so that he did not have to explain when he got back to base why he had not fired them. But Vitya is dead and so is the boy we'd left in the truck.

The hut turned out to be a Russian transmitting station so it was as well that we found out before we dropped grenades down the chimney. They won't have lit a fire since, but they won't freeze if they stay dug in and they'll get used to it. They have regular communication with lines behind so we were able to send our wounded back for medical attention, but the boy with the frozen toes and his companion, my friend were left in the snow.

I wrote for Donaldson even if there was no hope of getting the copy out – someday it would be found. At the moment, that is all I can hope. That someday it will be found out.

10 May 1944 The sound comes with the air – we are not aware of it at first – it is lost to the heave of our breath. Closer and the sound tells us what it is – it invites us into a copse – a tiny wooden church. The priest sings – the sound coats our ragged nerves – we sit in the long grass outside – Christian or not it heals and soothes. Later when we are sane again, and with as little noise as we can manage, we rise, refreshed and continue.

The amazing tiny wooden building with a steep roof and spire shaped like a double tear drop was embellished with exquisite wood carving: gutters, roof line, window and door frames, pilasters and capitals. Walls were covered with horizontal or vertical boards and even these had been moulded by skilled carpenters. Here and there were repairs, less finely done and it looked to my uneducated eyes as if it needed care and attention. There was no glass in the windows and I could see no shutters. It was probably not used in the winter, but today it was alive with sound. I felt as if my soul had been blown full of bubbles. No one spoke. No one disturbed the feeling. Did the others feel the same? We did not say. But for a moment, I felt in touch with my faith again. God had reached out for me. God had found me wanting.

Here I am, a pack on my back containing a small radio set, my spare socks, a little food, a water bottle and a rifle over my shoulder. How was God going to see me? How was I going to explain this to God? I looked over my shoulder at the lovely building retreating behind me. Would it survive much longer? Would I survive much longer? Would my soul be worth saving?

I made a decision all that time ago – a lifetime ago – that I was not going to engage in active combat. I was not going to join the military. I was not going to take part. How could I possibly justify what I looked like now? How could I possibly explain to God what I had done? How could I accept what I might be expected to do in the future? And that was the beating heart of my fear. What would I be expected to do? What would I be forced to do? But was it always by force? Did I have no free will left? Could I no longer make decisions about my own morals?

How far had I fallen? I had at last married the woman with whom I had been living, but that didn't make my earlier sins right. It wasn't even a Christian marriage; just a legal transaction. I've seen men killed in front of me and done nothing to stop it. I had done nothing to help them in their pain and their last moments. I had loaded the weapons in order for others to kill them. *Dear God. Why do You even speak to me? I am no longer worthy of Your attention. I am truly lost.*

But is that not the time when God finds us? While there is still time for a soul to be saved? Can I still be saved? Can I possibly end this and go back to being a decent Christian with morals and faith? There was a large silence in my heart. No of course not. There was no going back now. Even if I wanted to, I could not escape. I was in a huge machine that I could not influence. I could not get away from its power over me. I was trapped. Trapped in my own faithless desire for this woman and in the war's demands on both of us. I could not escape.

19

June1944

On a night in our village when there seem to be no night because of a strong moon, Vlad Ivanych Pronin, an informer came to Savarov with news. Like everyone else, he was thin. Even his hair was thin. But he was probably only about 30 years old. He wore the clothes of a peasant, but for all we knew he could have been a university lecturer. I had long ago learned that no one wanted to be noticed in this country. Everyone hid. He had found a dead German and brought us papers we might be interested in. Savarov handed the papers to me to translate. The dead man's identification card indicated that he was with a Chemical Regiment. I was naïve enough to be shocked by this revelation, but Savarov was not. He gathered us around. 'We must find where this,' he slapped the card on his hand, '... these ... where they are.' He was angry; I had seldom known him to be lost for words.

I was naive enough too, to ask questions. 'Is this news to you?'

'No,' he shook his head. 'We have known about the Germans and their chemical intentions for years. They have not yet used them, for which we are thankful, but now that they are becoming more desperate, they might do so.'

'What can we do?'

He smiled through his broken teeth. 'We can destroy the site.'

Somehow I knew that was what he would say. He called for Sasha who hurried up with Savarov's pack. Savarov rummaged in it and extracted a large map. It was old, but had enough detail to be useful. He laid it on the ground and we knelt around it.

He studied the map for a few minutes then pointed. 'We are here. Where was

235

the chemical site?' Vlad Ivanych studied the map and traced his way west before stabbing at the map. 'Here. It is a small place – ten to fifteen men can take it. But we must be swift. There are signs that they are planning to leave.'

'Well then…' I didn't realise that I had spoken.

Filat put his hand on my shoulder and spoke very quietly. 'Because they kill everyone who has worked for them to keep the work a secret. Then they kill everyone in the village in case they know what happens behind the wire. Maybe even let the chemicals go.'

I put my head on my knees. This war had to end. It had to end soon. The inhumanity in it had to stop. I know I had tears on my cheeks when I looked up again. The others were already discussing how to kill the right people and free the others and did not see my weakness.

'Fifteen men!'

'But there are only eight of us left.'

'The others won't be back for five days.'

'How can we…'

Savarov lifted his hand and quiet returned. 'We will plan very well.'

Those who know how to do these things then planned a search. We went out later in darkness and after two nights away from the forest, found the site, a large complex that had been a slaughter house and sausage factory in another lifetime. Those who know how to do these things, assessed the number of personnel on the site, what their weaponry was like, any defences they had and how well they were manned, especially during darkness. Others were sent to locate the best way for us to approach the place – there might be several pathways we could use and perhaps several simultaneous assaults might be possible. Although just how eight of us were meant to do this I dared not think. Then they looked for and planned our best withdrawal routes.

I was sent with Misha and of course Yeva. As usual she had the Mosins and pockets bulging with cartridges. She knew that no shots could be fired until the time came for the assault. The killing for now, if there was to be any, would have to be a quieter affair. But she was prepared. We maintained a watch on the towers around the perimeter. We had signals to use if it seemed that the others had been seen and an alarm was necessary. We retreated to our sheltered camp at dusk.

That night Vlad Ivanych disappeared and two shambling figures returned early the next evening. Vlad Ivanych and the Source - that was all we were

236

allowed to call him – who was tall, dressed in loose trousers and loose shirt with a flat cap like most of the rest of us. He carried a short coat and had a long strap over his shoulder with a bag that he carried against his back. When he reached us and was introduced to Savarov, he straightened his spine and accepted a drink of kvass. When he spoke it was apparent that he was an educated man. Now we were nine to accomplish this.

'I work on the site and in the morning, I took Vlad Ivanych into the compound in place of someone who was ill today.' Vlad Ivanych nodded and handed him the bottle.

The Source took another drink, wiped his mouth with the back of his hand and passed the bottle to Savarov beside him. 'The barracks are in a warehouse and the chemicals are stored in another storehouse at the back of the site and in the old slaughter house. The processing plant is in the old factory buildings. But there is little processing going on. Mostly we are packing up the materials and canisters for transport.' He drew a little plan in the dust.

It was my turn for the bottle. 'What chemicals? Would we cause much damage if we…? But I was interrupted by laughter.

'This man is chemist.' Savarov belted the man on the back. 'Is from Red Army. He knows his chemicals!'

The Source looked grave. 'Is good question. Most of the chemicals are components that could be made into mustard gas and others that rely on wind dispersal. Used in last great war.'

I shuddered inside.

'Things like thiodiglycol or phosgene.' Even in Russian I could smell through the language and taste the horror of what these might bring. 'There are also gas masks, chemical suits, empty chemodan – heavy shells.'

Bogdan, the musician leaned forward. 'Are they still planning to retreat or…'

The Source interrupted. 'They may bury it or destroy it after they have taken care of the workers. They may be taking it to a safer place in order to use it elsewhere.'

That brought silence and we knew how important this was going to be.

The Source went on. 'The workers come in each day from outside the plant. They come from the little village on the other side of the site and are transported by lorry. Entire village is heavily guarded as is the plant, but there are only a few at night. There is a double wire electrified fence around the plant; the electricity is provided by a generator inside small building by the administration building – the old packing house – now empty except for the generator.'

I sat up at the mention of the generator. But Yeva caught my arm and shook her head. There would be no time and it would be too big.

'Other smaller buildings are for stores, chemicals, food, munitions and other necessities. A lorry convoy arrives about 9 pm bringing what might be needed for the next day or weeks. Not much. It is parked overnight until the workers arrive at 6. We unload the vehicles and then reload them. The convoy leaves again about 4 pm and new one arrives again at 9.'

Yeva let go of my arm. 'The radio?'

'The radio is housed in the office of the old warehouse - near the entrance to the barracks - but manned only during day light hours. At night the gates are double locked and there is a patrol on the inside. Outside several hundred meters from the fence, are watchtowers with machine guns and observers with telephones wired to the main site. You have already seen these.'

'What about the villagers?'

'We will inform them to wait until they hear the explosions and then they can deal with their guards. There will be confusion. You can be gone by then.'

Savarov let the air quieten for a few seconds and then began the plan. Our Source and Vlad Ivanych would go into the site as usual but hide and remain on the site at the end of the day. The workers were rarely counted on the way out. At 3 am, he would disable the electric generator which would allow the fence to be cut and the rest of us to enter. The building was never locked.

Others organised the weaponry we had brought with us, planned the sequence of the attack. Still others planned our retreat and support to get us out of the area once the work had been done or if there was need for a rapid exit.

Once the Source had cut the electricity supply the watchtowers would be climbed and the sentries silenced. Others would dispatch the walking sentries.

Yeva and I were to get to the radio house as soon as the fencing was cut, steal whatever papers we could, especially code books. Yeva would then throw a hand grenade into the building as we left.

At the same time another team would grenade the doors of the barracks to confuse the men and keep them pinned inside. Others would blow up some of chemical machinery in the sklad cementa – the store house – to which the Source would direct them, but not the chemicals themselves. Also to be blown up, the munitions store and the lorries parked on the roadway, but only to disable, not to destroy. That might release chemicals. The first lorry and the last lorry would be the targets. They would be parked nose to tail and disabling the head of the column and the last would make it impossible to get the others out. The stored chemicals would be left for another group of Partisans or the Red Army to deal with later.

Then everyone would retreat in the dark. No one was to do more than they were sent to do. There was to be no heroics. Any Germans who escaped would be picked off later.

Planning done, Savarov leaned back on his heels. 'Proche parenoy repi,' he grinned. 'Simple – anyone can do it.' We were assigned to our tasks and retreated to assemble the explosives we needed from the heavy packs we had brought

The assault was perfect. It was all over in 30 minutes and we were on our way back to our village. No one followed us.

At night, in our own village while Yeva slept I stood at the door listening to the light wind in the trees above our roof and the light rain on the leaves. Tonight it was warm misty rain. The kind that felt like fog with menace.

I had to admit that I was not clever. I didn't understand people who were not what they led me to believe they were. I did not have a means to deal with falseness. The leaders of this country could do what they liked with people's lives regardless of what was the truth about them. On the say-so of anyone with a grudge or a differing opinion, someone's life could be ruined or taken away completely. Were the people who supported this kind of regime in their hearts false as well? Had they been convinced or had they convinced themselves? Perhaps not convinced; perhaps it was merely the safer path. Perhaps that was all. But it was all false. The whole country was false. It was true to nothing. Was the Laundry false? They still infested my thoughts from time to time. They had wanted me to transmit reports from a British spy and then wanted more – information about the financial situation in the country. It made no sense at all, surely their 'spy' would know better than I did.

I slid down the door frame and sat on the step, the rain landing in wisps on my bare feet. The weight of the reality was too heavy to carry. There was to be no end to this war. It was going to go on and on. Europe and this poor country Russia, were to be blown up and damaged even further, until there was no one left standing. More men and women were to die. Is that what they wanted? Is that how this would all end?

I went out to the main yard in front of our hut and let the mist from the rain cover my face and my bare shoulders. What could I do? I could not stop any of this and could hardly be successful in changing the opinion of the British Government. Who would listen to me? Me. A known CO. It was to be expected that I would protest against further violence. My opinion would count for nothing. Nothing at all. My head began to feel feeble. I went back to the step and put my head between my knees.

I had told no one what my deepest mission was. Not even Adrian knew. And I had failed spectacularly. I sent the few reports I had been given without knowing what they contained. Information from a spy – a spy for the British Government. If that was true – and I had no reason not to believe it was so – then why was my part such a convoluted way of communication? The Laundry wanted it this way. Why? Didn't their spy have better information than my displaced and probably misplaced observations?

For all intents and purposes I was very alone. I looked at Yeva with her blanket pulled up to her chin and her jacket over her feet. Not completely alone.

SA44 Western Russia to RT19 British Embassy 10 July 1144 115 Sent on reconnaissance more frequently Following retreating Germans Much area unoccupied But not ours Rogue groups of both sides exist

The air around us all was calmer now. Most of the German terror was fading. There were many groups still active of course and we had to maintain our usual high tension and caution. The front line was still somewhere to the east of us; our area of Western Russia was still technically occupied and in spite of our sense that the end was approaching, we could still be overrun by retreating German forces or Red Army ones chasing them. It was not yet over for us.

Russia North Western Front (Worcester Journal) Thursday 24 July 1944 *War Garden* by Royston Thomas

When the infantry had finished there wasn't much left. Only an old peasant woman and an old man standing at the edge of what had been their vegetable garden, staring at the devastation.

I saw what they saw – crushed stalks of not yet ripe sweet corn, row after broken row. Scattered and shattered greenery that was once the growing tops of potatoes and beetroot. Fine parsnips now ripped from the ground - twisted and split- they lay among the pulverised swedes and carrots. Salads, carefully nurtured to produce a second growth for the late summer were slippery, torn and flattened. Beans and peas for drying might yet be saved from a few unbroken pods among the ragged plants, but they would be few.

I also saw what they could not – the miles and miles of destruction around their tiny plot. I also saw the winter of hardship and hunger that was to come. And I saw nothing – nothing in their eyes or on their faces. It wasn't acceptance – it wasn't hate or blame – it wasn't hurt or anger – it was just nothing. Inscrutable nothingness.

Their ragged clothes would hardly be sufficient; their surviving animals were thin and few and would be fodder for the next army of one persuasion or another to come past. Their tiny mud covered hovel and whatever it may have contained was all they had left; it was too vulnerable to a shell or tank.

I saw him clutch her hand for a second and I knew that they saw much more than I could. They saw a lifetime of hardship – hard work on a hard landscape - a lifetime in which they had only each other. Whether there was love between them was a moot issue, they depended on each other and probably always had. Today was not hugely different than the thousands that had gone before. Each day was filled with just the need to survive. They saw today only as it leaned into tomorrow.

Then I saw a stake hammered into the edge of the garden plot on which was a sign in Russian that warned 'Do not enter – unexploded shells' – but who knew if either of them could read.

Then we walked on.

'Gleb?'

'Sorry, milaya? Have I kept you awake?'

'You are busy tonight.' She wrapped the blanket around her shoulders pulling it tightly against the autumn chill and came over to me. 'Who are you transmitting to? The Embassy again?'

I avoided the truthful answer. 'Just commenting on the Red Army's successes.' I coiled up the headphones and wires and put them in their box.

She stretched and yawned. Her hair tied loosely back, she looked like a child just woken from sleep. I opened my arms to her. I held her close and she leaned on my shoulder. 'They will not stop now until they reach England!'

A terrifying chill hit me between the shoulder blades. Russia may indeed win the war here and then…then what? Where? Maybe they could get all the way to Berlin; maybe all the way to Britain. The chill would not let my brain continue the thought.

In the morning, I sat at the radio set with a small pile of transmissions to send. With the headphones on, I shut out the world and retreated into my own head. Yeva's comment last night filled all the space in my head and I had to force a little niche in it in which to think. Is this what the Laundry's spy was telling them?

So why was the Laundry so happy to hear of their great advances in that direction? The question began to answer itself. The answer was not what I wanted to hear. The alternative. The alternative to democracy. With all its faults it was still a democracy. Wasn't that what this war had all been about? OK. I admitted I was naive. Not just about democracy. That was simplistic. There were lots of reasons why we fought this war. The objectives were never an issue in my mind. It was the means that I had issue with. But the why? Our way of life had been at risk. Was an alternative to this even to be considered? I got up and walked into the forest and then around the kolkhoz. The collective farm was quiet now. It was mid October again. The grain and hay collected and stored. It was readying itself for winter again. Would we be here? Would this kolkhoz continue? Would these people survive? Would they be swept into a new post war Russia? What would that be like? Would Stalin at last become benevolent?

I looked to the west in my mind. Where would the Red Army stop? And who would make them stop? If they did not stop ... if they were encouraged to continue ... waving crowds, heroes of the war ... warriors who saved us from ... from what? Hitler and fascism or from our own democracy? And what was the Laundry doing in all this?

I went back to my radio set. Sent the transmissions waiting for me: reports on surveillance.

Informants seemed to be coming to the camp at all hours these days. Today when I finished transmitting, I found Savarov in the meeting room with some others listening to an old man with a bent leg and a stick. I had seen him before and knew him to be an informant. The Germans were a little, if only a little, less likely to suspect a disabled old man or so we hoped. He came and went a lot more freely than most other people would be able to do. However he did it more slowly.

'… move towards the northwest.' He leaned towards the map on the table in

242

front of him. 'In this direction.' He spread his bent fingers across the paper. 'A column of lorries, men on foot and on transport ... a retreat, they leave only their wounded behind. They destroy the rest.'

Savarov studied the area carefully. And during the day I sent call after call to other groups we knew, asking for assistance.

The planning took most of the next day. This time there were Red Army regulars in charge

Late October 44 I was deaf for days and my ears bled. Then we got back to the village.

The shelling was an unemotional attack by the Red Army. It should have been over our heads onto the plain above us. Although the correct co-ordinates had been sent, someone got the elevation wrong and we were being shelled almost directly. The only thing that saved us from complete vaporisation was the wall of rock and earth that we sheltered behind and the little pocket we huddled in. It went on and on until the four of us were a tangled mass of people in a hole with the end of the world crashing around us, screaming at God, the universe and each other with no effect whatsoever.

The noise ceased when we could no longer hear. We dared to think we might not be dead when the earth stopped moving and the rocks stopped flying around us. The first man over the top into our hole might well have been shot had we heard him coming, but it was Savarov. He motioned us to follow and gathering what equipment our shocked limbs would let us carry, we followed him down.

When the dust and smoke drifted away, we saw that the Red Army had moved around the hill and were now attacking the unseen enemy from the side. No answering gun fire came in our direction but we would not have heard it if it had. I dared to assume that the barrage on our location and above had done its job.

It took four days to get back to the village. Besides the four of us there were several of our own wounded and some from the Red Army as well. Yeva had stayed behind in the village, as angry as I had ever seen her. She had a small wound on her upper right arm and would not be able to hold her rifle for a few days. No doubt she would then more than make up for time lost in stupid convalescence. The string of swear words she sent with us was impressive even for her. I hoped that this time, she would know how it felt for me seeing her disappear so many times, not knowing if I would ever feel her warmth again.

The vehicles were old and the track ways were rough and already partially frozen. We had to travel slowly. From time to time we stopped and unloaded the poor souls who no longer required transportation of any kind. They had found their own way to their destination.

Rain turned to rain combined with frozen, stinging slush, driven by the wind. Our clothes and kit got wetter and wetter. We sat in the back of the heaving lorry as it crashed its way over partially frozen mud and holes full of soupy slush. Very slowly the bubble of non-sound in my ears began to dissolve and after two days I could understand some speech if I watched the speaker's mouth. I wondered how long I had been lip reading like this. Was it part of normal speech and understanding? Had I always been partially deaf?

As we neared the village, the weather changed again. This time to flying wet snow that stuck to everything; made everything it landed on wet and cold and then froze it solid. The driver's door of the lorry froze shut, the windscreen wipers froze in situ and so did we. Most of the wounded were covered with canvas and kept dry but from time to time, we stopped and unloaded one more unfortunate who would never see our village or any village again.

About mid-day and three verst from the village we caught an unusual smell and saw a darkening layer of smoky air ahead. I felt Patya push the lorry faster. The roadway became harder and rougher as the vehicle responded. This was not smoke from a few tin stoves in low log houses – this was a great deal more than that.

It was, in fact, the remains of life as we had lived it. The little wooden houses had broken doors, missing windows, walls. Whole buildings looked as if they had taken direct shell hits; many still burned. Flames suddenly flashed up from beneath the remains of several ruins; other fires poked from mounds of earth and belongings with a sickening smell of wet smoke. Most of the ragged piles not actively burning were wrecked and smouldering. Everything inside had been thrown out onto the muddy ground where it was now freezing into the ice.

We crashed into the village – as far as the broken track would let us, and slid to a sudden and violent stop. The lumpy broken track through the village was blocked by exploded rock, broken timber, shattered trees and holes full of ice and water. Under the accumulating weight of the lightly falling wet snow, mud and rubble slowly slid down mounds of wreckage. Slow thin spiralling columns of smoke and steam rose from large piles of wreckage, fuelled by the timber structure and burning contents underneath that were once someone's safety and warmth.

Patya rammed his shoulder into the frozen driver's door and crashed out of the cab before it stopped. Without taking it out of gear, his foot suddenly coming off the clutch stalled the engine abruptly. He ran towards a pile of wreckage before the rest of us could leap from the back.

Men stood and stared. Others walked, stumbling with no focus on where they were or where they were going. Tanya Petrovna picked up at piece of torn and smouldering fabric and draped it carefully over a loose branch. A dog ran in hysterical circles around Maks' father who was picking up tiny pieces of wood to put in a small pile. Others worked frantically to pull burning and broken timber and trees off mounds that might once have been a hut or barn. They were calling to each other and looked up at us with no welcome; only relief that we could now help them. Elsewhere there was shouting, although I heard only enough to know that it was in anguish. Strips of clothing or laundry hung limply on broken burned spars of timber. Blackened and sodden, it was snagged on bushes tilted at unnatural angles. Pots, pieces of our rudimentary furniture staggered on door steps and pathways. The main building had only two walls still standing. The roof hung in space, swaying in response to any movement of air, however small.

The sharp smell of smoke and fire rubbed in the back of my throat like an illness. I stood for a moment on the muddy track trying to orient myself in a village I had once known. There was bile of an unknown emotion rising into my throat.

My own little hut tilted under several shattered larch trees. Two walls still stood; the others lay shattered, broken and buckled around the platform. The roof was folded into the building like a napkin into a box. I threw aside whatever I could to get in, calling for Yeva; the sound of my voice vibrated in my head and among all the others' muted shouting and calling for people they still hoped to be alive. Inside were a few of our things, my bag with the typewriter and my wireless was under the collapsed table in the corner. Our mattress and blankets were blown against the back wall; the floor boards were broken; in the corner and under the roof poles I saw Yeva's few clothes and her pack. With the strength of panic, I threw off what I could and found nothing. Yeva was gone and so was one of the Mosins and all the cartridges. The other Mosin was under a pile of broken wall timbers. Beside it was a clip with 5 shells in it. Why was I here? Why was I looking for her here? She above all others would have been the first out to face the invaders. She would have been defending what we had. She would have been in the front line of any attack like this. She would not be here, hiding in this hut. She would be outside facing them. She would be dead.

I crawled back out of the wreckage on my hands and knees. Outside I stood, staggering with limbs that barely functioned and with panic pulling all my senses into my body. My stomach filled with acid until I felt the need to vomit; my heart banged in the arteries in my neck. My breath rammed into my lungs. I ran from hut to hut, from the first pile of broken rubble to the next. I don't know what I hoped to find. I saw Sasha and his wife with the limp remains of their child between them. They were both wailing. Josef had located his wife and son. They were all on their knees in the snow and mud clinging together weeping. Vasili's house was gone completely and he stood in the back yard looking at the remains of the family cow. Others were digging into piles of broken buildings with their bare hands, calling, calling.

Anna Kolynova, came out from behind a door and frame, standing alone – the wall gone. Splinters fell around her as she tried, insanely, to push it shut again. She caught my arm. 'Gleb Alekseev.' I realised that I could hear her. I could hear everything. There were sounds here that would never leave my head, ever.

'What happened?'

'They came in the dark last night, with trucks and took all the men and women who had guns. They took them all.' She was weeping and I clutched her hands willing her to say more. 'We thought they were friendly, but then they took everyone.' Her babushka was wet and her hair stuck to her head. 'Then they – they ....' Her skirts were muddy and her boots were cracked. She shook from head to toe as she looked at the wreckage.

'Yeva? Where? Where did they go?'

She closed her eyes, shook her head and nodded down one of the forest tracks. I dropped her hands and ran to the trail in the forest – and ran and ran. But the snow and rain had obliterated whatever there might have been for me to follow.

I stood there, looking into the forest. My legs knew it was useless even if my logic and brain did not. Where would I look? Whichever direction I went may be the wrong one. I would lose time and the possibility of ever finding her. I needed someone else who would tell me what to do. I needed…I didn't know what I needed. The sun was disappearing - I needed daylight.

20

December 1944

We dug through the ruins, located the survivors and treated the wounded. We also found the dead. I prayed that Anna Kolynova had been right – that Yeva was not here. We searched for people we knew – parts of people we knew. We found them with faces in shock, in realisation that this was death; faces that were at peace. No faces at all, or no limbs, no clothing, no identity but known to us at a glance. We rescued what we could from the devastation. Whatever food could be found was collected and shared. Anna Kolynova found – we knew not how - and made tea. By nightfall, we had cleared what remained of the school house. Rurik and Leonid dug out some big timbers, black with smoke and broken on the ends, but sound enough and we propped up the corner of the roof. We piled what we could around it and made a shelter for all those who needed one, which was all of us. We needed to be together.

The rain now turned fully to dry snow. We could now dry out a little but the ground was now dark with sloppy slush, rapidly freezing into crumbled ice. Maks righted a barrel heater, banged it into shape with a stick and attached a few rusty pipes to the top. Then he lit a fire in it and we all sat looking into the flames through its missing door. Why was it, that after all the centuries of staring into fire, the human mind was still unable to understand it or know what it was? The flicks and licks of flame were now and would forever be a mystery. We looked into it as if our salvation and answers would come from within the small vision of hell inside. The larger version of hell with its bigger fire around us would be our final destruction. And we did not understand. We gathered the wounded close to the heat – treated what injuries we could and gave what pain relief we had to hand. Marie dug a chest of clean linen from the ruins of her house with her bare hands and then wordlessly tore everything into strips. Her strong arms making easy work of the thick fabric.

Mitya's wife was missing, her brother also. They were both partisans. Savarov looked strong although his voice was not when, in the silence, he chose to speak. 'This was a raid to collect guns and fighters to follow the retreating German bastards. Where they went we don't know. This ruination was done by our good friends in the Red Army.' There was little doubt of the acid in his voice and it seemed as if he no longer cared what his masters thought of his attitude. Pavel Nikolayevich was no longer there to hear. We did not miss him or need him. Savarov sat on a wooden plank from one of the houses now laid across logs of firewood and hung his head. 'What we do now I don't know.'

It was the first time I had ever heard Savarov admit that he didn't know what to do. He always knew what to do and it was always the right thing for the right time. This time he looked defeated, but he struggled to speak again. 'It was hard enough to fight the Germans with no reserves, no ammunition, no food and no support and then when we got those things we carried on and fought and beat them. We caused them real trouble; kept them from relaxing and thinking they had won the war in the marshes. We damaged their railways, we brought down their telephone and telegraph lines, we destroyed their trains, their bridges, their factories and their storage sites. We killed them in their thousands. We suffered for it and we lost friends. We could not relax.' He took off his cap and ran his hands through his sparse hair. I had never seen him without his hat. 'But when our friends do this to us.' He shook his head.

Mitya Nicholayevich wanted to track them all down, kill everyone. His brother Nikolai Nicholayevich wanted only to find and rescue what he had loved and lost. Leonid Antonovich wanted to stay and rebuild. He had no one to search for. Anna Kolynova wanted to find her large iron pot. Victor Victorovich wanted to find his children alive. We slept where we could or we talked…all night.

By morning, nothing had changed except that Savarov was again in charge. He began to put together search parties to go out in all directions from the track that Anna Kolynova had seen the soldiers use. They were to find where the Red Army had gone. They were the best trackers we had. I was to remain in the camp and receive messages from search party runners, transmit this to HQ and at the same time ask for medical supplies and food. I knew in the look that he gave me that he would allow no argument on the matter. I was to be trapped here relying on the skills of others. I wanted to kill him. I wanted to go out into the forest. I wanted to be doing something ... something ... anything ...

Others were ordered stay behind and try to rebuild enough shelters to keep the survivors alive during the winter. Livestock and fodder as remained would be gathered together into what farm shelters as were still serviceable.

I walked around the village time and time again, willing the search parties to come back. The little stream was beginning to freeze over. Thin ice formed around rocks and pieces of broken wood – translucent with holes in it, the sound of the water underneath bubbled and gurgled in unearthly ways. In another few days it would have to be broken to get drinking water again.

When the search parties returned, there was little to report. A group of soldiers of unknown size had passed through our village and others like it, taking able bodied men and women to pursue the retreating German forces. The Germans had decided to retreat by fighting at every step. The Red Army pursuing them were not about to forgive, now that victory was possible. They wanted to kill every German they came across and were not about to be kind in the manner in which they did it.

I spent every other waking minute on the wireless, trying to find communications from any district to which they may have gone, trying to locate who they were and where they were. There were hundreds of units moving westward, it was all but impossible to separate them or to know where they were now or would be tomorrow. But still I searched until I thought I would go mad. Then I made up my mind.

I went AWOL.

15 Nov 1944 I have no leads to follow. I do not know where to go. I just know that I have to do something. I hope that by getting into an active patrol or platoon I might learn something. Or they might just shoot me on sight. But anything would be better than waiting around in the village. My nerves and heart are …

So I took a little food, what clothes I stood up in, my typewriter and my small wireless, leaving the big one for Savarov. Maybe he would find someone else to do its work. I retrieved the Mosin and the clip of cartridges from the rubble and slung it over my shoulder. It probably didn't work. I wanted it only as part of a disguise. I needed to look like a lost soldier. The clothes I had were like all the others. Bits of uniform, jackets padded with wool, several pairs of trousers, boots stuffed with straw.

The group that I eventually found and joined were largely partisans who were being sent by regular troops to follow the shrinking front line with several cases of provisions. I told them the truth and they let me stay. Perhaps they only wanted the wireless, but I did what I could for them.

Russia North Western Front (Worcester Journal) Tuesday 9 January 1945 *Towards Poland* **by Royston Thomas**

We're making progress more or less in the direction our orders have commanded. We've replaced our damaged compass and maps but the new ones are years older than the ones we had, so we blunder along.

Our convoy is now a single badly overloaded truck, filled with fuel and ammunition. We carry our own food, any extra clothing we might be blessed to have and we walk.

The sky is silver as is the snow. The trees are grey like the fur of a wolf. The air is light; it feels like there isn't enough to breathe. We stand at the edge of the plain; the far horizon is missing in the darkness. A vivid moon floats from behind a cloud and slaps our shadows forward onto the snow, where their imprints will give us away. We stop to listen. Are we still safe?

I searched for her – was she still safe? Panic overtook reason. Urgency overlaid rational thought. I would never be a soldier like these. I cannot think clearly when my mind was searching for her. She filled my mind, my consciousness and my focus. I was empty if she was not beside me, even if there was a Mosin between us.

Information we received was so confused. I could not find my way. Details I had were not high enough quality to be useful. I was chasing dreams or ghosts. Nothing was real any more. I had no plan. I was lost in this eternal country without a map. I did not know where I was. I did not know where Yeva was. I had no way of reaching her – no way of finding her – no way of hearing her voice ever again. But I knew she was alive. My mind told me she was alive.

I knew I should not be going towards Poland. It was the wrong way.

15 Jan 1945 A group of ragged individuals came towards us out of the snow storm. We found them to be Partisans like us and from them, we learned much. No one had seen anyone who resembled Yeva. Skill with a rifle like hers could not go unnoticed. A long blonde plait would not be un-remarked. She was not there. I was not disappointed; I knew it to be true, I knew she was not there.

The others however had good news from the Partisans. I did not. They gave me food, a map of sorts and a compass. I left them the wireless and walked away to the east in the heavy snow. They had good news to follow. I had my instincts. I had a voice in my head – a voice from inside my soul.

The snow fell harder and a wind began to drive it into my face. It became hard to see where I was going. As the light levels fell, I struggled to see the track. I was in danger of being lost in the forest.

In the morning, translucent light of the sun filtering through the snow made a cathedral window of amber light; bright but wrinkled with grains of ice. I kicked the snow that covered the front of the little cave I had made under the tree roots and found the morning sun bright on the horizon as it broke through the morning clouds. If I believed in signs, this was one I wanted to keep in my heart for ever; warmth of colour if not temperature with hope of another day. It gave me hope for myself and I pulled the pack onto my back and walked toward the light. Later I would stop, build a little fire and make tea for myself.

This was the pattern day after day. I followed the morning sun where it existed and then the compass. The little map was useful to the point that it showed major roads and railway lines. But these, of necessity, I avoided or used with caution. I could not take the risk of being stopped, captured or questioned. I had a uniform of sorts, but it was made of what I needed to keep warm, not what marked me as anything that could be defined. It would be difficult to explain; walking to the east when there was still fighting in the west.

I had a fur hat that folded up on front and back with two long side flaps that I tied under my chin. Under it I had a scarf, the tails of which I pushed down the throat of my coat. This was a heavy quilted thing that came below my knees and was held together with a belt. All of its buttons were missing. I wore several pairs of trousers; some I was able to tuck into the big boots and the legs of the top pair hung outside where they became solid with snow. I carried a pack with my few possessions and a blanket. Over my chest was the strap of the dreaded Mosin that banged into my back.

The days seemed to get colder. The air became drier and it was harder to breathe. The hairs in my nose froze together and stung when I breathed and they pulled apart. Frost made my beard and scarf a single chunk of ice. The snow became deep and soft every time it snowed and it snowed often. It made an odd crunching sound as I lifted my foot high out of the softness and took another and another step. It was like climbing a ladder. My eyelashes were thick with frozen breath.

By night, I dug shelters in the snow, under trees or the wreckage of machinery destroyed beyond use by one side in this war or the other. I slept for

251

short periods until the cold woke me. I did not mind as it meant that I was still alive and had not yet frozen to death.

I tried to visualise the little cottage where I knew I would find Yeva. I knew that this was where she had gone and where she was safe. I had to believe that she would not be out in this wilderness looking for me. I knew that she would not, as there was nowhere in this country to which I would go except to find her. She was the focus of everything. It would be a little house; almost a peasant's house, but brightly coloured. There would be a huge chimney and smoke rising. Snow would be piled to the eaves by now and the garden covered deeply. It would be warm and safe. She would not be alone. There would be someone, an older woman with her. She would be safe.

In the first weeks, I kept track of the days and knew that January was finished and February had begun. Even though the winter solstice had long ago passed, the temperatures plunged even further. Normal winter temperatures in the marshes were below freezing, although not by great amounts, but the further north and east I went, the colder it became and the less it varied between day and night. Why had God deserted this country in the winter? Why was there nothing to be achieved? Why did everything, even war, come to a standstill? Why was the main energy of everything put to survival, only survival and not resolution or reconciliation?

Undated diary entry: I search for her with my heart. The little house is all that my brain can imagine and so I reach for her with my emotions. At times alone I feel despair and such loss that I set myself free. I leave everything around me and I search in a plane of consciousness that I cannot describe.

In these eternal weeks, I was helped by rural people as I encountered them. They asked no questions, but seemed to know, by divine providence maybe, that I was no threat, but a man in pain who needed to find his heart again. They fed me what they could spare and gave me directions that kept me from the major roads and rails. In return, all I could do was sing for my supper. For some reason, I could still sing. The old Welsh hymns remained in my memory but the meaning of them had deteriorated and I felt no emotion in the sound they made. But *Rhyfelgyrch Gwŷr Harlech* still brought me to my feet and tears to my eyes.

On a dark day in February - by now I had lost the date – I came to a narrow track way, used, but infrequently. I sat for a long time in the shelter of the forest, watching nothing. Nothing came. Nothing went. But there was something in my senses that told me there were troops nearby who used this track. I saw nothing and there was little to hear except the wind. Crossing the track would not be a difficulty; but what I might encounter on the other side was what caused me concern. How many troops were still out there? What mood might they be in? Who were they? Russians dug in for the winter? Bored and needing entertainment, namely me? Germans, cut off and desperate not to be located until they could be rescued? Partisans, suspicious and dangerous?

As I sat among the trees with a blanket that was white once pulled over my shoulders I bargained with God: I will repent. I will confess every sin – and there were many – that I had committed in this war. I will never commit any of them again so long as I lived. If, and only if, God, You are prepared to give me Yeva. Are You listening? If You do this and she is safe and well (by now I was adding caveats to the bargain), I will do whatever You ask of me. (Never mind what Yeva may want out of our relationship and how that might affect God's demands on me. I would discuss that with God later, when He had delivered up His side of the bargain.) What do you think God? Is this a fair bargain: my soul for her life? The air was very still. God? Where are You? If You don't like the terms of the bargain I propose, then You will have to say so. You will have to say something. I am too weak to hear You unless You are blunt. I am too stupid to understand the innuendo and parables You spoke in to reach peasants like me. That's what I had been taught God. Be blunt God, be truthful with me. I believed in you God. In another lifetime, I believed in You. If You want me to believe in You now, then speak.

I waited until dusk and then made a disorganised dash across the track, down it a short distance, to hide my blatant tracks among the others and then across a log, sweeping my tracks with the blanket to make them less obvious. Then I ran further into the forest. My blanket flapped around me, the pack banged into my back and the clips on the strap of the Mosin made more noise than an entire army on the march. I slid as quickly and quietly as possible into the darkness of the trees. Here I rested.

I realised that I was in poor physical condition, breathless, tired and weak. I had no idea how far I had yet to go, nor what was ahead of me. I pushed off the blanket and the pack, then took off the Mosin. For now I would have to carry it in my hand and stay as silent as possible. The feeling that I was not entirely alone in this landscape was stronger now. I pulled the pack back on and the blanket over it, knotting the corners under my chin. Who would see whom first? I couldn't ask God for help, there was no more room for conditions on my side of the bargain I proposed. I had pushed God as far as I dared already.

His breath must have made me turn. There had been no noise to alert me, but there was a human sound - the sound of breath. When I saw the movement, a cloud of breath in the cold air, I saw the man. This was not a peasant; this was a scout. He was armed and, like me, wore an assortment of clothes, but it was military kit. Russian or German? Impossible to tell from what he was wearing. There was a larger camp somewhere near and he was a forward look out. That was not in doubt. If he got to me before I got to him, I was as good as dead. I had no excuse for being where I was. I had no way of communicating with the Embassy to ask for their protection. Out here in the forest, looking desperate would not fill anyone with confidence. That was assuming of course, that I was captured. He could just as easily shoot me. In either case I was dead. He was probably from the Red Army, the damned Red Army. I did not think of him as friend. He had taken what was most dear to me. He could not also have my life. I had things to do that I needed it for. A branch cracked loudly in the stillness and fell to the snow in a great puff of powder. It startled him and he looked up.

I crouched down in the deep snow partially sheltered by a narrow tree. I pulled off my right mitt and, with all the strength in my hand that I could call on, I pulled on the knob at the back of the rifle bolt to release the safety catch and turned it to one side to lock the firing pin. I had seen Yeva do this thousands of times, but not realised how much strength it required. Whether or not the metal parts made a sound I don't know, but I felt, in my imagination, the cartridge slot into the breech. I pulled the butt of the rifle hard against my padded coat and looking down the barrel followed the figure as it got closer and closer. I knew that I had no skill in aiming at anything. When I knew I could wait no longer, I squeezed the trigger.

I didn't see what happened next, but I knew that the figure had disappeared and that there was a spume of snow rising into the air from where I had seen him last. I could not wait to find out if he were dead or merely wounded. The report from the gun in this still air would bring others from everywhere unless they too believed it was a branch cracking. And so I ran. Back to the path, where there were tracks of others to cover my own - with the rifle on my back.

Most of the recent past is missing. The bits don't connect. Shells shake the ground and suck the breath from my lungs. Trucks are on fire. Pieces of human flesh and bone hang in the air. Some of them might be mine. Time has stopped. It is like a snapshot in my head. But I feel nothing. This cannot be real. I am alone. There was no battle. Again and again, I see the man fall, my one shot jolting him and he throws his arms wide. But it is just my mind, I did not see him at all. But the sound of the bullet hitting him repeats over and over. Not the sound of the shot, but the sound of flesh. I could not possibly have heard it, but I did.

Then a soft white smooth blanket slides over my legs. It is warm. Like the warm flesh beside me. Her flesh, her warmth. Seconds of time in these days of noise and destruction. Under these blankets are peace, silence, love and warmth.

The white blanket stings my wrists and neck. It feels like ice. It is ice. The blanket is snow. I've been buried alive – or maybe I am dead. I can see only whiteness. But I can breathe. Maybe I am alive.

Her nose, cold as it always is, presses against my bare shoulder. I hear her laugh and see her hair falling forward. Her name? She is my life – I'd trade mine for hers in a heartbeat. But her name? Where is she?

My brain has stopped. Maybe I am dead. I can't feel my feet. Are they still there? No parts of my body seem capable of movement. Why can't I see? Has it gone dark? Is that why I can't see? I listen. It seems too quiet. Maybe I'm deaf as well as blind.

The man I shot lifts his hand then his arm from the snow. The horror of it makes me widen my eyes and I see body parts all around, rising from the snow. The snow disappears, gradually melting into the earth. The bodies rise from the snow. They are everywhere, frozen until now. Now they are free. But it is too late. They are blown apart. They are dead.

Yeva where are you? We were laughing then. You were beside me. Under the warm blankets. We talked about everything except the past and the future. In the past you were someone else – the mad woman with a rifle and a mountain of hate to unload. In the future we don't exist. Not unless there is a miracle and the war ends tomorrow and we survive within sight of each other. But in the present we are together and we can laugh. We have to laugh. Anything else is insanity. Then suddenly we are normal people again, not laughing, not talking, just walking behind the lorry. In the light of the first explosion I see your wide eyes look at me in shock. Then you are gone; I am gone. Only the blast hung in the air. But surely that is only in my mind.

I am not able, nor will I ever be able, to lift the vision of the man I shot from my mind. He will live there forever. But I feel calm. I have now committed all the sins known to man. I am free from the climb through them. I have achieved every one. I am free. I can begin again, but without God this time. But maybe that is part of being free – being free of God too. I don't know.

If I concentrate on my muscles one by one from my shoulder to my hand, I can move my fingers – some of my fingers. There is something hard and rough under them. Canvas? I hear something. The snow squeaks. Someone is coming. Do I shout? What if it is a German? No they have gone. Another Red Army bastard? The skin on my face stings. I'm face down in the snow. Covered? Maybe they won't find me. Still. Stay still. Let go of the canvas. Stop breathing. Pass out if I can. Die if I can.

They dig me out. In the dark. In silence. And they carry me through the snow. Under the noses of my enemies. In stealth, they secret me out. Me, a non-combatant. Why? They could have left me buried in the snow. No one would have ever known. They should have left me buried in the snow. But the Germans have gone. Where have they gone? There are no more Germans left here.

There are rough planks under my cheek. Noise like a motor growling over impossible broken land surface. Someone holds me against the planks in the back of a truck.

The thread between Yeva and me is thin. It sags under time and distance. Where is she? Where am I? There is no difference between us now. My war is lost. Love is lost. The skin that covered my emotion is thin. It is visible for all to see. It is ugly. It is drying out. Will it die too?

But I can see her in my mind or perhaps in my soul. I can see where she is and what she is doing. I lift my body from where it rests and let it fly until it floats above the snow and I see her. I try to speak.

Halt! It was impossible to miss the meaning of the shout – whatever language it was given in. Yeva lifted her hands slowly above her head. Turning with great care, she saw a person in a uniform and helmet approach her. Underneath them was a young boy – not more than 16. In front of him was a very long rifle pointed at her. However terrified the boy was, the weapon was steady. She tried to look convincingly terrified herself.

Stringing phrases of pleading together she wailed and cried. The chances that he understood her were remote, but that wouldn't stop him from shooting her. He waved the weapon to indicate that she should walk in front of him. She wrung her hands, slapped at her face and babushka, making as much noise as she could. Lifting her rag wrapped feet from the snow she made sure he could see that she wore no boots or mitts. Succumbing to hysterical crying, she fell on her knees in the snow and tried to indicate that she lived nearby and had been out collecting wood. Her pantomime escaped him and he tried to get her to her feet. She wailed louder and he dropped her back in the drift.

She sank back against her heels, pulled the big coat closer around her to hide the warm clothes underneath, pleaded and rocked back and forth.

He looked behind him, then all around. There was no one to be seen. No one to help either of them. She pressed her advantage, falling to her face in the snow sobbing and sobbing. When she looked up, she saw him retreating into the broken trees. Then she wept. Real tears. Tears of relief. Of loss, anger and hate. She sat in the snow, weeping until it was dark. Then like a wisp of smoke, she got to her feet, walked through the snow to a twisted and wrecked gun carrier with two pine trees broken over it nearly buried by drifts, dug her boots and rifle out of the snow and walked into the darkness.

White ghosts came and went. The air was warm and thin. It smelled clinical. There were screams and groans earlier in the night. Now there were only the sounds of sleeping. Yet I was alone. My head knocked on something wooden and my feet were cold. Then they were warm.

21

February 1945

The conjunction is alive. Snow has no movement, fire has all. At the edge where they meet, there is creation; light, smoke, steam, horror and life. No distinction among them. All is consumed – men, horses, arms, machines, armour and fabric, screams, silence, hate and love. Everything is gone. She is gone; they are gone. No one is left, but me. I, not allowed a weapon, only my typewriter, only I who cannot fight is left. I cannot seek nor have revenge – I have to live with it all forever. I cannot forget – I cannot write about it – no one will see what I have seen, felt my feelings; words cannot express, the emptiness, the hollowness of time…

In the silence, I see footprints. In the moonlight, I see footprints. They are obscured with flesh, with broken metal, with blood. But there are footprints - someone was alive here once. Someone was alive after, the ice preserves the track, the ice obscures the escape, the ice prevents my following. There is nothing to follow only footprints that go nowhere.

I feel the cold, bitter, biting cold. Again and again the cold. I feel the wind. I hear the wind in the trees. I feel life drifting, drifting away, perhaps forever. Sleep, please just give me sleep. I haven't resolved you yet. What do you want? I hear you. I know you can talk to me. But what the bloody hell do you want?

Where have you gone? I find nothing of you in the carnage – no body, no cloth, no hair, no weapon, no kit, no webbing, no footwear, no sound, no smile, no encouragement from you. No word. Only the footprints in the ice. Are they yours?

I woke up one day – I think it was some days ago. I was in a hospital of sorts. I had no idea where. My Russian was good enough to ask, but my head was not good enough to understand the answer. What has happened to me?

I had most of my limbs and my head seemed to be in order. But one leg is strapped with pieces of wood and tightly bound. I suspected it might be broken. Or missing? I didn't try to walk or even sit up. I was lying on the floor of a wooden house – some emergency treatment site. My canvas bag was beside me. It has been emptied and the contents placed on top. They saved my bag – and my typewriter. What possessed them to save me? What possessed them to save my typewriter? For a journalist – a silly unnecessary journalist? Why?

I saw Yeva. I saw her from a height. I looked down to where for four days she waited in a tiny broken barn. The wind had blown the snow hard and smooth and covered the tiny pile of logs that passed for a building, but for a fold under the eaves. She took off her boots and wrapped the rags around her feet to minimise her tracks on the packed drifts. In time the wind will eliminate them too. But an experienced tracker could find her if the orders were given.

She built no fire; she ate no food, but only snow for the water and that only sparingly. It takes body heat to metabolise it – heat she cannot afford to lose. She made no sound; she slept little and listened to every sound of wind, man, machinery and animal. When the blizzard began she left and, satisfied that the men and machinery noises were at her back, moved away in the darkness. She walked for six days and took shelter with a family living in a broken building like her barn. They made her rest and reducing what they had among them, fed her enough to bring back some of her strength. She stayed there until, weeks later, the air warmed and spring began again.

A doctor or whoever she was, told me that I had stepped on a land mine or a piece of unstable ordnance. The blast had caught my leg and arm. They had pulled most of the ordnance fragments out of my flesh, set the bones and sewn up the gaps. I would be able to walk again once they were sure that any infection was over. The cold had slowed down the bleeding and reduced the risk of infection, but fabric from all the clothes I had been wearing had been imbedded in my flesh. It had taken a long time for them to get the wound clean. Fortunately I had been unconscious for most of the operations. Now, however there would be pain… a great deal of pain.

I didn't mind the pain because I could get out of my body when it was at its worst and look for Yeva. When they checked the wound, or replaced the dressings, I was elsewhere. I was searching.

In all these days, I felt her searching for a connection between her mind and mine. I relived the laughter and pain we had between us. Would nothing we have ever be ours again? I saw her with the people who want to help her. I begged her to stay and be looked after. For her own sake and for the sake of the kind people who sheltered her, I begged her to stay. I know she could not sigh; she could not cry. Instead, I watched as she taught the old man and the children to read.

When the snow had stopped falling, but the roadways were still frozen hard, it was possible to travel and I knew she would leave. If the temperatures stayed below freezing for long enough, she could get where she needed to go before the mud stopped everything again. To where she would be safe. To where she could wait until I was able to find her again.

I could walk again now - hop on one leg, although I needed a stick to do so. But the jarring made the wounds in my damaged leg bleed. They told me I might be able to walk normally again in time and I was more grateful that words can say. My broken arm mended well, although it seemed to be a different shape now. However my fingers were strong and today, I got the little typewriter out and begging a sheet of paper from the nurses, I started to write again – with one finger on my left hand.

1 April 1945

Dear Mum,

I have no way of knowing if you will ever receive this. Somehow I suspect not, but I must tell you that I am in a Russian hospital. My rescuers found me unconscious and I really don't know where they have taken me. But although I have a smashed leg and broken arm, I am alive and it is because of them that I am so. I am getting stronger as time goes by and they tell me that I may be able to walk again soon. I am already able to hobble short distances.

I hear by the gossip that the war must be nearly over, that the Allies are advancing on Berlin from all sides. I pray to God it is so.

I stopped typing with those words. I hadn't spoken to God for weeks. I doubted that there was anything I could say to Him. Too much had happened to me and to others around me, for me to have any kind thoughts for a God who allowed it to happen. I know all about free will among men, but that was merely a justification in my mind. A rationale made by men who could not explain why God had let this happen. They could not and so they blamed men rather than God.

If God cared about individuals like we had been taught He did, then where was He? Why had He not stopped this? Free will? That was ridiculous. There was no God. There was no one to stop what had happened until we had all bludgeoned ourselves and others to the point where none of us had the strength to continue. That was what would finish the war. Not God. Not God at all. And He had not answered me nor commented on the bargain I proposed. Except for the blast that nearly killed me, but I chose not to read too much into that. It was just bad luck – an accident.

The men who brought me here or pulled me from the snow long ago moved on. I did not know who they were, nor where they had gone. I couldn't ask them where they found me; what they might know. I had no way of finding them. There was no one to ask. I could not even thank them for returning my life to me.

I tried harder each day to walk, until the pain made me weep and I had to go back to my mind. But I had goals: six boards across the floor, seven, eight, once a day, twice a day.

The snow was beginning to melt. Huge icicles developed along the eaves of the buildings. The melt water ran down the roof – there were no gutters – where it dripped , froze solid and now hung like deadly daggers. At some time during the day, I heard someone cracking them off and they fell onto the icy path with a sound of shattering glass. But around us, the snow levels gradually sank and on the day when there was a bare patch of earth, we all felt elated. It wouldn't last of course, because there was more snow to come, but the hope that it inspired could be seen in everyone. My neighbour with the missing shoulder has begun to write poetry!

In a few weeks the earth around the hospital became vivid with patches of green growth among the piles of snow. I saw that the nitrogen and bone meal in all that blood and death had given new life to the earth. But was the price worth the lushness, or was the colour just a trick of the light?

I continue to get stronger very slowly, and I can see Yeva wanting to leave the hut and the children.

When the snow begins to retreat, I see her struggling on. I know where she is going. I feel her determination and the fierce focus that she had on one end of her rifle I now see it focussed on her safe refuge - the cottage.

Over the next weeks I made myself get stronger. It was just a matter of will I told myself. I learned to walk on rough ground with the stick and then when I had confidence, I learned to walk without it. I also learned how to get up when I fell and how to fall so that I damaged my healing parts as little as possible. Time and time again I thought I had broken the weak bones all over again.

I also learned to type properly with one hand and how to write with my left. But the writing was just for me. I sent no reports to the paper; I wrote no letters, I had no means to send them and I did not want to let anyone into my private thoughts. I wanted to be left in the warm humid little cell that I now lived in. I wanted to be alone. Alone until I had completed the trek that I needed to finish.

On days when it rained or snowed and I could not get out to continue my regime to strengthen my broken parts, I begged maps from anyone who had one or could draw one. I gradually built up the information and knowledge I needed for the journey ahead. I added topography, road and railways, towns, cities, rivers and even military information. The more information I added, the more confidence I had that I would get to the end. There were still several hundred verst to go and I needed all the strength in my legs I could develop.

As the weather improved, I grew impatient. The nurses seemed to understand my urgency and worked with me for hours even to the point of training me with my pack on my back. My typewriter and what few possessions I retained would come with me. The typewriter could easily have been left behind, but it had been through so much of my life and it had been a gift from Yeva's heart; it had to go with me. I could not be parted from it. My few possessions amounted to very little. My pay book with my Russian name was still safe in the condom Gleb had been issued with, but the OTP in the other one had been thrown into the snow somewhere along the way.

A few weeks later at the beginning of June and after threats from me that I would leave anyway, they agreed that I was more or less strong enough to go. My first few steps away from the hospital gate gave me such a sense of elation it would be hard to describe. The air was bright and thick after months of weightlessness. The roadway was rutted but dry and there was fine dust in the air above it where the trees closed overhead. I could hear birds among the leaves and insects around my head. I was sure that I could fly.

The hospital had destroyed my old clothes of course, covered with blood, bone and probably a lot more. I now had another mixture of military and civilian pieces; a cloth wedge cap, formerly belonging to a rifleman. I did not wish to know what had deprived him of it. The shirt jacket was from a similar rank, but the sleeves were too short and I could not do up the cuff buttons. It was blessed

262

with pockets of various sizes and I put my pay book in the top pocket and secured the flap. The trousers were loose like ordinary farmers wore and my boots were the short ankle type with different laces. I did not ask for a rifle.

Across my back was my pack. They gave me what food they could spare, a water bottle and some money. I did not ask where the latter came from, but I hoped that the little bit of cash I had arrived with had gone to someone, like me, who needed it. My Bible had survived with me, but I chose to leave it behind. It had no significance to me now. The Mosin was left in a place known only to God. All I owned in addition to the typewriter, were my notebook and pencil, a small knife to sharpen it with, a spare shirt, underwear, socks, a razor and of course the map. Such a few things.

On the first day, I walked perhaps three verst. It was a pitifully short distance but I found a barn in the mid afternoon and did not wish to be in the open for the night, so stopped early to rest my leg. It was a good decision as we were both tired, it and I, and we would have not found another shelter for a number of verst as I found the next day. I slept with the animals.

I travelled a few verst each day, pushing myself to cover more every day than the one before. Where I could, I travelled in farmers' carts but still took care not to be obvious to anything related to military transport. There were still many of them about and I felt the need to be careful whether justified or not. Most people were helpful if distant and I passed on quickly from those who were not. I calculated that at the rate I was able to walk, it would take me about five or six weeks to get to the cottage.

There was little to occupy my mind as I stumbled over the hard dry ruts in the road. I made up observations that I could use to send to the Journal, but never cared to write them down. They were such trivial things in the large turbulence the world faced these days.

I wrote letters home – to my mother – in my head. Like the Journal reports, they would never be seen on paper either. It was only a means to help the time go by. I walked with others from time to time; men going home, men looking for home, men escaping from home. It was a time of great change I realised. How many people took the opportunity to be truly 'missing' – forever; to start a new life, with a new name, a new history? To never have done the things they did; or to tell the world the things that they did, but had not really done. It was such an opportunity. So much could change. I saw myself in them.

Dear Mum: I began another letter. I could not get my brain to stretch around the possibilities. I needed to rest.

It began to rain and I took shelter in a pile of timber until it passed. Would anyone in The Laundry believe what this country was like? Really like? What would they do if they did? Their requests for information were bizarre and I hadn't thought seriously about them for weeks. I watched the rain flap down in waving sheets.

Less bizarre or perhaps more so was the spy. The mythical person I had never met. What had happened to him? By now he may have been discovered. He might well be dead or had led everyone to Smythe and Johnson. Would Royston Thomas be next? What had he been saying to them in all those reports I transmitted? Who had he been spying on? He may not have been a single person; there were probably many of them, one after the other.

Why wasn't the information they wanted me to get not available to them through governmental or military channels. Surely they had access much better than I or even this mythical spy.

They asked me about the success of the Red Army, numbers and statistics of defeats, the wealth of the country. It was only good news. They were so pleased with my reports of German defeat and Red Army captures. Did they think that the Soviets were going to rampage across Europe with nothing to stop them?

Was that it? Did they think that Stalin would be able to conquer Europe... and did that include Britain? My mind collapsed at the thought. But was that what they wanted to know?

An oblique vision of the newspaper at the Carters a life time ago: *The Daily Worker*. Facts suddenly fell one after another into my head. Carter and Donaldson went to the same club. Donaldson knew that I could understand Morse code. Was that how it all began? Were they all in it together? Carter, Donaldson, Smythe, Johnson and who knew how many others. Was that how I came to be chosen? Were they all Socialists? What did they want? Total revolution in Britain? Dear God.

As the circle slowly closed in my thick brain, I could not quite get the ends of the arguments to meet. Smythe's lot wanted information about a Russia that did not really exist except in the minds of the rulers, the die-hard communists...the ends of the arguments met there, beyond just Socialism. Were Smythe and Johnson Communists? Living and working in the British Government? It was too large a leap for my malnourished brain to make.

When the rain stopped I stepped into the mud of the road. Precious little made any sense. My mind was not strong enough to make sense of any of it. I made my mind wander to other things to give the possibilities of the Laundry time to coalesce.

After the war, what would change for me? I would remain in Russia. It didn't matter what they did or who they were, I was safe from it all. They would never find Gleb Alekseev Rozhkov. How could they?

In all the time that I had been away from my home, I can't say that I ever felt loneliness. Yes, there were times when I was homesick, when I missed my father and when I missed Annie – poor dear Annie - but it was not what I would define as loneliness. On this long and limping journey I began to investigate my own soul and the space that it occupied in the life that I had been given. I began to feel more and more alone.

What would happen if I could not find the cottage? If Yeva had gone from the cottage and left no message? If she had never been there at all? The great hole in front of me when there were no answers showed me what utter loneliness was like. It was the bottom of an individual's soul. The dregs left when all else had gone. The nothingness that was me. I was nothing. I was a man with a limp and a bent elbow and a typewriter on his back. One who could not communicate, who could not touch another living being... I was alone in the universe.

I lost contact with the days of the week and the weeks of the months. And I walked. In rain, mud and blasting heat and dust, I walked. I endured blazing sun, insects and the questions of children. I did not yield to the pitying looks from people. If I spoke to people it was to buy a little food or to add to the map which, the further I travelled, needed more and more detail. I felt I had to be getting closer or perhaps I was going around in a very large circle and the world was altering the scenery just to keep me walking. I filled my water bottle from streams where I found them, or wells where I begged for it. I ate little, slept little, shaved when I felt like it and continued walking. Eventually I was able to discard the stick and walk. When my money was gone I worked as well as I could in return for a little food.

When the sun became unbearably hot, I waited in the shade of trees or buildings or rocks, washed myself and my clothes in whatever water I could find and used the heat to dry them and me. I was getting closer.

The cottage when I found it was exactly as I pictured it. The snow was gone of course and it was white not brightly coloured, but the little roughly plastered hut with a roof of ragged thatch looked over a sloping field to a stream at the bottom. The wide eaves put shade on the walls and a door stood open. There were vegetables growing in a well dug plot just outside the front door; a horse in a grassy paddock surrounded by a log fence and chickens in the yard. A line of laundry was swaying as the air slowly moved. All was silent. But I saw her. She came from behind some long sheets with a bundle of laundry in her arms, walked to a bush and put it down in the shade. She had her hair caught back by a coloured scarf tied behind her neck and she wore a white blouse and long printed skirt. She reminded me of a gypsy. When she stood up again, she glanced up and we looked at each other for a long time.

When I touched her face I didn't realise that either of us had moved. She put her hand behind my neck and we leaned slowly against each other. I put my arm around her shoulders. She lifted her chin and I felt my lips on her forehead, then her cheek and then on her mouth. It was a tiny kiss and it lasted merely a second. It was as if she had been gone for only a moment. The huge gap in my life had disappeared, all the pain had never happened. It had all been a dream. Winter did not exist, hunger, thirst and blistered feet did not exist. Life resumed.

She put her finger on my lips, drew away from me and walked to the bush where she gathered up the laundry. I shrugged the pack from my back and slung it in one hand to turn to the house. She held out her bundle of laundry and gave it to me. It was surprisingly heavy. I dropped the pack. Then she unfolded a corner of the bundle to show me a tiny pink faced sleeping baby.

I wept.

I had not wept since my father died. This was another kind of emotion and the only response my soul could command was tears.

It was not until we entered the cottage that either of us spoke. 'I knew you would come,' she said.

December 1945: It was very warm in his office. The heating had never been right in this building. Hot when it needed to be warm, cold when it needed to be warm. Smythe very much wanted to remove his suit jacket. But he didn't want his arm and the frayed lining to be obvious. He opened the window of his office and inhaled the wet, cold evening air. He was in august company with this disease – he and FDR. Struggle on – it's your brain that matters here. Poor man. Dead now and Truman in his place.

After a few minutes he was aware of the others coming in, helping themselves to tea and plain biscuits. He heard Neville. 'I can't help but wonder how different things will be now. War over, new government. Things should be changing and soon.'

Arnold Carter broke his biscuit in half, crumbs falling onto the table top. 'Probably years of the same now that we are nearly bankrupt.'

'I was thinking more of our objective.' Neville leaned on the table.

Robert looked at them all. 'The new government will be less of a threat, but can't be underestimated. And things will change sooner or later.' He leaned on his one good elbow.

Johnson stirred a cup of tea and knocked the spoon against the rim. 'Now that we've found him again, what do we do with him? Do we use him for anything at all?'

Neville Donaldson looked up suddenly. 'Where was he?'

Smythe spoke before Johnson could reply. 'He went missing months ago – after he left the Partisans, as we now know, and we found that he had been injured … don't know just quite how. He seems to be back to some sort of normality.'

Carter let out a long sigh. 'I know he's back to work at the Embassy, but we don't need him to work for us like he did before.'

Smythe leaned heavily on the table. 'No… the other operator's doing well.'

Donaldson leaned back in his chair. 'Has he tried to contact us?'

Carter interrupted. 'Does he know anything?'

Johnson looked up quickly. 'No,' he said sharply, then more casually, 'I don't think so. We've shut down the frequencies he used so he can't reach us.'

Carter took a handkerchief from his pocket and wiped his forehead. 'And if he knows something…? What then? Has there been any hint from him or… anyone else?'

'This may all falling apart gentlemen', Smythe rubbed his hand through his sparse hair. 'Let's be honest, if Roy does know something and talks to anyone but us, we could be in for some difficult questions. And he can't be got rid of quite as easily as…'

'But,' Carter's voice came from a slightly higher range. His face became flushed. 'Go back a minute. What does this mean? For us? What can he possibly do?'

Johnson's tone was brusque. 'Arnold. Do you know what treason is?'

Arnold Carter's eyes widened. 'Of course I do!'

'Then what the hell do you think we have been involved in for the past five or six years?'

'Saving our country of course!'

'Don't be naïve. Treason is treachery towards one's own country. Sedition by definition is words or actions that encourage people to rebel against the state. Just what do you think we have been doing? Knitting socks for sailors? If we aren't charged with treason, the Treachery Act will more than make up the difference.'

'Edward, for heaven's sake. You know better than most of us what this is all for. It is not treason if it is right for the reason.'

Johnson frowned and glared at the other three from under his thick eyebrows. 'Either way, it is punishable by death don't forget.' There was an oily silence around the table.

Donaldson pulled his chair closer to the table. 'We need to be careful here. We can try the blackmail route again, but that assumes of course that he can still be manipulated and hasn't gone completely out from under our control. Personally, I don't think we have much leverage over him now. Who will care that he was a conchie?'

Carter broke his biscuit into smaller and smaller pieces. 'So… how do we control him before he damages us?'

Johnson's eyes met Smythe's but he said nothing.

Smythe spoke into the silence. '…or we plan for our own futures.'

Carter looked at the pile of crumbs that had been his biscuit. 'He may not survive. He may not be allowed to leave Russia. Many things could happen between now and his return.'

Neville Donaldson let out a long breath. 'How will we know if or when he wants to leave?'

'The Embassy will know.' Smythe smiled. Perhaps it was all possible yet.

Johnson frowned and pushed his papers together. 'Gentlemen, you can leave Roy to Robert and me. More importantly, I think the time has come when we need to consider our futures. And I mean seriously.'

PART THREE

22

February 1946

'Mum, what about Roy?' Haydn took the coffee his mother offered and sat down again at the desk.

'I'm sorry it's not coffee as we remember it but maybe one day...' Miriam sat on the other side of the desk in what she called the visiting chair. It was usually occupied by people from the estate with a petition or problem. 'We thought rationing would end along with the war.'

In the momentary silence, Haydn ran his hands through his curly hair. 'Has he said anything yet? Anything useful?'

Miriam pulled a handkerchief from the pocket of her apron and wiped her eyes. 'No. Nothing that explains anything.'

'He is consumed with the child. He spends every minute with her – awake or asleep. He won't let her out of his sight.'

'All he has said is to tell no one he is here. He is adamant about it. Something is wrong.'

'He doesn't go out, so no one can know he is here.'

'We can't keep him a secret forever, and nappies have to be washed and dried.'

Haydn tapped the desk with the palms of his hands. 'He just shows up last night with a pack on his back and a baby in his arms as if it were a normal everyday event. How dare he?'

'Haydn! Please. He is not well.'

'Not well! A few days home cooking will see him right. But what do we do from here? And where does this baby come from? Whose is it and why does he have it?'

Miriam wiped her eyes again. 'I really must stop weeping. There has to be an answer to all these questions and we will find a way through. Please try to be patient.'

Haydn banged the desk. 'Patient? There is work to do.'

Miriam got up. 'I'll try to talk to him again.'

As she entered the corridor to the bedrooms, she heard the baby laughing. She stopped, smoothed her apron and drew a long breath. Laughter has a way of making life good, she thought. She knocked on the bedroom door. 'Roy?'

Roy opened the door. The baby was on a blanket on the floor and now rolled over and was trying to get to her hands and knees. Miriam smiled in spite of herself. 'May I come in?'

'Of course.'

'Roy...'

'I know. I owe you an explanation. This has been quite a shock for you I suppose.'

The baby fell forward on her hands and began to cry. In a stride, Miriam had caught up the child and comforted her against her shoulder. She put her cheek against the baby's head and rocked her silently. Her heart was suddenly filled with bubbles of joy. 'Please tell me this child is yours. I couldn't bear it if she were not my granddaughter.'

'She is my daughter. Her name is Efa. It's not her real name, but it is what I call her.'

'Efa?'

'For her mother.'

Efa was happily pulling the strings on Miriam's apron - she sat down and cradled the child. 'We need to talk.'

Roy nodded. He was wearing one of his old clothes. The shirt was loose around the body, but the shoulders were tight. The trousers were held up with braces, but they too were loose around the waist.

'You've lost weight.'

'I suppose I have.' He walked to the window and looked out.

'Can you tell me what has happened to you?'

Roy leaned on the window frame. 'No. There is much I cannot talk about...yet. Maybe one day, but not yet.'

'That you are here – and that you have brought a child – will not remain a secret for long. This is a community and while many things remain hidden in homes, the existence of a child is not one of them.'

Roy turned back from the window. His face was suddenly the colour of ashes. 'Not yet Mum, not yet.'

Later Miriam watched Roy walking in the orchard with Efa on his shoulder. The child was fretting. She had heard them during the night and the unease continued. She watched as Roy walked between the trees trying to comfort the crying child. Miriam went to the kitchen, then met him as he turned towards the house again.

'Try this.' She handed him a soft cloth smelling of cloves. 'Just rub it on her gums. It will stop the pain.' She held the child's hand. 'Teething is such a painful time. For everyone.'

The results were almost immediate. 'Thanks Mum. I don't know a lot about babies.'

'No one does until they have one.' She wiped the baby's tears from her cheeks with her thumb. 'Can you tell me when she was born?'

'15 of May.'

'And have you looked after her alone since then?'

'No. Since I left Russia in January.'

'Then you have done well. She is a healthy child. May I hold her again?'

Roy handed the now quiet child to Miriam. 'You are not alone Roy. We are here to help you.'

She recalled opening the kitchen door yesterday in answer to a call from outside. Against the early evening light it took her a moment to recognise Roy standing in front of her. He wore a British Army uniform – a rank she did not know – and had a bundle in his arms. A bundle that moved. She was too stunned to cry or call out. She just held out her arms and Roy leaned into them. The bundle was the baby and her shock trapped her voice still further into her throat. He dropped his large bag from his shoulder onto the kitchen floor and she drew them both into the warm of the house.

'Well? What has he said?' Haydn reached for the salt and thrashed it on his meat.

'Only that the child is his daughter and she is called Efa.'

'That's something I suppose. At least it is Welsh.'

'Haydn.' Miriam spoke in her serious voice. The one she had used since the boys were small. 'He needs time.'

'Time!' Haydn spluttered over his plate. 'What in heaven's name has happened to him? He spends all his time in his room playing with a baby! This is not Roy. I don't know who it is but it isn't the brother I used to have.'

Miriam sighed. 'I wish I knew Haydn. I dearly wish I knew.' She laid her knife and fork on her plate. 'He has been somewhere, seen something, done something that has changed him.'

'I'll say! He's fathered a child!'

'It's more than that Haydn. I know him. He is a decent person. I brought you both up to be decent people. Just give me time. We don't know what has happened to him.'

'Pah!' Haydn dropped his knife and fork on his plate and got up. 'Not too much time, Mum. There are things to be done.'

Miriam sat at the table alone for a long time. She needed to help Roy where she could, but she also had to be sure that Haydn didn't make things worse. She had to get Roy to tell her what had happened, why he had brought a child home. In part, the answer was in front of her. She looked through the long glass doors of the dining room into the garden. This was spring time and daffodils, the national flower of Wales, were in bud in the grass. Small pale yellow beacons of hope eternal. He needed his home and please God, he needed his family. That meant he needed the safety of both. Safety and peace. She folded her hands and putting her elbows on the table, rested her forehead on her hands. Dear Lord, give my son peace and give me a way to help him find it.

She gathered the plates and took them to the big farmhouse kitchen. She leaned on the sink watching the crockery sink into the hot washing up water. First things first. They had to agree on a story for the community that would soon know he was there. She pushed her sleeves up and put her hands into the hot water. First things first.

Over the next few days Miriam went to Roy's room as often as she could, played with Efa and accompanied them when Roy took the baby outside. She did not ask questions or seek resolution. She gave quiet advice on the care of the child or suggested what might be appropriate for her food or clothing or abilities. She cancelled her kitchen help for a few weeks and all events in her diary. Somehow she had to keep the other hired help away from the farmhouse until Roy was ready.

The farmhouse was part of a large complex of out-buildings. Some were formerly used for brewing, baking, laundry and cheese making, but were were used as storage. Behind them were sheds where the cattle for market were fattened and where machinery was kept. Haydn was tending to the animals, but sooner or later people would need to come for tools or tractors. She didn't know what to do.

Efa was a strong child who was cheerful, when teething allowed, and who loved being outdoors. On Friday morning while Haydn was in Aberaeron at the market, Miriam took the opportunity to be with them both in the spring sunshine in the front of the house. Efa amused herself by crawling off the blanket and putting stones in her mouth.

Miriam relieved Efa of the stones, and gave her back a wooden spoon that she had just thrown off the blanket. 'I will be going to Chapel on Sunday and I will see if anyone asks about you. It will mean that someone has seen something. And you know what Mrs Bevan is like. If she knows then everyone knows.'

'She always was the town crier of the area.'

'I am worried that we can't keep you and Efa secret for long. Why don't you come to Chapel and just get it over with.'

Roy snorted. 'Not likely.'

Miriam felt a wound she had not expected to be there. To deal with later, she instructed herself. 'I think we can say that you are safely home from being in Russia during the war and have brought your daughter home with you.'

Roy shook his head. 'That would be true, but I can't.'

'They will ask about her mother.'

Roy got up from the creaky wicker chair and walked slowly towards the drive. 'She is dead.'

Miriam got up and put her arm on Roy's. 'Is it true? I am so sorry.'

'No it isn't true. So far as I know and pray it isn't true. But I don't know.' He turned away from her. 'She might as well be dead.' The tone in his voice told her he was choking on emotion.

'Darling.' She felt such love for this quiet son. The one with the huge heart and strong morals. The one who had kept himself to himself ever since he was old enough to walk. Efa crawled off the blanket and Miriam picked her up. She handed the child to Roy. 'Tell me the most wonderful thing about her mother – about Yeva.'

Roy tucked the baby against his shoulder and kissed her head. 'She is the love of my life and she killed more Germans than anyone I know.' A note in his voice, told her to ask no more.

Haydn struggled not to confront Roy over lunch in the dining room but his discomfort was obvious to Miriam. Finally he came to the point. 'So, Roy. How much are you able to do with your leg like it is?' Roy looked up; his face showing no emotion. 'What happened? Did you step on a land mine or something?'

Miriam saw Roy compose himself. 'I don't know what it was – no one knows. The doctors didn't say.'

'They have doctors in Russia then?'

'Haydn. What do you think? That they are all sub normal heathens?'

'Well, they aren't exactly modern are they?' He smiled crookedly at his mother.

Roy put his knife down very carefully and retrieved a biscuit Efa had thrown on the floor. 'They have accomplished things that you can only dream of. And they saved my life.'

'What happened then? Come on we need to know.'

'Haydn…' Miriam intervened.

'Well?'

Roy got up and picked Efa from her high chair. 'No, you don't need to know…ever.'

It rained for the next few days and Miriam heard Roy working on the little typewriter he had brought with him. He worked in the bedroom while Efa slept and then in the living room while she played on the carpet. He never showed her what he wrote.

Haydn tipped the wash water from the basin into the sink in the scullery and reached for the towel. He dried his face and hands and rolled his sleeves down.

He buttoned the cuffs as he went back into the kitchen where his mother was putting up the plates for lunch.

'Well, what pearls of wisdom have fallen from his lips today? Has he said if he is home to stay? Or are we just here to feed him up until he says good bye?'

'Haydn, I have said before and I will say again, he needs time. Something has happened that he is not yet able to talk about... perhaps he never will. You will need to be more patient.'

'How can I be patient? We need to get on and I will need help soon. The farm workers will be getting suspicious. If he's going to stay I need him to pull his weight.' A shadow filled the door. 'Roy!'

'If you are concerned about the cost of having me and Efa here, I have quite a lot of salary that I have never used. You are welcome to the lot. I am not able to do much physically and I won't leave Efa, so you will have to make your own decisions about what to accept.'

'Haydn! Roy!' Miriam used the voice she had last used when they were boys, arguing over a game. 'Stop it! Stop it now!' She handed Haydn a steaming pot wrapped in a tea towel. 'Take that to the table please. Now both of you come and eat.'

When they had settled at the dining room table and Efa was in her high chair happily smearing gravy on the tray, Miriam spoke again. 'I need the two of you to put your differences aside.' They both looked at her. 'Until Roy is well again.'

'He's not ill!' Haydn glared at Roy. 'He may have a bad leg but he's not ill! I have a farm to run and it's not easy these days...'

'Haydn. You can speak to me. I am here.'

'Well then. What's wrong with you?'

Roy lifted the lid from the stew and then put it back. 'I... I can't say much. I...'

'Was it that bad? You weren't able to stop the war and save the world like you thought...'

'No. I promised ...'

'The Official Secrets Act I suppose. Oh for Heaven's sake. That old cop out.'

'Haydn! Stop it! If Roy is not able to tell us, we have to respect that he can't and that is the end of it.'

Haydn got up. 'He can't speak because he's fathered a child by some woman somewhere and is too embarrassed to talk about it in this stuffy little Methodist

277

community. He's ashamed. That's all.'

Roy put his head in his hand. Efa began to cry. Haydn slammed the dining room door on the way out.

Miriam put her hand on Roy's shoulder. 'Please tell me what you can. I will understand I promise.'

Roy lifted his head. His eyes were closed. 'She is the only reason I stayed alive. There is no one else in the world quite like her. But now I will never see her grow old. I don't know how I can carry on without her. I feel alone.'

Miriam got up and put her arms around Roy's head and shoulders, drawing him towards her. 'And, I am a wanted man.'

Yes?' Smythe had a way of answering the telephone that he knew startled his secretary. It was a little speck of immediate power that he enjoyed. Intimidation, but silly all the same. He loved it.

'Mr Johnson for you.' There was a series of clicks and snaps on the line and then 'Smythe?'

'Yes, Edward. What is it?'

'Is this a secure line?'

'Of course it is. You know that.'

'Just wanted to be sure. This is confidential.'

'Everything that comes out of your mouth is confidential Edward.'

'This concerns Roy Thomas.'

Smythe drew his chair forward sharply and banged his knee on the edge of a drawer. 'Roy?' he asked weakly.

'We think we've found him again. He seems to have fetched up at his home in Wales.

'We expected he'd do that, but after we lost sight of him in January... I thought maybe he was gone at last.'

Johnson interrupted. 'Someone who seems to have held him in some sympathy – don't know who – but when you find out... this is your bailiwick Robert. Someone got him on a train from Moscow at the very last minute before the police arrived and got him off again at some obscure place and then got him into the hands of the Red Cross. They got him home and he fetched up in Wales about a week ago.'

'How did you find out?'

'You don't need to know.'

'Do we need a meeting?'

'Yes, this is now serious Robert. All of our careers and, god help us, our lives may depend on keeping him quiet. We need to prepare a plan for him – which won't be difficult with your skills and mine - but then we need to talk about what we do after that. Organise a meeting will you Robert?'

'Do we really need the others? I mean Arnold and Neville keep each other informed. And if you and I...'

There was a pause. 'Yes, this time I think we do need to see them. We have to keep them quiet too. Absolutely quiet.'

Three men stood in Smythe's office, silently looking at the paintings on the walls, declining to take any of the tea from the trolley and feigning light conversation. It wasn't successful and their individual and collective nervousness was obvious to each of them. 'Where in hell is Donaldson?' Smythe muttered from behind his desk. He rubbed his arm. It often ached when he was under the most stress and when it was cold and wet. All three factors bothered him today.

'Start without him,' ordered Johnson. As they dragged chairs over the carpet to the table, Donaldson came in. 'Sorry everyone. Late report needed for the front page.' He looked around. 'What's the matter with everybody?'

Smythe banged his knuckles on the table. 'We found him.' That had everyone's attention. He held up one hand to quell the questions. 'He is at his family home in Wales. We are not sure how he got there or even when. But he seems to have arrived about a week or so ago.'

Carter spread his hands on the table and relaxed into the back of his chair. 'Thank the Lord for that. I was convinced he was lost. We had no word for so long.'

Johnson glowered around the table. 'Thank the Lord all you like. We now have a huge problem.'

Donaldson wrinkled his eyebrows in mute question. Carter was not so subtle. 'Why?'

Smythe got up and began to pace across the top of the room and back. 'Because you idiots, Pulmer is worried that Roy has worked out what he was sent to do. And he has probably worked out why. He may or may not have all the facts. But we can't take the chance. He is still alive, he still has a brain and he can still speak. So, if he knows anything at all...anything...' He left the rest

279

unsaid.

There was a moment of sick silence.

'He's now on his own... how much damage can he do to us? His word against ours...that sort of thing.' Arnold Carter pulled a large handkerchief from his pocket and wiped his forehead.

Smythe looked at him with a look akin to pity. 'Because someone in the Embassy helped him get out. Ask yourself why and then ask who? Then ask how high up is this source and what does he know?'

'Do you know who it was?' Arnold's voice was unsteady.

'No.'

Donaldson shifted in his chair. 'Has he said anything, Roy I mean? To your knowledge, Robert?'

'We don't know how long he's been there. He could have talked to the world and his wife by now and who can be sure he wasn't thoroughly debriefed before he left?'

'But what can he say that we can't attribute to a mind bent by events?'

'Plenty. He was lucid when he left Russia and even if his mind is awash, he can still make some sense. Enough for someone else to start asking uncomfortable questions. He may have kept some of the transmissions although that is unlikely.'

'There wasn't anything in them that would be incriminating, surely? And they were coded... surely he hasn't ...'

Johnson spun a pencil around and around his fingers on the table. 'Whoever we sent was not meant to come back. Ever.' There was a silence – the kind that precedes panic. Johnson went on quietly. 'As Robert said, even a little information to the wrong people will start the 'alternative intelligence service', sniffing around. A crumb of reality will have them dragging us in and then the net will widen to all the others involved. Some of them you know, but a great many you don't.' He broke the pencil in half. 'We are in the soup gentlemen. Truly. Unless we can shut him up. And then make it known that he lost control of himself a long time ago.'

Carter looked pale. 'And just how do you propose we do that? Keep him quiet I mean.'

Smythe actually smiled. 'Well, we have reason to believe – from Pulmer– that he was forced to leave something important behind – in Russia –something that

280

he dearly wants back. He may be open to some suggestion that if he really wants it, there may be a reasonable price he can pay to get them.'

Carter's colour became grey. 'What sort of thing?'

Smythe waved a hand dismissively. 'Facts not known at present – not firmly. We have more investigation to do.'

Donaldson cleared his throat. 'And if he is as honourable as I seem to remember him, what do we do if he refuses?'

Smythe looked quickly at Johnson. 'Leave that to Edward and me.'

Johnson did not return Smythe's look. 'In the meantime, I suggest that you prepare a strategy for yourselves if this comes out. Neville, you and Arnold are citizens of some stature in our little city. If you are questioned, you will have to have your plates clean...very clean. I leave that to you to do so, but I suggest you destroy anything and everything. And say nothing to incriminate anyone else... ever. Robert and I will have other issues to face.'

Donaldson's voice sounded more gruff than usual. 'I can destroy all my communications with the Party. It will mean a big bonfire, but...'

'Arnold?' Smythe looked at Carter. 'You probably have a bigger problem than the rest of us. But surely you have had some thoughts about a contingency position.'

Carter was looking pale. He cleared his throat and tugged on one of the wings of his collar. 'Yes, but much is tied into the bank records. A full bank audit could be difficult even though most of our resources are hidden. Redundant and dead accounts, that sort of thing. But a shrewd auditor... There will be problems there. An audit trail on outgoings... and conversions of...' His voice trailed off into his thoughts. 'I have work to do. It won't be impossible, but it does need time.' He looked at the others. 'I think we have all been too lax. We didn't expect to be challenged did we?'

The rain fell in sheets the next day - all day. Roy and Efa moved to the library. Efa played with a set of wooden blocks, a saucepan and a paper bag. Roy set the little typewriter on a small table and continued to work.

Miriam brought coffee in at mid-morning and found Roy with Efa hanging on his fingers, helping her to stand. 'She can almost climb to standing at the settee!' he reported happily.

'She will soon be bringing your table and typewriter down to her level if you don't watch her.'

He scooped the child up in his arms. 'She is never out of my concentration. Not for a second.'

'It is good to see a man so involved with his child. Most seem to delegate child care to the women and leave it at that.' She saw a shadow cross Roy's face. 'I'm sorry. That was insensitive.' She handed him a cup of coffee. 'Can you tell me about her? Her mother, I mean.'

'Her name was Yeva, Yeva Vilenovna Lavrentyev.'

'What was she like?'

Roy put Efa back on the carpet and gave her a biscuit. 'She was so complex. She...' he took a deep breath and looked out of the glass doors at the rain. 'She was funny. She was sensitive and loving. She was tiny. But she could be single minded and as hard as nails. She had skills and a mind that I never got to understand. She was a match for anyone.' Miriam leaned back in the big chair. How far did she question before he closed down again? 'When we married, I was the happiest I have ever been in my life. It didn't matter that we were living in the forest, surrounded by Germans and in fear of our lives every minute of every day. I could have Efa walked out of there on the tops of the trees.'

'Married? You married? In Russia?'

Roy turned abruptly. Some of his coffee spilled down the side of his cup. 'You didn't get my letter?'

Miriam shook her head. 'No, we didn't know you were married.' She looked at Efa.

'Cherta!'

She caught his surprise. 'Does Annie know?'

'I wrote to her...I hope so... I don't know.'

'Well, you can always write to her again... or telephone.'

Roy shook his head. 'No. No I can't. I can't let her know I am here. No one in Worcester – anywhere - must know I am here.'

'But Roy, I don't know how we can prevent it.'

He sat down on a hard chair and put his coffee cup on the desk. 'Mum. What I am about to tell you must never go any further. Ever.'

Miriam swallowed the dryness in her throat and nodded.

'Much of what I did must remain secret forever. Much of it is officially secret and will have to stay that way. But I can tell you some of it.'

'I worked with wireless radio – Morse code - but that will not be a surprise to you.' Miriam nodded again. 'I was asked to transmit for the Ambassador and others…but also for a group in Worcester. They were with British Intelligence and I transmitted reports to them from an individual who I never saw or knew, but who, they told me, was also with British Intelligence. But, I now know that the information was for quite another purpose… a purpose that had nothing to do with winning the war or British Intelligence for that matter… quite the opposite in fact. Now that I am home, those who did this will want me to be silent about it. And I am sure that they will try to silence me.'

Roy stood at the little bedroom window and looked at the unfolding spring season on the front garden. A yellow forsythia showed optimistic colours in its stark branches.

He had been standing at such a window but looking out at blowing snow and descending grey sky. It was only mid-day, but in winter in Moscow, it never changed. Grey and greyer; depressed and depressing. Even with the end of a war nothing had changed. Shortages and rationing continued with more of each to negotiate. The teleprinter clattered in the corner of the office and the whine from the radio and stream of Morse from his ear phones on the desk beside him, dulled the mixed emotions in his head.

23

The door to the office opened suddenly and the space was filled instantly by the bulk of John Bull. In a stride he tossed some transmissions slips onto the radio desk. He looked up and his face opened in shock that he quickly muted to surprise. 'Ah, Thomas,' he shouted and coughed lightly as if the name caught in his throat. 'I thought Fred was on duty today.' Roy picked up the slips.

'He has a stinking cold, so I said I'd help out.'

'Good. Good. Well, get these off as soon as you can.' He nodded at the slips in Roy's hand and left to shout at others in the corridor.

Roy flicked through the slips, counted them quickly and sat down at the radio. He put the ear phones on and fine-tuned the frequency for the first. Within seconds he was lost in automatically transmitting letters that had no meaning while his mind sought Yeva. Their little rooms in Moscow had become their home suddenly after they left the rural cottage where they spent the summer. That had been a time of calm discovery for them both. For the first time they had no crises to face, no death or loss a heartbeat away. They had time, the luxury of time, time of their own to find each other again and to develop as lovers and as a family. The baby, whose birth had been registered, was called Anya and they were both devoted to her. She was a happy baby and the summer seemed to go on forever.

But then the moment came when the cottage had to return to its owner and economic reality made them decide to return to Moscow. Roy hoped that the Embassy might provide him with some work while they established what would be their future. Yeva felt that she might be able to work in a children's nursery... there were plenty of them about as more and more women were finding they were expected to work and it would suit Anya. Uncertain it all was, but possible.

The Embassy was glad to find Roy small jobs, from putting up shelves to occasional radio work and Bull seemed glad to see him. Once Roy's extensive debriefing was over, Bull seemed satisfied with the long tortuous story and was even sympathetic about Roy's wife and family. Maybe it would all work out after all. Bull brought him more and more radio work, when there was no maintenance to do.

When he had arrived back to the Embassy, he asked Bull to see if there was a way for him to remain in Russia. It seemed best for Yeva and for the baby and if there was any way that he could continue to work for the Embassy, it would be a perfect solution. There was the question of him being married to a Russian national, but perhaps, he pleaded, there might be some way... In the meantime, here he was officially an employee of the British government, but not ... Bull listened but made no promises.

Today, the messages were all coded and the transmission routine. The fifth one had an unusual address and the code number leapt of the page. It was his mother's birth date 120496 which was why he remembered it, and the same as one on the little OTP he had hidden so long ago behind the panelling in his room. The possibilities made him take off the headphones. He put one hand on his wrist to stop his hand from shaking. It couldn't be true...someone else was using his OTP? Were they transmitting for the spy too? Who had coded this message? What was happening? Was it all just a co-incidence?

It was not a long message, but he copied it down, putting the paper down the front of his shirt.

When he finished the other transmissions, he waited in the radio room, with the headphones on, jotting down nonsense. Joyce, one of the typists now occupied Roy's old room and when she arrived in the office for her afternoon shift he slipped out of the radio room with the tool bag as if going to make a repair. He shut the bedroom door and lying on the floor beside the bed, he listened for any movement in the corridor. He pulled the little single bed away from the wall and with as little damage as he could, he pried the panel off. From among the dust he retrieved the OTP and replaced the panel. He did not nail it back on, just pushed two tiny pins into holes and bent them over the panel. Then he pushed the bed back into place. He left the transmitter where it was.

He went into the toilet and decoded the message. Amazingly, they had changed little of the initial cypher and after a few errors he had most of it written out on the back of his copy.

SA212 The Embassy to BR10 Worcester 27 Dec time 98 Shipment 25000 roubles 67000 gold plus gems value 5000 sterling dispatched today via route SKT Acknowledge receipt

Shaking with the knowledge he now had, he tore his copy and the code page into tiny pieces and flushed them away. He leaned on the cold tile wall until he felt he would no longer faint and his leg had stopped jumping up and down. With what confidence he could find, he walked back to the radio room, sat at his desk and held his arm steady until it too stopped trembling. Slowly, as if his wrist was stuck to the desk, he finished transmitting the message, then folded it and was putting it back into Bull's pigeon hole above the radio desk, when the man himself entered.

'Are you all right son?' Bull collected his papers, 'You look somewhat flushed. You aren't coming down with something too are you?'

Roy shook his head. He felt more than flushed. He felt ill; he could not speak; it all made sense now. Bull was the key. He was the spy. That was how Worcester knew where Roy was, when he came and went from the Embassy and what he had been doing. It was Bull who sent him to Smolensk and Kiev, gave him the old boots to wear and new wireless sets to use. The people he was sent to find may have been useful to the British Embassy, but they were even more use to Bull. They were wealthy and it was wealth that Bull needed. It also explained why the Laundry had no direct access to intelligence and why they wanted details from Roy on Russian finance. The bastards. He had been used... and used in ways that not only compromised his principles but also made him into a traitor. They used him because he could be manipulated and blackmailed. He felt more than ill, he was angry beyond belief. He stood up, took the headphones off his neck and dropped them on the desk with a great deal more force than was necessary. He wanted to tell Bull that he knew everything, but his voice had disappeared. He didn't know where it had gone. He turned and left. He tried, with a strength he did not really have, to look normal, but he was sure his eyes had said it all.

'What does it mean?' Yeva asked bouncing the baby on her hip.

'There is a group in Worcester, who are Communists and are collecting funds for some unknown reason... probably no good one. They are dangerous to the British Government and I have no way of warning anyone about them.'

Yeva looked at him and lifted both eyebrows. 'Why are they dangerous? They are just communists... like most of this country.'

'I know it is hard for you to understand.'

'I am not stupid you know.'

'That really is your word isn't it?'

'No, you are stupid. Why is being a communist, such a bad thing?'

'I'm not clever enough to know all the politics of this, but I know that in 1926 there was a national strike in Britain and it was found that the Russian government was sending money to some unions to support the strikers. I fear that they have been stockpiling money throughout the war.'

Her eyes flashed. 'So what is problem? Some of your communists have money from us? So what?'

'Britain does not want a communist government or a communist revolution, so far as I know. This is all probably illegal.'

'Why? Why does Britain not want a revolution?'

'You have seen what a revolution can do... and what harm it can do to people. Is that really the way you want to live your life?'

'But you want to stay here! What are you saying?'

'I want to stay because I love you, not because I love the government!'

She wrinkled her nose and frowned in frustration.

'This is a great deal of money and if it is going to be used to something bad to the government or the country... maybe for strikes that could bring down the country economically... I have to warn them... somehow.'

'How... how can you do that?'

'I have no idea. But I am very afraid.'

'Why? What for?'

'Because I think they know I have this information, and they do not want me to speak of it.'

He had pulled her to his lap, baby and all. 'They are dangerous men. I think they have killed already... to get me into the job here in the first place. They could well do the same again – and to you this time – if they think I have found them out.' He hugged them both. 'I don't know what to do.'

Miriam reached out to put her hand on Roy's arm. He took a deep breath.

Efa began to cry and Roy picked her up to quiet her. She gurgled happily, blowing bubbles. 'I didn't need to consider what to do, because the next day,

Yeva was arrested as being an enemy of the state.'

'Did she not have the protection of the Embassy?'

'Oh yes, but she was betrayed and arrested while she was out alone, shopping. I have not seen her since.'

Miriam felt tear sting her eyes. 'You could not save her?'

'Russian justice is very summary.' He rocked Efa who was now wiggling on his shoulder. He put her down on the carpet. 'We agreed long ago, that if something happened to her, I was to take Efa and save her. Yeva kept our marriage certificate, so she would claim British assistance. I have Efa's birth certificate. I had to get out and quickly.' He inhaled, his breath shaking. 'Or if something happened to me, she was to take everything and try to get to the Embassy.'

'Were you able to get a message to her?'

'Not directly, but someone at the Embassy helped me get out and if she is ever released he will tell her.'

Miriam sat up straighter. 'Have you told anyone else about all this?'

'I was debriefed when I got back to England, but I told them none of this. So, you see, as far as these people in Worcester are concerned, I am a loose cannon. I am a liability who needs to be removed or silenced. If not they could be arrested and charged… Treason does not have a happy fate.'

Miriam felt the blood drain from her face. 'So when you said you were a wanted man, it was more than just that wasn't it?'

Roy nodded. 'I suspect my time is running out.'

'So we must find a way to get you out of the country, into a new place, a new…' Miriam felt panic rising in her throat.

'No Mum, they will find me. They have skills and people, probably all over the world, who find out whatever they want to know. I don't know how many there are – or what they are capable of doing.' They both looked at Efa who was banging on the leg of the piano with the spoon. 'Whatever happens, I need to know that she will be safe.'

'Surely they wouldn't hurt a child.'

'Maybe, maybe not, but they can make her hostage to ensure my silence.'

Miriam felt fierceness boil over in her heart – a fierce protectiveness that she had never felt before. 'Not if they have me to deal with.'

Annie picked up the morning post from the door mat and flicked through the envelopes. As usual she looked for something from Roy and as usual her mind was elsewhere, knowing there would be nothing. There was nothing. She had nearly accepted her feeling of abandonment. It was not a feeling of anger. During war time all kinds of things were difficult. The letters she had received were in no particular order so she knew it was not a straightforward matter. But there had been nothing for over a year and that had been a short note. In Russia things were bound to be difficult. It was such a strange country, dark and frightening. She did little more these days than hope – hope that he was alive. The war was over; surely there would be some news soon. If he was alive, he would be home one day.

She tightened the belt on her dressing gown and opened the door to the hall, sorting the envelopes into those for her father and those for her mother or herself. Most, naturally, were for her father.

She stopped with the bundle in one hand and turned the knob to the dining room door. Before she had pushed it open more than a crack, her father's voice came through with the air.

'... back in Wales – on the farm.'

She inhaled sharply and pushed the door open wide to hear her mother. '... good idea to tell Annie?'

'Tell me what?' she demanded.

Her father looked at her mother and something passed between them. He cleared his throat.

'Well?' Annie demanded again.

'Nothing, darling. Just conversation between your mother and me.'

'No Dad. It was more than that.' She looked at her mother. 'Wasn't it?' Her mother said nothing. Annie turned back to her father. 'It's Roy isn't it?'

'No darling. We were discussing...'

Annie interrupted, the pitch of her voice rising. 'It is, isn't it? Don't lie to me – either of you. Is it Roy? Is he safe? Is he alive?' She leaned on the table and shrieked. 'Tell me Dad. You think Roy may be alive and back at the farm in Wales.'

'We don't know, dear.' Her mother, as always, tried to forestall any unpleasantness.

Annie threw the letters on the table. 'I must go – or call – or...'

'No! Annie, wait!' Her mother's voice was unusual. There was a sound of panic deep in it and it Annie stopped at the door. Her mother continued; her voice a little more calm. 'We don't know all the details yet. Please have some breakfast. Your father will tell you what little we know.' As usual, bribery of a sort worked and she sat down at her place.

Her father pressed the folded newspaper beside his plate, creasing the folds with his thumbnail. 'We aren't sure that he is there. There was a rumour – at the club – but it has not been checked.'

'Has anyone telephoned? Or gone there? How long has he been there?'

'No, no one has telephoned or visited yet. We heard last night. And we don't know how long he has been there.'

Annie's voice betrayed tears. 'Why hasn't he called me? 'She looked at the pile of post. 'Or written? Or come himself?' She got up from her place. 'Then I will call.'

'No Annie. You won't.' She turned and stared at her father.

The sun came out in the afternoon and Roy carried Efa into the walled kitchen garden where his mother was digging a small plot. 'Can I help?' She was working her way across the plot and beside her were a wheelbarrow full of compost, several garden forks and a shovel.

'Certainly. Will you be able to? With your leg, I mean?'

'I think so.' He put Efa down on a grassy patch and picked up a fork. 'What's being dug over there?' He gestured toward the corner of the walled garden.

'We dug a new drainage channel from the rain tanks and put in pipes to carry the excess away. It was just a french drain before and clogged up often.'

'I remember. It was always a boggy part of the garden.'

'The pipe is in and it just needs to be back filled now. The men had other work to do, so left it for another day. It isn't important.'

'This is such a nice place. Even on a windy miserable day, there is a kind of calmness here.' Roy pushed the fork into the vegetable bed.

'Yes, I often come here to work and let the world and its troubles go by.'

'Is that why you are here now?'

'In part.' Miriam turned over a forkful of soil and smashed it into crumbs with the back of the fork. 'I am worried about you.' She looked at him and smiled. 'Don't object, that's what mothers do. But I am trying to think of a way to keep you and Efa safe.' She spread a forkful of compost from the barrow and began to dig it in. 'Was there anyone in Russia who might have been able to help or might now help?'

'Possibly.'

Miriam drove the fork in, then straightened up, untied the headscarf tied under her chin, shook it out and put it back on. 'Are your instincts strong enough to act on if you need to, do you think?'

'One person, Adrian, helped me get out of the Embassy and onto a train at the last moment…. He may have been the one who had the Red Cross catch up with us at the port and get us on a ship home. But I don't know for sure.' ·

'That was a brave act. He may be the one to trust.'

'Perhaps he is the one who I can trust with this story, but I just can't be sure.'

Miriam closed the curtains on the long morning room windows. 'It will be nice tomorrow.'

Roy looked up from the typewriter. 'Why?'

'Because there is red in the sunset.'

Roy got up and went to the drinks cabinet. It was not likely that it had been opened since his father died or at least since Glyn Andrews read his father's will. He moved the bottles until he found what he wanted and poured a healthy amount into a crystal glass.

'Does that old wives' tale actually work?'

'Are you drinking?'

The horror in her voice was unmistakable. 'Yes, it's vodka,' he answered. 'Kept us from freezing to death in the winter. Anti-freeze in a way. Except that we never knew what the Russian stuff was made of.'

Miriam tried to arrange her face from one of shock to one of mere disappointment. 'I was just surprised, that's all.'

'Mum. I am not the person I was when I was here last. I do or have done all manner of things that would disappoint you and surprise you I'm sure.'

'You were so… so… well… committed to what we believed. I am surprised… I made a wrong assumption. I apologise.'

Roy pulled the little table and the typewriter aside and sat down. 'Mum. I saw so many things and did so many things that I knew God would never have permitted, that I can no longer believe. Losing my faith was the easiest loss to bear because it had become meaningless. Any God I had known would have intervened. So I concluded that He did not exist.' He sipped on the neat vodka. 'That is one of the reasons why I cannot go to Chapel with you. The other of course is I need to keep out of sight until...'

Miriam wanted to know, but was afraid to know. She wanted to share his burden, but dare not unlock whatever had caused him to make such a deep and fundamental decision.

'Can you tell me more about Yeva?' She saw the skin on his jaw become tight. 'Can you talk about any of it?'

'Yeva was an extraordinarily gifted killer.'

'Killer? What? How?' Miriam knew that the waters into which she was venturing were becoming seriously deeper.

'She was a sniper. She looked men in the eye and then she pulled the trigger. You would think that she had no humanity. But she had reasons. We all did.'

'Did you kill as well?' The question was spoken before she realised she had said it.

'Yes. Yes I did.'

Miriam sat down heavily in the arm chair, tears filled her throat. 'I am sorry – I keep apologising – I mean, I shouldn't have asked... I do know you well enough – even now – to know that it wasn't an easy thing for you to do.'

'On the contrary. It was simplicity itself. It was born of need – of necessity – of desperation.' He made small circles with the glass, spiralling the colourless liquid almost to the top of the rim. 'She had gone missing and I was looking for her. She was trying to find a place of safety.'

Miriam said nothing.

'There is an astonishing amount of distrust in Russia. No one trusts anyone else for any reason. Everyone is afraid of everyone. No one knows when they will be denounced on some – any – charge, rumour or simple grudge to the police.' Roy put the glass on the little table. 'People charged are dragged off, confined to prisons, questioned, tortured, and if convicted sent to prison in Siberia for years or a life time.' He put his elbows on his knees and with his head in his hands, he began to sob.

Miriam went to him, put her arms around his head and shoulders and rocked him back and forth. 'Is that where she is? In prison?' He nodded.

'You still have Efa.'

'Yes, I still have Efa.' He struggled on. 'Adrian at the Embassy... and the Red Cross...

'I don't remember much about the trip. I just looked after Efa as best I could. Winter on the sea in the Arctic...There were some women on board who helped. I took a very late train to get here. I didn't want anyone to see me.'

'Do you know for sure that Efa is still in prison?'

Roy nodded and wiped his eyes with the back of his hand. 'Yes. If they let her go she would have gone directly to the Embassy and I would have had some word.' He had tapped his temple. 'There is no word from her – here – in my head. No sound except pain. She is not free.'

'Smythe?' Arnold felt sick. He had tried all day to calm Annie without telling her why she should not immediately call Wales. He was not sure that any of his reasons had been successful. In the end all he could do was forbid her to go. He doubted that forbidding a daughter of nearly 28 to do anything would actually work. He prayed that he still had emotional control of her at least. But he still needed to warn the others. He had not seen her this morning, but heard her pacing up stairs. 'Look. There may be trouble. Annie overheard part of a conversation yesterday morning. She is determined to go to Wales immediately and find Roy.' He heard a sharp breath at the other end of the line and interrupted the pending blast. 'I have forbidden her, but she's 28, Robert. I don't know how long I can keep her here.'

'You idiot!'

'It wasn't intentional. It was an accident and she shouldn't have found out.'

'Bloody hell Arnold! That's too late now!'

'That's why I've called. You have to warn the others.'

'No, you warn the others. I have work to do.' The phone went down with a slam.

Arnold held the quivering telephone receiver in his hand. 'What did you mean "warn the others" Arnold?' He felt his wife's hand on his arm. Dear sweet wife. Uncomplicated, simple wife who knew so much and so little. Who stood beside him. Who heard everything.

The early afternoon sun had new warmth and the weight of the fork in Miriam's hands had substance. She needed some time and exercise to make Yeva a real person in her mind. A daughter-in-law she did not know she had and now might never know or meet. A woman who gave her tender son, love and happiness and then had given them all a lovely child.

She straightened and rested her back. Roy pushed the old rusty pram into the garden and into the shade of the raspberry canes. He looked calmer today. No less in pain, but calmer. 'Is Efa asleep?'

'Yes, I put her down a few minutes ago and she was asleep in seconds. She'll be fine for an hour or so.'

'Afternoon naps are God's way of giving parents a tiny space of peace.' She thought she saw a little smile on Roy's face. He took up the spade and began to cut the edges of the bed of dark earth. It would be a good vegetable plot later in the spring. A movement at the entrance to the walled garden made them both look up at the same time.

'Annie!' Roy dropped the spade. 'What are you doing here?' Miriam heard the panic in his voice – a sound between loss of breath and hysteria.

'Silly. I've come to find you.' She walked briskly towards them her arms reaching out. Then she became aware of Miriam and she put her hands in the pockets of her coat. 'Why didn't you tell me you were here? I would have come the minute I knew... Is this your mother?'

Roy seemed incapable of speech. He stared at Annie. Miriam could only imagine what the thoughts were that rampaged around in his head. 'How did you get here?'

'Train and then taxi. Why does it matter?' She stood in front of him and took his hands. 'Don't you have a hug for me?'

'Annie, I...' Miriam caught the glare that Annie gave her in reply. It said, 'Go away, old woman. Leave us alone for a few minutes.' Miriam did not move.

'Are you all right Roy? You look ... You haven't been injured have you? I am just so thankful that you are alive, it wouldn't matter a jot if you had been injured. I can look after you. Daddy will help us – find you a job – and we can get back to normal.'

'Annie, there is no normal, I...'

I'm sorry Roy. My thoughts were just tumbling over each other. I'm so glad to see you. Now that the war is over, we can be normal. Once we are married...'

That was the moment that Efa made everything easier for them all. There was a wail from the pram. Roy was beside it in three strides and snatched the grumbling child to his shoulder.

Annie's shock was total. She did not speak for several seconds. 'Who is that?' she finally whispered.

Roy turned to her. 'This is my daughter Efa...'

Annie's face turned to plaster. 'Your... your daughter... but...'

In a silence that resembled a vacuum on the sea shore, Miriam whispered to Roy. 'Would you rather be alone?'

'No!' Roy's eyes were on Annie. 'Annie, this is my daughter. You did not get my letter.'

Annie looked at Efa . There were red spots now on her cheeks. 'Letter?'

'The one that told you I was married. In Russia...?'

'Married? Wha ... Where is your wife?' Annie looked around as if anticipating trolls to leap from the earth.

'She is not here ... she is still in Russia.'

'Will she be coming ... here ...?'

'No.'

Annie visibly relaxed and let out a long breath of obvious relief. She smiled at Roy again, looking past the child. 'Well, that's all right then.' She reached for his arm. He drew back.

'What's all right? What are you talking about?'

'Well a marriage in Russia doesn't count does it? And if she can't come here, then we...'

Miriam could see the doors on Annie's' life closing one by one and watched her grab at any emotional possibility – reasonable or otherwise.

'Annie! What on earth are you saying ...?'

'We can carry on as we planned. We can find a place for the baby and...'

'Annie! No! No we can't. What do you mean - a place for the baby?'

'Roy. We can still get married, like we planned and make our own babies. I ...' Reality was beginning to replace hope into Annie's mind. She took refuge in herself. 'Roy. I've just been through a war – all the rationing, air raids, shortages ... it's been hard. You have no idea. I've waited ... and waited. I've suffered just like you have. We can ...'

'How dare you even suggest that you have suffered like I have? Your cosy life and all you've had to worry about was rationing. Don't you dare – don't you even dare!' He turned as if to protect Efa from Annie and saw another figure coming through the garden door.

This one was wearing a tweed suit and hat.

Roy pushed Annie aside. 'Smythe! *Kakogo cherta ty khoches?'*

Miriam did not know what the Russian meant, but the implication was clear. 'What the hell do you want?'

Smythe smiled as he walked toward them, but there was no warmth in it. 'Glad you made it, Roy.'

Roy said nothing. Smythe looked at Efa. 'So this is the child we have heard so much about. We need to talk, Roy.' Smythe looked at Annie and Miriam. 'In private if you don't mind.'

'I do mind. What you want to say must be said here in front of my mother.'

Smythe tipped his hat lightly. 'Mrs Thomas. Miss Carter.'

Annie stepped closer to Roy. 'How does he know who I am?'

'I know your father well.' Smythe looked at Roy again. 'In fact, he called me when he knew that you had gone. I got the same train. I thought I'd just let you have a few minutes before I interrupted.'

'What do you want? What has my father to do with …with …'

Miriam grabbed Annie's arm. 'Annie. Be quiet.'

Roy moved Efa to his other shoulder. 'I have nothing to say to you Smythe.'

'You may not, but I have much to say to you.' He reached to Efa and touched her cheek. 'It may involve this lovely child.'

Roy's voice remained calm. 'No Smythe. No it won't.'

Smythe sighed heavily. 'Roy, all the cards are in my hand. You know that you have things in your head that we want and we have the power to get them …' He looked at Efa again. '… one way or the other. So are you prepared to discuss …'

'Roy! What is going on?' Annie wrenched her arm away from Miriam.

Roy's voice was calm, but the words were deliberate, born of hostile intent. 'Shut up Annie. This is none of your business. Although your father may be able to explain.'

'My father …?'

'Smythe. I've known for a long time that you would come to kill me ...'

'Roy!' Annie's voice was shrill with panic. 'Kill you?'

'You should have stayed in Russia. You might – just might – have been safe there.'

Roy snorted in an un-amused laugh. 'Not likely – given what you did to Yeva.'

Smythe shrugged. 'Needs must, I'm afraid. We hoped that you would stay there and fight for her, but instead you ran ...'

Roy looked at Efa. 'You clearly don't know me very well ...'

'Roy? Who is Eva?' Annie's face was now flushed and angry.

Miriam grabbed her arm. 'Shut up Annie.'

'Will everyone stop telling me to shut up and tell me what's going on?'

Smythe put his hand in the pocket of his jacket and did not take his eyes from Roy's face. 'Shut up Annie.' When he took his hand from the pocket, it held a small revolver. 'Now can we talk?'

Annie and Miriam stared at it in shocked silence. Before she could draw breath to scream, Roy handed the baby to Annie. 'Mum, take Annie and the baby to the house.'

'No!' It was a scream this time but from Miriam.

Smythe wobbled the revolver in their direction. 'Go!'

Annie needed no other instruction and turned immediately to the gate. Miriam looked at Roy – there was a message on her face of love and understanding. Roy reached for her hand and squeezed it. She, too, turned toward the gate. Smythe's attention returned to Roy who continued to stare at him.

As she walked past Smythe, Miriam silently pulled a shovel from the earth they had been digging. With one stride she turned behind Smythe and with the energy of her forward movement, she swung the heavy tool. The corner of the blade struck him with all the force she could command. It smashed into the back of his skull. The cracking of bone was loud in the confined space and still air. Smythe pitched forward into the mud.

24

February 1946

In the library the sun was beginning to throw long shadows from the legs of the furniture. Haydn put a glass of whisky into Annie's hands. He folded her fingers around the glass to stop them shaking.

'I don't drink.'

'Shut up Annie and drink it.'

Miriam sat beside her on the settee. She too held a glass of peat coloured liquid – purely for medicinal purposes - and sipped at the liquor. She felt fog in her brain. There was no feeling in her hands or feet but she held the glass firmly, afraid of it falling on the carpet. Her breath was pounding from the top of her lungs. 'What have we done?'

Haydn poured a large glass for himself. 'It was the right thing. He would have killed Roy.' Roy stood at the long windows looking into the garden. He was tapping a large glass of vodka against the window pane. 'Self-defence.'

Annie sobbed. Her shaking shoulders made the whisky splash on her skirt. No one moved to take it from her.

Miriam tried to speak but her mouth would not form the words. She sipped the whisky. The fire in it calmed her internal organs and drove some of the fog away from her brain. 'What have we done? Dear God.' She squeezed her eyes shut to hold back tears of panic. 'What have we done?'

'Mum. You have saved my life and Efa's too. You don't know what he was capable of. I do.' Roy's calmness surprised Miriam. 'If you hadn't killed him I would have.'

She looked at him sharply. 'I don't think I know you anymore.' Roy turned

298

back to the room. 'I don't know how you can be so matter of fact about this. Do you realise ...'

'Mum. I've seen men killed for reasons a lot less than this.' He looked at Efa asleep in the pram. 'When you have reasons like we do I feel no remorse at all.'

'Roy,' Miriam felt her voice rise in tone. 'We are a civilised country. We don't do things like this. We have law and police and order, and, and...'

'The man was a bastard and so are all his cronies ...' Roy looked at Annie, who seemed incapable of understanding where she was or how she got there.

Haydn pulled a chair from the desk closer to Miriam and Annie. 'Now we have to be practical. We can't go to the police or anyone else. If we do we will be the criminals, not him. Do we all understand that?'

After a few seconds Annie appeared unable to respond. She looked down at her hands – fingers twisted together. Then she looked up and seemed to recognise where she was. Miriam nodded. Annie made no response.

'No one will question why the drain has been filled in. It was due to be done anyway.' Haydn swallowed a large mouthful. 'If he is ever found, none of us will know anything. We took everything from the body that might have identified him.' He looked directly at Miriam and Annie and then at the small smouldering pile of papers in the grate. 'We have buried the gun at the bottom of the lake. We don't know anything. Do we?'

Miriam took Annie's arm and squeezed it hard. 'We don't know anything, do we Annie?'

Annie's eyes were red. 'But, I ...'

Roy took the vodka bottle and sat down beside her. 'No Annie, you know nothing. You saw nothing. Because if you did ... Annie, listen to me.' Annie looked at him. Her eyes were staring and her face was white. 'If you ever, ever speak of this, your father and your mother will be arrested and charged with treason. Treason is a hanging offence.'

'Why?' Annie looked at the glass in her hand. 'I don't understand. Why?'

Roy emptied the vodka bottle into his glass. 'Because, Annie, they were conspiring to encourage a Communist revolution in England.'

'What? The two of them?'

'Don't be stupid Annie. There were many others ... probably hundreds ... maybe a whole country full of them for all I know. They may be stopped, but they may not. They are traitors Annie. Traitors. And your father is one of them.'

There was a long silence. Roy kept his eyes on Annie, watching as these facts settled into her brain, or not ... 'You must not speak of this. Ever. What these traitors might do to me, they could also do to you if they thought that you knew something.' He went to the little open desk and sorted through a few papers. He chose one, a magazine to rest it on and a pen. 'Sign here, Annie.'

She looked up at him without understanding. 'Sign it!' Roy handed her the pen and she signed a shaky signature at the bottom. Roy took back the document and sat on the edge of the sofa and looked at her directly. 'This,' he folded the paper, 'is a copy of the Official Secrets Act and you are now prohibited by law from ever speaking of what you have seen today. You must never tell anyone that you have seen me here or anywhere, ever. Do you understand?'

Annie nodded and uttered only a long sob. Roy continued, 'Do you know what happens to people who break the Official Secrets Act?' Annie stared at him. 'They are charged with treason and what is treason?' Annie's face took on the colour of cold ashes. 'A hanging offence,' she whispered.

'Do you understand? Really understand.' She nodded numbly and there was a moment of silence.

Miriam finished her drink. She felt warmer and there was some heat now in her hands. She felt weak but her brain was her own again. She took the glass from Annie. 'Come dear, let's get you cleaned up and then we will put you on a train home. You will be safe there.'

She tipped Annie's chin up so they looked face to face '... so long as you speak not a word of this. Otherwise you could be arrested or worse. Do you understand?'

Annie, still pale, nodded. 'Yes.'

'Good. Now come.' Haydn and Miriam helped Annie to her feet. Haydn picked up her handbag and handed it to her. She took it as if she didn't quite know what it was.

The women disappeared into the house, and Haydn looked at Roy. 'Can we count on her to keep quiet?'

'We have to hope so.' Roy turned to the drinks cupboard and opened the only other bottle of spirits remaining – whisky intended for Glyn Andrews. Clearly nothing had been touched since his father's death. 'There is little risk of her being charged with anything that her father did, but the "fear of God" is not a bad weapon to have. Keep an eye on her if you can.'

'When she gets home, they'll assume that she couldn't find you and that is the reason for the state of her.'

'They will put their poor darling to bed and in time she will recover.' Roy tore the document Annie had signed in half and then in half again.

'What are you doing? You need that!'

'It was a hire agreement for a radio set. Even I don't have access to copies of the Act and she'll never know the difference.' He threw the pieces into the grate.

For the first time, Haydn's face wrinkled into a tiny smile. 'What will her father do once this fellow – Smythe – hasn't returned? Surely he knows he came here.'

'I'm sure they will do the sums and come looking for him. On the other hand, they may be too fearful of their own skins to want to stir things up too much. They will know that I can still talk and be too afraid for their own futures. I am counting on that. But you will have to be ready and deny everything… don't give in to anything. For your own safety. And be very careful, whatever you do. These are dangerous men.'

'What will happen to you?'

'It may be better if you don't know Haydn.'

Miriam returned with Annie. 'Haydn, will you take Annie to the station and stay with her until she gets on her train? It is still early enough for her to get home tonight.' She brushed the shoulders of Annie's coat. 'Annie, dear, I would suggest you use the time on the train to rehearse what you will say when you get home. But always remember…'

Miriam found Roy sitting by Efa's cot in the dark. 'I know it's late but I brought tea.'

'Thanks Mum.' He took the cup and smiled. 'You still look after me. In spite of all the mess I've made of my life and yours.'

'This is not your doing. We can blame the war for a lot and whatever blame we put on it, it will be much, much less than it deserves.'

'How will you manage? Yourself I mean. This has been a shock that no one in a civilised country should have to take.'

'I will have moments when I wonder if God will ever speak to me again. But for everyone's sake I have to pretend. When I go to Chapel next, I will see if God wants to speak to me. If not, I don't really care. What happened was instinctive. It was not calculated from any religious understanding. It was a mother protecting her child. Just as you would.'

301

'Mum, I have guilt on my shoulders for so many sins, you can't possibly know. But this one... it is different because it happened here... in our so-called civilised country. I wanted so much to believe that home was safe and society was civilised. Perhaps it is, but there are parts of this country where it is not. I made the mistake of entering that area of life and finding out what it was like. Then I made the bigger mistake of trying to get out of it again. What that has done to all of you, I can't begin to know.'

Miriam put her hands on his shoulders and stroked his hair as she had done when he was a child.

'Someday the story will be told. Someday it must be told. But not for a long... long time.' Roy looked into the cot. 'I have to go. And probably forever.'

'I know. I may never see you again.'

'Mum. Over the last 6 or 7 years, I've lost everything dear to me and now I will have to lose the thing left that I love the most.' He looked at the sleeping child.

'She will be safe, loved and cared for. No matter what happens to you or the rest of us. I will make sure of that.'

'What will you do?'

'I have some people in mind. They have no children but have always wanted them. I will send Efa to them for a few years and then I will bring them here to the estate. I will make up a suitable story. He is a good manager and they can live in the cottage beside the house. I will not desert her. Anyone who may come looking for her will not find her; they will find a little girl who is the daughter of someone else.'

Roy nodded. 'It is for the best. Take photographs of her as she grows up ... keep them for me ... someday I will take them and get them to her mother.'

Miriam squeezed his shoulder. 'Of course I will. I will leave them at Glyn Andrews' office.'

'I must go. Tonight.' He stood up. 'I've telephoned Adrian. I think I can trust him. He is in London and says I can go to him. I will take the overnight train, and get him to send me out of the country or find me a place to hide in plain sight. He knows how to do these things. He spent a good deal of the war getting people out of Russia under the noses of both the Russians and the Germans. Perhaps he can do the same for me.'

'You have lost so much. Can you let me know if you are safe at least.'

'I will try to arrange something with Adrian. But to keep yourself and Haydn safe, you must know nothing of what has actually happened to me. Concoct a story – any story you like. But the less you have to pretend the better.'

'I already have ... Haydn and I will tell anyone who asks – it will not be something we go out of our way to tell – but to anyone who asks, you will have gone to Brazil or somewhere. We won't know where or what has happened to you. We will concoct a story for the paper ... we are desperately looking for ... etc.' She swallowed hard tears.

Roy looked into the cot again. 'I will not be able to send money for her support, nor notes for her birthday or Christmas. I can never communicate with you or her again. It would open a trail for someone to follow.'

Miriam nodded.

Later the next day, Miriam went upstairs with the laundry basket to the room that Roy and Efa had shared. On the bed were Roy's typewriter and a stack of typewritten sheets. She sat down to read the first page. 'Read this, destroy it and never speak of it.'

Wednesday 5 February 1941 Find myself in Moscow – at the British Embassy. The Embassy is on Sofiyskaya Embankment *. This is a street that runs along the side of the River Moskva in front of the building that the British acquired in 1931. It looks onto the activity of a busy river or it would be busy if it were not frozen over- and the Kremlin. Very much want to get out and SEE things.*

and then...

Haydn married a local girl, Moira in early 1947 and later in the year a daughter Hannah was born. She was their only child. Haydn and Moira developed an interest in breeding fine Welsh Black cattle and travelled over the world working to refine the breed.

Neville Donaldson, Arnold Carter and his wife continued to live in Worcester, never speaking about their attitudes to the English Government. They retired without ceremony from the newspaper and the bank respectively soon after the war and lived quiet lives in the city. They were, from time to time, visited by men in suits. Annie never married, but lived with her parents until they died.

Edward Johnson disappeared and was never heard from again.

John Pulmer was transferred to the British Embassy in Washington where he looked after administrative affairs and sorted paperclips until he retired.

In 1952, a couple named Bryn and Sophie Bevan came to live on the estate. He worked as the farm manager. They had a daughter named Haulwen. She and Hannah became firm friends.

Miriam kept a close eye on Haulwen for the rest of her life. She died early in 1975 at the age of 80 and left the manager's cottage to Haulwen in her will.

Occasionally, in the 1970s, when Haydn and Moira were away from the estate, a man visited Miriam. Haulwen remembered him because he walked with a limp.

Roy continued to seek Yeva and that may be the seeds for the next story.

Historical Notes

I wrote this because, coming from Canada, I have a certain enduring - and bitter - understanding of snow and cold, based on many years personal experience! I felt it might be useful in telling a story such as this. I am also fascinated by the history of World War II and so combining the two issues put the story in and around the invasion of Russia by Germany in Operation Barbarossa.

This is by no means a historically factual study: some dates have been stretched or moved slightly to fit the story. Characters and war time activities are all fictional with exception of great historical leaders and major events.

1. Russian Partisans: Partisans have existed since the beginning of time in conflict situations. It could be said that guerrilla influence has won and lost wars through their activities. Figures for the number of partisans in Russia during the Great Patriotic War - as World War II was known in Russia - are difficult to determine, but may have been as few as 140,000 or as many as 550,000. They existed all over the war zones from urban to rural and to active combat areas. The ones featured here are modelled on those in the Prip'yat Mashes of Belarus.

    Many of the Partisans, up to 30% were women and a large number, as much as 10%, were Jewish. Marriage was not encouraged during the war, but after, the number of weddings between partisans was considerable.

    As with so many sectors of Russia, the Belarus Marshes were encircled by the German advance and the inhabitants left to either starve or organise themselves. Disaffected or dispossessed, many formed themselves into groups of partisans and in time these groups became a formal part of the Red Army. In the marshes, as elsewhere, partisans relied on sympathetic people for their survival and in time, they had created their own villages and farms – many had their families with them, schools, a postal system and newspapers.

    As Roy found, they were disorganised and competitive in the early years of the war, but later were taken under the direction of P K Ponomorenko, Head of the Partisan Movement, a formal part of the Red Army, and so were better directed and equipped. Their communications systems were however weak at the start of the war and Roy would have been a great asset.

    Later in the war and once German occupation was waning they were used for reconnaissance work.

It has to be acknowledged however that neither the Russians nor the Germans had a monopoly on brutality. Ref: Grenkevich, *The Soviet Partisan Movement 1941 – 1944.*

2. MI9: There was a rescue section of British Military Intelligence called MI9 during the war. It was established to help escaped prisoners and others evading capture. There was a substantial network of people working in small secret sections throughout Europe, which moved people through a complicated, dangerous and clandestine system, eventually getting a great number back to Britain. Some of these sections helped downed airmen in Russia, particularly American airmen and especially in the area of the Balkans. I modified their remit a little to include the Marshes and gave the partisans a part in it.

   Large numbers of aircraft, tanks and other tactical machinery were sent to Russia as soon as Russia joined the Allies through a Lend-Lease program. Soon airmen from the allies were also flying from Russia. Ref: Foot and Langley, *MI9, Escape and Evasion, 1939 – 1945.*

3. Communist Plot: The issue of a movement to destroy the government of Britain during WWII is entirely from my imagination and not based on any known facts. The British Secret service did however know of Communist financial support for certain unions in the 1926 General Strike. I have used this in another time and place. Ref: Andrew, *The Defence of the Realm: The Authorized History of MI5* and Aldrich, *GCHQ, The uncensored story of Britain's most secret intelligence agency.*

   The Communist Party of Great Britain received impetus from the October 1917 Revolution in Russia but was founded formally in 1920 in Britain. It strongly supported the British General Strike in 1926 and, while campaigning for peace at the beginning of the Second World War, it gave its support after Russia became involved in 1941. Support for the party grew quickly during the war, in 1939 membership was at 16,000 and by 1945 there were 56,000 members.

4. Code and Cypher School: A substantial code and cypher operation was carried out at Bletchley Park during the Second World War. Training was given but how much of it was in Russian I don't know. It is a fascinating place to visit and I recommend it highly. I did not want to lose it in telling this story, so added a little, unofficially (I am sure) to its story.

5. Bombings in Worcester and Coventry: Worcester and Coventry were bombed as described in the story. Most of the facts are true.

6. Churches in Russia: Although Communist Russia was largely secular once Stalin took power, the Christian faith survived in places. During the war, Stalin acknowledged that the church was a calming influence, and a patriotic institution. It enjoyed a brief revival until the Khrushchev era. There was an Orthodox Church in Kuibyshev during the war, but it would, I am sure bear no resemblance to the one I created here.

7. Germans in the Prip'yat Marshes: The Germans retreated from the partisan areas in 1944-45. I have kept them engaged in the area, perhaps a little longer than was true, for purposes of the story.

8. Radios: Radio transmission at this time was by Morse code. Voice transmission did not begin until after but was used extensively by the time of the Korean War.

9. Treason and Treachery were offences which carried the death penalty until 1946. High Treason is a crime of disloyalty to the Crown but was difficult to prosecute. The Treachery Act 1940 also addressed the felony of treason, but proof was less complicated and it was easier therefore to prosecute. The last trial for treason which resulted in the death penalty was that of William Joyce, Lord Haw Haw, in 1946.

10. Lucy was the name given to an anti-German spy ring that originated in Lucerne. Information was sent to it by disaffected German officers. The information was of high quality and was sent by Swiss Intelligence to British SIS and to the Soviet GRU (military intelligence). Lucy was closed down in summer of 1944 when the German officers feeding information to it were arrested after the failed coup to assassinate Hitler.

11. The Worcester Journal: This is a real newspaper which is said to be the oldest surviving newspaper in the world. It appears to have been published as the Berrow's Worcester Journal since 1690. It has gone through various changes but is still published today as Worcester News, part of the Newsquest Media Group.

The role of Royston Thomas as one of its local journalists who became an ad hoc overseas correspondent, is an invention of mine.

Other books you may find interesting:

Ailsby, Christopher, *Barbarossa, The German Invasion of Russia, 1941*. Grange Books, Rochester, Kent, 2001

Aldrich, Richard J., *GCHQ, The uncensored story of Britain's most secret intelligence agency*, Harper Collins, London, 2010

Andrew, Christopher, *The Defence of the Realm: The Authorized History of MI5*, Vintage, October 2009

Beevor, Antony, *Stalingrad*, Penguin, London, 1998

Berton, Kathleen (text) and Freeman, John (photos), *The British Embassy Moscow, The Kharktonenko Mansion*, British Ambassador/Moscow, Butler & Tanner Ltd, London, 1993

Braithwaite, Rodric, *Moscow 1941, A City and its People at War*, Profile Books, London, 2006

Clark, Alan, *Barbarossa, The Russian German Conflict, 1941-1945*, Cassell, London, 1995

Denniston, Robin, *Thirty Secret Years, A G Denniston's work in signals intelligence 1914-1944*, Polperro Heritage Press, Clifton on Teme, Worcs, 2007

Enver, Ted, *Britain's Best Kept Secret, Ultra's Base at Bletchely Park*, Alan Sutton Publishing, 1994

Foot, M R D and Langley, J M, *MI9, Escape and Evasion, 1939 - 1945*, Book Club Associates, 1979

Gannon, Paul, *Colossus, Bletchley Park's Greatest Secret*, Atlantic Books, London, 2006

Glantz, David M, *Before Stalingrad, Barbarossa - Hitler's Invasion of Russia 1941*, Tempus, Stroud, Glos, 2003

Grenkevich, Leonid (Edited by David M Glantz), *The Soviet Partisan Movement 1941 - 1944*, Frank Cass, London, 1999

Hinsley F H and Stripp, Alan (eds) *Code Breakers, The Inside Story of Bletchely Park*, OUP, Oxford, 1993

Koschorrek, Gunter, *Blood Red Snow, The Memoirs of a German Soldier on the Eastern Front*, Greenhill Books, London, 2002

Macksey, Kenneth, *The Partisans of Europe in World War II*, Granada Publishing Ltd, 1975

McKay, Sinclair, *The Secret Life of Bletchley Park, The History of the Wartime Codebreaking Certre and the Men and Women Who Were There*, Aurum Press, London, 2010

Montefiore, Simon Sebag, *Stalin, The Court of the Red Tsar*, Weidenfeld and Nicolson, London, 2004

Neave, Airey, *Saturday at M.I.9*, Hodder and Stoughton Ltd, London, 1969

Rankin, Nicholas, *Churchill's Wizards, The British Genius for Deception 1914 - 1945*, Faber & Faber, London, 2008

Sakaida, Henry and Hook, Christa, *Heroes of the Soviet Union, 1941-45*, Osprey Publishing, Oxford, 2004

Smith, Michael, *Six, A History of Britain's Secret Intelligence Service, Part 1: Murder and Mayhem 1909-1939*, Dialogue, London, 2010

Smith, Michael, *Station X, the Codebreakers of Bletchley Park*, Pan Books, London, 2004

Taylor, John A., *Bletchley Park's Secret Sisters*, Book Castle Publishing, Copt Hewick, N Yorks, 2005

West, Nigel, *MI6, British Secret Intelligence Service Operations, 1909-45*, Weidenfeld and Nicolson, London, 1983

Winterbotham, F.W., *The Ultra Secret, The Inside Story of Operation Ultra, Bletchley Park and Enigma*, Orion, 2000

Welchman, Gordon, *The Hut Six Story, Breaking the Enigma Codes*, Penguin, 1982

Winchester, Charles, *Ostfront, Hitler's War on Russia 1941 -1945*, Osprey Publishing, Botley, Oxford, 1998

Winchester, Charles D, *Hitler's War on Russia*, Osprey Publishing, Oxford, 2007

Freeing My Sisters

The Welsh Marches Series, Book 1

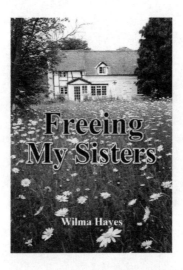

Bullying doesn't end in death... usually.

Just when Mary Mitchell begins to feel settled in her new but very old house in rural Herefordshire, she discovers that ghosts can talk to her.

At the same time her new best friend and neighbour Tim Spencer, discovers that his job as a structural engineer is systematically being destroyed. Trying to save his career, he and Mary find themselves drawn into the life-threatening world of modern day crime.

But the most frightening crime comes from the past. The history of Mary's house leads them to one so serious that the victims have come to tell her what happened and to deliver a warning.

Available via www.wilmahayes.co.uk or on Kindle

Things I Haven't Told You

The Welsh Marches Series, Book 2

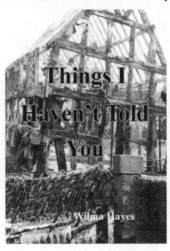

Everyone has secrets... haven't they?

Mary and Tim appear to have a perfect relationship – except for the secrets, a few lies and the odd legacy. With a relationship as perfect as theirs would seem to be, the world will conspire to prove otherwise.

She hasn't told him everything and he hasn't been entirely honest either. Neither of them is quite willing to confess all their secrets.

As they find their way in this new partnership, controlling, dishonest and unstable parents, a voice from the recent past desperate for help, and a murder, all intervene to damage or destroy it.

And then there are the children, one now grown up and the other not...

Available via www.wilmahayes.co.uk or on Kindle